MATTHEW JOHNSON

The Dark Song

Second edition

Editing by Nicole Carvagno
Cover art by Skylar Davis
Advisor: Nicole Carvagno, Hannah Price, Jordan Light, Olivia Hill, Levi Owens, Jade Dinger, and Sage Dinger: the Original Guardians of Lorial
Editing by Randal Meadows

This book was professionally typeset on Reedsy.
Find out more at reedsy.com

For my late Uncle Bob who never gave up on me.

Contents

Acknowledgments

I would first like to bring to your attention the outrageously long list of people who supported me and helped encourage me to keep writing. I would also like to thank all of you who read this first installment in the journey of the Guardians of Lorial. You are a true inspiration for me to keep writing the story that is to come. Most importantly, I want to thank my mother for all the love she poured into me as I wrote this and am writing the future book. You are a troubadour and one of the most important people in my life. I would, quite literally, not be where I am today without you. Finally, I would invoke the amazing "cast" of this story of my closest friends who played these characters in the DnD campaign that I ran for them. (And no, it did not go as smoothly as this book would have you to believe, as I am sure all the other DnD players understand. My heart is with you other DMs.) Nicole Carvagno, who played Esvele, Olivia Hill, who played Organa, Jade Dinger, who played Myrcle, Sage Dinger, who played Florie, Jordan Light, who played Brok, and Levi Owens, who played Talos. Each of you was/are a light in my life and has brought me so much joy, and I literally could not have ever written this story without your support. Thank you all so much for everything you were and are to me.

World of Lorial

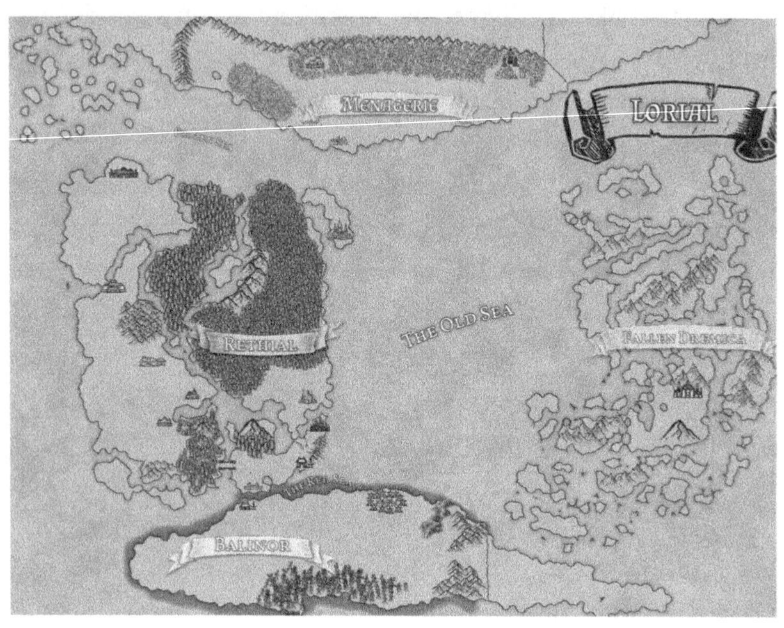

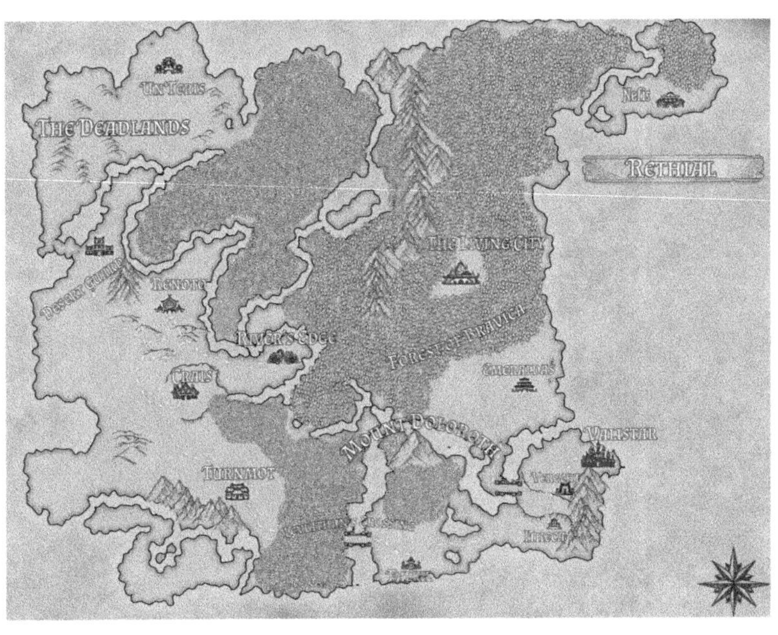

Un'Teris
THE DEADLANDS
Neko
RETHVIL
Desert Ruins
The Living City
Renore
River's Edge
FOREST OF DRAVICH
Caleindra's
Crius
VELISTIR
MOUNT DOLOROTH
Turnmot
Imeot

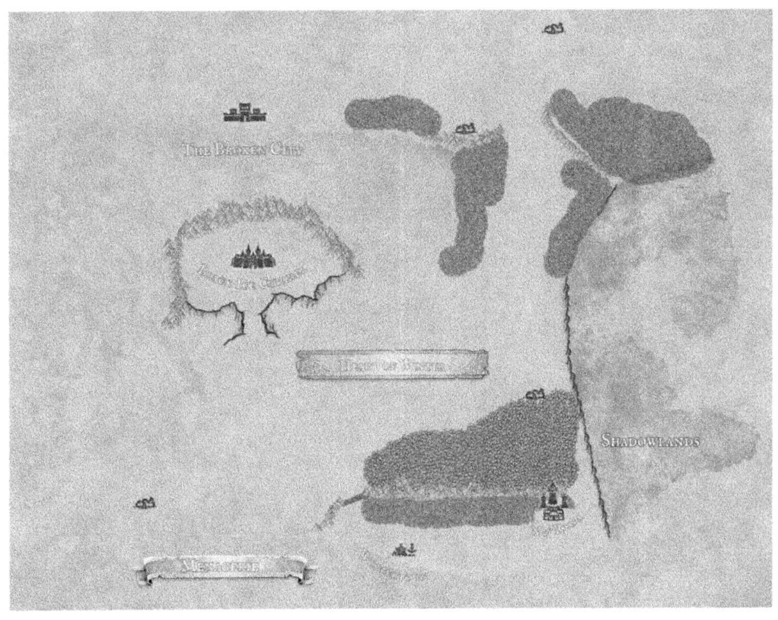

THE BROKEN CITY
Heart of Brivia
SHADOWLANDS
MENAGERIE

FARLEE
THE RED SEA
KALDAN
SINKING SANDS
SWAMP OF KALDAN
SHADOWLANDS
THE FAR LANDS

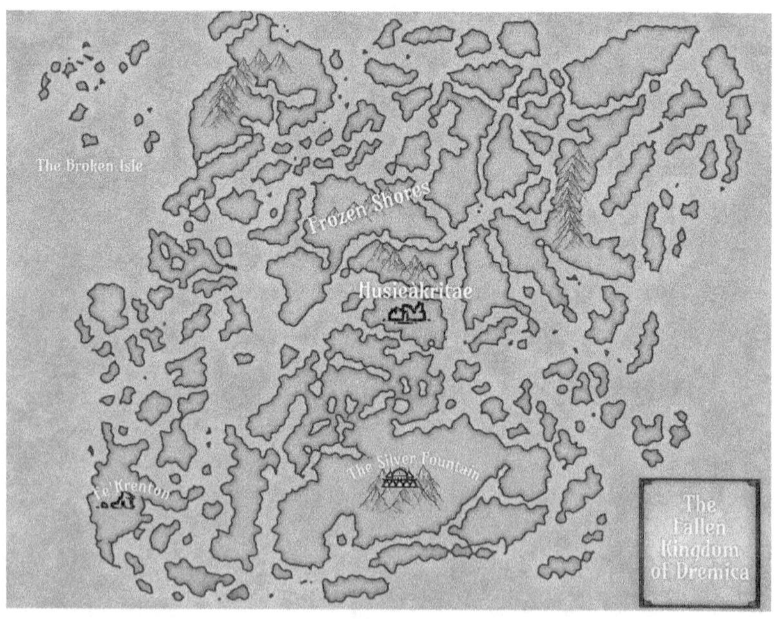

The Broken Isle
Frozen Shores
Husieakritae
The Silver Fountain
Isle Krenton
The Fallen Kingdom of Dremica

The Songs of Sorrow

This I sayeth unto thee, thou who wouldst heareth The Dark Song, heedeth mine own words, for the Cataclysm is nigh. Upon these words, beware, the one who walks in Light and Shadow is nigh. Darkness shall beest their burden and Light, their deliverance. Shadows will rise and fall upon the world. He who walks upon the Void cometh soon: the Herald of Hatred; the Vengeful Son of Sorrow; the Forgotten Brother; the Burning One; the Unending Flame of Chaos. Within his fire shall all things be devoured. This I sayeth unto thee, the Silver Kingdom will fall. Dremica will fall. Mine eyes have seen the coming of darkness and the coming of destruction; the coming of the Cataclysm. Fear the Dark Song, the Age of Shadows comes soon. The Days of Doom are upon thee. Yea, though I hearken toil and grief, sowing seeds of fear, there is still hope. Hope in the forsaken child of treachery, hope in the hands who wield the star-christened blade. Damnation is at hand. Salvation is Nigh. This I sayeth unto thee, the Cataclysm is nigh.

-The Prophecy of Shadows
The Scrolls of Ver'Keyth: Eye of Eternity
Volume I (327 FAoL)
Transcribed by Sorcerer Lord Mavius (384 AC)

Prologue

Flames devoured the City of Light. Once-gilded towers crumbled like dry leaves beneath a boot. The great marble walls that had protected Husieàkritae for a thousand thousand years now lay in ruins. The Gates of Peace shattered like glass across the cobbled streets as splintered wood and molten steel twisted under the weight of siege. Houses burned with writhing tongues of black, white, sickly green, and deep violet, ever-climbing toward the heavens they sought to sate with their hunger. The air stank of mangled corpses and blight-ravaged bones. Undead wings beat silently overhead as the Shadows of the North descended, unmaking all that stood before them. From above, they rained flame, pestilence, ice, and poison, drowning the eastern capital in a ruin of ages. Portals tore open wounds in the world, birthing abominations from the dark between stars.

A man in red robes, with blond hair containing streaks of gray, hid behind a mostly crumbled house. Claws scratching against the pavement echoed through the street. A creature of malice and shadows stalked around the corner with a *click, click, click, click, click.* The thump of his heartbeat sounded throughout his body. He was almost afraid the Rattler could hear it.

Across from him, Lukitas, the Lady of Light, hid behind another fallen bit of rubble. She looked at him with her copper eyes and nodded her head in agreement about what must be done. A message entered Bendrit's mind: *"Goodbye, old friend."* The sound of her breath exhaling drew the Rattler's attention, its *click, click, click, click, click* accelerating with a crescendo behind it as more of the demons gathered to the call of their brethren. Golden threads of radiance swarmed all around her as black flecks appeared in her eyes. She was letting the melody in. Yet, even with the power of the Shadow's forbidden song alive in her veins, she came alive like a radiant sun— resisting its hate as it tried to corrupt her. Every speck of darkness was banished from around her.

You are ours, Lady of Light. You cannot stop the coming Silence. The Dark One whispered through the Flux to her.

The pain of holding it back in the presence of such darkness made her scream as she rose to her feet, revealing herself to the blind creature, and sending forth a burst of brilliant bright light, banishing the creatures into the Void whence they came.

Bendrit ran toward the Citadel of Bal'Xani as she sent forth her power in a blinding beam of light. He would never know what became of Lukitas, but he hoped she survived.

The inner city was a maze in itself. The first obstacle of which was simply getting to the first wall of the great keep. However, the destruction that the Void had wrought upon that bastion made the way clear for Bendrit to follow. The path of carnage that led toward the castle reeked with the odor of a thousand corpses. Scattered pieces of flesh and bone were thrown around the streets like nothing. The blood of the innocent spilled on sacred grounds where such merciless violence had never set foot. Men, women, children, young or old, indiscriminately butchered by tooth, claw, tail, wing, and blade of the darkness that had befallen the eastern kingdom of Dremica. An unstoppable wave of crimson would wash over the world of Lorial should his mission fail.

The first gate into the Citadel of Bal'Xani was near. Smoke and fumes of ruin spiraled up into the starless night above him, with what the world would soon come to call the "Fire in Heaven" gashed across the blackness. The secret stair down into the crevasse that stood as the moat of the first gate was small. Barely able to stand upon the rocks, and carved just out of sight of any normal passerby, he felt the shift in its foundation as Bendrit carefully took each step. The sound of a small rock crumbling caused his heart to beat faster. With every inch forward, he descended into the maw of the endless drop below, the sound of the pebbles making light, echoing pops against the ravine's walls. Yet, within a few more passes along the sheer cliff, his feet found stable ground within a shallow inset of the cavern. Beads of sweat poured from his brow as he conquered the first of his tasks.

From within a pocket on the inside of his red robes, he drew forth the ivory key and used the small light that emitted from its surface to find the lock. Designs of swirling silver and gold carved with radiant runes that shone just enough to be noticed by their seeker. Following the designs with his eyes, he located the lock and removed the stones from their foundation, dissolving them like grains of sand in water. Before him stood a dark passage, but once his body passed through its portal, crystals of light cast away the shadows. The passage resealed itself behind him; the stones reforming as if never moved.

The damp air cooled his lungs as he walked through the corridor. He came upon an endless ladder rising through a vertical shaft. Bendrit touched the lay-lines of the Flux with the tip of his wand and cast a spell of flight on himself and ascended the way. He rose through the black gullet of the Citadel for a brief moment before coming to its end. Clinging to the ladder for support, Bendrit broke his own flight enchantment. Then, he used his open hand to lift the marble slab and place it on the floor, revealing the hidden passage.

Fires illuminated the interior of the ruined Citadel, and corpses lay upon it as Bendrit beheld the dead. Wild wind flew through the collapsing ruin, carrying the wailings of the damned innocents in the city below with it; dislodging some of the teetering stones in the walls. Bendrit pulled himself up a little further, pushing the slab off of him, just enough to see into the rest of the room and remain hidden. He placed his hand on the floor, weaving the Thread of Earth around his body as he drew it from the Flux. Each strand made the stones sing with every movement around him. Shifting bodies from the floor, crawling, standing, limping with broken bones, all moved with undeath surging through them. He could feel the scrape of a blade across the floor. Maybe an ax, a sword, or something else, but not held by anything living, as he could feel the footsteps but no heartbeat through them. He opened his eyes to see where the bodies once were, but they had vanished into the halls beyond.

Bendrit crested the opening. From his vantage point, he could see nearly the entire city. He could hear the screams of the dying, crying out for mercy from their fate, and the jubilation of the dead calling out into the night as they hunted. Huge portals in the distance with sprawling chains escaping their maws, grasping at the reality of the city, and pouring out endless hordes of evil beings, ravenous and filled with malice. Tears left his silver eyes as he looked upon what he once called home.

He felt his mind sink into itself as his sorrow and anger called to him. That familiar, promising melody wrapped around him like a cloak, warming, but cold; filled with the vow of vengeance. An assurance of peace and unlimited power to hold while he exacted his revenge. Everything he wanted at that moment for the price of letting go; to allow that song to fill him to the brim with direst cruelty. But the sound of a blade scraping up from the floor behind him drew his attention, and he turned around, launching a bolt of fire directly into the chest of a Soulless: a husk of someone once living now commanded by the Dark One's chorus of death. Its dark eyes of green fire diminished; the bones and flesh split apart, dissolving with the flames. He pushed aside the call of the Void he knew all too well with the thought of Lukitas—

Lukitas—

Even she, the Guardian of Inmost Light, has seen the truth and peace of Silence. Will you not join your wife in the blessèd nothing? The Dark One sang to him in a chorus of a hundred million voices.

Her smiling face gleamed in his mind.

If you have claimed her in your foul grasp, then she is not the woman I love. Bendrit felt the blood running down his nose.

Each of you 'Guardians' are mine... in this world or another... The Shadow's chorus of death faded as Bendrit held back the tide of the Void's hatred.

Running through the halls of the fallen Citadel, Bendrit searched every room he could find. Inside almost all of them were the corpses of the dead royal court, their families, soldiers, and servants to the Starlight Dynasty, but the queen was not there. He came upon a somewhat in-tact spiraling staircase that he cautiously placed each foot on, descending further down into the Citadel. The reek of death filled his nose as he left the archway of the stairs, seeing a pile of bloodied bodies, yet, even in the darkest hour of creation, the flies cared naught for any of it. The grand hall came into view around the corner, in shambles. Broken chandeliers and statues of the Soulflame Kings and Lady Magis riddled the ground. Splintered wooden tables and chairs, shattered glass, and fires around the room consumed the banners of the Dynasty. A foul creature stood at the far end of Sol Hall in the visage of a woman clad in black armor. Her white hair and green-fire eyes burned through its very soul as she gripped the side of its face, causing the beast to scream. Her words echoed with the voices of hundreds as she commanded the fiend. So overshadowed by its tones, Bendrit could not make out her command as she pushed the beast. It ran through a breach in the Hall's wall and back into the burning city to collect more souls. With a graceful twist of her wrist, she tore open reality in a torrent of white and black flames, passing through and returning to the halls of her master as the tear mended itself.

Bendrit left his alcove and walked down the long Sol Hall and through a door on the far side leading up to the throne room. A collapsed ceiling had destroyed the Crystal Thrones, scattering them like glass upon the rubble-covered floor. Through the holes, he could see Defilers flying above. Their shrieks and shrill overlapping voices filled the night as they circled overhead. Keeping to the shadows as best he could, Bendrit made his way toward the last door that would lead him to the Silver Spires, the homes of the monarchs and their advisors. Reaching the edge of the throne room, he saw the faces of crushed soldiers beneath the rubble, but passed by them quickly to continue his purpose. *May the Dawn Eternal embrace you in the warmth of the Shining One, brothers and sisters,* he prayed as he rounded the corner.

Bendrit ascended the stairs to a decorated wooden door with a broken painted glass window that once held the crest of the Starlight Dynasty. Moving the door aside, he walked across the courtyard, holding to the gloom once more to avoid the creatures that plagued the once-green gardens. He reached out his hand and dragged open the door that led up to the King's Pillar. The royal family should still be in the secret room Bendrit himself designed and cast the spells over.

A loud crash shook the foundations of the Citadel, and the sound of crumbling stone caught his attention as the Western Obelisk collapsed toward him. As it fell upon the courtyard, the sky rained enormous stones. The Lord of Flames held up his hands and created an orb of heat around himself. It burned so hotly that the collapsing stone melted into molten rock upon impact, forming a dome of lava that he took advantage of. With a swift motion of his arm, fringed tangles of fire formed a wave of ruin across the gardens, scorching everything that was unable to hide behind the rubble of the broken tower.

When his immolation had passed, he could hear it, that forbidden song in his mind once more. Tempting him once more with the power to save everyone if he just gave in.

There is no fight to be won here, Son of the Dawn. The Guardians are dead. You are alone in the darkness. You will only suffer should you press on. Yet, rest your head in the embrace of the Void, and we will give you peace and revenge. Be free. A chorus of a million overlapping voices called to him in his mind. He could feel its breath: colder than any frigid iceberg in all of Menagerie, yet, soft like a cat's fur. The Shadow Monarch's call coiled through his body like snakes; writhing and waiting for the perfect moment to sink their fangs into him and claim him for the Shadow.

For a moment, he almost gave in. But, Bendrit's resolve was solidified by his duty and the thought of the Lady Magis and the princess. He bolted across the gardens, into the tower of the King, and up the stairs, leaving the door open and allowing a hurricane of dust to shoot up through the twisting stairwell as something else collapsed in the city.

He came to the top and opened the door to find no one. Exactly as he designed it. He found the room in disorder, with shattered mirrors and torn family tapestries on the floor. Behind one of them that had fallen, he had hidden the secret room that he had made for them. He placed his hand on the wall and cast a spell through it, illuminating the edge of the doorway with light and pushing it forward, scraping on the floor. Behind the door hid the Lady Magis and one of her children, a daughter, who, like her mother, bore beautiful silver hair and emerald green eyes.

"Bendrit," she called out, running to him with her daughter shortly behind her. Her arms wrapped around him, nearly toppling him.

"It's all right, my Lady. I'm here."

"Have you seen my husband?" Her eyes glistened with false hope.

"Where's Kyriel?" the young woman asked.

Bendrit looked at them with despair. "No, I haven't seen him. But I am sure he got out of the city."

"He was with Dad in his war council chambers," the princess said as she held onto her mother, her eyes beginning to water.

"I have to get you two out of here," Bendrit panted.

"Not without Kyriel or father."

"Organa," her mother turned to her, "we have to trust in the Gods. We *will* see them again."

"I don't want to have to wait until I die to see them!"

"Princess," Bendrit looked at her with urgency, "I have sent my most trusted soldiers to help find him. Myrcle and Esvele are there as well. Please come with me," Bendrit pleaded.

"I told you, not without Kyriel and father! I'm not going to leave them here to die!" The walls of the secret room trembled as she shouted.

"Listen, sweetheart," her mother took her hand. "He's probably on a boat with your brother already. Please trust the Gods." Her daughter's face held trouble, and she heard that forbidden melody in her head. That need to find them. To protect them. The promise of saving them. But the thundering of the collapsing tower took her by surprise, nearly falling with the floor and the back of the King's pillar as it ripped away from its foundations.

Bendrit pulled her back from the edge quickly, and a dagger of shadows found his hand from a tangle of black threads. He pierced the veil of the Canvas of Creation, hoping it would open where he wished it to, and cut a tear. The chamber filled with blue and white light and the sound of crashing waves and more screams at the coast of the Old Sea.

The Dawn is still watching over us. Bendrit exhaled—but the sound of clicking rose up the stairwell.

"Where did you learn—" the Lady Magis glared at Bendrit, but his booming voice seized her.

"We have to go now!" he commanded.

"You first," the Lady Magis said with a weight to her voice that Bendrit knew all too well as she pushed Organa towards the tear. The princess waited a moment before begrudgingly passing through the magic she had never seen before. She passed through the light and landed on a grassy patch of land, seeing hundreds of people running for the ships that tossed and turned on the waves of the raging, stormy sea. Dark clouds above her nearly stretched to the horizon, full of ash and dark magic as the Void touched the world, devouring the light above them all.

"You are next, my Lady," Bendrit requested.

Click, click, click, click, click the Rattler sang as it entered the room. His heart thumped so loudly it should have left his body. "Now, my Lady!" And then she bolted into the tear. Yet, the demon moved faster than he could, taking the Lady Magis' neck in its jaws and biting into her flesh. Though Bendrit could not hear it, horror wrapped itself around the princess' face through the gateway.

His arms warmed as threads of fire manifested around them and he unleashed a scorching bolt against the Rattler, reducing it to ashes. The mangled body of the Lady Magis was a cold, gray, and crimson-painted slump on the floor. Still, Bendrit forced himself to turn from her and leapt through the tear, closing it behind him, and catching the princess in his arms as she battered and wailed for her mother.

I

Daughter of Starlight

"Will there come the day of peace?
Will there come the Second Age of Light?
When the stars have blinked their last;
When the noble die and suffer for the forsaken;
When the Shining One would turn its face from us;
Shall there be Silence?"
- The Songs of Sorrow
Author Unknown

Turnmot

Trickling rain pattered against the roofs of the houses in Turnmot as cutting winds swept down from the north, carrying the bite of a cold, dark night. Rusted, unkempt lampposts lined the streets, their dim flames flickering in protest against the gale. High above, the Element Moons gleamed in the star-strewn sky, casting silver and pale green light over the town. Piercing the blackness of night and swallowing the radiance of stars like a river of burning jewels, the Fire in Heaven scorched open the glinting sky.

Beyond the town's walls, the surrounding forest groaned as trees bent and swayed under the force of the storm. Compared to records of past tempests, this was by far the worst. Yet, despite the looming threat and the destruction that could strike at any moment, laughter and the clinking of mugs echoed from a small tavern: *The Sea-Old Wench.*

Inside, nearly fifty patrons gathered, at least half of them drunk beyond reason. Elves, Humans, Kalishtani, Dwarves, Orcs—folk of every sort—filled the air with laughter and song. Musicians played lively tunes as couples spun and stumbled across the floor, their movements clumsy but full of cheer. The Galsis Step, a simple dance beloved by locals, dominated the room as partners swung each other around.

Near the heart of the crowd, a single couple attempted an older, more intricate dance. Their performance drew appreciative chuckles and scattered applause. Nearby, a young Elf, grinning broadly, stepped lightly toward the bards. With a polite nod, the Elf requested a change in tune: *The Felionas*, the Song of the Mountains. The musician's eyes lit with recognition. Smiling, she leaned toward her fellow players and whispered the request; her bow already poised to draw the first notes.

An elegant song, long-noted and rich in contrasting dynamics, slowly built into a faster tempo more fit for dancing. As the viol sang the melody, the lute and other instruments simply followed its tune and moved with the dancers.

A moment of calm swept over the tavern, and the people watched in amazement at the flowing movements of the couple. Their feet easily moved together in a six-eight pattern as they danced around each other, grasping hands for a moment and then falling back from one another. Twisting and turning around each other, they smiled.

The light from the chandeliers and torches illuminated the Elven woman's silvery white hair, shining like a star. Her long beige sleeveless coat barely touched the floor in the back and extended up to cover her neck. Two descending sleeves, one a few inches shorter than the other, clasped at her neck and wrapped around her shoulders. The front of the long coat trailed down to the waist and fell behind her legs, exposing the brown leather pants covering the Elf's lower half. Concealed under this outer layer, a belt around her waist held two sheathed daggers with hilts made of white and brown speckled staghorn. Her tan skin contrasted with her timeless emerald eyes as they glistened.

The song tempo quickened a bit. Her partner was a taller half-orc from the wastelands of the southern continent of Balinor. His sea-blue eyes met his friend as he danced with her. He wore black leather pants with a short, light cloth tunic around his waist. His brown boots danced across the floor, dimly glowing through the light smoke from the pipes and candles in the room. A mostly uncovered torso showed his chiseled caramel physique that would have frightened the bravest soldier of the king's guard. Jet-black hair fell behind his pointed, elven ears; pulled in a small tail on the back of his head.

His feet flowed with ease as he twisted around the floor with his companion. Only the supremely dull-witted or thoroughly drunk could have failed to notice that every time the elven lady spun around, her hands sparked and a small white mist that blended into the smoke from people's pipes surrounded the feet of the Half-orc.

The tempo of the song was now at full speed. Feet pounded on the floor, and hands clapped in time, and a few out of time, as the song soared on in harmony and elegance. Spinning round and round, the pair came to a sudden stop with a stomp of their feet as a roar of applause echoed in the tavern.

The Elven woman took the hand of the half-orc, and he spun her round and round. As she spun on for what seemed like a lifetime, she abruptly, although gracefully, ended with the stomp of her own foot.

They both paused for a moment, panting and smiling at one another. A roar of laughter and applause filled the tavern. Everyone went back to their conversations and merry times. The duo found their way back to their table to rest as they recovered from their performance.

"So Brok, how'd you like your first proper Elven dance? Not like anything we got to do in the Living City, eh?" the Elven woman asked. Her voice was sharp, and the accent was clearly that of the people of Dremica, the lost continent in the East.

"It was… enjoyable." Brok smiled as he completed the sentence, and a look of pride crossed over his face as he smiled at her.

She smiled back, taking a long drink. "You are getting better and better every day at speech. One day it will be much easier for you. And those memories of yours might come back too." Brok glanced at his friend, the only kind person in all of Lorial that he had known. The only person who did not treat him as a hybrid or mutant monstrosity.

"Organa," he asked as he thought deeply to form words, "are you... happy... um... here?"

"What do you mean?"

"We could stay. Here. Live... in the forest, put... behind... the... troubles... of the past." he had a sense of desperation in his voice as if it were the only thing he had ever wanted.

"You know we can't stay here, Brok," she sighed.

"Why not... I... don't remember... small brain." Brok grunted with a kind smile.

"We're always going to be hunted by the Order. If we stay too long in one place, they'll find us. I am sure they already know we're here." As she continued to drink, a few eyebrows raised from the people within the tavern as they watched her easily gulp down the pint of ale.

A bard in the corner strummed her lyre as she sang of the Fall of Silver.

High, high, the flames burn high
The Blood of Stars has run dry.
Through ash and through bones,
The Shadow has come,
And we sing of the dream long past and gone.

The song resonated in Organa's mind—each word like a memory locked behind a pane of glass she couldn't break through—like her dreams she had in the Living City. Organa had heard of the towering cathedrals made of white marble and stone from the sea to honor the Pantheon of Dawn. Dreams of the City of Husieàkritae glistened in her mind like a perfect painting. There was something else…a sound…a scream…

"Organa," Brok's voice became clearer and more concerned, "Organa?"

"Sorry, Brok, I was daydreaming." Organa looked at him with a certain queerness in her eyes. He watched Organa hide her amulet of Valkiel beneath the cloth of her dress. Brok turned to see the way she was looking and saw the danger instantly.

The patrons all fell silent as three people, two in red cloaks and one in a blue cloak, entered the tavern. Mystic stitching embroidered the fabric just beneath the clasp. Four colored lines: red, blue, gold, and green, swirled into a tree of similar roots and leaves; the embellished crest of the Order shimmering like stars. The symbol was of the Eternal Cycle: *from the forests came all life of Lorial, and to the forests, life will return*, Organa heard the Lady Moonlight in her head repeating the mantra.

The man walked forward and looked around the room as Organa twisted her hand beneath the table and stitched a mirage of night threads around her and Brok. To everyone, the table where Brok and Organa sat was now empty.

The two women glanced at one another briefly and broke ranks to search through the building. They closely monitored the faces of everyone there as the entire room watched them in confusion and alarm. One held her hand out, as if she were gliding her palm down the railing of a stair no one else could see…feeling for something.

The man raised his voice. "There is an Elven woman who belongs to the Order of Valkiel. Who here has seen her?"

The man's voice lingered on her ears as Organa recognized him.

False bravado, she snickered to herself. *Of course they'd send him.*

Nobody answered.

A tapestry of wind gathered around him as his fists clenched and his voice boomed as if the volcanoes of Lorial erupted at once. "Who has seen the Elven Druid?" As his voice cracked through the room, clouds and frigid gales erupted like a storm-born beast. A loud high-pitched ring echoed in the ears of the people, causing some of the townsfolk to fall to their feet as if a gust of wind beset their chests, clutching their ears for relief.

An older woman in the back of the tavern stood with a look of defiance ablaze in her eyes, but a younger woman holding a tray with some cups of ale and wine kept the old woman down.

A few moments passed without an answer once more.

"Seal it. Find her." Their leader commanded, desperation lingering in his voice.

One of the red cloaks bent the wood of the floor with a few motions of her hand; *creaking* and *cracking* morphed into large vines that came to life. The roots coiled around and into the doorframe of the front exit, twisting themselves and growing a living barrier of sharp wooden brambles and bright leaves.

Suddenly, the bartender shouted to the trio, "Oi, quit your shit! We get it, you're a bunch of fancy tree magicians. Now, get out of my establishment,, please, before I set my hounds on you, and they'll be gentle compared to my chasin' youn's down." He rounded the end of the bar as he gave his command. An older gentleman, dressed in tattered clothes and had a white apron around his belly. The druids gave no response, only harsh looks to the old man. "Oi! Did ye's 'ear what I said? Get out of me tavern now before I make you. Don't make me ask again."

The man in the red cloak with the booming voice lifted his hand in retaliation as if to strike at him with a spell or maybe even just his hand until the old man said in a very clear, demanding, yet sarcastic voice, "Do try, please, I am beggin' ya, do try your luck."

The druid chuckled for a brief second and hummed lightly. Flickers of embers from the torches wove themselves in red threads against the rising wind held in the tangle of his left hand. As they touched, sparks jolted from his fingertips, *cracking* and *popping* with the waiting breath of thunder.

The bartender raised his own hands too and wove far faster without any song to aid him. A burst of flames and sunlight flew into the chest of the blue-cloaked man, launching him through the door of the tavern. Silence filled the tavern except for the bard's fearful strum. The other druids turned to face the old man.

"Got anything you'd like to try, ladies, because I'll throw your asses out too." The two women glanced once more at each other before singing to the earth and weaving spikes from the wooden floor beneath them.

"Bloody Dawns!" His fingers tickled the threads of fire once more.

One of the druids lunged and thrust her arms forth, commanding the sharpened wood against him with tangles of brown earth. The old man's flames devoured her might and threatened to engulf her as well. Yet, her sister-in-arms released her earthen threads and whispered the Song of the Sea into her palms.

The fire and water met in a cascade of reds and blues that gleamed with white light like a sun. Organa watched in awe as the old man seemed to be holding his own against the druid with a single hand raised to weave his patterns of ruin. His eyes blazed, as though he beheld the Realm of Sunless Fire itself…and there was something else. He was smiling.

Organa revealed herself. "Heard you were looking for me?" She pulled her hands inward, wind and water meeting in her palms in a blizzard. With the northern fury of an avalanche, a freezing, stiff wind full of shards of sharp ice threw the women out of the tavern. A sound echoed in her ears, the same one she was taught not to hear, its promises haunting her like a ghost. *Don't let it in,* she heard someone remind her from deep inside. *You have to hold it back with peace.*

The old man's voice broke her thoughts from it.

"Little lady, you've got some power," the bartender spoke, sounding impressed. As he got closer, his voice sounded familiar...like she knew him.

"I'm just getting started," Organa said as the forbidden melody continued to sing.

Organa stood under the small overhang over the entrance to the Sea Old Wench.

Covered in thick mud, the druids rose from the ground. As the leader wiped the filth off his cloak and the others attempted to pull the shards of ice from their thick cloaks, blood-stains smeared their hands. She walked down the few stairs to her old friends.

The man removed his mask to reveal a torn and burnt face, covered in patchy marks of semi-healed skin and one blind eye turned white as the snow. "Organa, you must return to the Living City."

Organa smiled and crossed her arms.

"The Lady Moonlight needs your help. She is trying to fix—"

Organa cut him off. "Shut up, Gerith. Just because I kept you from dying of exposure and frozen bones doesn't mean I want to hear you speak."

"Organa, come back with us," one woman pleaded.

"You show up all forceful and the like and now you ask nicely. I *can't.*"

"What are you talking about?" Gerith blinked.

"Gerith," she sighed, "I can't keep you all safe from me. The Council is afraid of me, and you should be too." Organa tried to look away from Gerith's deformed face, and with a simple flick of her wrist, tangles of winter air spun around the druidic trio, before she clutched a tight fist and flung them further into the dark and rainy night. "I'm sorry. I am not going back."

Her old friend raised himself from the mud. "You have to come back; we need you. The Void is—"

"Gerith…" Organa replied from the porch, "go home. Please. Just leave me be."

"We can't just *leave* you!"

"You will. Or you'll have to tear apart this entire town to get me. I'm—*not*—going back."

"We will return with the might of the Order then," the other druid spat.

"See you soon." Organa smiled back

"It didn't have to be like this, Organa." Gerith warned. Threads of earth bent to his will once more, and the ground swallowed the three druids whole into the caverns below.

Organa turned around and closed the door to the tavern behind her with another gust of cold air at the snap of her fingers. Roaring cheers and applause welcomed her return from the patrons of the Sea Old Wench. A humble smile glossed her face, and from across the tavern, Brok raised a mug in her honor.

The bartender shouted to the people inside, quieting them down, "Sorry for the little tiff, go about your business. Everyone gets *one*, and I mean *only one*, round on me tonight!" The people roared with excitement, and then he turned to Organa as the folk went back to their business of drinking and laughing. "What's your name again, little miss?" asked the old man, his voice still familiar.

"Organa, and this here," she pointed to her companion, "is Brok."

"The two of you seem bound for danger and trouble. Who were those people? Do you actually know them?"

"Yeah, just a little. Thank you for what you did for us." She stared at the old man for a moment. "I'm sorry…do I know you?"

"I wouldn't imagine," he lied. "And, to your point about the tree twisters," he laughed at his own joke, "That was an old lesson from a lifetime ago. I've dealt wit' worse."

"I was surprised by the power of your weaves as well, sir." The image of his smile as he commanded the flame lingered in her mind.

The man interrupted her. "Please, the name's Randy."

"Thank you very much, Randy. However, we must be off. The Order will come back for us soon, and we best not be here much longer."

"You're always welcome here, Organa, you and your big ol' friend." He nodded his head to Brok and Organa as he turned away and went back to work. Many people did not seem fazed by what had occurred in the last twenty minutes; they were all drinking and laughing away as if nothing had happened.

"All right, Brok, let's be on our way." Organa looked at her friend, and as they both walked out the door, an unlikely figure blocked their exit. A taller creature, a Firbolg, stood in the way. His maroon robes dragged on the floor just a few inches past his feet, and along the edges were blue symbols that looked like stars. Atop his head were two large brown horns, curled like those of a ram. Teal-water eyes dazzled in the light, and beneath them was a fairly large and flat nose. Two ears protruded from his hair a few inches and resembled those of a goat. In his right hand, he held a staff with golden wings that met at the center of firestone. Two silver discs separated the top from the sea gems around the neck of the staff before leading to a dark oak pole and a silver cover with four more bursting oval firestones at its base. His worn, tattered leather shoes looked like he hadn't changed or cleaned them in over six months. Despite white and gray hair covering most of his body, he kept his face cleanly shaven. Organa felt a gentleness from his presence; a familiarity.

"May I help you, sir?" Organa asked as she looked up at this giant of a man, who must have stood at least seven feet tall.

He spoke in a surprisingly tenor voice to Organa and Brok. "That answer remains clouded, young Elf," he paused. "I am Myrcle, a sorcerer of the northern part of Rethial. I might have need of your services and possibly to share in an adventure."

As he spoke, a Kalishtani, one of the People of the Flame, walked up to the group. Her light purple skin burned dimly in the light of the fires lit in the torches. Two blue and gray horns that turned into black tips emerged from her head of fiery red hair and arched back, turning up to the ceiling. On the right side of her face was a long scar that ran over her eye but did not affect it. Two bright violet eyes seemed to pierce the soul as she gazed at Organa. Her black cloth cloak flowed down just below her calves, and her deep red leather and hide clothes fit tightly to her. Resting in her left hand was a staff of twisted vines and wood with a green jagged crystal entangled permanently at the top.

"I told you not to come over here and ask these two, and what did you do? You didn't listen…again," she blinked.

"Excuse me," Organa sounded taken aback.

"Hush, let the adults speak, please." She turned herself and Myrcle away from Organa and Brok. "Myrcle, this is not a good idea. She is not ready, and this could end badly. Especially with the walking rock tumbling everywhere, which we never should have done in the first place."

"Be nice." He swatted the back of her head. "A little help never hurt anyone, EV. These two could be helpful in our journey," he said rather loudly.

"Excuse me, can my friend and I get going? We must leave before more of the Order comes back?" Organa tapped EV on the shoulder.

EV flicked away her hand and turned to her. "Hush, dear, the adults are still speaking." Organa looked at Brok, who simply shrugged his shoulders in confusion.

They both waited for a few minutes while watching the two in front of them bicker, then Organa interjected, "I hate to break up the argument, but we're leaving. Farewell and goodbye." Organa pushed the two apart with a quick burst of energy from her right hand. Organa reached the door and heard Myrcle chuckle and EV scoff. Brok followed his friend out the door into the night.

The night was beautiful and full of starlight. Bright orbs of every color strung across the sky like diamonds through the few holes in the great clouds of the approaching storm. The terrible Fire in Heaven overshadowed the two glorious Element Moons gleaming in the night sky behind them. Myrcle and EV walked closer to the door, watching the companions get closer to the deluge.

"Come, Brok," Organa said kindly. He took her hand, and she reached down to the wooden porch. Three twisting limbs spread out into multiple branches like a small tree sprouted and wrapped around one another. On top grew a large canopy of green leaves that shielded Organa and Brok from the rain as they stepped out into the night.

Myrcle looked at EV with a snarky look on his face.

"Shut up, Hairball," she rolled her eyes. "Oi, you two! Come back," Myrcle looked at her with disapproval, "Please…. we have a…. contract you might be interested in." Organa and Brok stopped under their device in the rain. They slowly exchanged looks with one another, and Organa turned around and grabbed Brok by the shoulder to correct his turn back to the ones in the tavern's doorway.

"What 'contract'?" Organa asked.

"Come inside and find out," Myrcle proposed.

After a few moments of deliberation, Organa and Brok followed the two employers back into the Sea Old Wench.

They sat at a bigger table and ordered a few ales paid for by Myrcle. A waitress came by shortly after, bringing their drinks. Her skin was covered in white scales, like snow, with a few sea-blue scales dotted around her. She was a Drakemen, the first people of Balinor.

"Enjoy," she said.

Myrcle chugged down his ale and then spoke to Organa and Brok in a quiet tone, "Well," Myrcle began as EV gave him an eye roll, "We've accepted a contract from an older gentleman who says that a Bandit Lord and his men stole his valuables, including a magic amulet he would like back."

"What do you need us for?" Organa questioned.

"That's what I've been saying!" EV exclaimed, putting down her mug.

Brok had gone through six mugs of ale and did not even seem fazed by his alcohol intake. Organa had yet to touch her drink. She murmured, only loud enough for her potential employers to hear her, "So, we're going on a scavenger hunt?"

"Yes," answered Myrcle.

"How much of the cut do we get?"

"Well, since there are four of us, then it's twenty-five percent each," Myrcle shrugged as he pitched the idea.

EV choked on her drink, coughing for a few seconds, and then recovering. "One moment please, Myrcle," EV cleared her voice and now showed high disdain. "I think the fuck not."

"Why not?" asked Brok.

"Stay out of this, Talking Rock," EV pointed her finger at him, "And to answer your question, Myrcle, because I am the one who has to bring back the amulet. That's why." Organa looked at EV with a curious expression.

"EV, calm down. You will get your money. It'll be an even split between all of us," Myrcle assured her.

"I shall repeat myself a little clearer." She cleared her throat and raised herself toward him. "I think not," she screamed in Myrcle's ear. He blinked rapidly for a moment, trying to recover as EV sat back down and took another drink.

"You know, EV, being the self-dubbed 'amulet holder' doesn't mean you get paid more," Myrcle corrected her.

"At least forty-five percent," she demanded.

"Thirty-five," Myrcle countered.

"Forty."

"Thirty-seven."

"Thirty-nine."

"Thirty-eight!"

"*Thirty-five. Last offer!*" EV snapped.

Myrcle raised an eyebrow. "An accord."

EV grunted and sat back down and propped her feet up on a chair nearby. She muttered something incoherently under her breath.

Organa giggled as she thought of their absurdity. How could these two be partners? She looked to Brok as he was easily downing his seventh round of ale. She whispered, "Brok... lay off the ale, okay? I need you to be aware if we accept this offer and not completely out of sorts, okay?" Brok looked at her as he put down the mug and simply shrugged, raising it again to finish the last few gulps left. Organa gave him a serious look but could not help herself and laughed a little.

Myrcle was watching in astonishment as Brok finished the most recent round of ale. "How does he do that?" he asked, pointing his finger at the half-orc.

"I don't know; however, I do think that might be why he doesn't understand much," Organa raised an eyebrow with a giggle.

"Well, he'll be our brawn, and we have two great and grand minds, so we'll be fine." Myrcle laughed.

"I had better be the other mind." Organa and Myrcle laughed together at EV's response. EV glanced her way with disapproval. "So are you the other one, then?"

"I could very well be," Organa said with a giggle. Brok laughed as well, his deep voice carrying through the room in obnoxious laughter at a joke he himself probably did not understand. Brok laughed only because his friends laughed. The entire tavern now looked in the group's direction. EV laid her head on the table, continuing her over-delivered charade as she lightly beat her head on the table.

Myrcle looked at Brok with an annoyed expression. "Brok," he said with no response except the giant's raucous laughter. "Brok!" Suddenly, strands of air wrapped around Myrcle's throat as his voice boomed as if a cannon had gone off in the ears of everyone within the tavern. The only one who did not react was EV, simply continuing to pound her head on the wooden table. Brok looked at Myrcle in total surprise.

With Brok now silenced, EV raised her head. "Thank you, Myrcle; you truly are a miracle on your own."

"I try, dearie."

"So, when do we start this adventure?" asked Organa.

"Well, now would be a great time," replied EV, like she was over-annoyed.

"EV, you really need to work on your people skills," Myrcle laughed.

"Shut up, Hairball, I don't need to work on them," she rebutted. "I am *very* sociable." She glared at him as she spoke slowly.

Myrcle looked back at her with the same intensity. "You constantly berate people about themselves and also attempt to steal or touch anything shiny."

"So?" EV asked.

"So', you need to learn to be hospitable and learn how to be nice."

"That doesn't matter. I am just brutally honest, and people need to hear that, plus shiny means valuable." Her demeanor changed again.

"EV, you can't always be that way. It will get you killed. You'll insult some king or royal person and you'll get your head chopped off," Myrcle retorted back.

Organa raised her eyebrows as a deep sigh left her lungs. "Are you two going to fight all night or can we go get some rest before this little shindig tomorrow?"

"I'd like to begin now," EV said, annoyed.

"In the dead of night? Dark creatures roam the roads at night, and some rest would do us all good," Organa rebutted.

"Myrcle," EV looked to him for support.

"I agree with Organa; the rest will be helpful. We will need our strength and cunning abilities not to be caught."

"Fine," EV rolled her eyes, "then I am going to sleep. Meet me in the room when you're done talking to these mountebanks."

EV stood, and her hand lightly brushed against Organa's wrist. Immediately, EV latched onto her like a shackle. Organa struggled to no avail, and she saw EV's eyes begin to turn deep blue and then change color to red, then white, then settled on silver. EV violently shook and suddenly stood as still as a statue, twitching every few seconds. The floor vibrated throughout the entire establishment, and a few lamps dropped from their hooks, lighting the floor aflame. Myrcle sprang into action, running and grabbing buckets of water near the sinks behind the bar. With her free hand, Organa created a sheet of ice over the fires, the heat melting it into water and drowning the flames out as Myrcle was about to douse the fire. Organa then felt a burning heat on her hand and looked down to see EV's hand ignited. Organa created ice to melt away the heat in her hands, but the water evaporated too fast, turning to steam as quickly as she could make the ice appear. Myrcle ran to EV's side, taking hold of her shoulder with a gloved hand, and creating a guiding glow as he chanted in a language that rang with odd familiarity in Organa's ears.

Brok reached behind him for his great sword and readied a swing to remove EV's hand. Organa screamed in pain, falling to the floor with EV still holding her. Myrcle thrust Brok to the floor with a burst of fierce winds, causing him to drop his sword. Brok then stood, took out a dagger from his sheath, and raised it to attack EV. As he raised his hand, Myrcle created an orb of light and plunged it into EV's chest. She released Organa's hand, and Brok's dagger missed. She tumbled onto Myrcle, and he caught her in his arms. She looked up at him and then pushed away rapidly. Organa saw a small tear come from her eye that dropped onto the floor after it trailed down her cheek. She turned to Organa with a confused but horrified look on her face. EV looked back at Myrcle, holding out his right gloved hand to her. EV turned from him and ran up the stairs, around the balcony, and into her room.

"She'll be fine in the morning," Myrcle assured Organa.

"What was that? What was she doing?"

"That is best left 'til later. Go get some rest; tomorrow will be a long day." Myrcle turned to the stairs and walked up them and around the balcony into a room where EV was pacing back and forth frantically. Organa sat in her seat and contemplated the events.

"Brok?" she asked. "Are you sure we should take this job?"

"We… need to… stay secret. Hide from… the Order."

"If we go with them, we'll keep the Order away from Turnmot, but we'd get dangerously close to the Forest of Bravica."

"We live… on danger." Brok smiled, laughing.

"All right, we're going then."

Shadow of the Past

The next morning came, and the sound of a rooster crowing woke Organa and Brok in their rooms. Brok squinted for a moment and looked to see Organa sitting up in the bed above where he lay on the floor. A few beams of light peeked through the holes in the curtains. Brok got to his feet slowly and noticed an interesting feeling. His head hurt, and he felt fairly weak. His arms and legs ached, and he felt as if he were going to vomit everywhere.

"Organa," he said with a deep, moaning grumble, "Why, why do… I feel… really… really… bad?"

"That, my dear, is called mornill, and you're not alone," she said as she yawned.

"Mornill?" Brok questioned with grogginess.

"We had way too much to drink last night." Organa placed her feet on the ground, stood, and stumbled a little. "I am going downstairs to get something to help you…and me."

"Help with what?"

"The mornill, moron," she said, pausing for a moment and sighing with a laugh as she walked out the door.

She looked around for a moment after rubbing her eyes. A long balcony extended around the back of the tavern, where ten rooms connected. She could see the door to Myrcle and EV's room open a little. The memory from last night's encounter with EV was still fresh in her mind, and she still struggled to understand what exactly had happened.

Her feet eventually found a staircase down to the main floor, which seemed to stretch on forever, each stair cracking as she crept down carefully, trying to control her dizziness and not play the fool by falling. Her hand gripped the rail on the right side of the pathway downstairs, but alas, her foot hit the next stair and slid on a wet surface. She tumbled down, crashing as she descended. Her body finally decided on its landing point and position—upside down and right at the feet of her new friend. She sat for a moment, sore and in pain, with her eyes shut. When she opened them, she saw a few people at the bar sitting and chuckling under their breath. A few feet away, a couple at a table were laughing uncontrollably. A footstep beside her creaked on the floor, and a long black shadowglass staff landed upon the wood with a clank. Organa turned her head to see a black boot with a couple of inches of thick heel to it and four buckles running up the side. As she followed the leg up, her eyes focused on the face at the top as the figure spoke.

"Have a little tumble, dear?" It was EV. The Kalishtani woman looked down at her with a smirk on her face. The glowing green orb at the top of her twisted staff gleamed in the light.

"Will you help me?" Organa groaned.

"No… I don't think I will," EV said as she walked away. A gust of wind came up from under her and her cloak slipped beneath her right foot as she walked, causing her to trip and fall flat on her face. Organa slowly rose as Myrcle walked behind her down the staircase with a wide smile. Turning over to see the amused pair and quickly leaping to her feet, "That wasn't funny, Elf!"

"I…," Organa tried to catch a breath, "It wasn't me."

"It was me," Myrcle admitted as he laughed a few more times.

"It's not funny hairball," she snapped at him.

"I believe," Myrcle corrected, "It was."

EV steamed and threw her cloak behind her, walking to the bar.

Myrcle turned to Organa, "Don't worry about EV, once she warms up to you and Brok, well, she does not get any better really, so good luck."

"I do not believe that will be happening anytime soon," Organa chuckled as she joined him.

Myrcle followed her. "A Tavian Juice for both of us, please, and a Red-Wine Cloaker."

A young woman walked over to the tap and poured out two mugs, filling them with an orange-red liquid. Organa took little notice of the new bartender as the drink flawlessly slid across the wooden bar and into her hand. She hesitantly took a sip and then transcended into a world of flavor. It was one of the most flavorful and beautiful-tasting drinks to ever have touched her lips. The sweet fruit of grapes and oranges clashed with the obvious taste of the Essence of Salt-Sage leaves and blended beautifully into a superb beverage. The taste instantly took the groggy feeling of the mornill away.

Behind the bar, a woman retrieved a clear glass bottle from the top of the counter. The bottle was empty, but not for long. With a snap of her fingers and a sudden *whoosh* of threads, a small flame appeared on the bartender's fingertip. She reached once more into the cabinet above the bar and pulled out a black pouch. Inside were a handful of red seeds, of which the bartender removed two. She placed them inside the bottle, took her flame-lit finger, and held the glass bottle above it. As the bottle heated, the seeds melted down to create a pasty liquid that was green and red. She set the bottle down on the counter and walked to grab a small vial, which had a label on it reading "Only 3 drops!" Three sparkling tears of glittering teal liquid ran down the neck of the bottle and collided violently with the liquid from the seeds. As they collided, there was a brief pause and then atomic reactions occurred in a split second. Then the bartender slid a purple liquid that smelled like roses across the counter into EV's left hand.

Organa was so mesmerized by the display that she simply stared at the bartender in awe. She was a young woman with dark skin and beautiful flowing black hair. Her eyes were teal, like the shallow sea of the southern isles of Rethial, and her skin was smooth as silk.

She looked at Myrcle and winked at him. "It's on the house, love," she said as his second drink slid into his hand. Organa looked back between the two and tittered.

"What's funny, little miss?"

"Nothing at all," she said, trying to contain her snicker. "It's just… she seems to have a fancy for you."

"That a problem?" Myrcle asked defensively.

"No, no, no, no, nothing wrong at all. I just never thought you'd be the lover type," Organa stated. There was something about him that reminded her of that fact.

"Well, I'll have you know, Organa, I have always enjoyed the company of others—on adventures or in bed," he chuckled as he took a sip of his drink.

He went on, but Organa quickly interjected, "Okay, this conversation is over, and I am going to get another one of these outstandingly tasty drinks for Brok, and we'll meet you in a jiffy down here."

"Where'd you get that scar?" Myrcle asked, pointing at a burn just above the collar of her top.

Organa stopped. "What do you mean?"

"That burn there," he pointed again, "what happened?"

"I don't know; it's been some time."

Organa walked away after grabbing the two mugs and then turned around. "Ah, miss?"

"Yes, ma'am?"

"Where's the old man from last night?"

"There are lots of nice old men who come in here," she laughed.

"Yes, but what about the older gentleman who said he owns this establishment?"

"Oh, Randy, he's upstairs asleep."

"When he wakes, will you give him our thanks for everything and that if more of them come looking for me, I am on my way to Mount Doloroth and to send them my way? I don't want you all paying for something that's my fault."

"Will do, dear," the barmaid smiled and returned to serving the other patrons.

"See you soon," Myrcle shouted to Organa.

When the door opened, she found Brok passed out on the floor, snoring away under an end table. A glass of water on the end table above him looked rather enticing. With a flick of her finger, the glass slipped off the edge and the water landed directly on Brok's face. Brok jumped, hit his head on the table, knocking it over with a loud bang against the wooden floor, and then slid out from under the furniture, rubbing his head. "Organa," he grunted, "What… what the hell?"

"Nice nap, sleepy?" she asked in a sarcastic tone. "Here," she handed out the glass. "Drink this."

"What is that?" Brok looked at her with disgust.

"It's for the mornill. Now drink up. We've got a job to do." Brok grabbed the glass and took a sip. The taste baffled him just like Organa, and he easily drank down the rest of the beverage in a few gulps. He took a deep breath after he finished his drink and handed the glass back up to Organa.

"Now, dear," Organa said, "get your stuff and meet me downstairs in five minutes."

He gave a nod and stood to his feet, gathering his things and checking the room as Organa left.

When she got to the main floor, Myrcle and EV stood near the entrance to the Sea Old Wench. Organa walked past the tables, weaving around them until she got to her new companions. As she got to EV and Myrcle, the Kalishtani noticed her approach and instantly stopped speaking.

"Organa, ready to embark on our quest?" Myrcle said brightly.

"Yeah, Brok will be down in just a momen—"

The crashing of something behind her cut her off.

Turning her head to see what the kerfuffle was, sure enough, it was exactly what she had thought it to be. Broken stairs and shards of glass scattered the floor, and at their origin was Brok, lying on top of a blue tablecloth rubbing his head.

He opened his eyes and looked at Organa in confusion. "Organa, why are you looking at me like that?" As he finished speaking, his eyes had completely focused on Organa's highly pissed-off glare.

"Brok," she spoke softly but with intensity, "this—" her voice rose with her next words—"this is the third time I am going to have to pay for damage costs!" She summoned her power, bringing branches from the floor that wrapped around Brok like snakes. With a swift movement of her hand, she sent Brok flying out the now-open door into a puddle of mud. Organa used her hand to close the door; simultaneously returning the branches to the floor.

Myrcle looked at her in shock. "Don't look at me like that," she said seriously. "He's used to it by now." She saw EV looking at her with her normal resting bitch face. However, this time, EV also held up a thumb of approval and a slight smirk to follow it. Organa laughed and then walked over to the bar. "I am very sorry for the display. How much for the three tables?" She asked, smiling yet still clearly annoyed by her partner's actions.

Suddenly, as the woman behind the bar spoke, a voice entered her head. *Just rebuild it. You've been trained by druids.* She turned around and saw Myrcle looking her way.

She spun back around. "You know what? How about this?"

Organa raised her hands and the wood trembled. Threads of earth wove themselves around her arms and into the broken table. The pieces shifted around and then sprouted golden trims. All three tables now looked as if they belonged in the palaces of the Dukes, Kings, and Queens. A Kalishtani man beside her on a bar stool clapped wildly. But through his clapping, she could hear that melody.

"Whoa," the barmaid's eyes were wide.

"Let go, Organa," Esvele cautioned.

The melody continued to sing in Organa's mind. For a moment, she was staring into someone crimson, blood-red eyes.

You... a voice echoed in her mind.

"Organa!" EV shouted, and the threads of the Flux dissipated like smoke in the wind.

Air rushed in Organa's lungs as she snapped back to her own mind. "I'm sorry, Master..." The words left her words before she knew she was going to say them. EV had already turned around by the time Organa looked her way—leaning on a wooden beam for support. Myrcle had a hand placed on her shoulder. His eyes were as wide a saucers.

"Does that help?" Organa asked the bartender.

"Yes, ma'am, it does."

"Good. Here's a little extra for yourself and your troubles." Organa placed three gold pieces on the bar and walked to Myrcle and EV.

Myrcle tried to say something, but he seemed to hold himself back and changed his words. "Please, please tell me you have not paid hundreds of silvers or coppers or even gold on broken wooden tables. You are a Druid who can control wood and most earthly elements."

Myrcle's voice was full of disbelief.

"Myrcle, this is not a good idea anymore," EV protested, her gaze burrowing through him.

"Hush, dearie."

"What's going on with you two? You acting odd," Organa blinked.

"It's complicated," they answered together.

"I need to go find Brok." Organa awkwardly nodded before making her way outside of *The Sea-Old Wench*.

Adjusting her eyes to the bright sunlight, she saw houses and people walking about the town. A human woman walked beside her three children and her Elven husband. The husband held her hand, and his eyes were full of love. Gleaming with passion and a heart full of joy, he picked up the smallest of the boys and held him in the air, then placed him on his shoulders.

Organa turned her head, flinging some of her silver hair to one side, and saw a man on his horse. His sword and armor gleamed in the light, illuminating a silver-and-gold crest on the breastplate. The crest was the Trinity of Arches, more commonly known as the Arches of Light, a symbol of Havithreal, the goddess of creation.

A groaning from nearby caught her attention as she turned her head to the left. Brok moved slowly in a pool of mud. He struggled to stand in the deep mud, falling every few seconds. Organa simply watched and enjoyed the clumsiness for a few moments. Brok finally stood to his feet and balanced himself. His friend stood on a wooden porch, laughing lightly. Gliding her hand in the air and weaving two threads, water and earth, the mud turned into clear, blue water that rippled around Brok's feet.

His leather pants clung to him and seemed to shrink around his legs. "Can you… uh… help?" She lifted her hand and pulled it back as if she were grasping something that was not there. The water in his clothes expelled itself in blue strands, and Organa returned it to the earth beneath their feet.

EV and Myrcle walked out of the tavern and saw Organa helping her dim-witted friend.

"So, where does this adventure of our lead?" Organa asked them.

"Well," Myrcle explained, "our destination is the base of Mount Doloroth. There is a forest that grows tall and strong. It there that they say the Golden Queen of Rethial lives. They are the ones who stole the old man's family heirloom."

"You mean the 'Bandit Queen'?" Organa let out a light chuckle.

"Basically, 'Operation Don't Do Anything Stupid and Don't Be Seen'—which we shall undoubtedly fail to follow," EV said, glaring at Organa.

"I have the strangest feeling that you really don't like me at all," Organa remarked.

EV's bravado fell away. "No, it's not that I don't like you. I am just…" her words trailed off as she donned her mask again. "I worry about your future and after how quickly you began to just flow with the Flux… your Balance of Chaos—"

"My future, Balance of Chaos, what is all of this?" Organa said.

"EV," Myrcle explained, "is a *Lananret K'Verel*, a 'Far Seer'—one who can see the fragmented paths of someone's life by touch."

"What did you see when you touched me? Did you see my future?" Organa asked.

"There are many paths, thousands, just like everyone else. Every choice you make creates a new one and destroys another. Everyone's life is like that to the eyes of people like me, the rare few left of us. Yet when I look into your future, it's as if something clouds most of the paths. Something blocking it intently. It's not that I don't like you, Organa, it's that I am afraid of what hides behind the fog. Dangerous things have happened when I cannot find the answers to the riddles of the future."

"You're a very strong Seer EV, but you still need work," Myrcle grabbed her arm firmly. "We need to set off on our journey. Come on!"

Organa looked at Brok who only shrugged his shoulders in response before they followed after their new companions.

As they made their way out of the city, Myrcle brought out a book from his bag and read from a tome full of arcane and ancient symbols. Organa leaned over his shoulder a bit to see the strange markings on the pages. Swirling characters connected to one another and then turned rigid before flowing once more.

"What's this?" she asked.

"This is a compendium of history."

"What about?"

"The Athenaeum Archive of Balinor and its many great wonders."

"How can you read it? Those symbols are not familiar to the languages the Order taught me."

"This is Stellevarian, the Language of Stars, and the dialect of the Lux." Myrcle explained.

"That's a dead language." Organa said.

"I have spent my entire life researching and decoding languages of the ancients and texts from the far past trying to find a way to help Lorial from falling into the grip of the Void. Many people have tried to lay the blame on someone—"

"Like the Cleansing?"

"Exactly. The fear that those Magiqas who could channel so much of the Flux to them was not an unfounded one. Many catastrophes were caused by the Magiqas. One could even lay blame for the Light-Kin wars of old Dremica given that the Queen Serefin, who swore herself to the Shadow Monarch to win against her brother's claim to the Crystal Thrones—"

"She was a Magiqas too."

"Yes. And, the most feared of them all—"

"The Lord of Shadows, Golgorot, the betrayer of the Silver Fountain?" the legends flowed through her mind in a river of images that seemed all too real.

"I see you do know some history, but yes and no," he chuckled. For a moment, he seemed almost in pain, but he quickly suppressed it. "Yes, his wrath was swift, and his cunning even more so. Evermore, he seeks to enter the minds of the weak and drown out their ideas of peace and replace them with his own vengeance. But his master is far more powerful and dangerous than any creature that has yet to enter this plane of existence."

"The Dark One," Organa said.

"'The Dark One', 'Formless One', 'Shadow Monarch', 'Betrayer'… all names for the evil that guided his hand and his servants. They had burrowed themselves so deep—" his concentration was broken by a sharp scream.

A woman on her knees beside an Elven man was calling for help as she held the man's hand. An enormous crowd formed around her, and people blocked the image out. Organa and the rest of her compatriots rushed over to the site of the uproar, seeing blood trailing underneath the crowd's feet like a small river. Myrcle pushed people out of the way and got close to the woman and the victim. EV and Organa walked to the center and saw the crying woman and the body on the ground. An arrow protruded from the man's chest, and Organa looked to his face and recognized it. The husband she had seen playing with his family lay on the dirt with an arrow sticking out from his chest, gasping for air as blood flowed down the edge of his mouth onto the ground. At the edge of the arrow waved a small scroll with an unbroken seal.

Myrcle ripped the scroll from the arrow. He unfurled it, and after he read it, then stuffed the note into his pocket. The dying man gasped for the last bit of air he could, and died with a few tears rolling down his face.

His wife called his name, "Malorian… Malorian!" He gave no answer. His eyes became devoid of life and light.

Myrcle got closer to the man's face and placed his hand upon his head, cupping his forehead. He closed his eyes and could sense the soul had not yet left the body. He roughly removed the arrow from the dead man, and his wife gasped in shock.

"What are you doing to him?" she asked, enraged.

"I am going to save him, my lady," EV answered.

She spoke in a language that caused Organa's head to ache. As EV sang lightly, her voice echoed around the crowd as streams of green threads of life poured into the man's chest. The water in the fountain nearby rippled with joy. The air danced around them, the ground purring with sensation, and the fire within the man's heart returned to him as his wounds managed to stitch themselves back together.

The man's eyes burst with life; his breath came rapidly at first before steadying out. His wife screamed with joy and hugged him. He embraced her, and they both cried together.

Myrcle looked at EV with judgment and disdain, but also understanding. He knew what that cost her. Myrcle reached into his pocket, took out the scroll, and stepped away from the crowd. Organa and Brok followed behind and watched him as he read.

"What does it say?" Organa asked.

"It is a letter from the Flames of the Sphynx, the royal guard of the Menitheal Dynasty." With a sigh he continued to read the scroll in a light whisper, "*Here lies a traitor to his kin, the High Elves of Dremica. Let ye who read this know, this is a royal decree and sentence from Lord Menitheal and his Lady Magis. Long may they reign.*'"

"Long may they rot in the Void," EV said and laughed as she came up beside him.

Myrcle turned and grabbed her arm harshly. "I have no love for the Menitheal Dynasty either, EV, but you must watch your tongue." His eyes looked about wildly. "You never know who may be listening." EV nodded her head in agreement.

"Are we going to tell the Warden of this town?" Organa pleaded.

"No," Myrcle shot back. "If he knew of the existence of this letter, he would tell the other Wardens of Rethial, they would then tell the spymasters, and it would roll into the jaws of the Sphinx."

"What did he do?" Organa asked.

"That woman over there," Myrcle pointed to the woman being held by other townsfolk, "is his wife, and she's human."

"What does that have to do with any of this?"

EV walked to Organa's side. "After three generations of the bloodline, they stopped the mixing of races, married only other elves, and forbade it among their people as well. So, there is some merit to this 'crime', if only from a legal standpoint. No…something else is brewing."

Organa nodded her head. "If they truly wanted to kill him for his 'crime,' they would have succeeded with an easy shot."

"The archer could have coated the arrow in dark magic to destroy or heavily damage the soul. Which begs the question, why is he not dead? Was it merely circumstance or was the archer's aim thrown off?" Myrcle pondered his question and walked over to the crowd where the elf had been shot.

Myrcle got back to the couple and tried to get their attention, but the husband ran past him to EV and hugged her tightly around her neck. "Thank you, my friend; you have given my family a great miracle."

EV nodded her head. "You are welcome, sir. I try my best. May I ask you something?" She motioned to Myrcle for the scroll.

"Yes, my friend."

"The shaft of the arrow that attacked you had a message attached to it from the Menitheal Dynasty. What do you know of this matter?"

"That is a conversation best had indoors in private." The Elven man led his guests to his rundown home across the courtyard. Myrcle kicked up some dirt behind him as EV scoffed, following behind him with Organa and Brok. The door opened, and the man called out to his children. Three boys ran down the stairs to their father. One boy was about twelve years old. His hair was like his father's, long and blond with small curls, and his eyes were like his mother's and father's; one of them was sea blue and the other a beautiful violet. The second boy was tall and thin for his age. He seemed about fifteen, and his hair was like his mother's, black as a raven and nicely trimmed. His skin was fair and tanned, and his hazel eyes sparkled in the slight light through the windows. The other boy was the one Organa had seen earlier on the Elven man's shoulders. One thing that they all had in common was their small Elven ears.

"These are my sons, my eldest, Manis," who bowed to the guests politely, "Forlin, my second son," who also bowed but not as well as his older brother, "and Valnias, my youngest son," whose atrocious attempt at bowing caused Myrcle to chuckle slightly. The father too bowed. "I am Malorian, and this," he pointed to his wife, "is Ynetia, my wife of five winters."

"Thank you for welcoming us into your home," EV bowed back to them.

"Boys, please go prepare dinner for this evening," Malorian directed his sons. They nodded back in response and went into the kitchen.

Myrcle took a bag of coins from his pocket and passed the purse to EV. She then walked to Ynetia and placed it in her hand.

"What is this?"

"That," he explained, "is seventy-four gold pieces to help you and your family, Ynetia."

She covered her mouth to hide her astonishment. "Sir, I cannot accept this."

"Take it, please," insisted Myrcle. "You will need it more than we do."

"Thank you, kindly sir." Ynetia walked away back to her husband, who was now in another room grabbing a book from a tall shelf. As she placed the purse in his hand, he opened it and poured out the money into a vase.

A simple expression of awe covered EV's face; she was dumbfounded that Myrcle had given away their money. Myrcle simply laughed at EV, who in turn moved to strike him, but Organa stopped her, placing her hand on her shoulder. "Not now," she said and walked forward.

Malorian walked back to the group. "Please have dinner with us tonight."

EV tapped Myrcle on the shoulder, and he turned around to see her shaking her head in disagreement. "We would love to, my friend." EV's eyes could not have rolled further back into her head.

Around the hearth that burned with a large fire, someone positioned a few rugged stools and other seats. Malorian motioned for his guests to sit, and they did. Myrcle took a seat in a large crescent-shaped chair that had a lovely cushion on the bottom. Brok found a tall stool, and Organa found another, taking a seat beside him. EV found her chair near the hearth, where the warmth of the fire was best. Ynetia walked into the kitchen with her sons. The oldest tended to the meat, trimming it with a large knife, cutting it into smaller pieces, and throwing it into a black pot over another hearth. Ynetia grabbed some spices from a very dilapidated cabinet and placed them on the table. She looked at her middle child and asked him to go fetch some water from the well and bring it back. Her son nodded, grabbed the pail by the door, and walked outside. The youngest sat on a platform near the window with a carrot in his hand that he took a bite of every few seconds. Ynetia grabbed the large kettle from the fire and poured its contents into the teapot.

Ynetia walked over with a tray that had a lovely and expensive ivory teapot and six wooden teacups, which sat upon small wooden saucers for everyone. "Would you like some tea?"

"Yes, please," replied Myrcle. Organa and Brok too accepted the offering, but as Ynetia got to EV, she passed by without an offer. Ynetia disappeared for a few moments, and an awkward silence came over the room that was then broken by Ynetia's return with a large goblet of wine for EV.

EV looked at Ynetia with confusion but much gratitude. "Thank you."

"So," Myrcle began, "why did you leave the royal court?"

"I beg your pardon, sir," Malorian said anxiously.

Myrcle chuckled, "You need to hide your mark better." He pointed to the black ink on Malorian's right collarbone. "The mark on your neck there is the crest of the Menitheal Dynasty." It was a great Sphinx with three heads, each of its faces like a lion's. The right breathed fire, the left snarled with rage, and the middle had a crown upon its head. Six great wings overlapped one another, and a long tail with a scorpion's stinger was dripping toxin. Small marks on the bodies resembled feathers and stopped at the calf muscles of the large lion legs.

"You've a good eye, friend," he said anxiously. "Because you saved my life, I will tell you. I used to be the apprentice to the Sorcerer Lord, m'lord."

"Oh," Myrcle stuttered, "I'm not a lord anymore, sir." Organa's eyes narrowed, but Myrcle quickly moved on, hoping to evade her questions. "So why did you leave?"

"Because of what I found," Malorian walked to a large bookshelf, placed his hand on the backboard, and whispered a spell. The wooden board radiated a golden and bright glow that shone upon Malorian's face. A seal appeared, the Arches of Light. He whispered another word, and the symbol changed, moving like snakes along the wall that retreated into the wood. The board opened inward, revealing a long cylinder. He took the scroll and rolled it out across the table in the center of the circle of chairs. Dyed with chromatic inks, the broken wax took the shape of a family crest.

Myrcle could not contain his curiosity. "Where did you find this?" He looked to Malorian with trembling confusion.

Malorian bowed his head in shame. "As I said, I was the Sorcerer Lord's right hand, the keeper of magical knowledge of Lorial in Rethial. I taught and created spells for the royal family. The ones I created, however, rarely ever worked, and if they did, they were turned and used for war." His voice trailed off and a sense of shame came over him. Ynetia walked over to him and rubbed his shoulders with her hands. Malorian reached for her, and their fingers intertwined. He gave the top of her hand a kiss before he took in as much air as he could and released it slowly. "My friends, I have seen many wars. I have seen hundreds of dead bodies, people killed by magic, some of it from spells I created myself." He held up his hands as he let go of Ynetia's. "They may not seem so, but these hands have spilled blood. Even more would have been in danger if I had not left."

"What exactly happened?" Organa asked Malorian.

"Well, m'lady, though it was not the first time someone had asked me to do something rather unsettling while in the family's service, this was the worst by far. The Lady Menitheal sent a messenger with a small scroll, which was passed to me. The Lady asked me to meet her in the throne room of the castle, so I did. When I got there, she and her youngest daughter were waiting for me, and she asked if I could find a piece of information in the High Tower, where all the records were kept. She said that her daughter was curious about the architecture of the castle. I found the request odd, as people said the first Lord and Lady had destroyed the castle and city architectural plans. However, I went to look."

"And you found this," Myrcle asked.

"Yes, and to my great surprise."

"Where was it?"

"I searched for over three days in the High Tower, skimming through hundreds of small parts of the records of the design of the city and the great pyramid, but never found a single piece of a schematic for Castle Black Rose."

"Castle Black Rose?" Organa asked.

EV turned to her, and a very unsettling tone of fear gripped her voice. Clearing her throat and looking as if she was about to cry, she spoke softly. "Bal'Xani was the original name. All of the details in the entire city were designed to be a replica of the city of Husieàkritae, the capital of the Silver Kingdom. However, the name of the palace in Dremica was not called something so foul, but far more ethereal, 'The Starlight Citadel' which in the old words of Stellevarian was *Bal'Xani*. This new place was no replica or possible resemblance of the grace of the ancient monarchs and their customs."

Organa felt a slight twinge in her head at the mention of the name, but she pushed it aside. "So why was the name set to mock the old ways?"

"'Castle Black Rose' was decided upon from the first of the Menitheal Dynasty to mock the Starlight Crown." She continued, "You see, the Menitheals were one of the higher families in Dremica and still believed themselves above all other people. Many times, the family would try to challenge the throne in a ceremony called *'Forntera'*, which in the common tongue means 'Battle of Kings', a battle to the death. The winner of the battle would be the new bearer of the Starlight Crown and thus become the new monarch of Dremica and its people. Each time the Menitheal family tried to overthrow the ruling house, they failed."

"You know your history. EV, was it?" Malorian asked.

EV nodded. "So then, how did you find this?"

"That's what I do not know."

"What do you mean?" asked Myrcle.

Malorian stood and walked to the new kitchen. He grabbed a nice mug from a cabinet and filled it with water from the brown wooden pitcher. He walked back over to the group, speaking as he did, "I finally took a day of rest in my chambers in the Western Obelisk, and when I woke up, I found this scroll sealed with this." As he finished, he passed a second scroll to Myrcle.

Upon the parchment was a broken white wax seal split into two halves. Myrcle put the two halves together to form the image. A triangle with three lines stretching to the center, giving the appearance of a three-dimensional form. The lines met at a purple crystal in the center, from which a liquid dripped and landed on the horizontal line. Around the crystal and hitting the edges of the triangle, a cube-like figure seemed to form.

"What house is this?" Organa asked. "I've never seen this crest."

"That, Organa, is the crest of the old Menitheal Dynasty."

"Why the change in crest?"

Myrcle sat silent and pondered the scroll, and EV stood and did the same. They gave no answer to Organa for a few moments until Malorian broke the silence with a slight quiver of fear in his voice.

He sat up straight and cleared his throat. "A rumor circled about the continent long ago that the Menitheal Dynasty was a part of the *Vul'Denitier Xir Revin*, which in the common tongue means—"

"The Cult of Blighted Souls," Myrcle interrupted. "It is better known by another name in a fouler tongue, that of Vodrian. *Blenturi*

Valis Fearnis, which then translates differently to the common speech as Order of the Valiant."

"Valiant, as in courage?" asked Organa.

"Like every cult," Myrcle confirmed.

"Why is that more well-known?"

"The title they operate under is more appealing, and through the initiation, the initiates discover the true nature of the cult. Throughout their training, they are brainwashed to be mindless servants of the elders and powers that control the cult."

"So, they lure people into a false faith and corrupt them to the point of no return?"

"Correct," Malorian confirmed.

Myrcle continued, "They say that Vexian, the Kalishtani elder, created it when he and his closest followers offered their services to the Void before the Cataclysm. It changed them into the Heralds of Darkness on Lorial. A revolution against Vexian and his cultists began from the other Kalishtani, who saw his pact as an abomination to the Pantheon of Dawn, which it was. After the Cataclysm, when the people of the east fled to the other lands, three noble houses arrived on Rethial and began a feud amongst one another over the rule of Rethial and the refugees of Dremica. They saw this land from the west as primitive and beneath them, except for one, House Fultan, who tried to convince the others that a life of work and plenty would be more prosperous than the old monarchy that ruled the Fallen Kingdom. House Menitheal, House Fultan, and House Xelith began a six-month war over the new world. Obviously, the rule was given to the triumphant Menitheal family, who killed off the other two houses in a single great battle near Valistar. Thus, their dynasty began."

Myrcle pointed to the seal on the scroll which he held in his hand, "The crest they originally owned was this one, but due to the information and rumors of the dark magics within Castle Black Rose, the family changed their crest to the one we know now. Many believed the original crest to resemble the Blitinas crest, a long-dead family from the beginnings of Lorial. Some say Blitinas was the first family and the first of the Fallen Souls who began the Cult of the Blighted Souls." Myrcle held out the scroll that was attached to the arrow that pierced Malorian.

When put together, the halves of the dark purple broken seal formed another crest. An enormous diamond with four triangles connected to it surrounded a smaller. One triangle was on the inside of each corner, with strange symbols that Organa had never seen before. Strict lines and dark purple wax traced the runes. Inside the enormous diamond were smaller runes, somehow darker in nature and more definitive. Below the darker runes was another diamond with small lines connecting the edges and, in the center, a small swirl made up of many pyramids.

"This is the new crest?" Organa asked.

"Aye, and it's only been changed in the last hundred years. That, my dear, is, beyond any doubt, the crest of the Cult," Malorian concluded.

"If I were to open this scroll, what would I find?" EV's voice trembled.

EV and Myrcle exchanged glances and then opened the scroll. Written in silver ink, a passage in the center was made of strange symbols unlike any seen in three thousand years since the First Age of Light. As their eyes followed the trail, it led to a great black pyramid with shiny sides and strange purple markings on the edges of each of the four sides that connected at the summit. Then the entire picture was realized. The base of the black pyramid linked to a much larger base of a white pyramid with gold lines along the edges and a great gold apex. Dead bodies littered the bottom of the scroll, and then the purple flame came alive on the parchment, stretching to the bodies and bringing them to life. Some became undead minions filled with the fire, and others fused themselves together to create great monstrosities. The great pyramid above them shattered at the top into millions of pieces and slowly became more disassembled. A large purple, red, and black crystal formed in front of the pyramids, and it too shattered the same way. Ultimately, the shards became connected by a trail of white light that then covered the entire piece of parchment, and Myrcle dropped the scroll.

Malorian went and poured glasses of wine for them all, then spoke. "This is one of eight scrolls like it."

"What did we just see?" Myrcle asked.

"I showed it to a colleague of mine. He disappeared just two days before I left, and he said it matched the description of the Cataclysm."

"So, these scrolls are what, visions of the past?" EV asked.

"These are keys, keys to the lock of the mystery of the darkness under Castle Black Rose, the royal family, and maybe even the secrets surrounding the Cataclysm," Malorian explained with excitement. "This is one of the eight Writs of Sight, the seeing scrolls that have seen the past, present, and future."

"The world knows what happened," EV went on. "The Fire in Heaven that tore the night sky, the endless armies of the dead that slaughtered the people, and the great Shadows of the North, flying down upon the city drowning it within their dark flames and torment. They slaughtered millions in seconds, cities turned to ash in minutes, and centuries of people were wiped out in a few days."

"You speak of it as though you were there, m'lady?" Ynetia questioned.

"Everyone knows the Songs of Sorrow," she brushed it off.

Ynetia had a fair point. The tone in which EV spoke seemed like she lived it, as if she was there. However, most who had lived through that time were long gone and their bones turned to dust, given back unto Lorial. Rarely few who were alive then still draw breath.

Malorian grabbed the scroll from Myrcle's hand, holding it over a small bowl of liquid that had been mixed. With a snap of his fingers, the liquid burst into flames, and he placed the scroll a few inches above them. The parchment cracked, but no fire spread to the page. Instead, the flames burned away, and the bottom right-hand corner revealed more symbols. Malorian took the scroll from above the flames. "Read this, my friend." Bright red and green runes shone upon the parchment as the language revealed itself.

Myrcle took the paper and looked back to EV, motioning for her to come to his side. She walked across the new wooden floor, and her boots made loud *clops.* EV crouched down beside Myrcle, held the right side of the scroll, and looked deeply at the runes, trying to decipher them.

"These are designs for the city of Husieàkritae." EV looked at Malorian alarmed. "Where did you get this? These were all destroyed."

"Not all, it may seem, dearie," Myrcle retorted.

"As I told you, I was studying some scriptures, and, in my studies, I found a journal. The journal was that of Lord Kan'Dravis. In his notations, he described the Fire in Heaven and his flight into the west. He took up the position six years after the current Soulflame King and Lady Magis began their tyranny of Sorcerer Lord once more, and this time recorded everything. Including the location of the last of the schematics for Husieàkritae. Which you might note, is the same for Valistar. The capital is a copy, one gigantic memorial to what was lost." Malorian ran into a nearby room, opened the dresser against the wall and pulled from within the drawer, the journal. Myrcle stood for a moment as Malorian got closer to them and grabbed the book from his hands.

Over eight hundred pages filled with sketches of artifacts, symbols, and other items. Pages of notes and daily things that the Sorcerer Lord would write about. As Myrcle flipped through the pages, one caught his eye. Looking back at the parchment, he saw the thing he had feared might be underneath the city.

"You see, a darkness lies beneath the city, and I both believe you and know what it is. If a Sepulcher has been found and it is the reason behind the ever more corrupted heart of the Lord and Lady Menitheal, only pain and death have come from trying to open that prison, so we must destroy it."

"Nevertheless, should we shatter it, the darkness within will be freed. We are warriors, but we cannot take on what is coming should it empty its treasury," Myrcle said, his voice quivering.

"That is why I believe I was shot today. I know of the Sepulcher, and I am afraid the Lord and Lady Menitheal are trying to cover up their plans. I believe they mean to open it."

"Let me see that scroll," Organa asked Malorian. She opened it and saw the image restored to its original form. A closer look at the image of the black pyramid revealed another mystery. "Myrcle," she shouted to him. "Myrcle," she said this time louder. Still no answer. "Myrcle," she said as she hit his head. He took notice, and as he turned to his friend, she saw within his eyes a dark purple glow and a moving blackness.

"What was that for?" he asked.

"You wouldn't shut up and listen. Here, look. Look at the black pyramid," she said as she handed him the scroll. "What do you see?"

"The amulet the old man described to us. EV, look," he said as his finger pointed to it on the page. At the base of the pyramid was a circular amulet with blue, purple, and red crystals, which hit the points of a black crystal in the center. "This is a key," he breathed.

"And keys… uh… unlock… things, right?" Brok asked.

Organa walked to him and patted his head lightly. "Yes, Brok, yes they do."

"Looks like we're not abandoning that quest after all," EV said.

"Then we best be off." Myrcle was already at the door and ready to walk outside to begin the journey. The others saw him walk out and followed him. As they did, they saw the day was turning into a bright evening and the sky was a vibrant purple and orange.

Myrcle motioned to the others, and all three of them followed EV with their gear for the journey.

"That," Myrcle spoke and pointed to the northeast, "is Mount Doloroth, where we're headed."

Just above the treetops, the great snowy white peak stretched toward the sky and could have been mistaken for a cloud. Its grandeur was like a stairway to the heavens.

With a simple nod of his head, EV came to Myrcle's side. Both of them raised their hands and moved them closer together, hovering a few inches apart. Tangles of white and golden threads emerged from the space between their palms and began to wrap around them. The web of light expanded until it had made a dome. Organa heard their words and somehow knew them, as if they had been sung to her long ago.

Lead us into fate,
Lead us into Destiny.
Guide us to where we seek,
But where we need be.

As their unison lyrics ended, the orb expanded around the quartet. The bright light within stayed still as the surrounding orb expanded past them. The white light that danced in the middle grew in size, intensity, and a droning sound followed the growth. "Hold on, dearies," Myrcle shouted. "Things are going to get a little bumpy.

And try not to vomit. These robes are new-ish."

"Well, Brok, this will be one interesting tale to tell when we come back."

Then they were gone in a bright flash.

Drowning Flames

Each of them felt a sharp pain against their backs as they hit the ground. All of them let out loud gasps for air as the white light faded from their eyes. EV opened her eyes and saw the bright purple, red, and orange sky of the sunset. From the far horizon and the gleaming star behind it, long clouds stretched into the heights of the sky. EV marveled at the eternal stretching of the universe, and she simply lay there on the ground, catching her breath and staring into the semi-night sky.

"Organa," Myrcle called out, "are you okay?"

"I'll be fine," she said with a chuckle after she gasped for air.

"Good, good, and thank you for not vomiting on my robes. Now, stand up and help me make camp," he said. Organa shot him a confused and frustrated look that he did not see, as he was already turned around to set up their tents. Attempting to stand but failing miserably, Organa looked over to Brok, who was stumbling everywhere and unable to maintain his balance.

Brok fell face-first and hit the grass with a light thump. He hit his head and fists on the ground many times, creating dull but loud bangs on the earth. A resonance from the magic that they had passed through remained as she made her way to him.

Brok held up a hand to stop the approach. He hit his head

on the ground many times along with his fists, creating loud but muted bangs in the ground. Organa hesitated for a moment, trying to overcome her dizziness, and then finally processed what was happening to him.

"Shit," Organa shouted, running to Brok's side and moving his great sword away from him. She anxiously laid her right hand on the back of his jet-black hair. She muttered to the wind as his fist pounded the ground. Myrcle ran to Organa's side, but she too held up a hand to signal him to halt. Brok let out a loud bellow, and his rage grew more and more.

The wind caught her angelic voice as she sang lightly. The wind responded and picked up, and the grass became like waves. Leaves from the nearby trees flew and spiraled around Organa and Brok as they diminished into ash and concentrated into threads of verdant life. Small, dancing sprinkles and sparkles of light shone from Organa's hand, flowing into Brok's head. His tenseness fell away, and he stopped hitting the ground. As he relaxed, Organa's singing trailed off, and she fainted, falling upon Brok's back.

* * *

In her mind, Organa saw Brok standing in a never-ending field of tall ash, surrounded by a large forest lit ablaze. A voice on the air beckoned her forward.

As she got closer, she heard the voice on the hot winds. "I am your fate." It was a solitary voice, dark and malicious. "I am your destiny."

As the phrase ended, a great explosion sounded from behind the forest. A blinding flash of pale blue light came through the trees, and the ground beneath Organa's feet rumbled. The roars of five terrible beasts sounded from behind her as she watched the mountains around the forest blow away from the force like leaves.. Their presence seemed familiar as she watched them fly above in the sky and lay waste to the trees with different colored flames, ice, and shadow. From their wings came a rain of fire, a violent blizzard, or a black cloud of death and blight. As each of the dragons flew over the forest and Organa, their darkness fell upon the world, and from that darkness came green, white, and purple flames that drowned out the life of anything living.

The sounds of screams on the wind, dead things, dying people, and monstrosities of the Void and Deep pierced through the air with a terrible song of death. Suddenly, conclusively, booming, and shattering, an explosion of immense proportions threw massive heaps of stone, earth, marble, and other structures into the sky. As fast as the flames consumed the world around them, a winter blew them away with a massive blizzard that turned the very earth beneath her into solid ice. But it too was stopped before it could claim more of the world as the ice retreated into the few standing trees of the forest that managed to cling to the earth.

Organa ran through the trees and bushes, using her power over nature to move them from her path. As she reached the end of the forest, a great crater waited, at least twenty miles across, and in its center was a dark, black-and-white flame.

"Now, I will have vengeance," the voice said again on the wind.

Organa turned to her right and saw Brok, Myrcle, EV, and two figures made of light fighting off the shadowy demons. As they laid waste to the ranks of the darkness and the creatures lay lifeless upon the ground, maniacal laughter echoed from the central fire of the desolation.

From within the dark flame's depths, a figure made of dark, smoke-like shadows and white flickering lights stepped out with burning eyes of crimson red. Heavy, dark, plated armor sat on their body, and long black and white hair flowed from the top of their head. A crown of gold rested at their feet, the inner band swirling with the light of a hundred-thousand galaxies. One dark wing and another of radiant light unfurled from behind the mysterious figure as it rose high above them. Suddenly, the crater around them was gone, as were Myrcle, Brok, Esvele, and the two figures of light.

Rising from below, another massive forest grew in place of the previous, but it would not remain standing for long. Organa and the dark figure stood above the forest and, raising their hands, smirked as they flung them down. A stream of bright red and orange fire extended, and the forest burned. Hundreds of people ran from within the forest.

The streams of fire broke off from one another, and with a single ancient word, the flames burrowed into the corpses and their souls. The figure twitched violently, and its eyes burst into red flames. Within seconds, the dead became undead. They stood individually at first and then as one mass. The forest burnt away, and the souls of the dead appeared before a solitary tower of black and jagged stone. A rift in the sky above it pulled millions of green souls into the maw of the Void.

* * *

Organa lurched forward from her sleep in a cold sweat. Strands of wet hair clung to her face as she panted with a racing heart. The light from the fire cast the shadows of three figures onto the tan cloth. Seeing them and knowing their forms, her heart slowed. There was something about them, something she knew but did not know. Like something she used to know. A feeling of peace and friendship. With that, her heart steadied, and she wiped the sweat from her brow. Organa rose to her feet, hunched over because of the size of the tent. She walked to the slit in the cloth and pulled it back, revealing the others gathered around the fire.

EV held a cast-iron skillet with some meat in it while Brok sat with his legs crossed on the grass. He stared into the fire in deep thought, with what little he could think. Organa looked up at the stars and saw The Fire in Heaven glowing red and deep crimson. Myrcle was floating in the center on a column of air as he scoured through six of his books. He spun around, glancing at the different tomes. He turned the pages with his fingers, controlling the surrounding wind.

EV sighed, "Don't stare too hard; you'll only boost his ego."

"What do you mean?"

"You think he doesn't know he is one of the smartest people on this planet."

"I can hear you, Esvele," Myrcle said with a chuckle.

"Esvele?" Organa questioned.

"That's my real name, Esvele."

"It's really pretty."

"Thank you," she paused, "but don't be calling me that. I'll stab your eyes out," she said defensively. EV got up and went to her tent.

"Why doesn't she like to be called that?"

"Because it is her birth name, the one her parents gave her," Myrcle said as he floated lightly in the air reading his books.

"What were they like? Did you ever meet them?"

"No, no, no. They died about…" He paused. "Two hundred years ago," Myrcle said with ease.

"Two hundred years ago? What do you mean?" Organa asked.

"EV is much older than she looks, my dear. How old do you think she is?"

"Late twenties, early thirties?"

Myrcle snorted at the number. "Dearie, she is well, *well*, over two-hundred-and-fifty years old."

"What?" exclaimed Brok. "That's not…. hm… oh, possible." Brok looked to Organa for reassurance in his vocabulary.

"*impossible*," Organa smiled.

"Yes, my friend, it shouldn't be. However, it is." Myrcle said.

"Wait a minute. You mean to tell me that EV was alive during the Cataclysm?" Organa asked.

"Yes, dearie, and she watched it happen," Myrcle's voice had changed tones to solemn and sad.

"Did she tell you what happened? What does she remember? How old was she? Where was she? Who was she with? Did she see the Shadows of the North—"

"I was in Husieàkritae," Esvele said, her words weighing down her throat.

"And you're alive?" Organa blinked.

"My father was a Kalishtani Master of Arms and War for the Soulflame King and the Lady Magis. We—"

Esvele, we have to be careful, Myrcle's words echoed in her mind. *We can't push it too hard too fast. Lie to her...*

Esvele eyed Myrcle for a moment, but she knew he was right. "Anyway," she trailed off, weaving the tale together with slight truths. "We lived in the Citadel of Bal'Xani. At the time, I was training with my father and the High Druid, Master Corthal, in the courtyard." EV finished her sentence and then paused. She gazed deeply into the flames of the bonfire as the memory flooded her mind. "You've heard the stories, right?"

"Yes, ma'am," Brok said as he cuddled close to Organa like a small child, which he was nowhere near the size of.

"The tales of the great cities of Lux and the white crystal halls and buildings. The Cathedral of Dawn, how it beamed over the city and shone the brightest light of all creation on Lorial." Myrcle rose from his seat and walked to EV's side, sitting down beside her and wrapping his arms around her shoulder comfortingly. Esvele sighed, "I wish you could've seen it."

"I had a dull, makeshift fake version of a blade in my hand, and my father held a sparring greatsword. We battled throughout the whole courtyard. I used my skills and small size to slide under and around him, dodging his attacks and landing a few hits now and then." She watched the flames closely as if she could see the images inside her mind through them as they crackled. "I landed a blow to my father as he missed his last chance to win the match. I had slid around him on the grass and then turned around, ready to put the fake knife to his throat with the victory won with honor. Then, I changed my mind without even knowing it, wrapping him in a vast number of vines and thorns that protruded from the ground, created from the blades of grass and from the roots under the earth. It was at that moment that the High Druid stopped the fight and told my father to train me as a Magiqas"

"So that's where your powers came from?" Organa asked.

"I didn't even know I had them 'til that moment," EV said. "It felt like such an honor. I was the youngest Magiqas initiate ever to be trained at the Silver Fountain outside of the Guardians or royal family. I spent the next ten years there; it's where I learned to master my powers and studied the histories of Lorial and the cosmos. Following my training, a great contest determined the next High Druid. "Every two hundred years, the ceremony was held, and the next High Druid was chosen from the current *Retoura*. Each of us had to demonstrate our skills in three days, showing we could control the elements, hand-to-hand combat without magic, and finally, on the last day, we fought an incumbent."

"You had to fight the High Druid?" Organa asked.

"Not necessarily, but yes, I did, and all to prove that we were worthy of the title and could protect the royal family. And I fought him and won."

"Did he die?" Brok asked.

"Gods, no," EV shot back at him. "We were not savages. The High Druid would be granted a second life with the royal family and would continue to serve them as their *Wareliétae*, 'Scribe' or 'Great Scholar,' a master of healing and knowledge who would record the events of the Royal Court and be the person who would stay in the *Husvostus*, 'The Place of Healing,' as the master healer."

"You never told me that." Myrcle gave her a jealous, but clearly false, glance. "Sounds like my kind of job."

"You would have loved it, Myrcle," she assured him with a glance, "but you're not a druid, so you can't."

"Fuck that, I'll do what I damn well please," he remarked with a loud laugh. The group followed the laughter for a few moments and then recovered.

They are odd, Organa said to herself.

EV continued the tale of the Cataclysm. "I spent only a few months in the service of the royal family as their children's *Retoura*, then it happened. The Cataclysm began and devoured the entire continent in a matter of days."

"I watched, powerless to stop the terrible beasts of the Void. Trying to save the people I could within the gates of the Citadel of Bal'Xani. The people ran through the courtyard and into the castle while I and the city guard ran to the towering Gates of Calikan. As we got there, we saw some of the other guards who were barricading the entrance to the city. I saw my father there, the last time I'd see him breathing. Within a few seconds of our arrival, the gate turned to solid ice and then shattered into millions of pieces. Through the gate was an eternal blackness, like a void. None of the blizzards touched it, nor did the cold come from it. No light, just an endless expanse. Then the shards vibrated and rose from the ground, turning into spears. I ducked down and created a barrier of vines and wood around my soldiers, and the ice advanced. When I pulled the barrier down, I saw the slaughter that had ensued. I saw my father with three of those spears in his chest." EV was now almost fully in tears. Myrcle held her as she took a moment to recover. Organa looked at Brok's head as it rested on her shoulder. The idea of her losing a loved one was unknown to her. She never had a family except for the Order of Valkiel, and they all betrayed her.

EV spoke again now that she had regained her composure. "I watched it all burn under the tyranny of the Shadow Monarch's forces."

"'Shadow Monarch'?" Organa asked, the name echoing in her mind with whispers she barely heard.

"The ruler of darkness and all evil creatures. A culmination of all evil actions and intentions. The last thing I remember I regret, but it was necessary." She cried into Myrcle's shoulder. She stayed there for a while and then composed herself, rising from the grass. "So that's my story, and now you know what happened in the City of Light. I am going to bed. I shall see you all in the morning… goodnight." EV walked into her tent and sealed the seam once more.

"I can't imagine what it was like to live through that," Organa said solemnly.

"I can't either," Myrcle lied. "I looked in all my books for anything I could find as to what the great explosion could have been, or what had caused her to not age or die whilst she slept; however, I found nothing of the sort."

"What stopped the… Cataclysm?" Brok asked.

"I don't know, Gentle Giant. But I thank the gods for whatever it was."

"Nothing much ever came out of the gods, from what I've seen," Organa scoffed. "For all we know, all of this messed-up world is their fault." She nudged Brok and rose to her feet, walking toward her tent, and Brok followed behind her. He entered as Organa held the curtain for him. "Goodnight, Myrcle," she said, smiling at him.

"Goodnight, Organa," he said.

Leviathan's Crossing

Myrcle and Esvele broke through the tree line first. Before them lay rolling hills, mere footholds beneath the towering shadow of Mount Doloroth. Spanning four miles to the King's Isle, the Leviathan's Crossing—a massive bridge wrought of stone, wood, and metal—stood as a proud testament to mortal craftsmanship, though humble beside the feats of old. In ages past, great sorcerers, druids, and wizards could have summoned such a wonder with magic alone, crafting the glory of Rethial to bind isle and mainland. But when the Cataclysm sundered the connection to the gods and the Fire in Heaven marked their fall, the light that flowed through the blood within the veins of the peoples of Lorial diminished, and no more Magiqas were born in Lorial.

A broad span of stone and metal links formed the way across the Coiling River, the maw of which was just shy of the length of the passage. One of the great wonders of Lorial, the Leviathan's Crossing has never failed and will endure until the last days of the world.

"Well." Esvele pointed. "There's the mountain. That great frosted peak towers over everything. Let's get going. I'd like to reach the edge of the Forest of Bravica before nightfall. We need to be fully rested for our mission in the woods and the Golden Queen's camp." They all marched down the hillside together and made their way toward the bridge.

Warm air and a cool wind blew on a pleasant springlike day. Long stalks of wheat swayed as Esvele ran her hands through the golden stems and felt the breeze caress her cheek; as every warm day with its cool wind did, it reminded her of the days in Dremica. Endless fields of beautiful farms and tall forests. Buildings made of pure marble, gold, and silver. She thought of the Silver Fountain and her students, feeling their spirits as if they were right beside her. She could see the vast markets of goods from all over the continent. The Crystal Throne room and the thrones themselves, shining brightly with their sky blue hue falling down from the ceiling like a waterfall. She remembered the little girl she'd grown very close to and the girl's courageous, strong brother. She never saw that child after the Cataclysm, and she would never see that same child again.

They walked forward onto the great stone bridge, their shoes clopping lightly against it. "How did they make this bridge?" Organa asked.

"Carefully and patiently, my dear," Myrcle laughed, "Even before the Cataclysm, there were those who had ventured into the Old Sea and found the Four Lands. The furthest west currently known being where we stand now, for few dare to go beyond the veil of the Far Lands. Those who were here long before us built small villages and fishing towns like the town of Nefis on the Lonely Isle. It is said powerful sorcerers of great stature built Leviathan's Crossing, but no one really knows." Myrcle walked over to the edge of the bridge and peered out into the river that led out into the sea. He could see the waves of the Red Sea, the small ocean between the two lands where the waters of Rethial met the Balnorian clay sediment and turned a deep crimson. Legends told of a mighty, unbeheld beast, smitten by the gods and cast down from above into the sea, leaving its trail of blood to wash up on the shores forevermore. But just beyond the western coast of Rethial, green and blue waters stretched to the edges of the world along the great fog of the Far Lands. The ever-looming veil of mist and clouds shielded all eyes from what waited behind it. He returned to his original story for Organa. "It is quite a structure, is it not?"

"It's enormous. I didn't realize just how big as we passed over it in the night."

"Some legends say the name 'Leviathan's Crossing' comes from the great beast of the river that dwelled in these waters before the bridge was made. That those who traveled by boat were met with a serpent of great magnitude that would bring ships from the sea it had caught into the mouth of the river, where it would devour all those it could."

Organa smiled at him. "Then how was the serpent captured?"

"As all good tales go, a wondrous magician, Ecthelias, Lady of the Red Sea, took a company of two hundred soldiers just over there"—he pointed to the far-off riverbank— "and made battle with the beast of the river. They fought for seven days and seven nights before the beast was finally tired out and Ecthelias had exhausted her soldiers and resources. Then, when the last night had fallen, and the beast was ready to make its final assault, a sorcerer, Bendrit, Guardian of Lorial, Flame of the West, cast a spell on the beast and bound it into the cage beneath our very feet."

"What a load of rubbish," Organa laughed at him.

"Do you not believe in the beasts of the old days?"

"They existed, of course. They have found great skeletons of them, but none still exist that are that dangerous. And if it was that long ago, how could such a beast still be alive?"

"Because the Guardians of Lorial are meant to protect all living creatures and banish the darkness from this world."

"Clearly, they failed," Organa whispered under her breath.

"Don't you dare," Myrcle shot back. "If you had seen the devastation of the Silver Kingdom and the endless legions of darkness, you would not dare to speak such blasphemy of the sacrifices the Guardians made."

"I'm sorry." Her hands shot up. "I didn't mean to offend you."

"It is not me you have offended, but the memory of those who died to stop the Cataclysm from spreading across Lorial." His eyes flashed bright green and purple as a flame within him sparked for a moment.

"Myrcle," EV shot at him. Their eyes met, and he felt something within him subside before it took control.

Myrcle contained himself. "I am sorry for my rudeness."

"It's all right, I was being rude as well by insulting them." An awkward moment of silence fell over them until Organa broke the ice. "May I hear the rest of the story?"

"Yes, my dear," Myrcle smiled back at her, but she could still see the frustration in his eyes as he tried to calm his power. "Bendrit captured the creature on the bridge to preserve it. All accounts of the beast said it to be a majestic serpent of a magnitude hitherto undreamt of. When they made its cage, they carved runes inside that would allow the beast to rest in a dreaming sleep of freedom as to keep it from attacking sailors or innocents passing onto what would become the King's Isle."

"I hope it is still alive. I would love to see it."

"If we're not careful, maybe we will," Myrcle laughed at her.

Organa laughed at him as well, and the group continued on their way over the bridge. She caught up with Brok, who had continued alongside Esvele, who was speaking to him of the different magics of druid-craft. Slipping her hand in between his arm and torso, leaning her head on him as she walked.

"How long have you two been together?" Esvele asked.

"What?" Organa raised an eyebrow, "What do you mean?"

"How long have you two known each other?"

"As long as I can remember, although that isn't much."

"What do you mean?"

"I don't remember anything before the Order of Valkiel. They took me in, trained me, and that was where I met Brok. I was already a young adult when they found me in the Living City. Gerith told me that they had found Brok the next day."

"Why did you leave?"

"It's not important," she quickly replied. "I left, and I will never go back. They will have to drag me by my hair before I go there willingly."

"Fair enough." Esvele nodded and continued on.

A voice entered her head—the voice of Myrcle. *Do not pry, EV. We do not want to reveal much before we reach Mount Doloroth.* They walked for about three hours and, finally, were almost at the end of the great bridge. The rushing water of the river splashed over the banks of the shore.

As Brok reached the left of the two great columns at the end of the bridge, he saw a symbol carved into its stone: a great wave, colored blue, and a piece missing in the center. Running his hands over the stone column, looking for anything that might be able to be removed, he scoured the ground and saw a small green gem hiding amongst the grass at the edge of the stone walkway. Brok walked forward and, taking it in his hand, turned back toward the symbol he had seen. The gem hummed with an emerald radiance as he held it close to the vacant space on the pillar. It matched the shape of the piece missing from the symbol on the wall, so he placed it in the socket.

The gem radiated a bright, pure green light from within, and the waves of the symbol moved like the ones in the Old Sea, large and crashing on the gem and releasing a small mist of a scalding liquid. They spilled over the side of the railing and down onto a large round crest of the Menitheal Dynasty. Without delay, the acid ate away at the Sphinx and devoured it quickly. The crest dissolved rapidly, and the acid moved along the metal toward more crests; four more were burned away by Brok's mistake.

Suddenly, a substantial shift beneath their feet shook through them and the earth around the bridge. The quake loosened rock and metal, tossing them into the river as small pebbles or large boulders of fused material fell into the waters below. The quakes only got stronger as the foundations of the bridge cracked and shattered. As the middle of the bridge collapsed, the companions rushed off, and the rest of the structure quickly followed into the river. Shooting into the sky, a plume of thick mist was all that was left in the wake of the collapse.

"What did you do?" Esvele shouted at Brok, who only gave a shrug of confusion.

A large ripple in the water became visible as the curtain of mist subsided and the beast was unveiled. Myrcle frowned and sighed. "You know, sometimes—just once in my life—I want to hear about a legend or a myth and have it not *actually* be true."

A great snake, at least seven hundred feet long, with most of its length reared back as it glared at its next meal, rose from the cliff face. Its scales were blue and green to let it hide in the water of both the sea and the river that met it, and the bottom of the beast was a very light brown color. It had four golden eyes full of rage and heat, seeming to be inflamed. The maw of the beast opened wider than that of seven Sand Striders of the Western Wastes. Four great fangs, two on the bottom and the top, protruded like great spears as thick as oak trees. A long, quad-forked tongue, covered in small spines that looked like teeth, flicked out. Seven large fins lined its spine in fiery colors all the way down into the water and up to the tail of the great beast, which rested on the surface near the shore. A large, barbed stinger that was curved and sharpened to a point gleamed like a polished blade in the day's sunlight and a black and blue ooze dripped from its edges and tip, forming a pool of the liquid on the shoreline of sand and rock.

Myrcle ran at the beast and whirled his staff around him in blazing arcs. Threads of emerald fire danced in his wake until they gathered at the top into a burning orb of ruin. With one final swing, he unleashed the fireball, and struck the great beast.

A cloud of dust formed in the air around them as the serpent jerked about. All of them dodged out of the way of the swinging head as the serpent moved about wildly. Esvele and Myrcle were able to anticipate the movements of their foe, but the others were not so fortunate. Organa landed on the grass with a *thud*, hitting her head on a sharp rock.

Staggering for but a moment, Organa rose to her feet and searched for Brok. The thick brown cloud surrounding them blew away with a wind from Esvele's staff, revealing two great big hands clinging to the edge of the cliff. Organa ran to him, and as she approached, a loud roar sounded from their foe as it struck at her with its great mouth, just barely missing her. The serpent sank deep into the earth. Organa watched in horror as it tried to pull itself free from where she had seen Brok's hands.

After a moment's struggle, the ground gave way to the force of the leviathan's bite, and it reared its head back into the sky, taking the earth it had punctured with it. At the very bottom, near the corner of the mouth, she saw a figure dangling and heard a cry for help.

Brok barely clung to the edge, losing his grip as the chunk of earth collapsed within the serpent's maw. It shook its head wildly, throwing Brok from its mouth, and he landed on the creature's hunched back. He saw his moment, and hysterical laughter filled the air as Brok removed his weapon from his back and sliced deep into the hide of the mount beneath his feet. A rush of thick red blood poured from the wound of the creature, and it shot its head up toward the clouds and let loose another loud roar of anger and pain.

Snapping its head back to its attacker, the serpent *hissed* and shot a scalding spray of purple liquid forward. Rotten, burning flesh sizzled on Brok's shoulder as he dodged out of the way of the acidic rain. As the rain fell upon the serpent's scales, it trickled into small rivers, running along its back like smaller snakes and falling into the river below. Enraged, the constrictor lurched forward, sinking its fangs into its own body as Brok jumped out of the way and slid down to another spine.

Esvele saw the opening and gathered the threads of the Flux around the crystals of her staff. Fire and air wove themselves within the jagged glass and sparked to life with lightning. Thunder roiled around her as the flashes grew in intensity until Esvele thrust her staff forward and a blinding bolt of heavenly fire struck the serpent.

The great snake lifted its tail from the waters below and shot forth a rain of black and blue boiling ooze upon the ones still on land. Luckily, each of them was able to move out of the way before the poisonous and acidic liquid could touch them as they watched it melt the grass, dirt, and stone that it landed upon and then caught fire. The leviathan prepared for another bite upon them, hoping to fill its empty stomach.

Myrcle bolted and brought emerald flames to life in his hands. As he breathed, the strands of the Flux sharpened themselves into a single point that he channeled through his grand staff. The firestones came alive, and a single beam of verdant ruin erupted into the waiting jaws of the leviathan.

As the monster shot its head back in pain once more, Brok made his move. He sheathed his great blade, took out two daggers from their sheaths at his side, and plunged the blades into the skin of the beast, ascending the creature with each sinking stab.

Organa watched Brok climb up the snake, thrusting his blade into the creature with each inch gained. The serpent hissed as Brok's sword cut into it, and it turned its head to see the thorn in its side. But, before it could snap its jaws around him, a cloud of frost covered its eyes as Organa wove threads of air and water around its brow.

Brok finally made it to the head of the beast, barely hanging on as it thrashed about.

Esvele took a deep breath and looked up to see the raging swordsman atop the leviathan's head. "You've got to joking," she sighed.

Brok sheathed his smaller blades and took out his great sword as the creature writhed in agony. Black veins crawled up its body and pierced through its hard scales like a knife through butter. Seeing the raw flesh, Brok leapt from the creature's back and dug his large blade into the leviathan. It roared with terror as the scalding heat of the sword tearing through its body slid down and released a boiling flood of blood upon the ground below.

Brok descended from the beast and landed solidly on the ground with perfect grace and prowess, to the others' amazement. His glory radiated off of him as he vanquished the mighty foe, then a gushing wave of blood fell upon his head and drenched him in a hot, thick crimson liquid.

The leviathan remained motionless for a moment before the base of the body sagged into the depths of the river. Its upper body followed into the water with an enormous splash. Geysers of water erupted as Brok landed with a brutish grin across his face, covered in the beast's blood and other dead parts. Myrcle looked at him with horror and amazement at the same time. Organa ran to him, getting close enough to smell the foulness on his body before backing away and giving him a thumbs-up in congratulations.

EV steadied herself and simply clapped for them all, her careless facade returning, with a slow speed and no roaring applause. "So, we destroyed the only bridge connecting the western part of the continent to the King's Isle. Great."

75

The Serpent's Ring

By the end of the day, the group had made their way to the edge of the forest on the other side of Leviathan's Crossing and made camp after their battle with the beast. Myrcle woke from his nap to the smell of fire in his nose. He looked around and saw nothing but a light shadow on the cloth of his tent and a small beam of light from a little hole in the side. His nose was ablaze now with the smell of what could only be described as an interesting meaty stew. *Ah, EV's cooking again*, he thought to himself. Uncovering himself from the furs, he walked to the entrance of his tent, pulled back the hide, and straightened himself, stretching to the bright sky.

EV knelt on one knee beside the pot over the fire, stirring the liquid within. Organa and Brok emerged from their tent and took a moment to stretch in the setting sun's glow. The rising Element Moons glistened in the east across the world where they had already touched the soil of the once-green country of Dremica. For a moment, solemnity fell over Myrcle as he remembered his homeland. But he pulled himself back to reality and walked over to the fire.

"How did everyone sleep?" asked Myrcle.

"Pretty okay, I guess," replied Organa, and Brok nodded his head in agreement.

"EV," Myrcle asked, "what about you?"

"I got enough," she said with an interestingly perky tone in her voice.

"What do you have there?"

"A spoon and a cauldron over a fire, hairball."

"Who'd have been able to guess that?" Myrcle laughed. "What are you cooking?"

"My famous rabbit and squirrel stew."

"Sounds tasty," Brok added. Myrcle looked over at Organa and shook his head lightly in disagreement, eyes wide. Organa giggled softly in response.

Organa's curiosity sparked. "How long have you known each other?"

They didn't answer at first; instead, they thought long and hard, then began laughing to ease the awkward silence.

"Myrcle was the healer who took care of me while I slept, so I was two hundred and twenty-three." She trailed off, doing her calculations, cutting off Myrcle as he was about to answer with a single finger, "two hundred and fifty-four years, give or take a few?" EV looked at Myrcle for reassurance, and he nodded.

"So how old are you, Myrcle?"

"Um, I was fifty-three when the Cataclysm occurred, but I was in Balinor at the time, training to be a healer. I met and took care of EV when I was fifty-six after I traveled to Rethial looking for a position as a healer in an infirmary. Took care of her through all of her sleep, so that puts me at two fifty-six?" Organa could hear the uncertainty in his voice. After all those years, it would be hard to remember so accurately.

Organa replied in amazement, "Brok and I are like children to you two."

"Literally," Esvele whispered under her breath.

Myrcle cleared his throat with a chuckle. "See, EV just gets a plain, old, boring death from disease or what-have-you, whereas I will take my place as a Dire Bear in the forests with the others of my kind. Living out the rest of my days in peace."

EV smirked and said, "Well, I am glad I get to die peacefully. I'll just join the stars and the heavens above us and see the world from up there. Who knows, maybe I'll leave a widower behind." A pause came over the camp as the only sound was the crackling of the wood under the cauldron. EV and Myrcle's outrageous laughter broke the silence a few moments later, and Organa and Brok quickly joined in.

"Can you see it?" EV struggled to get the words out, gasping between every few words and cutting them off early. "Me in a long, flowy white gown, walking between the trees as the birds sing and flutter their wings around me with some idiot at the end of the fucking aisle waiting to be the husband of a psychotic bitch." EV's laughter roared even louder.

Their cackling eventually subsided, and the group broke their fast together around the fire. The sun was about halfway set, casting light through the trees and holes in the clouds, illuminating them with gorgeous colors. The hills behind the camp stretched for miles, covered with dense forest, and the mouth of the Coiling River beyond them. A few miles away, Mount Doloroth loomed. The group rested for a few hours and then packed their belongings into their bags.

Not taking the main road through the forest, the group traveled as lightly and swiftly as possible without making much noise, walking like cats in the night. Myrcle walked close to EV and Organa at the front of the group with Brok at the back holding his great sword ready. The dense forest of green, red, orange, and yellow leaves on trees that stretched thirty to sixty feet into the sky creaked in a light breeze that blew from the east. Dancing beams of sunlight shone through the openings between the leaves like a trail to the mountain. Myrcle held up his hand to signal a halt as a sound to the right of the group in the forest echoed through the greenery. Organa moved her fingers, turning them pale as white and blue crystals formed, and eventually turning her hands into solid, freezing ice. Brok walked to the center of the group and clutched his weapon tightly. Myrcle's hands began to flicker with blue and green flames as the threads danced on his fingers.

The sound echoed again, louder and closer this time. EV rolled her eyes and took her staff off her back, charging the crystal with electricity. "I really don't feel like fighting right now," she whispered.

The third and final sound echoed as the bushes moved. Twigs snapped and leaves fell to the ground. Esvele met Myrcle's glance, and they advanced slowly like sentinels. Reaching her hand out, Esvele took the branches of the bush in hand and yanked them back.

As the veil of leaves lifted, the group found a small creature. Its skin was light green, and long ears extended from its head, held back by a pair of goggles with red lenses. A semi-long nose with a pointy end trailed back to a pair of large, bulbous blue eyes. The creature's short body stood only about three feet tall, and dark brown leather pants covered its scrawny legs, connecting to its shoeless, three-toed feet. Four long arms extended into hands with four fingers, each tipped with black claws. One arm held a large red cloth sack over his shoulder while the other three gripped silver daggers with white blades.

As the creature looked back at the feisty four, it smiled and spoke in an obvious northern accent. "You want some fine wares?"

Myrcle and Organa exchanged confused glances, and Brok laughed at the short creature. As he did, the little one used two of his daggers and sliced at Brok's right arm, spreading two large gashes on the forearm.

"Say somethin' 'bout me fuckin' size and I'll fuckin' cut your bloody eyes out next, you overgrown potato."

"Witherspoon, shut the hell up, please," EV shouted as she shook her head in disbelief and annoyance.

"You know this thing?" asked Organa.

"Oi! Mind your talk, lassie. This 'Thing' is a goblin merchant from Wintertown, and I only have the best shit for my customers," Witherspoon retorted, "and I know Esvele here from the good old days back in Dremica."

"How do you know him, EV?" asked Myrcle.

"We first met in the trading markets of Husieàkritae."

"Aye, and I had my own shop and family back then."

"If you call whores your family, you need a new one," EV scoffed.

"Oi! Who are you to judge, you big she-devil?"

"Shut it, Witherspoon, we're trying to get somewhere, so we're going to just run along. Go away," EV shot at the goblin.

"What about your friends 'ere, they might want some fine wares? I got plen'y in me bag. One moment, dearie."

"By the bloody Dawn!" EV walked away mumbling to herself and then heard Organa speak.

"Who were you again?"

"Me name's Witherspoon."

"'Witherspoon?' That's an interesting name," Myrcle said with a laugh as he watched the goblin open his red sack. With his arms, he untied the silver knot around the opening. As he did, a shimmer emitted from within onto a nearby tree. He grabbed the edges of the bag with two hands, holding it open, and then with his other two, lifted himself inside, sinking within easily without the bag showing the slightest give or contortion to his body. Organa gasped as she saw the goblin disappear and looked back at Myrcle with a confused look. "I'm going to assume it's enchanted."

"No, the bag is over a hole in the ground that the goblin jumped through for dramatic effect to show off. Of course it is enchanted, dearie," Myrcle said, shaking his head. Brok walked closer to the bag and reached into the bag to inspect it. As his hand got closer, one of the green arms of the goblin reached out and slashed it with a dagger. The cut went a few inches across, but not too deep.

"Don't touch me fuckin' bag, ya bug-brain twat," Witherspoon's voice echoed from within the bag. Organa hit Brok on the back of his head and shook her head, smiling. Myrcle simply laughed at the brute and walked over to EV, who was distressed. His boots shuffled a few leaves across the forest floor, and he laid his hand on EV's shoulder as she paced back and forth.

"EV, what's wrong?" Myrcle asked her.

"I don't trust that little fucker, that's what's wrong. He's always been a trickster and a thief and a liar. He works for the highest bidder. He could jeopardize everything we're trying to do!"

"EV, we have no reason to dislike him."

"Why, exactly?"

"Well," a momentary pause came over him as he thought.

"Yeah, that's my point." EV rolled her eyes.

"He's done nothing *yet*. When he does… I'll set him aflame, okay?"

"Fine," EV paused, and Myrcle took his right hand and placed it on her head between her two horns. In a few swift motions, he moved his hand, ruffling up her hair.

"Stop that, you great hairball," EV laughed. She cleared the hair from her eyes and she saw one of Witherspoon's hands extended toward Organa, holding a silver box decorated with red metal along the edges. EV burst into a quick sprint across the short distance between them. Earthen weaves obeyed her command as a whirlwind of vines, twigs, and thorns enveloped Witherspoon. Twisting around and around as the greenery wrapped around him tightly, leaving only his head visible.

"What are you doin', bitch? People ask for a date first, usually before we get into the interesting things," the goblin chuckled.

"What's in that box, Witherspoon?"

"I don't know."

"Don't lie to me," EV tightened her grip. "I know that you swore—"

"I know better than to lie to you ol' she-devil," Witherspoon said with a chuckle. "It's a Wishing Chest. You pay the price for the key and wish for whatever and then, if the chest can provide it, the wish appears within and it's yours."

Myrcle set fire to the vines with a snap of his fingers, and the group watched as they burnt away. *Stand down Esvele. You are going to ruin all we've planned.* The wrath in her eyes disappeared.

Witherspoon looked back at EV and gave her a smirk as he walked over to Organa, "As I was sayin', if you got the coin, you could use one of my keys to open this box, just have to pay the price."

"Don't trust him, Organa," EV cautioned. "Goblins are tricksters and will betray you the moment things don't go in their favor."

Organa shook her head and unlatched her small white cloth pouch at her side.

"Is this enough?" Organa asked as she handed him the purse. Witherspoon took it from her hand, bowing kindly a little as the exchange happened.

Witherspoon looked back up at Organa. "That'll do it, dearie." He walked back over to the bag swiftly and crawled inside.

"*Ugh,* I told you, you can't trust goblins. You're making a huge mistake." Esvele's voice shook, and another called out from within the bag.

"Oh, shut it!" cried Witherspoon. "Don't get into such a farce, you annoying devil!"

"Stop calling me that," EV shot back. She looked back at Organa. "Please let's just leave and forget this goblin thief."

Organa questioned, "I just paid for that."

"I'll pay you back," she paused, sighing with a light laugh, "someday. But let's go, please, Organa." As EV finished her plea, the goblin emerged from within his bag holding a large key ring. At least a hundred golden, silver, red, and green metallic keys. Each of them had unique symbols carved into the round heads. Organa noticed one with a roaring dragon, another with a great Kraken, one with three feathers, and another with a green gem glistening with starlight, which Witherspoon then pulled off the ring. He put the green gem key in his right upper hand and, with his left lower, tossed the ring back into the bag. Witherspoon shuffled some leaves around as he walked to his client. He then held the key out to Organa.

"Are you sure you want to open that box? You never know what's going to come out of there," Esvele's voice trembled.

"Have you done this before?" Organa asked back.

She gave no answer as she simply looked away from her.

"Once you wish and turn the key, the wish shall come to thee. But think long and hard before you choose—you could find you will lose."

Thinking long and hard for a few seconds, Organa twisted the key.

As the key turned, several gears clicked, and cogs moved. The chest opened on its own, and a white mist overflowed from within. The mist hit the floor and spread like water through the grass. Witherspoon continued to hold the box in his hands without fear. As the box revealed its treasure, a multicolored glow emitted, blinding the group for a moment, and then the light receded back into the box, revealing its treasure.

A band made of pure silver with green metallic vines and red thorns along the edges sat in the center of the chest. As the vines crept up to the head, they morphed into two green snakes with blue sapphires for eyes and two claws that held a purple gem containing a dancing red flame inside. Witherspoon looked at the ring and watched as it glimmered in the light through the trees. Organa reached out to the ring, and EV waited in anticipation of what was to come. As she extended her hand, the two snakes moved their green and red vine bodies.

The serpents' blue eyes glowed wildly with blue flames. As her hand met the ring band, the snakes then bit into her ring finger, leaving four wounds in the skin with small streams of blood flowing down. The snakes took their metal tongues of silver and licked up the crimson on her finger. As they assessed the blood, the blue flaming sapphire eyes morphed into fiery red rubies that the flames followed with their color. The heads of the snakes gave a noble bow, and they returned to their state upon the ring, keeping their ruby eyes.

"What?" Organa looked back at the others.

"I don't know," Myrcle said, his voice shaking as he lied.

Organa took the ring from within the box and slid it onto her finger. As she did, she felt a burning sensation through her hand and fell to the ground, grunting with pain and discomfort. A pair of scarlet eyes flashed before her as she closed her eyes, taking in the pain—and a feeling of rage, of revenge yet to be had.

Brok went to her side and helped her to her feet. EV and Myrcle exchanged terrified glances as they sprinted to her as well. Witherspoon muttered a few words, and within a few seconds, the box turned to sand. "Well dearies, if youn's ain't gonna buy anythin' else, I'll be on my way," Witherspoon walked over to his bag and looked back to his new client, "Oh, and dearie, be wary of that Kalishtani, she's a real firecracker, that one. Maybe I'll see youn's again." As Witherspoon finished, he hopped into his bag, and it spun faster and faster, all the while getting smaller until he disappeared in a golden flash.

Still processing the events of the last few moments, Brok looked at her with a curious expression. "What just… occurred?"

"You don't have to try to use big words all the time, Brok," Organa said with a laugh, "and I have no idea."

"I do," Myrcle said. "You wished for memories, didn't you?"

"How do you know that?"

Myrcle's eyes scanned back and forth as he thought of his reasoning. "Serpents are the guardians of memories and the masters of lies. Sometimes they work hand in hand. A Serpent's Ring is an enchanted item of old magic. Meant to restore memories forgotten, lift the veil upon lies told, or keep the truth from those who wear them. Did you see anything?"

"No," Organa lied.

"Maybe it will take time to affect you." Myrcle allowed an awkward silence to come over them but broke it quickly. "We need to continue on. The southern border of the Forest of Bravica is not far now."

Organa walked to Brok and whispered softly, "We need to keep our eyes out. I feel a change in the wind, and not for the better." Brok nodded in agreement, although he did not really understand what she meant. They walked on together with a suitable distance between their companions.

The Waking Forest

Morning came, and the group departed their camp, leaving it intact as they traveled off-road toward the base of Mount Doloroth. Brok took his blade and kept it mostly unsheathed, ready for any danger as he walked in front of Organa to guard her from their employers. As they wandered, Organa could feel the serpent's ring itching slightly, but she never felt compelled to remove it from her finger.

Hours passed as the midday sun beat down upon Esvele's bare brow now that she had removed her hood. Her horns had a shining gleam that reflected the sun, and her black cloak seemed to soak up the heat along with her hot leather clothes.

They all walked on for another five hours and the sun finally crept toward the western horizon, illuminating the sky with gold, orange, purple, and red. Clouds looked like flames, and the sky above them had a few bright stars whose light shone brightly enough to break the night like shattering through a glass barrier. The Fire in Heaven burned as it rose overhead, and so did the Element Moons. Their combined glow of sky blue and silver shone like sparkling diamonds in the heavens above. The two celestial bodies were a beautiful companionship in grandeur and color.

Esvele went into the forest to find wood for the fire that night and came back with large logs and long sticks while the others made camp. With Organa's permission, Brok rose from his seat on a fallen tree, took his sword with him, and raised his hands above his head. He swung his great sword down, the blade easily separating the wood into four large chunks. After fifteen minutes, Brok came back to the center of the camp, stacked the chunks of wood together, and laid some grass and leaves throughout. Esvele took out from within her satchel a fire starter of flint and steel, lighting the grass and leaves, which, with Esvele's help, burst into flames, alive with full orange and white glory. As Brok chopped the wood for their small fire, Organa thought of a plan to extract the information she needed from Myrcle.

"What is a Magiqas?" Organa asked.

"Beg pardon?"

"I've heard you all say it before. What is it?"

"My dear," Myrcle said with a laugh, "you surely know what Magiqas are. The gifted beings of this and probably other worlds whose magic is much stronger than others. Anyone can learn magic through years of study and practice, but their magic will never be as strong as a Magiqas. We are born with our powers, and our magic flows with our blood. But such strength comes at a cost; their powers are much harder to control. Esvele, you, and I are all Magiqas. Being so, we *must* keep our powers under control. If not, you will lose yourself to the Shadow."

His words resounded in Organa's mind like she was remembering them as he spoke. "Will you teach me?"

"You would have already learned how to control the powers of the Magiqas if you had stayed with the Order of Valkiel." Esvele's venom cut deep, almost intentionally.

"I had to leave. You wouldn't understand."

"I'm sure I won't, and I don't honestly care, but I'd rather you had stayed and learned how your powers work and suffered whatever it was, so you would be of use." Her words seemed too targeted, enough to rouse more of Organa's suspicion, but Myrcle stepped between them.

"EV and I will teach you together. I am not a druid. My magic is mainly pyromaniac; however, I'll do what I can."

"Don't do this to me, Myrcle," Esvele grumbled, her eyes cutting through him.

"What happened during the Cataclysm?" Organa asked, changing the subject.

"I already told you my story," Esvele glared at her. "Your turn, hairball."

As Myrcle mused to Organa, Esvele imagined it in her mind.

The Guardians had barely stopped the Cataclysm from spreading last time, and that was against a few thousand of the forces of the Void. What was coming was far more terrifying and dangerous than the Cataclysm. She thought of the Fire in Heaven and its great tear in the night sky. The ground beneath the continent opened up and swallowed everything. The mountains burst with molten rock, and towers of black ash climbed thousands of feet into the sky, blocking the sun for days. Esvele remembered her father's face when he died. She remembered the freezing cold and the great blizzard that fell upon Husieàkritae. Kethir, the Lady of Bones and her legions of undead fiends and monstrosities rushed over the fallen gates of the city, slashing, piercing, and tearing everyone and everything that they could.

Some sailors say that the Silver Shadow still looms over Dremica, and that the sun has not shone upon that land since the fall of the Silver Kingdom. They say that not even the beasts of the sea nor its great leviathans will venture near the deepest parts of the ocean near that land, nor will the great schools of fish dare settle in the reefs. The trees have either turned to mounds of sludge and rot or stand as charred remnants of the once lush green land. The magnificent temples and cities near the coast are nothing but ash and ruin now, with the Tower of Endless Steps turned to a heap of rubble.

Those fools who dare step onto the ground and into the once Living Lands cannot survive. For now, many demons crawl above and below the ground, and the very air they breathe is a noxious poison that burns their lungs with each breath. There was an old tale of a company of brave men and women who sailed to the shores of Dremica and barely made it that far as the sea revolted against them and tried to save them from their fate. A single young Drakeman returned from that voyage on a broken and barely floating ship. He told his crew's story of what they saw in the Silver Kingdom. He spoke of mounds of bones and charred corpses around the gates of the cities, their limbs reaching for the gates, clawing to enter the safety of the walls, unknowing that more people were trying to escape the city as death consumed them all indiscriminately. He said he had seen the Mountain of Shadows with the Great Forest of the Damned before it and the gigantic stone wards with spells carved into them in Stellevarian to keep back the evil that dwelled there.

Perhaps one day the sun may shine there again, though not very likely. As long as the shadow is on Lorial, it will never stop trying to devour life. One day, not even the Shadow Towers will be able to hold back the decay and rot beyond their massive walls.

Myrcle waited for Organa to catch up and spoke with her. "Organa, the darkness that has fallen over Lorial won't go away easily, and no one knows where the gods went after the Cataclysm. I believe that they are rebuilding and making ready to march to war against the Void. You and Esvele need to learn to respect one another and get along."

"I can't get along with someone who wants to stab me for breathing."

Myrcle laughed. "Aye, she is quite the piece of work; however, I believe there may be more than meets the eye to what unsettles her about you. Why not ask her, try to mend the bond? I already told her we cannot win the war to come if we're already at war amongst ourselves."

"What war is to come? Brok and I are just here to help you on your contract and then return to Turnmot so we can collect our reward and go from there as unlikely acquaintances."

"Organa, you must know that the Menitheal Dynasty is an utter dictatorship. They rule over Rethial as tyrants who do whatever they please while their people starve and kill one another every day. Turnmot used to be a proud city, a hub between the west and the east. Then, when the current Lord and Lady took over as the Soulflame King and Lady Magis, the land fell into ruin. You have a duty to protect those who can't protect themselves."

"We will not be a part of any 'glorious revolution' because we have no part to play. If there were to be a great uprising against them, it would be crushed immediately. The people would be slaughtered by the thousands, and then the Soulflame King will have no other choice but to rule by fear. The might of the Flames of the Sphinx is unmatched.

"Organa, the war we speak of is not some revolution. It is much bigger than that and will end far beyond our lifetimes. We're doing a simple contract; I'm only making a point. The wheel of power spins on and on, but eventually, someone needs not just to stop it, but to break, shatter, and destroy it. Down to its very foundations. "But this is a feeble and minor inconvenience to the greater plan of Arratir," Myrcle said solemnly.

Organa stopped for a moment and then walked back to Brok. "Arratir is a myth, and if he or she were real, they would have died when the Cataclysm wreaked havoc across Lorial and decimated the east."

Myrcle sighed as he watched Organa walk to Brok in the back of their train. He whispered to Esvele, "She'll learn one day, and you have to teach her."

Organa slipped her hand through the hole between Brok's arm and his torso. "Brok," she asked, "do you think we should have left the Order?"

"They… would kill you… if we… had not left."

"Yeah, I know."

"Will we help them?"

"I don't want to be a part of some great revolution. I don't want to be anything to anyone." She laid her head on Brok's shoulder. "I just want us to live and travel the world."

"We can… travel… to the Far Lands… one day?" the giant asked.

Organa chuckled. "Gods, wouldn't that be quite the adventure, huh? Maybe one day."

They followed Esvele over the hill, and when they reached its apex, they saw the Forest of Bravica. Trees that stretched at least one hundred and fifty feet high into the sky. The bark was as hard as Blood Iron from the heart of the deepest mines of the Endless Maze. Their bark was as hard as Blood Iron from the heart of the deepest mines of the Endless Maze, as white as snow, with dark brown streams flowing from the ground up. The leaves were as large as Brok's head and always in an eternal state of fall color. The great wall of trees perfectly divided the plains of the south from the forest. Mount Doloroth loomed in the north, and its snowy peak gleamed in the light of the noon sun. Small puffs of clouds gathered around the peak, and some of the trees grew up the mountainside.

"Look there," Organa pointed to a light column of smoke rising in the air.

"That must be the Golden Queen's camp," Myrcle concluded.

They walked for another hour or so into the forest, and Organa did not like the awkward silence. She walked close to Esvele and whispered in her ear, "What did you see when you touched me?"

Esvele waited a moment, looking to Myrcle as if waiting for permission to speak, and when he said nothing, she sighed. "Broken glass that reflected your image, a ring that coiled around a finger, a large stone on a hill, and a city on fire. Some of those could be repressed truths in your past; others could be the future. It's very hard to distinguish the difference between you and them as you're an Elf, and your beauty, unlike others, it won't fade or change quickly. Therefore, there are so many paths that it is naturally clouded, but yours is almost intentionally hidden." Esvele retreated from her last words as if she was hiding from them. She quickly recovered and went on, "The others are vague. I don't know whether they're in the past or in the future."

"I thought you could only see into the future."

"I believe it's the future, but sometimes I have seen the past. Once I saw Myrcle's childhood. He lived in Dremica for a long time. He studied magic, art, and history, and even taught as an instructor of healing and fire magic. An odd combination, I know, but he was strong, powerful, and kind. When word of his teachings in Fe'Krenton reached the Soulflame King, he had him brought to Silver Fountain, where he taught a young Elven prodigy."

"You boast too much, Esvele, and you doubt your abilities too much. Young Organa here just stumped you once. I am sure that it's nothing to worry about." As he spoke his last sentence, he became slightly sterner in his tone. "We've only a couple of hours left to the base of Mount Doloroth."

"We've a few hours to spare till sundown," Organa noted. "Let's rest for a few hours to make sure we're ready for what is to come."

"I think that is a good idea, Organa," Myrcle agreed, with nervousness in his eyes.

The evening came soon, and the sunset was a gorgeous red and purple, casting some of its light through the tops of the trees. A slight breeze blew, and the leaves of the large trees rustled, sounding once more like the waves of the ocean. Organa and Brok stayed warm in their tents under their covers with their warmer clothes on, as did Esvele and Myrcle. As the night fell, the temperature dropped drastically, and one of the coldest summer nights swept through the southern part of Rethial. It almost felt cold enough to snow, but they were all able to sleep thanks to their warmth.

* * *

Esvele fell asleep against a tree. Her mind was filled with death and suffering. A burning city, the great Shadows of the North laying waste to the people, burning, freezing, and screaming in pain. Darkness and blood covered the world. She was standing near the east gate of the city, where the Xurinal should be but was not. Mounds of marble rubble as tall as the houses stood like sentries. She turned her head and saw what was behind her—another pyramid, where the Xurinal once stood. But it was not a place of worship and safety like its predecessor. Instead, the structure was of darkness and fear. Its surface was that of black glass and stone that moved with red and purple within it. Above the pyramid was a towering crystal. It radiated a pale and purple energy and felt like hatred and destruction. Just as Esvele looked up, she saw it shatter into millions of fragments that held their place above the dark structure beside her.

The ground around Esvele then shook violently as a blizzard suddenly appeared around the city, engulfing it in snow, ice, and freezing winds. The earth cracked like an egg beneath her, pulling itself apart in the wake of such power. As it slowly dissolved, the black pyramid glistened, exposing a shadow being with fiery red eyes. Golden chains within bound the creature to the realities of the Sepulcher. Then they shattered, and a silence fell over all creation, banishing the blizzard.

The Shadowlight had come.

* * *

Esvele woke in a cold sweat, panting and shaking.

Myrcle jumped to her side. "Are you all right, EV?"

"Yes," she panted, "I'm fine." *No,* she said in his mind.

The next morning came, and they packed their things and began walking once more to Mount Doloroth. It was not far now, and they could see more details as they got closer. To the north, the great Mount Doloroth towered over everything in its domain. Within the forest, small glimpses of its majesty peeked through. The snowy peak gleamed in the sunlight, immune to the melt the sun wished to force upon it. The leaves of the trees around them rustled in the wind, sounding like the ocean. Waves crashing down upon one another and spreading shells and sea-worn stones across endless, beautiful golden sand. Myrcle loved the ocean, and he loved its sound, the smell of the salty water in the air, the feel of sand under his feet and between his toes, and the warm sun upon his face. He had not seen, smelled, or touched the coast in thirty years, searching for his old friends and hoping they had survived the Cataclysm for all that time. He and Esvele had traveled thousands of miles over Lorial and sailed across the Old Sea, voyage after voyage, and now they were close.

"I can hear those thoughts of yours, Myrcle. The idea of seeing the sea again before we die would be nice, if you actually think we will make it that far," EV quietly whispered.

"We've made it this far and maybe still have some time to go. Who's to say what the gods have in store?"

Esvele placed a hand on his shoulder, and he turned back as she spoke to him, "We're near the end of the road, Myrcle. You know that the *Vitu'Lux* is leaving us."

"That doesn't matter right now. All that matters is getting them back."

He laughed, "And we will, my dear. Have faith in the Gods. They will let it all play out as it is intended."

Organa shouted from far behind them, moving through the foliage, "How much furth-"

As the first words exited the elf's mouth, Esvele quickly ran to her like a mist with great speed and covered her mouth with her hand. Organa resisted, and her eyes grew wide with anger and annoyance. "Hold your tongue, Organa, or I will rip it out myself." The desperation cut through his words. "You should know better than any of us what creatures the Order has guarding its borders.

The leaves that were once flowing and rustling in the wind had instantly stopped, and the air grew very thin. Myrcle looked around the greenery wildly, holding a small orb of fire in his right hand, ready to strike. Brok could feel it as well and held his great sword in both his large hands. A commotion in the forest up ahead caught Organa's attention.

A large, bark-covered hand erupted from the earth, and a powerful gust of wind rushed through the leaves, pushing a tree over with ease. Esvele slowly crouched down into a nearby bush, bringing Organa with her and the others doing the same as her. As it emerged, they could see the blooms of the flowers receding back into themselves to hide from the beast. The trees lost their color, and the grass crept back into the ground. Branches fell in fear of the creature and attempted to hide within the bushes. A loud *thump* echoed in the forest as the tall beast stood only a few feet below the tallest of the trees. It looked like a tree itself, covered in a dark red and black bark, with a few small flames between the joints. Its eyes burned with red rage, and a crown of dead leaves and black twigs lay upon its head. Long and monstrous arms dangled just a few inches above the earth and, as it walked forward, large roots extended from within its feet and dug deep into the earth, grounding it. Its head turned from side to side, scowling over the greenery, its rage-filled eyes burning with intensity. A leg detached from the ground, and its roots settled in another spot a few yards ahead. It continued down this path until it disappeared into the forest from their view.

"What was that thing?" Organa asked.

"You don't know what that was?" Myrcle was confused.

"No, should I?"

"I would hope you remember avoiding them when you ran from the Order?"

"Wait," Organa pondered, "I have never told you I was running from the Order of Valkiel. I disregarded it the first time you mentioned knowing about my connection with them, but this is the second time. How do you know?"

Myrcle jumped in quickly. "We overheard your conversation with the tavern owner. We were at the table behind you. That is why we hired you; you would know how to get past those." He motioned in the direction the magnificent beast went.

"That's oddly convenient." Organa motioned to Brok, who drew his weapon. Myrcle laid down his angelic staff on the grass and held his hands up in surrender as Esvele readied a spell within the crystal of her own.

"Stop, EV, stand down before you make it worse," Myrcle whispered angrily so as not to attract the attention of the beast. Esvele reluctantly laid down her staff as well and surrendered.

"Tell me now, or I will get that thing back here," the Elf demanded.

"That 'thing' is a Ghast. A sentinel created by the Order of Valkiel to guard their realm," Myrcle explained.

"You're Watchers, aren't you?" Organa's suspicions brewed further. "The Order won't ever stop, will they?"

Esvele sighed, "No, Organa, we're just-"

Organa interrupted, "Just what? Lying to me?"

Myrcle hissed in a sharp whisper, "Our chance meeting was anything but chance." Esvele shot him a look of disapproval.

"What do you mean?" Organa asked. As she questioned, she twisted the blades of grass behind her into small vines, freezing and molding them to a point. The sharp blades extended only a few inches, small enough to keep hidden, but ready to spring into full spears.

"Organa, hear us out, please," Myrcle held his hands up as if to show that he bore her no ill will. "I, we, had to find you. There is something happening across Rethial, and we needed to make sure you were safe."

"Why? Why do you care what happens to me?"

"Because you don't even know who you are."

EV had gotten closer, and Organa saw her reach for something behind her back. With a swift forward motion of her right forearm, Organa sent spears of ice from the ground flying toward EV and Myrcle. Brok grabbed her hand and ran into the forest. Tree limbs smacked their arms and shoulders as they sprinted through the thick bushes and trees. The ground rumbled, and from the dirt shot up an immense wall of stone that stood around twenty feet tall in front of them. Organa looked as she saw EV's eyes far behind her glowing a radiant, fiery yellow, thrusting her hand into the earth, creating trailing mounds in the dirt forward to block their escape. Organa extended her hand and touched the new wall before them, freezing it to solid ice instantly. Brok took his greatsword from behind him and cut the wall with one swift stroke. The duo continued to run farther into the forest.

Organa looked over at her companion, and then they both walked slowly and quietly through the forest. Brok wandered a little in front of Organa with his great sword drawn and ready to attack. He looked back at Organa to check on her, and she nodded as if to say she was okay. The duo continued farther into the woods. The forest's trees stretched completely around the mountain and further to the north, far beyond what they could see.

After going for some time, Organa and Brok skulked through the forest. A sharp pain scratched Organa's head, and a light voice, a man's, entered her mind. *Organa,* it whispered. She did not recognize it at first, but then it continued on, and it was clear who it was. *Organa, please come back. You do not understand!* It was Myrcle. Ignoring the call, Organa rushed to Brok's side and stayed close.

"You see, Brok, you can't trust anyone. Not even those you think are your friends," Organa said, sighing.

"I can…. trust…. you can't I?"

"Of course you can," Organa said with a sharpness in her voice. "You can always trust me." She leaned on Brok's shoulder as they walked. The ever-expanding denseness of the woods stretched almost to the very summit of Mount Doloroth. She saw the great peak of the mountain, and its white snow gave Organa an idea.

"Brok," she looked back at him, "put on your warm clothes and wrap yourself in those skins."

Brok nodded and changed his expression to a menacing scowl as he scanned the forest. Organa then placed her hands on the ground and spoke in the northern language of Nestrian. Her voice carried through the air with ease even though she whispered. The winds rose, and the air became harshly cold, as the threads of air and water wove themselves around her into a frozen storm, dropping the temperature with each passing heartbeat. The ground became frosted, and the grass itself was white within seconds. Great showers of ice and snow rained upon Brok, who gripped his sword with both hands and still watched for any intruders. Organa completed her spell and then her attention went to the Ghast bursting through the ground near Brok.

Its large arms ripped the earth apart as it emerged, and its eyes were fixed on Organa. It bellowed a deep sound out, like that of a whale and a crumbling building at the same time.

"Brok, run," Organa shouted. He followed her in the opposite direction of the Ghast but as they made their escape, the beast shoved its right hand into the ground. Its vines flowed through the earth like fish in water, creating a wall of wood and leaves and blocking their exit. The Ghast removed itself from the ground and slowly stomped forward.

Organa placed her hands on the wall as Brok turned to face the great beast. Drawing forth his great sword, he held it high in both hands, ready to strike, and walked toward the beast. Organa attempted to freeze the wall. Slowly, the places she touched turned to solid ice and began to spread across the surface. Brok moved out of the way of a strike from the Ghast. The ground thundered as the great arm hit the earth. Brok swung his blade at the appendage of a wooden monster and missed, having to roll out of the way to dodge another swing from his foe. The Ghast's blazing red eyes grew brighter, and from its mouth came a river of flames and molten rock. Organa removed her hands from the wall and pushed forward a stream of snow and ice from her hands, holding back the immolation, and creating hot steam where they met. The trees around them burst with the heat of the fire, creating a pillar of smoke thousands of feet high. Organa's touch on the wall was doing little to nothing when she was there, and now her effect had faded away completely. She held her hands up for as long as she could, keeping the blaze from touching them. Nevertheless, she failed, and her power waned. Her blizzard ended, and the Ghast looked back at them with its raging eyes.

A high-pitched whistling sound echoed through the forest as a great ball of flame and smoke flew through the forest and landed upon the gigantic wall of vines the Ghast created. The beast shot back in pain and roared loudly as its trap shattered like glass. Organa could see Myrcle lowering his staff and running her way, with Esvele only a few feet away, another spell ready to attack the Ghast.

Esvele got in between Brok, Organa, and the Ghast, holding the emerald orb of her staff toward the sentinel of the forest and unleashing a stream of flames at it. Instead of the Ghast recoiling in pain, this time it made a shield out of its vines and absorbed the flames, sending them back upon the group. "Move your asses!" the Kalishtani shouted.

Organa and Brok bolted away, following Esvele, and made themselves ready to attack the beast. Myrcle now joined them and generated a force field of blue light to defend them from the flames. They looked up at the Ghast. Its charred body gleamed with flames, standing nearly as tall as the trees above them.

"Oh, this is going to be fun," Myrcle nervously laughed and jumped into battle.

He channeled threads of fire into the rubies along his staff. Each of them came alive with stronger and stronger blazes until they reached the top and met between the golden wings. The staff stood on its own, held aloft by the smoldering breath of the heated air. Myrcle pulled his hands back, and shaped the strands into spears of flame that he sent forth in a ruinous barrage of desolation. Some missed, sparking emerald wildfires around the Ghast, but the ones that met their mark nearly threw the Warden of the Forest on its back.

Esvele plunged her staff into the earth and gathered a tangle of brown threads from deep within world. A coil of roots erupted from the ground as she attempted to bind it, but the Ghast quickly swatted her away and ripped up the vines, burning them upon its fiery bark.

The Ghast raised its right hand and slammed it into the ground, its fingers thrusting themselves into the earth and causing a tremor beneath their feet. Then the charred fingers moved through the ground once more and wrapped around two other trees nearby, penetrating the bark and wrapping around the hearts of the trees. They came to life, their roots erupting from the ground and moving like snakes. A loud, whale-like cry rang through the forest.

Brok dropped his greatsword and fell to the ground, holding his heart and screaming in pain. Organa crouched beside him and placed her hands upon his head, emitting a golden glow and calming him. He shook his head, regaining his composure, and reached for his blade before running toward one of the newly living trees, slashing and hacking away at its large tendrils of roots. Organa turned to the Ghast and raised her hand into the sky, darkening it, and bright red flashes lit up the clouds. With a thrust of her hand toward the ground, four red lightning bolts from the clouds struck the Ghast, causing it to catch fire, and the creature seemed to revel in the flames, growing larger and more powerful.

Myrcle ran behind it and held the firestone a few inches away from his left hand. In his hands, heat appeared, but Myrcle was unaware of the power the Ghast would be gaining. The small flame between them grew uncontrollably, and Myrcle threw it at the tree that was attacking Esvele, making large swoops under her feet and vertical strikes that she barely dodged. The tree burst into flames and shouted in another high pitch, this time causing Esvele and Brok to fall to the ground, holding their ears and screaming.

The Ghast reached deep within the earth once more and pulled a great boulder from the ground. A cloud of dirt and dust blinded Organa for a moment, then she saw the shadow of the large rock and dove away from the attack, rolling on the grass and landing on her back. Looking up, she saw the large wooden foot of the Ghast descending upon her and rolled quickly out of the way but was scratched by the splinters on the edge of the foot. She ran to Esvele, who was still screaming in pain from the shrieking of the trees, and jumped over the large roots of the tree attacking her, and placed her hands on her head as she had Brok's, ceasing her torment.

Myrcle dodged an incoming attack from the Ghast's right arm and cast another spell. From his staff came a host of lightning that penetrated the defenses of the Ghast with ease. The bark exploded, revealing a single large piece of amber and a red flame within it burning so slowly it looked like time was stopping. The Ghast let out a dark roar of pain and fell backward onto the ground, releasing a cloud of dirt and displaced grass. Thrashing its arms about, the Ghast threw Brok and Myrcle into the grasp of the living trees, allowing the roots to envelop them like the tentacles of a Kraken of the Old Sea. The Ghast stood back up and rooted itself deep into the crater of broken earth beneath it, and around the area vines covered in thorns and sharpened their ends. The snakes of the earth coiled around Organa, but when she placed her hands upon them, their composition turned from wood to solid and transparent ice, which she shattered in an instant. Esvele rose to her feet and saw Organa and the power building in her.

The air around them became cold and harsh, the wind speeding around them like a twister of ice and snow. Organa's companions shivered, and their breath became visible; almost freezing, they exhaled. The living trees recoiled from them, their roots releasing Myrcle and Brok from their grasp and freezing like stone statues. Her companions fell to the ground with a *crunch* and saw that the grass was frosted and had turned to solid ice near Organa, ever-expanding as the temperature plummeted. Myrcle held up his hands to guard him against the blizzard, and Brok followed him toward Esvele, behind a shield of heat and flames.

Organa lifted into the air and came face to face with the Ghast. Though it had no discernible expression, she could feel the fear in its heart, and the small flame inside the amber began to die. The burning eyes of the beast diminished as it looked at Organa's magic. Her skin had become like the frost she created on the ground, her hair a solid wave of ice, her clothes frosted and draped in icicles. Her power flowed through her body, and she felt invincible. Nothing had ever felt like this before—the all-enveloping rage of power, and in her ears, she heard a melody, dark and deadly, but beautiful and smooth.

"Organa," a thousand and one voices called out from around her. She could feel the intent of it, drawing itself ever closer through a resistance her magic generated. "Organa," they called again, slightly louder, and she could feel a pull as she lowered herself from the air. The melody rang louder as if to block out the voice as it called one last time before she touched the completely frozen ground. She looked and saw Brok to her left. He was stuck in the frozen ground, and it slowly entangled him, gradually turning him into a frozen sculpture. Behind Brok, she saw Myrcle and Esvele backing away from the expanding frost, trying to escape behind Myrcle's shield of flames.

Brok ran out of the warmth of the ward and toward Organa. As his shoes touched the frozen ground around her, he felt himself stop against his will. Looking down, he could see that his shoes were now made of solid ice, and he could feel his bones and skin transforming. He continued to try to move, but to no avail. The ice was now at Brok's lower torso, still creeping upward. He called out to his friend, though she could not hear him. Her eyes were fixed on the terrified creature in front of her, its eyes. She stared into its amber heart, the flame now dead, and, in its place, an ice crystal formed. The corruption spread into the bark of the beast, and the Ghast cried out in pain. The flames within his eyes died as the frost touched them. After a few moments, the beast had transformed completely into a sculpture of snow and ice. Organa held up her hands and placed them together.

Brok was now almost completely like the Ghast and gave the last call to Organa before he turned into a sculpture as well. The voices faded as her friend's covered them. She turned her head from her prey and looked at Brok, a few seconds from completion. She felt the power recede and diminish, and she allowed it. The frost from around the area faded, and Myrcle lowered the ward guarding him and Esvele. Brok thawed as well, but as the winter storm thawed, the Ghast and its flame began to re-ignite. Organa conjured another wave of killing frost within its heart, and the Ghast froze entirely once more. With a mass of cracks webbing along its form, Organa shattered it like glass, sending shards of ice speeding in every direction, but, as they exploded, she recalled them into a single orb of ice and melted it away before further damage came to her friends.

Organa's blizzard receded into her. The ice upon the hundreds of trees she affected melted, and so too did the ice that had crept toward Esvele and Myrcle along with what had already taken most of Brok. The gentle giant sprinted to Organa as she stood to her feet.

We finally found you...Daughter of Starlight. Something echoed with a hundred thousand voices in Organa's mind.

Her eyes found Myrcle and Esvele standing with terrified expressions. A searing pain echoed in her mind, along with a fading melody. Brok's sturdy hands held her up for a moment, but he suddenly dropped her as bandits bashed him over the head and seized the others, binding them in rune-carved chains.

Cold Blades

Organa blinked her eyes a few times as the world came into focus. A few bonfires crackled with intensity and heat. The tents were large enough to hold at least four people, and each of them bore the banner of the Golden Queen: a knife through a shimmering, yellow, burning heart.

Pushing up, Organa tried to stand but found herself hunched over because of the size of her room. Metal bars lined its edges and reflected some of the light from the fires. The gray metal was tightly sewn together, allowing only enough room for a toddler's finger between the cross-hatches. As she looked out, she saw a large tent in the far back with two apexes that stood twelve feet high. Fine crimson-and-gold cloth, richly decorated, danced in the wind, revealing the figure of a woman in silver plate armor with a golden crown on a pedestal beside her. Guards donning leather or iron armor, wielding blades, staffs, spears, and axes were on the watch or sitting around the fires of the large encampment. Towering over them all, Mount Doloroth stood exalted but small under the shadow of the Fire in Heaven, screaming across the night in its grand, crimson, and scarlet glory of the agony of ages past.

"Pst," a voice called. Organa looked around to find the origin but saw nothing. "Psssst," it sounded again, but longer to give a better sense of direction to the origin. Organa looked to her right and saw many more cages like hers, a few dozen of them with a tiny one at the end. As she turned her head to the left, she saw a few more people caged, and Brok within the closest one. He was still asleep and snoring loudly. It was a wonder that whoever their capturers were got Brok knocked out and scrunched up inside his cell.

"Pst. Oi, over here." Organa followed the voice this time and turned around to see six more cages behind hers. Within one of them was EV, who glowed dimly as the light of the fire hit her ashen skin. Myrcle leaned forward in the cell beside hers, his gray horns and eyes catching some of the light.

"Good evening, dearie," whispered Myrcle.

"Can I not get away from you two?" Organa sighed.

"Organa, we never meant to frighten you. We didn't prepare ourselves, we didn't prepare you—I'm so sorry. I never meant to frighten you." EV shook her head. The face she had been wearing of bravado and wit had shattered and now, she only looked at the young druid with terror alight in her eyes.

"I wasn't scared of you." Her walls came up.

"Organa," Myrcle kept his focus on their mission, "don't you think these cages look withered?"

"What do you mean?"

"These cages were not made by any guards of the Menitheal Empire, nor were they the making of any skilled blacksmith among any of the races," he hinted.

"And?"

"And that means the cells' construction was poor. So how do you think we shall get out?" Myrcle asked. As he did, Myrcle crept back into the shadows of his cell. In an instant, the metal behind him glowed with light. A blue flame emitted from his hands, burning away at the rope. It sizzled away, and the darkness returned around him as the flame died.

"What did you do?" asked EV.

"I am free of my bonds, and now we must figure out how to get out of this cell and get you three out as well." Myrcle pondered for a moment, thinking about the possibilities.

Organa opened her hand, moving her fingers lightly, and the ground stirred as the threads of earth plunged into the depths. The earth under the cages came alive as four thick roots grew up into the lock on the right side of the cage and inserted themselves like a key. Rust quickly enveloped the lock, and it fell from the cage. The roots sank back into the earth and then reappeared in front of each of their cages, opening the cells.

Organa crawled out of her prison, and so did EV. Myrcle untied their bonds, freeing their hands from behind their backs. Organa looked at her left hand and saw that the snake ring was still there. She ran over to Brok's cell and tried to wake him.

"Brok," she whispered, but he gave no answer. "Brok," she tried again. He still did not wake from his sleep. Organa sighed, took her right hand, froze it solid, and placed it upon his face. The extreme cold woke Brok immediately, and he hit his head on the top of his cage. He blinked his eyes a few times and focused on Organa. As he did so, he saw EV and Myrcle to the left of Organa. He sprang up and shielded Organa behind him.

"Go away," he boomed.

Organa ran around in front of him as he growled and almost released a roar of anger. "Brok, wait; we'll deal with them later. Right now we have to be very silent." The giant looked down at Organa with confusion, deciding to comply.

Organa turned to her old friends. "We will work with you for tonight and tonight only. After that, we are gone, and you leave us the fuck alone." Her voice was sharp.

The four of them walked slowly and quietly to the edge of the lines of cages, hunkering down out of sight in the shadows. Myrcle looked around for a moment and looked back at EV. She pointed behind him, and something grabbed his shoulder, nearly causing him to scream if not for the same hand wrapping around his mouth.

"I didn't mean to scare you, mister," a low female voice spoke as the hand let him go.

"It's fine," Myrcle said as he caught his breath.

"Who are you? What are you doin'? Why are you here? Do you owe some money to the Golden Queen too? Are you okay? Are you—"

EV cut her off. "Will you shut up?" she glared.

"Sorry, I couldn't help myself. It's been so long since I've been able to talk to another person," the voice apologized happily. Her black feathers hid her very well in the dark, only revealing bright, glowing hazel eyes illuminating from the blackness of the night and the cage.

"What is she?" Organa asked.

"She is a Hawkina," Myrcle answered, now steadied. Then, suddenly, excitement filled his voice. "Descendants of the people of the Spine of the World in Menagerie. I heard of your race nearly passing into legend."

"My name is Florie, for your information, and yes, most of us died out when the Cataclysm came," she said somberly. "My great-great-great-great grandmother told the family of how the mountains of Menagerie shook as the Corruption spread from Dremica. The demons and dark fiends slaughtered everything they could see."

"Esvele, if you would kindly release her from her prison, dearie," Myrcle nodded, and she replied with a quiet rumble of moving dirt. Three vines from the brown and green earth twisted around and coiled into the lock, expanding until it broke into pieces. The little bird-woman crept from the shadows, her black feathers now better illuminated by the bonfires around the camp. She had muscled arms with three-taloned fingers, and her legs and feet were the same. A long black beak connected to a black and silver feathered face with beautiful hazel eyes.

"Now that you've set me free, I owe you a debt. Even though that debt has yet to be decided, I still owe it, because you saved my life, and now I am in debt to all of you and—"

EV cut her off once more. "Your payment to me can be not to talk quite as much, okay?" she said, shaking her head.

Myrcle slapped the back of her head with his left hand, looking at her with annoyance. "Don't be so rude."

"Ouch," she whisper-shouted.

"Oh, hush. I didn't even hit you that hard."

Organa whipped around, holding a finger to her lips, her eyes burning a hole through them both. Within a few moments, three bandits passed by their hidden prisoners, unknowing of their new freedom. Walking up the hill to the grand tent with the symbol of the Golden Queen, four daggers in a cross formation meeting a golden band in the middle, the bandits pulled back the curtains and went in. With a few glances around them, Organa noticed something wrong. "Where's Brok?"

EV pounded her head with her palm, and Myrcle rolled his eyes at her. "Stop doing that." He took her hand from her face and slapped it hard enough that the sound actually echoed a little in the camp. Organa looked back at him with anger as the slap sounded and then looked to see if the bandits had noticed. Thankfully, they had not.

Myrcle looked at Organa and whispered, "Okay, where is the giant fellow?"

"I asked you, how am I supposed to know?"

"Maybe he's over there?" the Hawkina pointed with her feathered hand.

Brok was creeping along the ground on his belly. Organa nearly burst into flames with disbelief, and EV went back to pounding her head, this time lightly against a nearby wooden chest. A light chuckle left Myrcle as he watched the great half-orc attempt to be stealthy and then realized the immediate danger. Brok was heading toward the Golden Queen's tent.

The group watched, helpless, as Brok entered the tent where the three bandits had gone inside. As he reached and began pulling back the drape, Brok noticed Organa flailing her arms and waved back at her with a bright smile.

Organa pulled a gust of cold and freezing wind from the night, sending Brok flying into the air, tent curtain in hand, onto a nearby tree that sounded with a few snapping branches. As he flew, the tent's material went with him, ripping a large hole in it and alerting the bandits.

Each of the men and women inside grabbed their swords, bows, axes, and staffs before running out of the tent looking for the culprit.

Brok raised his head through the top of the branches, took a deep breath as if to bellow, and the tree came to life. Through Esvele's magic, it swallowed him up in a rush of leaves and branches, letting out a small yelp as it devoured him.

EV looked at Organa with a smirk. "Nice going. Now watch as I show you how this is done." She stood to her feet and flicked her hands a few times to warm them up.

"Now is not the time to show off, Esvele," Myrcle furrowed his brow.

"Oh, hush, dear. Organa, watch and learn what your powers could really do." EV then burst into a full sprint, leaping over the boxes and landing on her feet with a loud thud. The rogues took notice and ran at her one by one, taking out their weapons, ready to attack.

A younger man took his spear and slashed at the air around Esvele, missing each strike. Attack after attack came, and EV finally decided to put the poor boy out of his misery. With an upward thrust of her arm, a boulder from within the earth to meet his face, knocking him cold to the ground.

A Kalishtani woman rushed her with a wooden, brass-tipped spear. Once again, EV dodged each stab, save for one of them that struck her back with the pole.

Myrcle rushed over to the crates where they were all hiding, and the Hawkina girl followed along. Brok rushed from the tree line quickly and grabbed a man, throwing him across the camp into a nearby tent.

EV got up with the help of a hand from Organa. "Nice going. Let me show you how it's done." Graceful, swift fingers pulled from the Flux a blade of cold blue ice, and the weather answered the call of her left hand with a rumble in the skies. A swirling vortex of clouds formed overhead as the storm charged itself with energy.

The forbidden melody sang to her. Organa's eyes radiated a crackling, thunderous sound as she called forth from the clouds' radiant streaks of blue and white lightning. Passing through the bodies of the growing number of bandits, it sent millions of blue and purple streams of volts running through their veins before they fell to the ground as thirty dead, smoking ruins.

"Organa," the sight stole Esvele's breath.

"Watch out!" Myrcle shouted.

Running from behind EV, a man holding two curved blades leaped into the air to strike down the Kalishtani. Spinning the icy blade in her hand, Organa threw it into the man's shoulder and thrust him to the ground with a cold force. He tumbled along the earth and removed the icy dagger from within himself, then rose to strike again. Organa wove another cold cutlass from the air around her and caught the assassin's iron with a sharp ringing of blades that harmonized with the melody in her mind.

He dropped the dagger into his free hand and went to strike again. As he moved, Organa called forth a final blade to catch his hand, severing it with a burning cold. His cry of pain pierced the night around them.

His eyes met hers: unfeeling and merciless. Tears rolled down his face. "Please, please, m'lady, I was just doing my job. Have mercy, please."

The chorus whispered again, *See his fear...*allowing her eyes to pierce his armor, flesh, and bone, revealing a quivering soul.

"Please, m'lady!" he pleaded again.

A feeling of joy flowed through her as she felt his terror exude from within him. And that melody...sweeter than the brightest tune and the ripest fruit...yet darker than the midnight-black above, filled her head.

"Organa," a muffled voice called out. She gave no answer, not even an acknowledgment. Her eyes focused solely on her victim. She felt the power coursing through her, filling her with endless possibilities. Myrcle slowly approached her to calm her; then, with a strong, stiff gust of wind, she sent him flying against a boulder.

Within a few moments, Myrcle was on his feet again. He grabbed his tome from his side and turned the pages, flipping through them as fast as he could. With each page turn, he looked up to see Organa, who was getting closer with every turn. The servant of the Golden Queen jumped back up and wrapped his wounded arm around her, seeking to pull her to the ground, but found only an icy blade lodged in his heart.

The man's body fell with a thud to the ground.

They will betray you again. They will hurt you. You must stop them, Organa...the Shadow tempted her.

Turning back to Myrcle, Organa called another blade from the Flux, and music boomed in her mind, but it was no longer the one she typically heard. Its melody had changed, promising her not power, but revenge. She raised her hand to bring down the knife on the old sorcerer, but Brok stood in his place, instantly stopping her motion with his presence.

"Organa," he looked at her with his kind eyes. "Don't." But the seductive melody was stronger than her now, consuming her from within with hatred…wrath of a hidden birth in her mind.

"Move, Brok," she muttered.

He did not. But a torrent of strands of air cocooned him and threw him from his defensive stance. Using her right hand, she wove the air and unsheathed the great sword from his back. Raising it high over her head, she began its descent toward Myrcle. Her eyes held no remorse, no question, only hate and a lust for chaos and power.

Kill them all… save him!

"Organa, no!" Brok cried out with a cannon's boom as he rushed her way. His feet moved with undreamt speed, and she turned her head to see the horrified look on his and EV's face.

The crashing of metal against the pebbles from the great sword echoed throughout the dead-silent camp. The song sang no more.

"Organa," EV looked at her with what compassion she could find.

"I…," she stuttered.

Myrcle stepped to her side, helping her sit down on the ground. Brok stumbled back. Even with his simple mind, his eyes were as wide as the moons.

Light swam at the edges of Organa's vision, and the world tilted, weightless. The gray dusk dissolved, replaced by towers that pierced the heavens; colossal spires of marble veined with gold and silver, each catching the light of a sun that glowed like a captive star in the midnight sky. Its radiance bathed everything in a warm, impossible dawn. Along the cobblestone streets below, markets spilled with silks, fruits, and glittering wares, their scents of spice and sweetness rising like incense. The air itself hummed, too perfect, too still.

Organa's eyes darted all around her. A voice called to her…called her name. There was a warmth to it of familiarity, but an echo of venom on the tongue hidden among it, waiting to strike.

As the vision faded, Organa ran into the real Myrcle and fell into his arms. Esvele bolted to them and looked to Myrcle and then back to Organa. "We need to tell her the truth."

"Let's not argue about this now."

"Hello, Myrcle," a light alto voice said. "It's been some time."

More of the Golden Queen's forces emerged, surrounding them with spears and swords.

"This was a mistake. She's not ready. I was—"

A quick glance from the Queen brought a swift blow to the back of his head, and darkness took him.

A Song of Vengeance

Myrcle sat tied to one of the support beams in the grand tent of the Golden Queen. EV lay next to him, and Organa lay on the floor unconscious. A few braziers illuminated the room, and a light wind stirred the red tent cloth around them.

As Myrcle came to full consciousness, he saw a human woman with golden blond hair and sky-blue eyes donning heavy brass and silver armor with gauntlets and greaves to match. Her right hand sat upon a pointed golden pommel that connected to a black leather hilt. A great sword carved with silent holy symbols of Stellevarian punctured the ground. The Golden Queen watched him with a worried look she tried to hide.

An enormous figure stood on the woman's right. Two long, curved blades lay sheathed and strapped to the back of their dark silver armor. Two war axes rested on each side of the person's waist, held by a long brown leather belt. A great cloak of dark fur draped behind them, and upon their head was a large helmet shaped like a dragon's head, made of dark silver and shadowglass horns. Where the eyes should have been, there were only two glowing red flames.

Esvele struggled to break free of her bonds to no avail.

"Hello, Esvele," the Queen said.

"Velkin, she's not ready." EV shook her head, focusing her eyes on the Golden Queen. "We were wrong… so, *so wrong.*"

The flames of the braziers danced in Organa's eyes as she opened them. The frightening man in armor in the corner was like a great shadow behind Velkin, nearly enveloping her.

"Why did you kill my soldiers?" The Queen looked to Organa.

"You know she has no control over it," Myrcle said, glaring at the woman in armor. "Esvele is right. I—*me*—I was wrong. I pushed to far. She is—"

"I know, Myrcle!" the Queen glared before her gaze returned to Organa. "Why?"

Organa gave no answer.

"She's not ready to know!" Myrcle pleaded. "Let me rebuild the walls. There's still time!"

"Ready to know what?" Organa asked.

"Nothing of your concern right now." Myrcle snapped back.

"It is her concern; the blood of one of my men is on her hands, and she doesn't know why." Velkin's sharp tongue cut at her.

"Please don't," Myrcle pleaded again. Myrcle and EV tried to break their bonds as the great armored beast moved forward and unsheathed one of the war axes from its side. As it raised the ax to take the first swing at Esvele, Organa screamed her reply, her voice just barely reaching the woman's ears through Esvele's terrified wail as the armored woman walked out of the tent.

"Stop!" the mistress shouted, holding up her fist, which glowed dim green. In an instant, the creature had ceased its action and returned to its post. "What did you say?"

"Please, you heard it. Let us go," Organa begged.

"No, say it again."

A long pause of silence echoed, and the woman snapped her fingers, giving the creature a signal to kill EV. However, Organa refused to let her die.

"I wanted to!" she shouted.

The mistress snapped her fingers again, turned to her pet, and motioned for it to return to its post once more. She sat back down in her chair and whispered a word, too quiet to hear, and the bonds turned to purple mist.

* * *

Brok woke in a cage again and hit his head as he tried to sit up. Two guards stood in front of his prison, whispering to one another. Brok reached through the space between the bars and smashed the men's heads together, causing a crimson spray to paint the grass. The jingle of the keyring rang as he lifted it from the dead guard's body. With a click, he unlocked the cell door. He kept his head down low and remained hidden behind large trees and stacks of rations and resources. As he made his way through the camp, the large tent of the Golden Queen flowed with wind on the high hill. About twenty men and women in long black duster coats stood near the fire at the foot of the hill.

"Hey, big man," she squeaked. Brok did not hear her the first time, so she tried again. "Hey, over here." That time he heard her but did not see from where. "Look this way," she called to him from the night. He looked around but did not see the source of the call. "Brok, over here, you thickhead!" This time she got him, and he walked over to her, hunched over like an old beggar. "Where are the others?" Florie asked.

"I do not...know," Brok replied as he placed his hands on the bars.

"Well, open this thing; let's find them."

* * *

As the bonds dissolved around their wrists, the prisoners rose to their feet. Organa tried to reach for the Flux without the woman seeing, but to no avail.

"No need for that." The woman motioned to Organa's hand. "If you don't teach her how to control her rage and her magic, it will consume her."

"She will learn in time," Esvele scolded back.

"Esvele should have taught her to control it long ago."

"You know that I taught her, but we hid all that from her for a reason, Velkin," EV spat.

"You're not as much of a problem. She is." She pointed to Organa.

"I am sorry I killed your people; I…I…couldn't control my power."

"Well, it's not the first time that the Dark Song has called to you," Velkin pressed.

"The what? What does she mean, Myrcle?" Organa's frustration was clear.

He took a long pause, with no answer to the question. "Organa… I'm sorry," he finally spoke.

* * *

The duo stood a few hundred feet away from the great red tent. Brok walked forward, and Florie grabbed him with her taloned arm. "Brok, you can't just go in there, because there are bad people here, and we don't even know if the others are in there or alive, and there are dangerous people around and—"

Brok cut her off. "You…need to be…more quiet."

"A) quieter. B) I know, I'm just so flustered and I get overwhelmed and I—"

"You need…to…breathe. Don't act stupid…like usual." Brok placed his hand on her shoulder.

"You're not good at this, you know."

"I try." Brok's deep voice loomed in the night.

"How do you plan to get around those crazies around the tent?" The great brute shrugged his shoulders and moved, but Florie slapped him. Brok whimpered and recoiled from her hand as he sat down. "That wasn't me saying 'fuck it, let's just go for it,' buddy," she blinked. Florie turned from him, looking at the multiple routes and plans to the tent, and thought of likely outcomes. The scenarios played out in her head. "We could go all the way over there and hide behind the crates of supplies as we had done before, sneak up that hill and into the tent, hopefully finding the others in there. Or we could run to the hilltop head-on and take out the guards around the tent, alerting all the bandits to our presence. Or we could…," Florie trailed on and on, leaving Brok's simple mind very bored, so he left Florie to her plans and ran up the hill to his left, through the woods.

* * *

Myrcle paced as the Golden Queen eyed him. "You tell her. She needs to know. She *deserves* to know about *him*."

"Who?" Organa turned red.

"She's not ready." Myrcle shook his head. "I need to reinforce the barriers we put there and we need to wait longer."

"You keep saying that. She has to be. If any of us wants a chance at having back what was lost…" her mind seemed to become lost in thought before she returned. "There's no going back now, Myrcle. Tell her about him."

Myrcle took Organa's hand in his own and tried to think of the right words to say to her. "When twins are born, a link forms. Both of them feel each other's emotions and pain and have a bond beyond what any could imagine." Myrcle sighed and placed his gray fur-covered hand on his head, exhaling heavily. He turned back to the young elf and spoke, "Organa, you have a twin…and your brother caused the Cataclysm."

The words echoed in Organa's ears, and a sharp ringing and excruciating pain came over her mind. Her heart nearly burst from her chest as her body heated, threatening to catch fire. Then, she screamed as a tsunami of memory drowned her thoughts.

"Where are my tomes?" Myrcle shouted to the woman in armor. She gave no response, only a horrified look as she witnessed Organa's collapse. "Velkin, where are my tomes!"

* * *

Organa opened her eyes and saw a black cascade of night and empty nothingness. Standing and walking, her footsteps echoed down a long corridor. White marble walls formed around her from the blackness, and a booming voice shot through the darkness in a vile language that made her stomach churn. *"Karven."*

Organa felt her mind ache, and a sharp pain and ringing echoed in her ears as a choir of voices repeated the words the single voice spoke.

"Karven, trum vel nihtra!" The words coiled inside her mind, and

from within the darkness, a bright green light shone in the distance. *"Xeliv Minach!"* She did not know the language, and the ensemble repeated the same words over and over.

The green light revealed itself as bright flames atop eight pillars of shadowglass. Large pillars held the ceiling of the bowl-shaped room up; two strong, carved stone doors stood at its entrance. People were calling to the night, covered in black robes with red linings and purple symbols that matched their leader's. Red and black half-skull masks covered their faces. All of them circled around a shadowglass table where a body lay covered with a red cloth.

A Kalishtani man with brown horns ascended from his black hair that covered most of his pale face and upper torso. Covered in a bright green and red skirt with many symbols of an ancient dialect, he held out his hands. Bursting forth, red and purple flames danced there, and soon black flames danced in his followers' hands.

With the congregation chanting alongside their master, an unseen voice suddenly extinguished the bright green flames, saying, *"Selvat vis Solvitasra."*

In their place emerged newly lit purple and white flames that emitted little to no light. The now darkened room became still and cold and, as winter seemed to arrive within the room, the congregation became quiet, leaving only their leader to chant. The flames trailed down the pillars, onto the floor in between the congregation, up the side of the shadowglass table, and under the cloth cover.

The cloth burst with the flames of the pillars, throwing its ashes into the air. As they flew, they became still, solidifying and connecting to one another and then swooping down to the table. As the first of the trails touched the table, it shattered into millions of pieces and reformed itself with ashes. It covered itself in dark shadows, and large spikes extended from the arm supports. The ashes and shards of the altar came together and formed a dark throne.

* * *

"Where are my tomes, Velkin?"

She gave no response but motioned with her left hand to a chest near the chair she sat in. He threw open the closed top of the chest and rummaged rapidly through a large bag, ripping out his books.

"Myrcle, what are you doing?" Velkin glared.

"I'm going to save her. I will rebuild the walls I put up a lifetime ago, and we…she will be safe."

"Where is she?!" Brok roared as he cut through the tent.

The armored guardian of the Queen met Brok's blade, disarming him with a single parry and holding him in a tight grip.

Velkin knelt down beside Myrcle. "You need to let him remember too."

"If he remembers, then Organa has to remember! That's the wall I built."

"How has she not remembered by now on her own?" Velkin grit her teeth.

"I had a contact in the Order that constantly rebuilt her psychic walls against her own memory. Masix, and his sons after him, would reset her every twenty years for me while she stayed there. When she and Brok ran, Gerith let us know, and Esvele and I began searching for her. We found her in Turnmot."

"They have to remember Myrcle!" Velkin insisted.

"We can't!" Myrcle's voice was like thunder. "She's not ready! She needs at least another year before it's time. She can't handle the Dark Song!"

"Velkin's right," Esvele shot at him.

* * *

Organa watched as the figure beneath the cloth became visible. A young Elven man levitated in the air before the dark throne, donning clothes made of darkness and shadow that writhed around him. His long silver hair flowed as if submerged in water, and his eyes were full of a raging crimson fire that spread across his body, creating great wings of flame.

The young man looked down at the Kalishtani and spoke in hundreds of thousands of voices. Men, women, children, beasts, and demons echoed as he spoke in the common tongue to his servants, "Well done, Golgorot, my Lord of Shadows. You have brought us the Child of Starlight as you promised, and we shall fulfill our end of our bargain." The voices paused, and the Shadowlight descended to the floor as an echo of many voices shouting from beyond the great door to the chamber. "Who did you tell of this summoning, whelp?"

"No one, my Lord! I swear it on my Salvation," Golgorot spoke with fear.

"If you forsake this ritual because of your incompetence, our bargain will cause the same fate as Nashindris." A colossal explosion sounded beyond the great stone doors of the ritual.

As the dark flames upon the pillars burst into bright red, lighting the room completely, a legion of armed soldiers of the Light surged through the room's two great stone doors and surrounded the cultists at the top of the stairs. Their armor was bloody and burnt from the raging battle above against the forces of the Void.

As the soldiers finished spreading out, three figures walked through the ritual room doors. A Kalishtani woman with gray skin and fiery red hair held a wooden staff with a bright green orb on top wreathed in green flames. A Firbolg ran behind her, his white robes gliding over the floor and clinging to his gleaming staff, with two tomes strapped to his side. Trailing after them was a half-orc man with two curved swords sheathed around his waist, clanking against his silver armor. Esvele, Myrcle, and Brok all stood at the top of the stairs.

The Kalishtani man fell to his knees before the Shadowlight in the center of the room, who lifted himself up above the floor enough to be at eye level with the burning red flames upon the pillars.

The Shadowlight spoke, "Come 'Guardians,' let us see if your power can stand against the might of the Void!" As he finished his taunt, his arms became wreathed in flames and he thrust them forth from his hands as the fire coiled around his arms like snakes. The trio dodged aside, but the fire caught the few soldiers behind them, reducing them to ash and smoke.

Myrcle ran, stood to his feet, and shouted to Esvele, "We have to stop him, Esvele."

"No, I thought I would let the Shadow Monarch take over the world and the Starlight Prince's body. Sounds good to me. I might have a few glasses of wine while I'm at it," she sarcastically and loudly remarked.

"Now is not the time for your snide remarks, Esvele." Brok spoke with the clearest voice Organa had ever heard. "Myrcle, you need to distract him. Esvele, go around the left; I'll go around the right; we'll use the Bonds of Light and bring him to his feet. Myrcle, you then sweep in and excise the Shadow Monarch from Kyriel."

"Do you think that will work?" Myrcle asked.

"It has not yet taken full hold of the prince," Esvele began. "We have precious little time to bind him. As long as he is bound by the magic of the Light, Golgorot cannot complete the summoning." The others nodded in agreement, and the plan was in motion.

The Shadowlight sent his dark fire in great streams toward the soldiers, dissolving them and adding to his throne. The stone pillars that held the ceiling toppled and turned to rubble, and the ceiling cracked and shattered. Large chunks of stone and marble fell to the ground and almost hit the Shadowlight himself, but with a simple motion of his hand and arm, the rubble moved from its course. The gaping hole in the ceiling now revealed the great cathedral's roof in the City of Husieàkritae.

Chunks of marble, stone, and glass fell from the crumbling ceiling and walls of the Xurinal above them. The sounds of the screaming, dying, burning, and slaughtered people in the city above flooded the chamber like a drowning sea of death. High above it all, the clouds of darkness and endless night closed over the stars, going out one by one as the Void consumed it all.

Suddenly, through the darkness, a great beam of light appeared in the entryway of the chamber where a woman in silver and star-sown runes manifested. A circle around her brow held two gems, one for each of the Element Moons that radiated her sienna skin and metallic silver eyes. But tainting her angelic visage, scars and splatters of blood had painted her with crimson.

"Servants of the Dawn, rise against this Shadow!" She proclaimed.

Moving her hands over one another, Lukitas, the Lady of Light, brought forth golden chains of radiance, binding the Shadowlight.

Esvele and Brok appeared in the openings on the side of the room and with a few simple words and moving of hands, created great, brilliant, golden chains, binding the Shadowlight's arms, and the dark fire smothered.

Myrcle ran with haste and opened his tome to the page needed, levitating it in the air before the Shadowlight as he screamed in pain and agony from the burning restraints.

The chorus of death wailed through him one final time, echoing into the cathedral and through the apex of the great pyramid, shattering it, and throwing the pieces into the night sky. Booming thunder drummed overhead, and flashes of white lightning brightened the clouds above. In a single moment, the young Elven man Myrcle, Esvele, and Brok knew, was gone; replaced by the husk of the corrupted child they were sworn to protect.

The chains dissolved, withering away like dust, and Kyriel's body became limp as Myrcle took him in his arms, giving him a brace on his knee. Brok and Esvele rushed to Myrcle's side along with the radiant woman.

"Is he still there? Is his soul still there?" Brok worriedly asked, his voice clear as water.

"Barely," the woman replied.

"Lukitas, can you save him?" Myrcle trembled.

"You have a valiant heart, Myrcle, and you are blessed with compassion, but I dare not return him to our world." Lukitas bowed her head with sorrow. "A part of the Shadow Monarch lives within him. Part of the ritual was successful. If he lives, he will wreak havoc upon all of Lorial as a tool under the influence of the Dark One, if not consumed by the Deep."

"Then take his memories." Myrcle suggested. "If he does not remember the events of tonight, he'll never know of the Shadowlight and the power within him. The hybrid will be nothing but an old fairytale to frighten children."

"Organa won't remember either; we can hide them away from one another, separate ends of the world if we must," Esvele begged.

A silence fell over the room for a moment, and Lukitas stood to her feet. She walked away, and as she did, she heard Myrcle humming the broken melody of the Psalm of Amity, cradling Kyriel in his arms and rocking lightly as his breathing became weaker and weaker.

Lukitas turned back to Kyriel and knelt beside him. Myrcle's tears wetted the prince's face as the sorcerer sang to him. She looked at the others. "If I bring him back, he must remain hidden, far away from the sight of the servants of the Shadow Monarch. Far from us as well. We will keep our memories of the child and the power within him and his sister. Myrcle, you will remove the memory from his family. Organa will not remember him, and I will hide him away in the darkest prison in the darkest world at the very gates of the Abyss if I must. None who seek his Sepulcher will ever find it. If they find him, the world will fall."

"A Sepulcher? You can't be serious. He's just a boy," Esvele shouted.

"A boy who possesses more power than any other being in the universe, and his bond connects that same power to his sister. They will both need to be hidden away in prisons, under eternal watchmen."

"I won't let you damn them both," Esvele grasped Lukitas' arm.

"Let go of me." Her eyes glared back. "Now."

"You will not subject her to eternal torment," Esvele glared.

"Then what would you have me do?"

"I don't know, but placing them in an eternal, dark, torturous prison is not the answer," Myrcle could feel Kyriel slipping away.

His rage will burn the world, and Organa's fury will shatter it. If we leave the world to chance, the Void will destroy everything. The very fabric of the Canvas of Creation will be unwound." The screams above in the burning city fell upon them. "We have no other choice."

"Forgive me, Kyriel. I have failed you," Myrcle cried over the dying boy.

"I'm sorry, Myrcle," Lukitas said, placing her hand on his shoulder. "Let him go."

With tears streaming down her face, Esvele helped Brok remove Kyriel from Myrcle's arms, placing him on the rubble as comfortably as they could. Lukitas raised her hand, ready to cast the ancient Luxian spell.

"Wait," Brok shouted, "what if we let him die?"

Myrcle's rage built up within him until he nearly snapped his staff in half. His eyes burned with bright green fire as the Dark Song called to him and he went to cast a spell, but Esvele stood between them.

"If he dies, the power will not fade. It will pass to his sister directly through their bond," Lukitas replied. "Their power is interchangeable. It will only make things worse. We have only this choice, and in three hundred years, the Sepulcher will manifest once more. The Glass Key created will be required to cast it back into the Void once more before he is resurrected."

"Who will do that?" Brok asked, "We'll be dead."

"Not if you're imbued with the Vitu'Lux."

"Only Guardians can have that power."

"And so you shall be them. Guardians of Lorial and bound to keep the Shadowlight in check."

"And if we fail?" Brok interjected.

"We're all dead," Lukitas sighed.

As the last few words of Lukitas's voice echoed within her ears, the world grew bright and blinding.

* * *

Velkin's voice was harsh and collected now. "What we did to this poor girl, can it be undone safely?"

"Yes, that's why we're doing this, remember? Don't worry about her; you need to get your people out of here. This is either going to go really, really bad or extremely bad. The power I can feel welling up is strong and untamed. Many will die." Esvele shouted to Velkin over Organa's screaming. Myrcle was speaking the words from his tome that he had spoken many years ago.

As he muttered, Florie burst through the tent, ready to slay any who dared prevent her escape, but she found Organa seizing on the floor with Myrcle over her, speaking his ancient words. Brok stood there, held by Florie, and watched as his best friend thrashed and gasped for air, exhaling terrible screams.

Myrcle turned to Esvele. "Continue the incantation. Wake her up and restore her memories, I will restore Brok's. They both have to know if we want there to be any chance of either of them living past this night."

He ran to Brok and placed his hand on his head. But before the past could be unveiled within Brok's mind, Organa exerted a wave of power across the tent, throwing Myrcle and Brok away from one another. Her body thrashed wildly, and her screams shot through the night.

With a thrust of her right arm, she unleashed a blast of powerful energy, setting the tent cloth ablaze and throwing the others across the hillside. Esvele held her staff, allowing it to take the brunt of the force, splintering it across the hillside and throwing her against the ground.

Organa stood, her eyes full of red flames. "You deceived me! You betrayed us both! You stole everything from us!" She turned and raised her right hand. "Now, we will have our revenge." Many voices sounded through her own as a blaze of red immolation burnt the ground and spread down one section of the hillside and into the camp, setting fire to every tent and burning the bandits alive within an instant.

Six of Velkin's forces ran up the hill to escape the inferno. One of them ran toward the Elven girl with her spear, ready to thrust into her chest, drawing Organa's gaze. With a single glance, large tendrils breached her chest like the spears she held. Her blood sprayed into the air and poured out of her throat and onto the ground like a waterfall. Twisting her hand, Organa caught her assailant's blood aflame, trailing it back into the woman's mouth and body, melting her from within. More tendrils erupted from the ground, piercing the other soldiers of the Golden Queen.

She twisted the flames within the bodies into living forms and summoned forth large cobras that circled an area around her and her deceivers. Their flames hissed and roared with fury and rage. She sent the serpents into the burning camp, and they went to devour those left alive.

"Organa, everything we did, we did to protect you, to protect the future," Esvele swore to Organa over the raging fires.

"I forgot a brother, someone I would protect. I forgot my family!" she screamed back. "You should have tried to save him!" Her voices overlapped themselves. Her body enveloped itself in writhing red flames, yet she did not burn. Her clothes were unscathed, and her body was unharmed.

Velkin shouted to her through her screams. "Organa, what they did was wrong, but it was also the right thing."

"I don't know you; your words mean nothing to me!" Her power engulfed everything around them, and her Balance of Chaos was discarded as a song of vengeance and unknown dark powers flowed through her. "No," whispered. Then again, "No," and once more with as the chorus sang more hatred around her. "No!"

As she rejected Myrcle's words and his spell failed, a dome of red, black, and white fire surrounded them all, dominating the hill and devouring some of Velkin's forces, turning them to ash.

Myrcle stood to his feet. "Repeat my words now!" He began his incantation, speaking old words of the Stellevarian language.

As Myrcle continued his incantation and the others joined him to subdue her, Organa screamed, "No, no, no, no!" Her hands clutched her head as she cried out in agony, and then she could take no more. Organa gazed into their souls with enraged eyes, lifting them into the air. "Get out of my head!" Revenge filled her heart and soul, flowing into her and redirecting it back at Esvele as deep blue and purple lightning. Esvele drew forth from the Flux a shield of radiant light around them, but it shattered like glass and threw her across the hillside.

Organa reveled in the power she had as the melody played in her head. One warmer than the sun and dark as the space between the stars, where light treads not. Brok raised himself from the ground and walked forward to his best friend.

"Organa," Brok called to her. His voice filled her head, and she shook her head as his warm voice caused her pain, forcing the Dark Song from her with his words and presence. Kill him! He betrayed us! Then her rage reignited, stronger than before, burning across the eastern face of Mount Doloroth. "Organa," her friend shouted once more. Brok coughed as he got choked on the smoke from Organa's ruin. Death moved across Mount Doloroth and consumed all things in flames. Brok was getting closer, and he could see more of the devastation of the flames engulfing more of the mountainside. "Get away from me before I kill you!" Organa screamed at Brok, who was shoved back a few feet by the power of her voice.

Esvele kept her hands upon Myrcle's head, trying to repeat her incantation to return Myrcle, but her mind faded with the exertion of power and she fell backward onto the ashen grass.

Velkin woke, squinting her eyes and trying to see through the smoke, and coughed to keep it from smothering her to almost no avail. Burning wood and flesh mixed in the air, choking her with each breath she took. Death was surrounding them on all sides. She reached for the steel great sword on her back but did not find it. With pain, she held out her hand and could feel the pull of her ancient blade as it raced toward her hand. From within the fires of the hellscape, Silverlight came to her hands and flew past Organa, consumed by her power. As the hilt met her hand, she pointed the blade at the ground and plunged it into the charred earth. A great shield of flickering light surrounded Velkin, Esvele, and Myrcle, clearing the air of foulness and springing life into all of their bodies.

Organa saw the paladin's challenge of her might and reveled in the thought of her power crushing the life of those who would oppose her, their traitors who bound them.

Kill her!

A foul grimace appeared on her face, and she extended her right arm and sent forth a burning beam of raging fire toward Velkin's shield. As her power reached the edge of the barrier, Velkin clutched the hilt of her blade and kept it from giving in to the flames' oppressive weight.

Organa's eyes darkened, annoyed with Velkin.

Kill her now! The chorus commanded.

Suddenly, a second inferno erupted from her hands with the strength of a volcano, breaking and burning away the Paladin's ward.

Brok held out his hand to her. "Organa, stop, please!"

"No, they will pay for what they did to me. What they did to us!" Her magic intensified and began not only to diminish the shield but to surround it, burning through the divine magic and turning it red like heated metal. The globe shrunk around them, and she pulled back all her power and thrust it willingly through her body. A single stream of fire struck Brok in the chest, sending him flying back as the globe broke. Sending him across the hillside, Brok's head contacted a boulder near the others. Velkin was nearly drained of her power but thrust her blade once more into the dirt to form her ward again, and Organa unleashed her fury.

Esvele held her friend, rejoicing that he had survived. Myrcle saw the Ward of Dawn weakening and on the verge of collapse. He channeled his power into two streams of light that shot from his hands and reinforced the shield.

"Myrcle," Velkin shouted to him with a grunt, "We have to restore her full memory."

"Brok is the only one who can get close to her." Myrcle moved over Brok's unconscious body and placed his hands on his head once more. All the old days of adventure with Organa, growing up together in Dremica, in the royal courts. All around Brok. A white, blinding light covered Brok's eyes as his memories flooded into his mind at a wildly rapid pace. Brok's eyes opened to fire and destruction.

"Save her." Myrcle moved aside, and Brok walked to his best friend. Organa's burning eyes glared at him as he got closer. She held up her hand and pushed a wave of power all around her, throwing all of her 'friends' to the ground.

Brok rose to his feet slowly, and Organa saw him. Her fiery eyes seemed to dim slightly as she looked at her closest companion. "They betrayed me! They took everything from me! They hid my brother away in some cold and dark prison! And you, you were there," she raised him from the ground. "You didn't stop them! You let them do this! They stole your past too."

Organa looked at her prisoners. Myrcle and the others hung in the air, dissolving slowly in agony. Brok held out his hand. "Vengeance is a powerful tool, and an even worse ally," his voice clearer than water, without struggle and without hesitation.

Myrcle, Esvele, Florie, and Velkin fell to the ground. Their ashes returned to them as if time were reversed. They all lay on the grassy hill, groaning from the pain they endured. Velkin pushed through her pain and saw Organa holding Brok's hand. The dome of flames disbanded and diminished, but as it did, she felt it, the last of her energy, the last few measures of the Dark Song echoing in her mind.

Her hands and arms began to radiate the heat and flame of the sun. Velkin called back to Brok, though her words were not able to be understood through the chaos around them. Brok ran as fast as he could, seeing Velkin raising her sword up to make her last shield against the darkness. A field of sparkling energy circled around the traitors and closed just as Brok got to the others. But the magical barrier had sealed itself. Velkin's eyes grew wide and her face went pale; however, a somber but peaceful smile graced Brok's face.

The last eruption came swiftly and violently. Time sped up and slowed down; ran backward and forwards. Her eyes became like lightning and flame. A scream of agony echoed through the night. A vast wave of light enveloped the mountain.

Beautiful

Organa opened her eyes to the somber rage of the Fire in Heaven above as ash fell on her face. Her hands crumbled the burned, ashen grass, scattering it to the wind. "BROK!" she screamed as she stood.

A horrible, wet choking sound came from near a large boulder that had broken through the earth during the quakes. The gargling of a thick liquid in someone's throat echoed lightly in the air. He was gasping for air as a slow stream of blood fell from his mouth, flowing slower when he breathed in and much faster when he exhaled. The rotten smell of burned flesh and other disgusting odors filled their noses as they all gathered around Brok. The right side of his body was burned black from the rage and fire, covered in bloody gashes and bubbling pockets of blood beneath the skin. His entire body trembled with each slight movement he made.

Organa felt a sinking weight in her stomach and heart. His beautiful eyes shone faintly in the night, but a web of bloodshot veins overtook them.

Blood trailed down from his mouth. "Organa," he smiled, and a thicker flow of blood ran down from the corner of his mouth.

Myrcle, Esvele, Florie, and Velkin moved up behind her. A light hand rested on her shoulder, which she shoved off swiftly. "Don't touch me, Myrcle!" Organa shouted. Esvele began to speak but stopped herself and brought her hand back to her side.

"Organa," Brok said more clearly, then choked, letting out a bloody cough and speckling crimson across Organa's face. She did not wipe it away but let it stay there, as her focus was on the last moments with her friend. Brok let out a sigh and began to fade.

"No, no, no, stay here, you big lug. Hey, look at me." Organa's voice cracked a few times as she cried and got his attention. Her hands trembled as she reached and lightly touched his shoulder. Brok winced and recoiled from her. "Brok, I'm so sorry. I didn't mean to. Please don't go. I'm sorry. I didn't mean to. I'll fix you. Just hold on for me, eh?"

Organa tried to smile but found her lips quivering as she looked into his vacant eyes and burned face. The smell hit her again as she beheld the cost of her ruin. Her heart skipped a beat or two, and she reached out, touching the brightest schisms of the Flux and pulling the holy energies of eons past and the last few years to come through her fingertips. "I'm going to heal you. You're going to be okay." She placed her hands over his wounds and filled his body with life magic. Golden rays of light fell from her hands and thrust themselves through his body. However, his wounds did not heal, his eyes did not regain their gleam, and his breaths were precious seconds. "Myrcle," Organa said worriedly, "Myrcle, why is this not working?"

"When Darkness consumes a Magiqas, their power comes from the Void, and now so do they. Every burst of energy is filled with the darkest power and evil in creation. When a being is damaged by this—"

Organa cut him off. "Spare me the details, Myrcle!"

Myrcle's voice was calm and understanding. "Darkness damages the soul. With enough dark magic, the soul is beyond repair, and without the soul, there is nothing but a husk, a shell that will simply linger on. The soul is like its own being; it is its own being—"

"Myrcle!" Organa's voice boomed across the hillside.

"Unless you can heal the soul, he will be gone."

Organa stood and shouted at Myrcle with rage and hatred, "Fix him then! Save him, heal his soul. You're powerful; you know more magic than me!"

"He can't, Organa," Velkin said, grabbing her arm as the crying girl turned to face her. "No one knows how to heal the soul—only the gods, and the gods are gone."

Brok's left hand raised and cupped her cheek. "Hey, I'll be fine." His voice was liquid, and blood flowed more than he spoke from his mouth. "I did my duty. I protected you as they tasked me." Brok looked at Myrcle, Esvele, and the others. "Keep her safe, 'til I see you again."

"You're not going anywhere. We're going to get you better; just hold on a little longer. I'll find a way. I'll make it right. Brok, I'm sorry. I never meant to. Please, Brok, I'm sorry." Organa fell against his burned flesh, forcing a painful groan from within him, and she jumped back from his body. All at once, she felt her face drop and her chest palpitate as she gazed into his burned but cold face. Her whole body shook as if her own winter flowed through her, and she held Brok's hand. Esvele knelt down beside him as well, along with Florie, each of them kneeling before their fallen friend. Esvele laid her head on the gray boulder near his mostly intact ear and allowed the tears to run down her face as she sang to Brok.

A few moments passed with only Esvele's song filling the silent night, and after that Brok sighed one last note and spoke lightly, "Isn't that beautiful?" Then, stepping out from his body, he looked back to his lifelong sister and his friends as he walked on into the brilliant light of the Dawn Eternal, greeted by a soft choir of warm voices entering his mind.

Welcome home, Child.

And so, Brok passed into that great, beautiful land of the wonderful and peaceful beyond.

Dawn came not long after the companions left Mount Doloroth. As the sun peeked over the edges of a great mountain, shining brilliantly upon the snow and land, it slowly crept up the hillside and lit the trees' leaves ablaze with orange, fiery radiance. The light brushed against the tops of the burned forest, turning the black and charred bark to a red glow, that of a hot ember. As the sun hit a newly grown green hill, a great oak tree towered over the decimated land, where a newly formed tablet of stone marked the passing of the warrior.

Brok the Brave.
Defender of the Starlight Dynasty.

II

The Road to Valistar

"Weep for the fallen.
Weep for the brothers.
Weep for the daughters.
Weep for the Land of Silver,
Lost so long ago."
- The Songs of Sorrow
Gavrel Ul'tar, Court Poet of Valistar
10 AC

Solemn

A s they manifested, the surrounding air smelled odd, like a roasting fire but foul, as the wind carried the death from the mountain behind them down along the land. Fractured earth burnt black and smoldered on the eastern face of the great Mount Doloroth. Organa felt a crushing weight over her heart, and she fell to the ground. The beating drum of her blood rushing through her body concussed and threatened to burst through her ears as she cradled herself. Brok was gone, and the memory of him was the only thing keeping the Dark Song at bay.

Esvele watched as the girl who was once her student wept into the earth. A firm hand grabbed Esvele's shoulder as Myrcle held her back. Wrapping his arms around his oldest friend, Myrcle held Esvele in his arms as they both felt the same hole in their hearts. Dawn broke over the trees of the Forest of Bravica. Rustling leaves blew in the wind as it passed through, pulling that awful smell closer, and allowing it to linger. They waited for a few hours until Organa fell silent, and they departed from the hillside with Florie keeping Organa on her feet.

Bright, clear blue sky gleamed overhead as the morning came. Rolling hills of the King's Isle's plains tumbled over one another toward the God's Way. The great plateau of the isle stood tall like a magnificent wall of stone, transforming into a land bridge the further north it went, connecting to the northern part of Rethial where Gavis Vel'Statis was barely discernible from the tops of the great Forest of Bravica.

On a hill far away, they rested a moment before making their trek back toward Turnmot. The sound of the chirping birds as they flew above, singing their songs of grace, pleased the ear. Esvele tried to distance herself from Organa, who simply sat on a rock, looking up toward the sky like she was waiting for a sign from the gods. Florie never left the poor girl's side either, always making sure she was in between her and the other three. After their break, they continued on until, after a few more hours, the afternoon sun had begun its descent, Myrcle had them make camp. He and Velkin set the tents while Esvele gathered some twigs and sticks that she found around the area. By the time evening rolled around and the gleaming stars began to reveal themselves, along with the crimson Fire in Heaven, Organa had found herself another rock to lean on and silently peered into the beyond above them.

Florie went and offered her a cooked plate of the rabbits that Velkin had caught for them, set it beside the silent girl, and waited a few moments before lowering her head and turning to leave. Sitting back on the ground, Florie glared at the others, "What did you do?"

"What we had to," Velkin snapped back defensively.

Myrcle raised his hand as if to calm her, "What Velkin means is that we…well, we did do what we had to. You wouldn't understand."

"Try me," Florie scoffed.

Esvele retreated back into her tent as Myrcle explained what had happened on that fateful day. The darkness that devoured everything, the hungry earth, and sea that swallowed mountains, the lightless night sky without a star to show the way, hordes of demons and tormented things that butchered everything in sight, and the fire that rained down from above as the volcanoes woke from their slumber. He recounted the Songs of Sorrow: the Fall of the Guardians of Lorial, the Visions of Ver'Keyth, and the Battles of Salvation on Verimon's Hill. Everything he could remember about those terrible days of death and destruction would have spread across all of Lorial had they not done what they did. And so, he told her of Kyriel, the brother of Organa.

"How did he get wrapped up in all that?"

"He was a student of mine at the Silver Fountain, and Organa was Esvele's. We trained them separately for the majority of the time but brought them together to spar and test their power. During his tutelage, Kyriel grew close to another instructor at the school, Vexian Brentori, who was better known as Golgorot, the Lord of Shadows. At the time he hid under the guise of the sorcerer, under our very noses, and his plan was to recruit Kyriel into the ranks of the Cult of Blighted Souls. Eventually, Kyriel requested a transfer from my guidance to Vexian's, and the Council of Masters granted it. The Lord's deception was so deep that we could not detected the slightest hint of the darkness inside his heart. Years went by and I took on more students, the Organa was Esvele's student, and the twins wished to continue to spar together. The longer Kyriel's tutelage under Vexian lasted, his power grew and grew. When *Frei'Esvera*, the day that the students graduate and their catalyst chose them, Kyriel refused one. He believed he could control his power with sheer will alone, which wasn't uncommon for the students of Vexian. Though we pleaded with him to take one, Kyriel wouldn't, and against our better judgment, we allowed him to continue on without one. The years went by, and Kyriel swore himself to the study of the Shadow. That was when Vexian made his move.

"Kyriel was taken from the scholarship and filled with delusions of the Void's ultimate goal 'Salvation' they called it. But to do so, they must swear themselves as a Forlorn to the Dark One. It granted these few limitless power and allowed the Dark Song to willingly take over Magiqas. Kyriel was raised as one of them, and all he had to do in return, was be a part of a summoning ritual to commune with the Dark One. Unbeknownst to him, their plan was to use Kyriel, not as a conduit, but as a vessel, and bring their god into this world to bring about 'Silence'. That day, the Shadow Monarch touched the mortal realm for the first time and the Cataclysm tore through Dremica, opening rifts into the Void and pouring out the forces of darkness onto creation."

"So, he is why the world is broken," Florie sighed.

"And he's her brother," Myrcle looked past the Hawkina to Organa, still silently gazing at the sky above.

"What about you, Velkin?" Florie asked. "Where were you when everything happened?"

"I was… I was there." Her voice seemed weighed down.

"So, you all are old, old—like really old," Florie giggled.

"I don't think now is the time for jokes, my dear," Myrcle shook his head.

The night went on, and the fire Esvele built died out into glowing embers surrounded by a few rocks to contain their heat. Organa could not sleep, only watch the night go by as the stars overhead gleamed in the blackness between each of them, as the Fire in Heaven threatened to burn away everything, and as the Element Moons stood guard over Lorial with their bright blue and silver glows. Yet no matter how far they moved from Mount Doloroth, no matter how much she tried not to think about what she had done, the smell of burning flesh mixed with charred wood filled her nose. The smell of Brok's dying body, the sight of his mostly burnt corpse, the smell of the blood that flowed from him like a river. Throughout the night, her eyes stayed fixed on the sky above.

Dawn crept over the trees behind the camp near Leviathan's Crossing, illuminating the plains and the scarred eastern face of Mount Doloroth. Florie came out of her tent to find Organa wide awake on the rock. Silently, she walked over to the side of the boulder and hoped that the young girl might turn her head to see her. But the young elf did not even acknowledge her presence and simply stared at the orange and blue sky.

"Would you like some breakfast?" Florie asked.

Organa gave her no answer.

"Would you like me to leave you be?"

Still, she gave no answer.

Florie left her there and went to gather some berries for herself and the others.

Myrcle and Esvele came out of their tent and restored the fire a moment before Myrcle began to wander over to the boulder until Esvele's hand gripped his shoulder. "Don't, we shouldn't."

"She needs someone."

"We aren't the ones she should be talking to right now."

"Then who will she talk to?"

"I don't know, but that will happen in time. Let's just get her back to Turnmot so we can figure out how to get to Valistar properly, like we planned to."

"Our plans are already awry. I don't expect any of them to go any better." The two of them packed up their tent and things, pulling out some rations from their bags and waiting for Florie's return.

It took some time for Velkin to come out of her tent, and to Myrcle's surprise, she was back in her full armor, clean and spotless from the events of late.

"Velkin," he called her over to them.

"How is she?" Velkin asked.

"As you'd expect," he sighed.

"Something had to happen to harden her. She must be ready for what is to come." Velkin's stone gaze never broke from Organa.

"What?" Esvele glared. "You see this as a good thing?"

"No!" Velkin turned to her. "Brok was a valiant man, but she was living a lie and she needed to be woken up. I wish it hadn't taken him to do so. You all know what's at stake—"

"She needs time to grieve, Velkin," Myrcle eyed her.

"Wallowing in grief never did anyone any good." Velkin said coldly. "We need to get to Valistar."

"Velkin," Myrcle scowled, "as someone who's lost those closest to them, I am sure you understand what she's going through. So shut it." The paladin shook her head and packed up her tent as Florie arrived with a small bag of wild berries.

"I got blueberries, strawberries, blackberries, elderberries, boysenberries," her list went on and on until EV cut her off.

"Lots of berries. Got it."

"We need to get moving," Velkin shouted to them.

"What is your deal?" Esvele shot to her feet. "What are you so impatient to get done, Velkin? You act like Brok didn't matter to you!"

Myrcle felt a twinge of fear as Esvele said that name, afraid it might send Organa back into her darkness again, but it did not. Organa simply sat there staring upward silently.

"Of course, he mattered to me," Velkin dropped her sack. "I trained him in combat. I was closer to him than any of you, just shy of Organa."

"Then how can you stand there trying to push this beyond what she can handle? You lost your husband and your sons in the Cataclysm, and you didn't just get over it!"

In that single moment, Velkin seemed to move faster than light itself. Like a passing shadow, she gripped Esvele's neck and held her up high. Myrcle ran to Esvele's side and tried to push Velkin out of the way, but she wouldn't budge. "Don't you dare!" the paladin shouted at her. "Don't you ever presume to tell me what I've lost!"

"Velkin put her down." Myrcle held an orb of light in his hand, ready to send it into the champion's chest. "Now!"

And the paladin dropped her. "I'm sorry, EV," her eyes paced back and forward from the coughing woman on the ground. "I fell," she whispered to herself.

Myrcle helped Esvele to her feet and nearly watched as EV almost lost control of herself as the Dark Song called to her. "EV," he turned her to see him, and the Dark Song faded, "You have to be careful. You lost your catalyst." Esvele slowed her thoughts and stomped off from them. Waiting until she was far enough away, Myrcle hit Velkin on the back of the head. "What the fuck was that?"

"What? I didn't mean to; I just got angry."

"And so do I, but I don't just choke people out."

"Myrcle, it's no big deal. I didn't mean to."

"You're a paladin of Calikan, God of Protection; act like you retain some of that decorum please." He shook his head at her and left her there.

The morning went by, and everyone packed up to walk the rest of the way to the forest before Leviathan's Crossing, where they would rest for the night. Florie coaxed Organa from the rock with a few words but was greeted with nothing. The sky above them brought a few dark clouds, providing moments of reprieve from the warm sun. Organa traveled in the middle of the pack with Florie as Esvele and Myrcle led the way and Velkin guarded the tail end.

"Are you all right?" Myrcle asked Esvele.

"I'll be fine," she nodded. "I was out of line bringing up her boys. I think she's also sad about everyone she lost on the mountain too."

"I'm sure she is, but she should know better than to do that."

"It's fine, Myrcle, we're all just stressed."

"Oh, and you're the mind expert, are you?"

"Shut it, hairball," she giggled.

A gathering of large boulders on top of one another stood like a house between two hills. "We'll rest here for a moment and continue on toward the crossing."

"I'll go find some water," Florie said.

"Let Esvele," he nodded at Organa. "You stay with her, all right. Look after her for us." Florie nodded back and walked over to the slouching Organa.

"Would you like a snack? I've got lots of berries," Florie smiled at her. But she gave no answer and simply stared at the sky above them. "You need to eat something, Organa." Still no reply. "I'm going to go sit down over in the shade, come on," and she had to pull the young girl with her to the rocks and out of the sun.

After a few minutes, Esvele returned with few full water skins that leaked a few drops onto the grass below. An idea struck him, and Myrcle twisted his fingers, molding the earth in front of him. A Celestial Rose appeared from within the fertile soil, a beautiful white and blue flower with small specks that looked like stars. With a motion of his fingers, the stem was cut, and he lifted it into his palm.

He trudged forward, but Esvele placed a wet hand on his shoulder. "Do you really think it wise?"

"We need her to trust us if we're going to train her for what's coming." He walked on.

"You're talking like Velkin, Myrcle."

"He's trying his best, it will be the hardest change she will ever go through, not to mention her memory crisis. We need to keep her faith in us," Velkin explained.

"I do not need lectures from you of all people on sympathy and much less loyalty," Esvele kept her voice down, but her tone was stern. Myrcle began to slip away as Velkin shot back.

"I have been trying to help you all this whole time."

"You've been a manipulative bitch! Pushing her farther than she can handle—and look where it's gotten us!"

Myrcle quickly walked back to them. "If I hear another foul comment out of either of your mouths in the next few hours, you are both in for a jolly good smacked bottom." He turned in the dirt, creating a small cloud, and walked away to Organa. Kneeling down beside her on the dirt road, he slowly and cautiously placed a hand on her shoulder. Florie watched him with fear and worry about Organa's reaction. He placed his open hand upon her. The one holding the Celestial Rose moved forward slowly, and he attempted to set it down in front of her. As his hand got closer, he could feel something queer about the surrounding air. When he got within a few inches of her to place the rose on the ground for her to see, he watched it transform. The petals became clear and blue as ice, and his hand slowly succumbed to the winter as well. The hand that once held on to Florie grasped Myrcle's swiftly. Her head rose, her eyes a sky blue, and a white mist of cold air streamed from them. She bared her teeth and saw the fear in Myrcle's eyes as her grip tightened and the gray fur from his hand transformed like a rose and quickly spread. The top layer of ice now almost completely consumed his forearm, webbed and cracked. A loud grunt of pain left his mouth and was followed by a shout. Esvele and Velkin quickly ran over to Myrcle and Organa. The young Elf's grip solidified around Myrcle's arm, and he screamed in agony as the ice webbed, creating a cracking sound like glass ready to shatter.

"Organa! Let go," Esvele screamed at her. Instead, Organa flung her away with a single, effortless glance. The Kalishtani skidded across the dirt of the hill, kicking up a large cloud of dust surrounding her.

"I'm sorry," Florie winced as she unsheathed her dagger, cutting

Organa's hand deep enough for her to feel it. The cut bled, and a few drops stained the ground as Organa released her prisoner and turned to Florie. "It's just me," Florie shouted.

Organa looked at her sympathizer. Her rage subsided, and she resumed her weeping. Myrcle fell back onto the ground, screaming in pain as his hand slowly reverted back to its original form. Velkin moved to him and placed her hands above the wound, looking for the damage. The bone in his forearm had splintered. Myrcle was moving from side to side on the ground, trying to distract himself from his pain.

"Myrcle," Velkin warned, "this is really going to hurt." She pressed down with force. Myrcle jolted and let out another scream. He continued to move as Velkin's hands radiated a golden light as she spoke an incantation, burning away the ice and restoring his hand back.

Esvele got up from the dirt and ran to Myrcle. She slid across the ground and quickly pulled a tonic from her bag. A small glass vial held a maroon liquid. She quickly removed the cork from the lip and placed it in front of Myrcle. "You need to drink this." He did as he was told and took the vial from EV's hand, swallowing the tonic. In an instant, he had stopped moving and relaxed. As his breathing slowed and he recovered, Esvele placed her hands on his arm as well and assisted Velkin with Myrcle's healing.

Organa calmed down, and another one of Velkin's spells put Myrcle to sleep with help from the tonic that Esvele gave him.

Florie stayed with Organa and helped her to a tree nearby and sat her up against it. "Stay right here. I'll be back." Organa gave no verbal or physical reply. She simply stared into nothingness. Full of regret for harming Myrcle and full of sorrow for Brok.

Florie made her way to the other two. "How is he?"

"With a little rest," Velkin reassured her, "he will be all right."

"Fucking idiot," Esvele grunted. "I told him not to do that, and yet again, he did not listen to me."

"He was trying to help her," Velkin rebutted.

"I know," Esvele snapped at her. "What did he think was going to happen, though? We just turned that child's world inside out. We brought her so much pain, and she killed at least seventy of your people."

"And I should be angry, but I'm not. We've known for some time that her power would awaken. When it burst, it was always going to be devastating."

"You made it unpleasant when you continued to push us to restore her memory before she was ready."

"I recall that you agreed with me, Esvele. She was already remembering something before we restored the rest. Imagine if we hadn't."

Esvele bit her tongue to keep from saying something she knew she should not have. "Let's just get the fucking camp set up. We all need a long rest after last night," Esvele suggested. She raised her right hand as Myrcle's limp body floated in the air as Florie, Velkin, and Esvele pitched tents and gathered wood for a fire.

Night came slowly, and until the Element Moons appeared and the red Fire in Heaven was shining in the sky, Organa had sat against that tree without saying a word. Velkin sent Florie to her to get her to eat with them by the fire, but as she placed her feathered hand on her shoulder, Organa gave no response, simply staring into the night, drowning in her own thoughts. Florie thought about trying to speak to her, but decided against it and returned to the camp. Esvele had placed Myrcle in their tent and let him rest for the evening, giving him a Night Pearl to help him sleep.

Velkin looked at Florie as she got closer to the fire where she and Esvele sat. "What are you going to do now?" Esvele asked the

Hawkina.

"I might go and find my way back to Menagerie to find my old tribe. We were once the strongest, but the elders say that during the Cataclysm our tribe was closest to the Silver Kingdom's borders and sailed across to aid them in their escape. Thousands were sent on at least a hundred ships, but only fifteen of them returned. Now, we are scattered and divided."

"Weren't you supposed to be stealing from me in the last few years?" Florie hesitated and gave an awkward smile. Velkin raised her eyebrow. "Oh, and what were you after?"

"That little amulet you carry, someone wanted it."

Velkin laughed. "Well, you failed."

"I didn't notice." Florie darted back but then gave way to laughter as well. Esvele smiled but did not laugh along with the others. Her mind was too focused on her best friend, still asleep in the tent. After they calmed themselves after a few seconds, Florie asked a tough question: "What exactly did you do to that girl?"

Velkin looked to Esvele for the answer, but she nodded and gave her permission for Velkin to explain it herself. "When the Cataclysm swallowed the east, and I watched many whom I loved die, it broke me. I had sunk into my own self-loathing, thinking I was a failure. But I saved—" Velkin looked to Esvele, "*we* saved millions of people escaping Dremica, and billions around the world when we tried to take back the capital. It gave the ships full of Dremicans time to escape."

"But why did you have to hide her memories?"

"Because of her brother, Kyriel," Esvele interrupted and continued the story, "he was used in an attempted ritual to create a vessel and fulfill the Vow of Murtin, the first Lord of Shadows. *Starlight shall birth to us our Savior; the Shadowlight cometh.* They were to use the boy as the vessel, as Myrcle said. Instead, only a fragment of the

Shadow Monarch had time to take hold of him and tear open the boundaries of the realms."

"What was it like?" Florie asked.

Velkin lifted her head, offended by her words. "You wouldn't understand. The hordes of demons, undead, and monstrosities of death and decay burst forth from the broken, bridged schisms of reality, setting cities ablaze, crumbling the old temples, and slaughtering all in their path. The tearing of reality strained Lorial so much that it cracked and fractured. Consumed everything it could. It was a bloodbath. It only stopped after the Fire in Heaven tore across the sky on the third night, at the fall of Husieàkritae. The demons were instantly banished, dissolving like sand in water, and cast from the mortal realm back into the Void. But the damage had already been done. Dremica was lost."

"So, will the Silver Kingdom rise again?"

"Ver'Kyth the Oracle, the most gifted Far Seer to ever have been born and one of the strongest Magiqas, saw the Cataclysm six hundred years before it happened, and I saw him die during the Battle of Utisi, fallen to the blade of a Shadow Priest."

"How is it you've stayed alive this long? You're all over four hundred years old!"

"It was only after the Cataclysm that the Light of the Dawn, the *Vitu'Lux*, left most of the Dremicans But our light still shines within us with the blessing of Lukitas, the Last Guardian. I miss her," Esvele sighed.

Velkin remembered her sons. Their beautiful black hair and hazel eyes, their smiles, the memory flowed through her. She would sing to them every night before her watch with the Luna Guard in Husieàkritae began. She had often hoped that they would grow up to be Magiqas. That one day she would come home to find that Melik had cast a spell on Ilinta, or the other way around, and neither of them knew what was going on. Velkin wanted them to be like her so badly, but they were much more like their father. Absolute, kind, and gentle.

The closest they got to magic was when the Fire in Heaven lit up the night sky and she and her other Luna Guard failed to safeguard the city. She lost her child. She never saw them board the ship from Menagerie at Nevis. She looked for her twins, but never found them. During the second night after the Silver Kingdom's fall began, she watched as the Shadows of the North lay siege to the Spire and crumbled it from the white and golden tower into a pile of rubble and a gaping crater as the flying and necrotic beasts burned the land to the ground.

When the Guardians of Lorial rallied the people on the third day, built an army of fifteen thousand Dreminise, and rode to the capital with what little weapons they could muster. The road they could not recognize the road. Strange vegetation and living nightmares roamed the walls, mutating the animals that used to graze and hunt across the plains and in the forests beyond recognition. The buildings were displaced within one another, and large catlike creatures with long tendrils on their backs that moved independently from one another roamed like watchdogs. Their flesh clung to their bones so tightly that it would tear and sometimes drop from their bodies to reveal decomposed bones and rot wyrms moving through them like snakes.

Two pairs of glowing yellow eyes moved separately from one another and inspected their prey. She remembered her husband's shout of pain during the siege of the north gate when the Lady of Bones sent forth her legions of demons and Unvardin, the Soulless, husks of flesh and bone that devour and kill all in sight of their burning green eyes. She saw one of them rip out his neck, and she saw the river of blood that rushed from within him and flooded the ground around his corpse.

"What was it like—to be in Husieàkritae when it fell?" Florie asked Esvele.

"Hell…" Myrcle answered as he exited the tent. A black cloth had been fashioned into a sling to help hold his arm, which could not be fully healed by magic alone. Time would need to pass for his magical blood to repair him. "We both entered the city through a secret passage connected to the palace, alongside Velkin and Brok." Myrcle tried to whisper so she could not hear, but Organa's keen ears heard him and she rose from her seat against the boulder and walked further away to escape her late friend's name. "The Shadows of the North and the Lady of Bones had already desolated the city. The Lord of Shadows, Golgorot, had retreated deep within the Xurinal of Husieàkritae and prepared a ritual. Some dark spell that would summon forth the Shadow Monarch from the Void into the material world via a vessel. But such a being would need a powerful vessel to inhabit. The spell has only been performed this once, and it almost succeeded, if we hadn't been there to stop it." Myrcle explained what had happened. He spoke of their assault on the ritual and the Shadowlight they subdued. With much regret, he told Florie about the walls he had to build inside Organa's mind.

"Well, at least you all defeated the 'Dark One,'" Florie smiled.

"Defeated?" Myrcle raised an eyebrow. "No, my dear—only subdued and imprisoned… It is more dangerous than anything we could imagine as one mind alone. Something that has only been defeated once in all of time's significant history. When the goddess Havithreal, Lady of Creation, threw the fiend down from the Great Beacon and sent him spiraling into the Eternal Abyss."

"The gods are gone," Florie rolled her eyes.

"Many people believe that nowadays, but they are wrong. Velkin's power alone is proof, a paladin is nothing without the might of the gods behind them."

"In the darkness, we are made stronger and may shine our light the brightest," Velkin's eyes fixated on the fire as she recited the ancient adage of the ancient texts.

"It is said that the Fallen One, *the* Dark One, was her twin brother. Together, they formed our universe and breathed life into our lungs. But Maltheil believed that the chaos of evolution and chance was too much and desired a true and final form of creation. Bound to one fate and one mind to keep peace and order and tranquility. However, Havithreal did not agree and saw the Balance of Chaos as a wonderful creation of choice, of free will. Maltheil, determined to create its Final Form, tried to overthrow his sister and Arratir themselves, but inevitably failed. For his sins, he was cast into the Void as a beast of shadow and death, and thus the Shadow Monarch was born."

"How can something so evil exist?"

"It was not by the will of the gods that such darkness was allowed to creep into our universe. Maltheil chose of his own accord and fell."

"All right, I think that's enough depressing topics for the night. We all need to get some rest and be ready for the journey to Turnmot tomorrow." Esvele looked around for a moment, and her eyes went wide. "Where's Organa?"

Organa had wandered far from their camp under the trees and felt the cool night breeze against her cheek and her hands. When she held them up, small, black and burnt areas on her palms, slowly scarring, would stay with her until she died. It instantly reminded her of Brok's burnt flesh and his dying body. Her eyes flowed with a river of tears, and she fell to the ground, attempting to remove the spots on her hands to no avail. She sprung up, ran in many directions, and came upon a small stream. Dipping her hands into the water and violently rubbing them, she attempted to wash the death from her hands. Yet, it would not leave. Death stained her hands and would follow her until the end of her days until her body returned to the universe and she passed into the Dawn Eternal. When she pulled her hands from the chilly waters of the stream, she gazed at her sin and wept more, screaming into the night. She could feel and see the fire in her veins stir as her rage swelled. The surrounding ground rumbled, and the trees shook violently, but within a split second of realizing she was using magic, it all ceased. *I will never use magic again*, she thought to herself. *I will never use magic again.* The words echoed over and over in her head like a never-ending whirlpool that would eventually consume her. Dragging her into the deepest depths of the ocean of her mind. Swimming in pain and misery of memories stolen and death. She could see the faces of those men and women who tried to defend their Golden Queen from her and how she turned them into ashes, tossing them into the wind without care. She could see the flames gorging over the camp like wolves among sheep. Into their gaping mouths fell people and animals alike, her rage consuming it all. She could hear coughing from around her, the sound of someone choking on blood. She saw Brok against the boulder again. His body burned almost unrecognizable and that waterfall of blood was in the corner of his mouth. Organa tried to run from this and attempted to shut down her mind, to let go and be free, but a hand pulled her from the stream and up onto the grass.

"What the fuck are you doing, Organa?" Esvele shouted at her.

"Why did you save me?" she coughed through the water.

"Why did you try to drown yourself?"

Organa moved to a large rock against the bank of the stream. "You had no right!"

"To save your life?"

"Yes," Organa's answer was immediate, and then she took a pause and began again, "If you knew what I felt right now, you'd understand."

"If I knew?" Esvele furiously shouted back as a few tears dropped from her face. Organa looked at her, and a confused expression passed over her face as she stood from her seat against the rock. She had seen her cry before when she talked about the Cataclysm before, but not like this. Esvele glared at Organa through her tears..

"I lost my entire family. I watched as my father was killed, my sister was ripped into pieces before my eyes by the Soulless, and my mother had her throat cut and her head mounted on a spike near the gates of the capital. I saw it there when we went to save your brother, and I saw my brother get drowned by a Death Knight in a pool of blood. You think you have seen horrors and you have not."

Esvele's voice had become deep and hoarse as she went on, and she cried.

"What we stole from you, your memories was to save you! From pain, and suffering, and to save your life. If you had had your memories while you were with the Order, you would have been on constant guard for yourself and Brok. The Elders would have become suspicious and looked into your mind to find the source. And once they figured out who you two were, they would have killed you both or given you over to the Cult to save their people. Your past is dangerous for everyone involved, and we needed to give it to you when you were ready, but Velkin pushed too far, too early, and as a result, Brok died. But that is what it is. He's dead, Organa. Make sure he does not die in vain. You were not the only one who lost a friend."

Both of them stood there for a few moments, and silence draped over them like a great cloak. Organa spent her time thinking of the many ways to apologize but was too afraid to speak. Esvele had turned around now, facing away from her old friend. Regardless of what Organa thought of her, she believed Organa was still her old friend and student. So, she expanded the truth to Organa and turned to speak to her. "Once, I had a student. Well, he wasn't mine, but I did teach him a few things. He was really Myrcle's prodigy. Such power was grand and beautiful, and your brother was the first one since the earliest days of the Silver Kingdom."

"You taught him?"

"The students I 'taught' at the Silver Fountain were brother and sister, twins."

"You taught us," she understood.

"I did what I could. I mainly taught you, which wasn't much, I am sorry to say, but I taught you both well, I guess. I watched as his flames grew higher and bolder and saw your winter storms blow stronger and more swiftly. It wasn't till your first sparring lessons with your brother that the strength revealed itself. You were both using every bit of power you had. Eventually, you won as I knew you would, but both of you were highly competitive, and thus he used everything he had. Then, I felt the ground rumble, and slowly the marble and stone dissolved like ash. He pulled it toward him and formed a long blade. I don't know if he intended to strike you, but I didn't allow it and took the vines of ivy growing over the canopies of the courtyard and bound him within, and your duel was finished."

"Why did you protect me? I thought you hated me."

"We used to be close once. I loved you more than anything, like my own daughter."

* * *

Organa looked at her with great confusion and then she remembered. In her mind, she saw radiant fragments of her days in Dremica, her and Kyriel arriving at the Silver Fountain.

A massive fortress with great towers made of white and gray marble, gold, and silver—the traditional foundations of its structures. A large archway with two huge silver doors opened as their mother and father, who smiled down at them with much pride and joy, guided her and her brother. Her memory jumped to another moment when she spoke with other students there at the temple and she saw Brok, a young, strapping, and much less muscular version of himself. Speaking with all his wits about him and she remembered them doing tricks with each-others magic and playing pranks on other students and her brother.

Her vision shifted again.

She was speaking with other students at the temple, and then she saw Brok—a young, strapping, and much less muscular version of himself.

"Begin your spar, Organa and Brok." Master Esvele commanded.

Organa gathered her frozen threads of air and water but the Dark Song was already taking control.

"You have to be wary, Organa. If you use too much of your magic, it will consume you. The Dark Song calls to all of us Magiqas. We must know our limits."

Her memory moved forward again, and she saw herself and Brok—much more like she knew him now—sitting outside the Silver Fountain upon the edge of the nearby cliff.

A golden sunset glowed in the sky, and red, orange, and purple clouds reflected the wondrous colors of creation. Their feet dangled over the steep cliff. Above the forest below, and in the distance, they could just barely see Husieàkritae. Organa was going to travel one day.

"Far off to the cold and wild north, and the rolling plains of the south, and the grand forests of the west. Maybe one day, we'll sail into the Far Lands beyond Rethial." She heard her own voice speak now. "Maybe one day, Brok, but we've much work to do here first".

She jumped up and held out her hand to help pull him up. He obliged her, and they stood. Her own voice echoed in her head.

"Come on, if we want to travel the world, we best get to our duties before Master Escele has our hides."

They both walked back into the temple, and the memories shifted again.

Esvele's voice shot through her mind as the images came into focus. "Tomorrow is your trial. Are you ready?"

Organa was in her room pacing back and forth in white and gold combat robes while Esvele stood near the door wearing red and green robes that had an upward collar and long sleeves with a bottom that touched the ground lightly. It was the most formal she had ever seen her mentor, and she was beautiful.

"I don't know Master Esvele. What if I go too far?" Organa asked.

Esvele walked forward and stopped her student in her pacing.

"The Dark Song will always be there, and we will always be tempted by the wonderful melody it promises. But we know that we can't give in. You are strong and powerful. You will know when it is time to stop yourself. Don't let yourself get too emotional, remove all thoughts of fear, and kick your brother's ass tomorrow."

Esvele laughed and hugged Organa. As they embraced one another, the memories faded, and Organa returned to reality.

* * *

Her eyes opened, and she saw EV looking down at her. She could feel the grass's dew soaking into her hands.

"Organa," EV kept repeating as Organa's eyes came into focus. The bright and twinkling stars of the night shone cold and seemed so far from her.

Organa felt her sadness return to her as she came back to reality. She was seeing her old days with Brok, and now, he was not there.

Organa sat up from the wet ground. She placed her hands on her face and felt the tears that had dripped down from her eyes. A cold draft swept in, chilling her tears and inflicting a slight, yet sharp pain on her cheeks. Esvele sat on her knees watching Organa, patiently waiting for a few words from her old friend, but she could not utter any more wisdom to her student that she didn't already know herself.

Organa's hopeful spark in her eyes, waiting for those absolving words, diminished, and she stood, dusted the morsels of grass off her, and walked back toward the camp, retreating once more into her solitude.

Shadows of Turnmot

A part of Organa simply wished to scream within those trees and bring another Ghast upon them—to punish herself for Brok's death and to punish those who had stolen her family from her mind and caused his death. Yet, within the deepest recesses of her mind, she could not help but want her old mentors and friends safe. Something was there, thanking them for her life being returned to her. *They killed him;* that's what she tried to tell herself. But she knew the truth. It was her flames that singed his skin. Her rage burnt him nearly to ashes. Her hatred buried him.

She could still hear the sound of him choking on his blood when she tried to sleep. Every time she closed her eyes, his charred body and mangled flesh appeared before her. The smell of burnt skin and death filled her nose when she sat around their campfires. His death plagued every waking moment. The only solace she was granted was when the wind blew so loudly in the trees that the sound of the leaves drowned out the gargling of blood; when the smell of great oak and pine overtook the scent of death and decay; and when the sight of light falling through the canopy made it all bearable.

It was in moments like these that she missed the Living City. Tall towers of oak and pine inside the trees themselves manned by the Forest Guard. The Sanctuary where she was trained to master the snow and ice. The markets of the commonwealth in the lower hallows of its domain. The beating Heart of the City, a font of magic so pure that it manifested into a singularity, pulsing and sending radiant splendors upon all those who beheld its majesty and throughout the Living City itself. All of this was broken from her concentration when a few giggles drifted from the campfire the others had set.

The group had set up camp later in the evening on the other side of the forest. That night, they sat by the fire, now another common, quiet night of silence. No one spoke to Organa as she stared away from the flames as if the light of them offended her or somehow harmed her. Yet, to her it did. Every *pop* and *crack* that the fire made reminded her of the sounds of that night. That night when her Brok died. The heat from the flames was almost enticing, though, as a punishment, a way to relieve herself of guilt, shame, and pain.

Florie made her way over to her friend and sat down beside her as she stared into the night. Organa did not look at Florie. Something fixed her eyes upon the darkness between the shadows of the trees from the Element Moons. The blue and silver moons filled the sky and peeked over the mountains. The Tears of the Sun echoed its crescent light down upon the Serpent's River and the glistening water reflected that light upon the banks of its shores. The Snow Moon looked exactly as its name described, a pristine silvery white with small black and gray spots upon its surface. Florie's silver crown of feathers gleamed from their light.

She spoke and at that moment, Organa glared at her. Without a single word, Florie could hear the young girl scolding her, but she spoke anyway.

"Organa," she whispered. But the girl gave no answer, her emerald eyes staring into Florie's soul. She had tried this many times over the last few weeks and each time she got no answer from Organa.

Florie continued, "You know, considering what has happened," she paused and thought carefully about what she was about to say, afraid it might send her into another raging inferno, "At least you now remember him as he was. The friend you've always known."

Organa did not respond. She sat there in silence as Florie stood to her feet and placed a feathered hand on her shoulder briefly before walking back to the center of the camp.

Organa only slept every few days, spending most of her nights staring into nothingness. Esvele kept a watchful eye on her old student in fear of what had happened a few weeks ago. She and Florie had agreed to take shifts watching over her.

Myrcle woke from his sleep the next morning with a sharp pain in his wrapped arm, to the sound of crying nearby. He tiptoed to the entrance of the tent, trying not to wake EV. The morning sun hit his eyes and blinded him for a moment. Myrcle held up the hide flap to block it. Tall trees nearby framed a beautiful scene as he looked upon the rolling hills and the sun rising over the Southern Shields. From there, he could see the God's Way, the great plateau that led to Valistar. Myrcle thought to himself about the future task, the journey back to Turnmot, and going to the capital to uncover the mystery of the Sepulcher. He heard the crying again from within Organa's tent. Walking by the burnt-out fire, Myrcle moved to the young girl's tent. He extended his good arm toward the tent and recoiled. Questioning himself for a moment, he pulled back the flap.

"Organa," he lightly called.

She gave no answer and continued crying.

He walked forward across the way, passing by Florie, who sat up in a tree, watching her friend. "Organa, you need to talk to us."

She gave no answer and continued crying.

He reached out again as he had done before with no regard, but Florie's black wings unfurled from behind her and she shot down to him, swiftly pulling him back.

"Don't Myrcle," she glared at him, and the bubbliness of her voice disappeared.

He whispered back, "She needs our help Florie."

"Not yours. She almost killed you the last time you tried. What makes you think she won't do it again, hm?"

"She'll learn to control it in time."

"And that time to push her to do so is not now." Florie glared.

Myrcle reluctantly agreed with a nod and walked back to the camp.

Florie followed him and left Organa to herself, her bubbliness returning. "Why don't we just Flash back to Turnmot? It's much faster than traveling this way."

"I fear using more magic around her is not wise, plus my arm is not fully healed yet. It shouldn't be long, though. We're only a day away."

"You think magic will hurt her? We flashed just after the hilltop." Florie blinked.

"And I regret that. We forced her to leave that place, which would have helped, but also removed time in her grieving process. The long road gives her time back, to some extent."

"EV hasn't told you what she did, has she?" Florie's tone fell away once more.

"What do you mean?" Myrcle eyed her.

"Myrcle…Organa tried to kill herself. She tried to drown herself in a creek three weeks ago. That's why EV and I have been doing watches on her at night."

Myrcle's fury boiled in his blood, outraged at the thought that Organa would dare do something so reckless. He turned to where she was sitting and began to hastily walk over to her. Florie tried to pull him back, but with a simple motion of his hand, he sent her flying away. Florie landed with a crash into Velkin's tent and woke her with fear. Esvele bolted through the curtain of her and Myrcle's tent and saw him walking toward Organa. She ran toward him to try to stop him, but he pulled Organa up from the ground enraged.

"Why in the world would you try to do that, Organa?" he yelled at her, tears in his eyes. "Do you regard your memory with so little care?"

"Myrcle stop!" Esvele shouted at him, but he did not.

"You are worth more than you can imagine! You have such a life ahead of you! Why—by the Dawn—why would you do such a reckless thing?" He finally placed her back on the ground. Fear gleamed in her eyes as he walked away from her and paced back and forth. Esvele rushed past him and wrapped her arms around Organa. The poor girl cried again and allowed Esvele to comfort her.

Organa hid her face in her hands, and for the first time in weeks, she spoke. "Look, I know it was stupid, okay? But can you blame me?"

"Organa," Myrcle stopped in his tracks and looked at her. "When I watched our land burn in those few days, I failed. Esvele failed. Velkin failed. We all failed! By the gods, the Guardians were even slain! I followed the Guardians into the Void itself when we tried to take back the capital. I watched as the Citadel collapsed into rubble and the Xurinal imploded as we rescued your brother. We've all lost, but we have to! Else, we're all the same people throughout our entire lives. Loss empowers us as much as a victory. In time, you'll come to see it for what it is."

"And what's that?"

"A sacrifice. A sacrifice of love, as pure as the stars in the sky! Brok knew what was going to happen. He had to have, otherwise, I don't think he would have laid his life down to save you. He knew he could have died at any time when he volunteered to protect you 'til we were ready to find you, 'til the Sepulcher manifested. 'Til you were ready to be brought back into the life you had forgotten and help us end this."

"Wait." Organa's eyes narrowed. "Did you know that my brother was in Valistar?"

"No Organa. But Malorian confirmed that for me. The Sepulchers return to the plane of their host's origin to be either opened or recharged every four hundred years. Esvele and I knew the time was coming, so we began to plan out extraction. But when you fled the order, we had to track you down and get to you before the Valiant somehow found out who you were and what you were capable of."

"Murder. That's what I can do," Organa screamed at him as she winced at the melody in her mind. "I will kill everyone."

"That's not true. You can learn to harness this better and become more than they ever could have hoped to stop. You could bring a new Dawn."

"I am not some pawn for you to use in whatever hope you have of restoring the Golden Order!" Myrcle trembled with the rhythm of the ground beating through his body as she shouted.

"Forgive me, my lady," Myrcle fell to a knee. "I did not mean to anger you."

Organa then felt her heart sink. She stood in silence until she met him on the ground, holding his shoulders with her hands. "Esvele told me almost the same thing that night." She glared at him. "How 'We've all lost.'" She paused for a moment to contain herself but cried once again. Through her tears, she spoke, "That doesn't mean I don't have the right to be sorrowful. He was with me for so long, and I didn't know him as I once did. It's only after he is fucking dead that I know him truly! That night I remembered more, and at first, I thought it would help me get through this." She gasped for air and collected herself for a moment, then continued. "I thought it would help. Instead, with each hour, more of my memories return, and I see more and more of him. Training at the Silver Fountain, riding horses through the forest beneath the mountain, studying magic with Esvele, sparing one another, all of these bring more pain and suffering than what I could ever have wanted to feel in my lifetime because I know he's not here!"

"It will take time, but you have to forgive yourself."

"Forgive myself?" she shouted in rage and rose to her feet. As she did, a gust of wind moved through the camp, waking the others from their sleep. Her tent's anchors were picked up, and her tent was thrown down the hill. "You think I can forgive myself!" Esvele moved forward, and the others mirrored her. Myrcle held up his hand to stop their advance, and they did, but they stayed ready to sprint to his aid if need be. "I can't forgive myself! Brok is dead! My magic killed him, mine, and there is nothing I can do to bring him back! I was supposed to protect him as he was to protect me, and I murdered him in cold blood!"

With each sentence, the wind picked up more and more, and a blizzard howled. As she came unhinged, she saw the others circling around her and remembered the scene from the night before, waves of flames in a sea of death.

Velkin rushed forward and placed her hands on Organa's head, filling it with the memory of Brok.

Isn't that beautiful?

Organa screamed and then fell to the ground, limp, and as she did, the blizzard ceased. Velkin pulled back her hands and looked at the others. Esvele ran to Myrcle to help him up, and Florie fluttered over to Organa.

"She's fine, just asleep is all," Velkin reassured them.

"You can't just do that to avoid her power," Myrcle scoffed. "When she loses control like that, we have to help her come back. The same goes for us all."

"Well, we haven't been able to help her. You two keep antagonizing the poor child," Florie shouted at Myrcle and Esvele.

"We're trying to help her," Esvele rebutted.

"By trying to force her through the loss of her closest friend?"

"We don't have time for this," Esvele chuckled. "We need to get her under control, or we're all lost. She's the only one who can beat her brother if the Cult manages to bring him back."

"No, she's not, and we can't expect her to."

"Oh, and who else can?"

"Us," Velkin interjected.

Esvele laughed. "Us?", she looked at Velkin, raising her eyebrows in astonishment at the suggestion. "We barely contained him last time, and Lukitas did most of the work. Unless you know where she is and whether she's even still alive, which I highly doubt, Organa is our only option."

"There is always a chance. The gods will watch over us and come to our aid," Myrcle promised.

"The gods?" Esvele laughed. "They are gone," she spat out. "They died in the Fire in Heaven. When that happened, they were killed, and we lost everything. If they were alive, they'd be able to smite down the demons and the evil in Dremica and help us reclaim our home. So where are they, hmm? I refuse to believe that Havithreal, Calikan, Dunivas, and all the rest of them are alive because it's the truth. The gods have been dead for a long time now, Velkin, take the hint." Esvele stormed off into the woods.

Myrcle knew that she had believed that for a long time. "She just needs time. If any of us had lost what she did in the Cataclysm and watched as Dremica burned, we'd all be the same."

"She can't truly believe that, can she?" Florie asked.

"None of us has been the same since the Cataclysm; we're all broken. But there is a way to come back. There has to be," Myrcle said as he followed after Esvele.

Florie sat on her knees near Organa in silence while Myrcle passed by them to join EV in the forest and comfort her.

"Go get her tent back. We'll put her inside for a while and let her rest." Velkin nodded to Florie, and she went over to the hilltop to find the tent.

* * *

In the forest, Esvele marched and stomped on the ground heavily, her anger and frustration building with every step. In her ears, she could hear that melody, sweet and promising, but knew it to be deceiving and deadly. The melody grew in her mind, a crescendo louder and louder, flowing through her veins. Some of the strong brown bark gave way to the unrelenting strength of Esvele's power. It overtook her, consuming her like a wave of the Old Sea consumed the eastern shore of Dremica when they were sailing away from their burning home. Images, moments, and memories all flashed in her mind as the Dark Song sang to her, forcing her to remember, and refusing to let go of the trauma it dangled it front of her like bait. It drew her further into her own reality as if she had shifted herself from the mortal plane to another of living nightmares.

Her brother's gray body drenched in his own blood, demons slaughtering the innocents of her home like lambs, the laugh of Kethir in her false body as she engulfed her victims in black and white fire, and the burning red eyes of the young prince gazing back at her as they attempted to overpower him. With each vision of carnage, Esvele felt the weight of her guilt splitting her skull, shattering her mind into a thousand pieces. Organa's smiling face blinked by and the Dark Song quelled itself, unable to touch the purest form of all things. But a sudden explosion of fire wrapped itself around the young woman, and her brother's bright eyes burst through the peace.

Esvele's guilt swelled to its apex, beating her resolution against the magic of the Void.

Without her knowing, Esvele's hands thrust into the ground, digging her fingers deep within the earth. From within the cold ground, vines erupted—larger than the tentacles of the Krakens of the Old Sea—ripping out of the forest floor and binding the tree. They crushed it with brute force and tore it apart, sharpening themselves to a point and thrusting their edges into the tree, tearing it limb from limb. Esvele's radiant eyes burned like fire as she pressed deeper into the earth. As she did, so did the vines. They splintered apart, the roots deep beneath the tree, and pulled it down into the earth She could feel the ground giving way to her will, and the power tasted as sweet as red wine. Soon, the tree was almost completely consumed by the ground.

A sudden but quiet tremor crept through the ground beneath Myrcle's feet, bringing a warmth to the soles of his boots. He turned back to the forest and saw a light like the flame of a candle from within the treeline. Myrcle burst into the woods, running as fast as he could until he appeared at the source of the disturbance.

When he saw her, he ran to his friend and attempted to place a hand on her shoulder to get her attention. Instead, she felt his feet pounding against the forest floor far behind her, took one hand from within the earth, guided more vines from within the ground to him, bound him as the tree was, and they slowly prepared to impale him and bring him into the dark and cold ground of Rethial. Myrcle shouted in pain as the tendrils wrapped around him with great might that threatened to crush his bones. Myrcle felt like his body was nearly broken in two. As he was about to release a scream, the Dark Song was cast away for another moment, but it forced itself back into Esvele's mind, enjoying the rage within that would bring about destruction.

From within the forest came a great orb of fire that struck the tree and flung Esvele against another nearby. The vines she summoned instantly fell limp, releasing Myrcle. The flames that devoured the tree were recalled to their master and returned to his hand swiftly. The summoner walked to Esvele and placed his hand upon her head, sensing for life. "She'll be all right, just hit her head real good." His voice had a northern accent, that of the Menagrians.

Myrcle thought the man sounded familiar and listened intently to place the face, but could not. He slowly rose to his feet from Esvele's small crater, bringing the man into view. An older gentleman in green and white robes hunched over Esvele, whispering an incantation of healing.

A black hood covered his head as he rose from there to see Myrcle. "Hello," he nodded kindly.

His face was wrinkled lightly, and he had shining gold eyes that looked like the sun. His hair that fell in front of his face was white as snow from old age, and his groomed facial hair was the same. A kind smile moved across his face.

"We'd better get her to your camp nearby for some rest," the man said.

"Yeah," Myrcle agreed, "we'd better." Confusion filled his mind like fog on a cold and wet morning. The old man held out his hand, and Myrcle took it as the gentleman muttered another incantation. In a bright flash of light, they were gone.

The midday sun shone brightly overhead, and the warm summer blew with a gentle breeze. Florie and Velkin re-established camp and built another fire, ready to be lit once the sun had faded. They waited around the edge of the waiting pyre, silent and waiting. The bushes *cracked* and *snapped* behind them as three figures emerged. Organa jerked back the hide of her tent opening to see Myrcle, an unconscious Esvele, and a robed figure. Velkin ran to Esvele with

Florie behind her and helped put her in her tent. The robed man pulled down his hood, revealing his face completely.

The old man from the tavern in Turnmot stood before her. "Hello, Organa."

"Randy?"

"Well, not exactly," he chuckled.

"What do you mean?"

"I lied. My name is Bendrit of Dremica, Guardian of Lorial."

Myrcle shot up to his feet and turned to the old man. "Bendrit," he said with astonishment. "The Flame of the East?"

"Aye," the Guardian responded with shame.

"You were all said to have died in the retaking of Husieàkritae."

"Some days, I wish I were—" he fell solemn.

Organa felt a twinge of pain in her mind as she recalled him saving her from the crumbling castle of the City of Light. "Where's my mother?"

"The Lady Magis," Myrcle's eyes lit up. "She's alive?"

"No," Bendrit lowered his head. "She died before I could get her out of the Starlight Citadel. I'm sorry." The memory came back to Organa; watching that creature ripping her mother apart through some sort of rift opened by her robbed savior. She stood there, powerless, helpless to stop it. Organa's tears ran down her face and brought her back to reality. She wished she could change it, turn back time for so much, and the Dark Song offered it to her through its melody, singing in her mind as she relived the death of her mother. But Bendrit's next words nearly brought it through her fully. "Where's Brok?"

Myrcle's eyes went wide with fear as the ground beneath them trembled in the presence of such power flowing through Organa. Winter itself came to her side, and the hill became as cold as a tundra. The very ground froze into solid, clear blue ice. Tall trees turned to glass, ready to shatter at a forceful exertion of wind. The clouds above rumbled with her anger and swirled, threatening to descend upon them all and wipe them from existence.

For the first time in forever, Organa felt nothing. No pain, sorrow, or revenge. She felt nothing at all. She stood there, motionless and speechless. Staring into Bendrit's eyes. Florie stood, moved in front of Organa, and tried to get her attention, but the Elf never responded. She felt nothing as Florie shouted at her, nor heard anything. The world around her shrunk, the surrounding sky lost its blue glow, and the sun seemed to die. Cold air blew through the camp, and Esvele now stood with fear alight in her eyes. She ran to Organa and pushed Florie out of the way, falling to her knees and taking Organa's hands in her own. Organa could see Esvele shouting something at her but could not hear it. The icy wind blew harder, and the trees moved with it. Bendrit looked at her with curiosity and caution. He held up his hand and slowly created a small flame. Its flicker caught Organa's eye, and she turned sharply to him. Small patches of ice grew over her skin as her eyes turned from emerald green to a cold, deep blue.

Esvele blocked Organa's view of the messenger of her mother's death. She tried to shake Organa, but found her to be as still as a statue. Her eyes shifted to Esvele's with a sign of question in them. Esvele had seen that look before. The question lingered in her mind as well almost every time she looked at her own reflection on a reflective surface. "Why?" The answer was always the same: "I do not know." Except in this instance, Esvele knew the answer. After many centuries, she had walked on Lorial, seeing the Cataclysm, the death of her family, and other horrible things, the answer would change.

Gazing into Organa's cold eyes, Esvele said, "I don't know why things like this happen, but you are here, breathing, living, and powerful." Organa heard again, slowly as Esvele continued, "Death has taken so many that we love. My sister and brother, your mother, father, and best friend. It has robbed us of the joy and love we deserve. But we're here, and we have lived in our lungs and power flowing through our veins. If we could find a way to beat death and bring back all the ones we lost, we would in a heartbeat. But that is not for us to decide. We must live now and cherish the moments we are given. Please, Organa, you've lost yourself to the Dark Song before; don't let it consume you again. The Void will entice you. It promises power over everything in creation, but it is only a deceptive fallacy that causes more death and destruction. Real power is not allowing your emotions about the past to control your future. We can only protect only those who are still living."

Organa's voice echoed across the space. "But why should I? I have no love. I've been the reason for the death of my family, the imprisonment of my brother, and the death of my closest friend. I deserve no love, and you should fear me as much as you hate me."

"I never hated you!" Esvele shouted back. "I missed you so much. I remembered all the days we had spent together. Every day I traveled with you, I remembered the person you used to be, the one I would never see again." Esvele was now crying, and Myrcle watched the scene and felt himself fill with joy for his old friends.

Tears leaked from Organa's eyes, and she felt again. "I can see everything when I am like this. When the Dark Song enters my head, I can feel the beating heart of Lorial, the rush of the oceans on the coasts, and the wind against the tallest mountains in Menagerie. I can see and feel it all. Endless power and endless peace in the darkness with Final Form. I can feel all of time and the foundations of creation within my hands, able to create and destroy." The surrounding ground froze as it did before, and then it burst into flames, slowly spreading around the area. Esvele backed up from Organa's immolation, and Organa began again, "Seeing the spread of the flames and the melting of ice, creation, and destruction in my hands and the power of life and death. I am a goddess among mortals in this form."

Esvele removed her cloak and laid her staff on the ground. Myrcle grasped her shoulder. "What are you doing?"

"I am going to save my old student and friend. Fire doesn't hurt me much—'People of the Flame,' after all," she said with a nervous laugh.

"I can't let you!"

"You can't stop me," she said as she closed her eyes and jumped over the spreading flames, running toward Organa. Myrcle reached for her but could not restrain her, so he prepared to join her in the flames, but Velkin and Florie pulled him back. Bendrit stepped in front of them, placed his hands against the firestorm, and held back Organa's destruction by giving into his own darkness.

Esvele could feel the flames against her clothes and the singeing against her skin, but she pushed through the slight pain to get to Organa. The temperature rose as she got to the source, and she held out her hands in front of her arms to block as much heat as she could. Esvele smiled at Organa, and tears of joy flowed down her face like a river as she hugged her student. Organa slowly raised her hands as they thawed, and she embraced Esvele for the first time in centuries, the Dark Song fading in her mind. Organa could feel her grief, anger, and sorrow swelling, but it did not affect her. She could no longer hear the dark and promising melody enticing her with vengeance. The warmth of her old mentor's arms enveloping her forced the Dark Song to recede from her mind.

The two separated, and Esvele wiped Organa's tears from her face while smiling at her friend. The flames died out and diminished as the ice melted and restored life to the surrounding land.

In the darkness that Organa was creating, she saw Brok again at her side as he had always been. In a clear and gentle voice, he spoke into her mind, *You can't let go now,* he said softly, *They will need your help, and you will need theirs to get through this. Stop!* and the storm faded. Time was turned back, but not through the power of darkness, only through Organa's will to honor Brok's memory. "I'm sorry," she said to them, "I didn't mean to frighten you. I just need to be alone for a bit." And she retreated into her tent.

Esvele woke and put a hand on the back of her head, where a sharp and throbbing pain echoed. Myrcle heard her groan and knelt back down to her and recited an incantation to heal her. Her eyes focused, and she saw the robed man speaking to Velkin behind Myrcle.

The paladin knelt before the Guardian. "My Lord."

"No," he shook his head. "I'm not that man any longer."

"You were the leader of the Guardians of Lorial."

"Exactly, I was. Now the Guardians are gone. Dead, reduced to ash and returned to the earth. And yet, I live."

"Why?" Organa asked as she walked forward. Florie turned to the young child and grasped her hand to keep her from getting too close, afraid of what Organa might do. "Why are you alive?"

"The *Vitu'Lux* is with me still, just like you."

"But that should have faded by now; even Myrcle and I are feeling the effects of its waning," Esvele squinted.

"I have no idea," Bendrit shook his head. "You're right—it should have left me long ago. But here it is, moving through me."

Velkin looked at the child with horror, turned to Myrcle, and, with a whisper, said, "We should have never awakened her mind."

Myrcle shot her a disapproving glance. "That pertains to nothing we were just speaking about. Why would you say that?"

She took Myrcle by the shoulder and drew him into the woods behind the others. Bendrit caught wind though and intently listened. "That girl is not ready for the power she has. She will kill us all. The grief she harbors…" Velkin's voice broke. "None of you can imagine what it is like to lose the ones you love the way she lost her brother. The way my sons were taken from me."

"Esvele would." His eyes narrowed, but he set his suspicion aside. "Velkin, you have to understand. If we had not given her back her life, she would have never known who she was, and eventually, there would have been no way to calm the storm inside her. Look at what Esvele just did," he pointed to the two talking and Esvele smiling down at her old student, "She was able to bring her back because Organa remembered. If she had not had those memories, we could have all died."

"Myrcle," Velkin shouted through her whisper, "I have seen the power of Magiqas. We have seen the power. Her brother nearly killed everyone in Lorial with a single spell."

"That was not him. That was the Shadow Monarch. He was possessed, unable to control his power."

"Nevertheless, what if that happens to her? You told me a few days ago about the danger of Valistar, that you think the Cult of Blighted Souls is involved. What if they know that she's traveling with us? What if this is all a trap? They could use us all to get control of her and use her as a devastating weapon. They could tear Lorial apart piece by piece and create a portal directly to the Void. AH," Velkin fell to the forest floor as a flash of purple light shot through her blue eyes.

Myrcle raised her to her feet. "Velkin, are you all right?"

"I'm fine," she said, pushing him away, leaning on a tree. "I just get these headaches, you know," she laughed it off.

"I could heal them with some mag-"

"No," she snapped back. "No Myrcle. There's no point." She left him there at the tree and walked back toward the camp.

"Velkin," he called after her.

"What, Myrcle?" she rolled her eyes, turning to face him.

Myrcle shook his head and placed his hands on her armored shoulders and uncurled his fingers, revealing the Dawn Ward of Calikan that fell from her pouch on her belt. "Velkin, you are worrying too much. If the Cult of Blighted Souls is involved, they wouldn't have the power to conjure such a ritual. Their leader is dead and gone. They wouldn't be able to, even if they wanted to." He walked back to the group, and Bendrit's eyes followed Velkin as she slowly made her way over as well. Florie had now run to Organa and given her a hug, with her head only reaching Organa's abdomen. Her crown of silver feathers shone like the metal itself as the sun hit her, and she embraced Organa.

"That scroll," Myrcle turned to Bendrit, "the one with the Sepulcher on it. It is in Valistar." Esvele instantly turned around and pulled Myrcle's shoulder to get him to stop speaking, but he ignored her. "We must return to Turnmot and gather more information from Malorian. Once we have that, we can decide whether to intervene. But Organa, if this is your brother's Sepulcher, we cannot free him." Esvele released him and looked solemnly at Organa.

Organa felt her heartbreak, but showed no outward expression.

Bendrit walked forward and knelt down on his knees again, not as bowing, but to look at her. "Organa, what your brother has been transformed into cannot be allowed to escape."

"He is my brother," she whispered back. "I have to get him back."

"I know, Organa, I know, but the power to do so is not within us mortals. Until the gods intervene, he is lost," Velkin assured her.

"We can't go back to Turnmot either, my friends," Bendrit's voice was heavy.

"Why not? Did those beasts of the Dynasty infiltrate and take over?" Myrcle asked, anger in his voice.

Bendrit rose to his feet and walked over to Myrcle. "Turnmot's gone."

At that moment, time seemed to slow down around them all. In fact, it did. The wind blew slowly, and the trees swayed with little movement. The blades of grass moved like snails, and the clouds above ceased their traveling across the sky; darkness gathered within. Rain descended upon them. Myrcle looked at his old friend and saw her eyes filled with gray and white fog as Esvele projected her mind through the forest before them to Turnmot.

Large columns of thick black smoke rose into the sky like dark tendrils toward the sun, hoping to block its radiant light. Familiar fumes of burnt and seared flesh and death filled her nose as she manifested between burnt homes. Singed and inflamed trees littered the land, uprooted by the magic of the tyrants. Corpses piled high as if trying to escape. Men, women, pets, livestock, and children were thrown over the top of one another like discarded rubbish. Cold air blew, and the dark clouds above wept for the great loss of life. To her, it felt like she was there.

She walked across the center of Turnmot toward the house of Malorian and his family, stepping over the charred, scarred, and mangled bodies of the dead. As she got closer to the house, she could see a figure against the wall, near a window on the left side of the home. For a moment, she hesitated to look, afraid of what she was about to see, but she could not avoid it.

Before her was the corpse of a woman who had been crucified on her doorstep. Long, thick black nails were driven into her wrists and feet, spreading her limbs apart. Unending rivers of blood trailed down her arms and chest to her feet, where a scarlet pond had formed beneath her. Her raven hair had fallen in front of her face and dripped blood into the pond below from a few gashes in her head. A once-deep blue dress was now stained a dull, bruised purple. Esvele extended her hand, moved the woman's raven hair aside, and saw a battered and bruised face. Long cuts ran like caverns on her face, and mountains of swollen yellow and purple bruises formed near her eyes. More bloody droplets dripped from her face and collected themselves in the pond below. She looked for a resemblance to who she might have been, and when she looked down at her neck, she saw the silver chain with the emerald star on it and knew it was Ynetia. Esvele turned her head in horror and disgust at the image before her and gagged. After she collected herself, she turned back to Ynetia, and when her eyes lifted to the window, she saw words written in blood.

"Hybrid Whore."

She reached out, took her necklace from her, and watched as time in the town turned backward and she could see the people of the town rising from death and their wounds being healed. Their bodies were whole once more, and she turned and Ynetia was gone. The trees that were broken and the burnt homes of the town were restored.

The sun shone brightly above with beautiful radiance. People were walking through the market from stand to stand. A group of small and young children were playing around the center fountain in the courtyard. Among them was one of Malorian's children—the youngest, Valnias—playing with some of his friends. Esvele looked around, seeing the tavern where they all met, and felt a sudden heat. From behind her came an enormous ball of fire that crashed into the tavern, exploding in a massive rage and launching shrapnel everywhere. When she turned back around, she saw a full legion of the Flame of the Sphinx, donning black and silver armor crested with a Sphinx in its center. Their arrival was like a shadow cast over the land, and darkness consumed the town. A woman with dark hair and armor like the others of her company, but for a helmet that looked like a dark crown upon her head and the skin on her face that seemed to cling to her bones, rode into the center of the town on her white horse clad in matching protective clothing. Esvele looked for Valinas and saw him still near the fountain, but he lay lifeless and cold. Most of his body was burnt black, and bloodshot eyes gazed back at her without a trace of light within them anymore.

The woman on the white horse sounded a high-pitched horn and raised her voice. "Malorian, come forth and face judgment for your sins!"

Esvele moved toward the woman on the horse and readied a spell, preparing to kill, but the ground beneath her feet did not respond to her call. The roots would not move, for one cannot change the past.

Malorian exited his home with his wife and other sons behind him. He saw the tavern burning in ruin and then gazed his eyes over the other people, watching in horror as the legion began seizing him. As they pulled him from his porch, he saw Valnias at the fountain, burnt, cold, and lifeless. Enraged, he shoved the guards off him, ripped the helmet off one, revealing his clinging skin, and struck his face with his helmet, knocking him to the ground and hitting the other the same way, denting the metal of his adversary. After his opponents fell, he ran to his son and held his limp body, screaming in agony. The woman on the horse smirked at his pain, and Esvele tried again to cast a spell at her, but to no avail. The woman dismounted her horse and walked across the courtyard to him, her boots clicking and rattling as she made her way.

Malorian was holding his son close to him, and Esvele could see Ynetia, who had fallen to her knees, holding her sons on the porch, all of them gasping for air and feeling their hearts being ripped out of their chests. The woman was now standing over the father, and reaching down, pulled him from his son, but he resisted. She tried again, and this time he went to strike her, but she held up her other hand, met his fist with her palm, and squeezed tightly. Esvele could hear the bones in Malorian's hands breaking. He screamed in pain as he dropped his son's body; the woman lifted him into the air with her free hand. Bursting past a man in red robes who Esvele now knew to be Bendrit, Ynetia kicked up a cloud of dust as she sprinted toward her husband. Bendrit started after her before raising his hands to protect her and her sons.

The woman used her other hand and held Ynetia up in the air. "These two have sinned. The bond between High Elves and other races is forbidden! The tainting of the Pure Blood is an abomination. Captain," she looked to a man in dawn-red armor and a black cloak that covered his sheathed blade, "cleanse them." The man in the red armor drew his black blade from its sheath and walked toward Bendrit and the children. The Guardian held up his hand, and a bolt of flames shot forth, throwing the captain across the courtyard. "You dare stand against the royal legions!" the woman shouted.

"Against this tyranny? Always!"

The armored man stood and went to strike Bendrit with his dark blade, but the woman commanded him to stop. She lowered her prisoners and commanded the captain to hold them where they were, then she walked toward Bendrit. "Who are you?"

For a moment he paused and then answered, "I am Bendrit, Flame of the West and Guardian of Lorial."

As he uttered his name, the soldiers of the legion backed away from him, and Esvele saw a smile creep across the woman's face. "A Guardian? Well, that can't be true. You all died in the Cataclysm."

"Forgotten, yes, *died*, no."

"Well then, let's see if the legends are true." As she finished, she launched a wave of black arrows from her hands at him, covered in dark shadows and purple flames. Bendrit made quick work of her spell and raised a ward to block them. The woman lowered her hand and smiled again before a crack of thunder and blue lightning shot from her palm at the Guardian, which he reflected up to the sky with ease. *Maybe they were true.* She looked at Bendrit and cast another spell, but there was no effect, only a small puff of smoke from her hand that lingered there for a moment before she blew it toward him. Bendrit's confused look surprised Esvele, and she watched as the smoke reached him and he instantly fell to the ground.

He tried to cast another spell, but could not. With a heavy breath, he spoke, "What have you done?"

"I see I was wrong. The power of the 'Guardians of Lorial' was just a myth," she laughed as he choked on the smoke, coughing.

Trying to speak through the thick and draining smoke, Bendrit called out to the people of Turnmot, "Will you stand for this? A tyranny that crushes all!"

The people looked at one another, waiting for someone to be the first. No one stepped forward. No one spoke. No one did anything. Until a young man, an Elven young man, no older than sixteen, stepped out, "No."

The woman raised an eyebrow. "Return to your parents, boy. Before you can't."

"No," he shouted back.

"Very well," she held out her hand and saw another person step in front of him. "Move, peasant," she commanded.

The older woman answered, "No."

"Then you will both die."

And as the woman readied a spell, another young female child stepped in front of the others. "No." Now, many had formed a line of people to shield one another. Young, old, frail, and strong, they all stood together. No weapons, no armor, but together nonetheless.

"Fine," the woman looked to her legion and smiled, "Kill them all! They're traitors to the crown!" she calmly commanded, and her soldiers carried out their order without question.

The Flame of the Sphinx slaughtered the people indiscriminately.

Some met their death by cold steel or iron blades of axes, swords, daggers, or pikes. The spells of the woman and her mages' flames, ice, and dark spells caught many who escaped their mortal death.

All the residents of the town were dead, slaughtered like animals, and the woman approached the Guardian. She squatted down beside him as he gazed in horror, powerless to stop the murder of innocents, and pulled up his head by his gray hair. "You see, Guardian, you are weak. Your kind failed long ago, and now you have failed once more." She laughed as she walked away and kicked a cloud of dust into Bendrit's face. Bendrit cleared his eyes and could see the town in ruins. The same columns of smoke Esvele saw when she projected here spiraled into the sky and the mounds of bodies piled high.

Esvele watched as the woman threw Malorian onto the ground. "Kill his whore and his bastard children. Make him watch, and then he'll die. She paused as she walked away. Make it last and hurt. Such creatures deserve no pity." The guards did as they were bid, seizing Malorian and dragging his weak and feeble body away. Other soldiers took their blades and cut down the children, and Esvele was forced to watch as they nailed Ynetia to the side of her home.

The Far Seer returned to her body and found the others almost as they were when her mind had left, though she had experienced what felt like many moments. They had barely moved. Her power subsided and diminished, and she fell to the ground, sobbing.

Bendrit walked forward and looked down at her. "You see, there is no Turnmot anymore."

The Black Riders

A few hours of silence from Esvele passed as night rose above them. The Element Moons shone brightly overhead, and the stunning stars twinkled in the blackness between each other. Velkin spent that time praying and holding close to the voice she heard in her head. Florie and Organa traded stories about the things they had done throughout their lives, and for the first time, Organa could speak of Brok without losing herself to her own rage and hatred.

The duo laughed by the fire as Organa explained, "Once, Brok and I snuck into the pompous hall where the Elders convened, and we took some of their belongings, hiding them all over the Living City. There were some in the tallest treehouses and in the lowest parts of the forest floor. We hid one tome from the Elder of Storms, and he was furious. We thought he was going to disintegrate the whole city. Thankfully, they found it before he completely lost it." Florie and Organa laughed loudly, and Myrcle smiled at them, happy to see Organa enjoying herself for the first time in weeks.

Esvele's eyes were fixed on the flames, her mind playing the images of the slaughter of Turnmot over and over in her head. Bendrit thought about asking her questions, but he knew better than to disturb her.

"So, what was it you were after in the Golden Queen's camp?" Bendrit asked.

Velkin took out the dragon's eye pendant. "This," she said as she passed it to him.

Bendrit examined the artifact closely, and as he did, his eyes got wider. "How did you come by this?"

"I found it during a raiding party at the House of Eris, sitting on a pedestal in a tower on the mountain called the Spire of Stars. Though I could barely read it due to the withering of time, the plaque before it called it an Astral Compass"

"Didn't you two say the old man said it was stolen?" Organa glared over at Esvele.

"Well," Esvele bit her lip, "Not exactly."

"What do you mean?" Organa asked.

"You see, we lied about that too," she said with a nervous smile. "We… um… well…" She continued to pause, but eventually got the words out. "We conjured up a fake 'contract' and approached you back in Turnmot to get you on the road to remembering."

"And when you got that Serpent's Ring," Myrcle interrupted, "and you wished for memories, the wishing chest brought you your brother's ring. Out of fear, we sped up the plans and messaged Velkin here to kidnap us all and bring us back to camp. We told her where we had hidden the Compass and had her retrieve it for us so we could continue our 'quest'," Myrcle gave a nervous smile.

"Why did I see my brother's memory and not mine? Why did the memories show me something that I wasn't there for?"

"The Dark Song can do many things, though its limits are unknown. One of its effects—"

"The short version," Organa grinned.

In rare cases, the Dark Song of two people is connected—uncommon, yet not impossible—among *twins*. That weave within the Flux allows them to experience the other's current memory, dream, or even life right then and there. He's in the Sepulcher, and he's trapped in his memories. I thought you might get a glimpse when you wished for memories and obtained the Serpent's Ring, and when you slipped into the darkness of your mind, it showed you the most repressed memory of them all—the day your brother was imprisoned, and the last day of the Cataclysm—because you wore his ring. There could be other things that your connection will allow you to do. But I believe it in our best interest not to dwell on it." Myrcle explained.

"Kyriel is reliving that night over and over again while he is tortured within that thing?" Organa's voice cracked as she swallowed down her tears. An uncomfortable silence lingered over the camp, broken only by the *pop* and *snap* of the bonfire they had gathered around.

"Kick the habit," Florie smiled as she swung on a branch. "Her brother's prison—do you all actually know if it's there?"

"Malorian's scroll confirms that they have a summoning circle under the Xurinal, but I don't know if it's there yet or not."Myrcle sighed.

"So why does anyone still need to search the Western Obelisk?"

"That," Myrcle stopped and pondered, "is a really good point, Florie."

"I do my best." She tilted her head with a smile.

"There is still a reason enough to search the Western Obelisk," Bendrit assured them. "I know of no spell or rite that can banish a Sepulcher once it is bound to the plane. If there is, then it is likely in that tower, or in Gavis Vel'Stratis. What you have here," his fingers caressed the silver amulet. The Crimson dragon's eye at the center gleamed with fire, waiting to be unleashed. "This is a Glass Key."

"Bendrit," Esvele asked softly, her voice trembling as her eyes gazed into the embers of the crackling fire.

"Yes?"

"How did that woman cut off your ability to use the Flux?" Her eyes peered deep into him.

"One can easily cut the weaves or unravel magic from an area or a person's hand. But to extinguish the ability to reach into the Flux of another? Especially a Magiqas? That is an exceedingly rare gift entirely. A blessing of the Dark One, mayhaps?"

Esvele raised up from her seat and began pacing. "You are a Guardian; you should have more power than any of us combined! Why didn't you save them? I fought beside Lukitas in the very heart of darkness, and she was able to call upon the Light even there!"

Bendrit gave no answer, and the others sat in silence. Esvele continued to eye the Guardian, waiting for some response, but none ever came. She scoffed as she walked away into the forest. Myrcle stood to follow her, but she held up her hand for him to sit. She wanted to be alone. Velkin walked over and sat on a stump beside Organa and Florie. No one said a word for quite some time.

Myrcle finally interjected, "Bendrit, she knows that you and the others were strong; she meant nothing by it."

"But she is right. I should have known that such spells could one day exist and should have prepared myself for them. If I had not gone into hiding, Rethial might not be what it is."

"How do you mean?" Organa asked him.

"We all know of the 'Great Cleansing' that the previous Soulflame King and Lady Magis brought a hundred years ago, that rid the world of Magiqas. But the tyranny of the Menitheal Dynasty goes further than you know. The northern free cities were pulled into the kingdom forcibly in the last few decades. The Western Wastes were just conquered by the legion sent forth calling themselves the Flames of the Sphinx, the very ones who were redirected on their way back to the capital to deal with Malorian at Turnmot."

"Why do they want the Western Waste? There is nothing out there. The name is 'Waste' for a reason," Organa asked.

"Resources, the few out there. Taming Sand Striders. Amber gems hold great power but are very rare, and so are the soldiers they could recruit from the tribes. They are planning something, but what, I know not. Maybe they're looking for something to help expand their reach across the world if they dare. I don't know."

"We might," Organa replied. She pulled from her satchel the scroll Malorian had shown them back in Turnmot. Bendrit took it slowly and, likewise, revealed its information. As it unraveled, his eyes gazed over the few words and then met the image of the great pyramid, the Xurinal, and the dark reflection. His eyes went wide with fear, and he shot a gaze at Myrcle, who explained how they knew of this. He recounted the attempted assassination of Malorian and Esvele saving him, further explaining how Malorian was once a Sorcerer Lord and fled Valistar after discovering the secret.

"If the Sepulcher has already manifested, or at the very least been anchored to this plane, then the Glass Key will be their next target. It will allow them to open the Sepulcher and unleash Kyriel. All Sepulchers are prisons that continuously shift a being through the realms. That is why they are even more dangerous. If one were to try to force it open, the magic that kept the being moving from plane to plane every second would explode all at once, unleashing a massive amount of energy, killing the thing held within, and shattering the world around it. These amulets have the power to peer through and pass through the other planes, allowing the process with Sepulchers to slow down, acting as a sort of key. Once the Sepulcher has manifested completely, power must be channeled into the eye there, causing the bonds to break and the being within to be set free."

Velkin shot up from her seat and looked directly at the Guardian. "Then that is why my convoy was attacked on our way back from

Turnmot." The others gave her a curious look, which she responded with, "Golden Queen, remember?" She paused for a moment and went on, "When I acquired the amulet we were attacked by a small battalion of the Flames of the Sphinx. Why do they want to free Kyriel?"

"I told you," Velkin cut Myrcle off.

"I wasn't asking you."

"They want Finality. Perfect silence and nothingness. The idea being that there was no creation, thus, the perfect form was the Void," answered Bendrit. "We must make our way there, and if we are to get into the city without someone taking too much notice, we're going to need a smuggler."

"And how are we going to manage that?" Organa curiously asked.

"Itheca," Florie answered.

"Where I caught you?" Velkin raised an eyebrow.

"Shut it," Florie shot back and giggled slightly. "It's a rotten city, full of thieves, pirates, marauders, and many other unsavory folks. If you're looking for a smuggler, that's where we'll find 'em. If we leave by dawn, we should be able to make it there by midday tomorrow."

"Well then," Myrcle stood from his seat, "best be gettin' some shut-eye. I'll go find Esvele," and he walked off into the night after his friend. The others waited about an hour for them to return, but heard only their raised voices.

"Myrcle, if you had seen what I saw, you would be just as upset," Esvele shouted at him.

"Dearie, I know I would be, but you need to rest."

"How can I rest when I know we weren't there to help those at Turnmot?"

"How have you rested since the Cataclysm then?"

"*I don't!*" Her voice boomed through the night and across the nearby hills. She stared intently at Myrcle and then sighed, holding her hands to her fiery red hair, pulling it back from her face. She walked around slowly and turned away from her companion through all these years, "I have not had a single night where terrible dreams have not come to me in my sleep. Every night I am reminded of the fall of Dremica and the burning city. I see my brother drowning in a pool of his own blood. My sister was gutted like an animal for slaughter. I see it all repeatedly in my mind. I can't end it! It is always there."

Esvele wept as her knees hit the forest floor, her shoulders weak from the weight of guilt and regret. The cold air blew on her cheek and surrounded her body as the light of the Element Moons shone down upon her. Myrcle walked forward and placed a hand on her shoulder, and for a brief moment she could feel the weight lift, but it returned swiftly to her, as it always had.

"Myrcle, I watched them kill children in Turnmot. A small boy, Malorian's charred and burnt from an explosion of flames. They nailed Ynetia to her home and let her bleed out and die. They murdered the few who resisted in cold blood and the others who simply ran. We were hunted down and slaughtered. There are no survivors." Her silver eyes shone back at him with the light of the moons as she looked his way. "I am so tired of failing, Myrcle. I need a victory at last."

"We had a victory, EV," he whispered into her ear. "We have Organa back. We found a Guardian who can help us unravel the mystery of the scroll from Malorian. We have had a few victories."

"And each came at a cost. Brok, when Organa returned to us. Turnmot and the death of innocents when Bendrit returned. These 'victories' are all in vain and have had a great cost to them."

"Then we need to make them mean something. We learn the scroll's truth and figure out how to overthrow the Menitheal Dynasty."

"You actually believe we can do that?"

"Four Magiqas, one being a Guardian of all things, a Paladin of Calikan, and a swift and sneaky little Hawkina. They stand no chance against us." Myrcle laughed as he finished, and Esvele smiled at him in disbelief at his optimism. Myrcle rose to his feet and helped Esvele to her own. "You'll see, when we finally bring justice to those who steal, murder, oppress, and destroy their own people, a true victory will be had." They walked back to the camp and found the others gone and the fire nearly burnt out. With a quick flick of his fingers, the embers died, and they retreated into their tent.

* * *

Dawn came not too long after they had all fallen asleep. The golden sunrise gleamed over the treetops and through their branches onto the forest floor. Red, yellow, purple, and orange clouds loomed overhead, mirroring the glorious light of the new day. Birds in their trees chirped and flew around in the morning air, a few of them swooping down to the grass and drinking the dew from its blades. A far mountain range in the southeast gleamed with white tops of snow and ice, its barren sides devoid of trees and green life. The God's Path, a great plateau of rock and stone dividing the King's Isle, radiated like gold from its great wheat fields atop its cliffs. Florie watched all this light scare away the darkness of the night, and she smiled and thought of its grand beauty. Velkin exited her tent to find Florie already awake, perched on a tree limb. She giggled to herself as she remembered capturing her in Itheca a few months back for trying to pick her pockets.

"Morning," Velkin called out.

"Good morning, you gorgeous hag," Florie replied as she glided down to the ground from her perch. She landed gracefully on the damp ground and took a seat beside the paladin.

"For a sleazy rogue, you are terrible at pick-pocketing, you know."

"I would have gotten your coin off your belt if you didn't have incredibly fast reflexes."

"Sure," Velkin laughed. She stood from her stump, dismantled her tent, and packed it into her bag. Organa exited her tent and, holding up her hand to shield herself, tried to block the sun from her eyes.

"If it isn't the ray of sunshine herself," Florie giggled.

"Not in the mornings, I can tell you that, especially this freakin' early." They both laughed as Organa took a seat. She saw Velkin packing and looked for the others. She saw the knot on the entrance to Esvele and Myrcle's tent tied with twine around it but did not see the Guardian around. "Where is Bendrit?" she groggily asked.

Velkin turned and looked for him as well, confused that he was not there. "I don't know," she answered. "Did you see him this morning, Florie?"

"No."

Organa called out his name and heard only her own voice echoing across the surrounding land. She shouted several times before a voice called back to her, "Oh, for the love of all things, shut the hell up! Some of us want to sleep!"

"Well," Florie laughed, "Esvele is up."

"And highly annoyed," Esvele replied. Organa and Florie laughed as Esvele pushed the curtain aside of her and Myrcle's tent. She groggily walked over to where the fire once was and sat on a stump. "It is too fucking early for this bullshit."

"We had best get to packing," Myrcle rubbed the sleep from his eyes as he left the tent soon after her.

"Hey," Velkin called out, "Have you seen Bendrit?"

"No, I can't say I have," Esvele grumbled back.

"Down," Myrcle commanded her like an animal, which she took great offense to and opened her mouth to answer, but he held up a hand and continued, "No, I have not, for the same reason Esvele has not either. I assumed he had gone into his tent." Myrcle looked for it, and it was nowhere to be found.

Velkin walked over to where his tent was and found a small scrap of parchment. She took it in her hand and held it up to show her companions. Myrcle walked over to her and took the note from her, unfolding the piece of parchment. He read it aloud to the others.

Dear Friends,

I have decided to part with you for a while. I have traveled to the old tower, Gavis Vel'Stratis, where I shall be looking for the answers to the Sepulcher in that scroll you showed me. I will meet you in Valistar at the Morning Glory Inn, on the west side of the city, in two weeks. Hopefully, by then, I will have some answers. I will be under the name of Verit.

My best to you all and see you soon,

Bendrit.

Esvele gave Myrcle a weird look. "Why would he leave? He said last night he was going to accompany us."

"Before you stormed off," Florie laughed at her.

"Shut up, bird," she glared back with a smirk.

"Now, children," Myrcle interjected, "play nice." He paused a moment to think as Florie and Esvele backed down from one another. "Now, we need to head to Itheca, and find one of Florie's old friends."

"'Old friends' is being very kind. We're all more like, 'I won't kill you if you don't touch my stuff, but if you do, no one will ever find your fucking body,' kind of friends." Florie blinked her eyes mockingly.

"Are we going to die when we go there?" Esvele asked worriedly.

Florie laughed. "Yeah, but it was a while back and I was on a solo contract."

"You know, that is not a comforting thought," Esvele laughed.

"Can we get going now?" Organa asked.

"I suppose so," Myrcle agreed, and they finished packing things into the bags and went on their way toward Itheca.

While the warm summer sun beat down upon them as they walked, Florie explained more about the town of Itheca. It was a dark place, near the sea, and made most of its wealth, in the first era of Rethial, on the materials mined in the depths of the Shimmering Hoard, now known as the Red Falls. The Dwarves of the town delved far too deep into Lorial and found the heat unbearable. Great waterfalls of fire and lava came from the sides of the mine, killing three hundred of the workers in the mine that night. No one went in there but those who wished to die in the most painful ways possible, or if the King of Thieves sent you there as a punishment for your crimes. "Trust me, if we get entangled with them, we're fucked," Florie assured them, and went on.

Plagued by storms every other day, the town was mostly a dark and cold place. Velkin had interrupted to point out that during her stay there she had met the King of Thieves and offered a bounty. She wanted him to send a team into the Red Falls and claim the Necrotic Emerald, but he did not want to sacrifice his own people for such an insane task. The Red Falls were like a dark legend to Organa, almost like those in Dremica. There were the Shadow Hounds to watch in the Dark Wood leading to the mountain where the Silver Fountain once was. The Grasps of Darkness were large leviathan-like creatures with black and red slimy skin and countless tendrils that sought to drag you into the crushing abyss of the sea surrounding Dremica. In the places where holy power once held great sway, darkness now crept into the once heavenly hearts. But now, instead of simply a legend of some far-off land in the east, it was her home. Four hundred years ago, she was taken from there, her brother imprisoned, and her family dead. Four hundred years ago, when the Silver Kingdom fell, she lost her home. Even though she felt no sincere attachment to the land where she grew up, she still felt that small hole in her heart, a need to return one day. She heard it in her head, the melody of vengeance, but instead of heeding its call, Organa let her memories run through her head and drowned out the Dark Song with ease.

They walked for about twenty more miles. "How far is Itheca?" asked Organa, her breath short and legs tired.

"Well." Florie landed beside her and, with a calm breath, said, "Four hundred miles."

Organa shot her an annoyed glare. The Hawkina laughed at her and took back up into the sky, flying onward.

"Days like these, I wish I had wings," Organa sneered.

"Don't we all," Velkin laughed, trying to catch her breath. She took a seat on the grassy hill they were climbing. From there she could see the King's Road slowly being overtaken by a black shadow from the clouds above, with the radiant light of the sun shining through minor breaks in it.

Organa pointed out, "It would be a much easier walk if we took the King's Road to Itheca."

"Yes, it would, but the dangerous eyes of the Soulflame King and Lady Magis are ever watchful on the King's Road," Myrcle explained, "Not forgetting to mention that the Order of Valkiel is more than likely still hunting you my dear. With our close call with the Ghast in the Forest of Bravica, we must avoid the main road at all costs."

"What path are we even taking, Myrcle?" Esvele asked.

"Our own," he simply smiled, "the one less traveled and the one that is sure to lead into the jaws of the Sphinx." In the distance, he could see a small column of light brown dust rising from the west as he turned and looked at the surrounding land. The cloud grew in size for a few moments and swiftly approached like an oncoming storm. Small black figures moving fast beat against the dirt road as their hooves pounded the ground, creating smaller clouds of dust.

The black horses shimmered with silver and black armor, and so did their riders, save one. A woman with raven hair blew in the wind as they galloped forwards along the King's Road. Beside her were three riders on each side, captains of the Flames of the Sphinx, and further behind them their legions of soldiers came into view. Hundreds of enormous banners strung up on flagpoles, decorated with the image of a red, two-headed Sphinx with streams of purple fire coming from its mouths within a silver circle on a black piece of cloth. The legions marched forward toward Valistar. Myrcle became alarmed when one rider next to the woman slowed and the others eyed him with confusion. The rider pointed directly at the hill where the group of companions was resting, and Myrcle saw them blow a horn, forcing the legions of soldiers to halt dead in their tracks. At that moment, the seven riders made haste toward their hiding spot, and Myrcle shouted, "Run! Run now!"

"Why?" Organa looked at him with annoyance.

"Black Riders! Run!"

They all shot up and sprinted away from the hillside. Florie took to the sky with her black wings beating against the white clouds, making her an easy target. A rider locked an arrow onto his bowstring and let it loose into the sky. She dodged out of the way, diving toward the ground with ease through the air as another arrow swiftly followed its predecessor. Arrow after arrow, the rider shot, each one missing its target, and then one hit. The sting of piercing and searing pain as an arrow burst through Florie's flesh, thrusting into the muscle and tissue of her lower leg. She continued to fly away from her attackers as she noticed they were gaining on her friends, but she struggled to maintain focus through the pain. As she realized this, her vision blurred and darkened, and she fell from the sky toward Lorial.

Organa looked up as she heard a shriek of pain from above them in the sky and saw Florie struggling to stay in the air, then watched as her friend began her descent. Stopping where she stood, she cast a spell and summoned a cold and winter wind to Florie that blew from the clouds above and caught her unconscious body just above the ground. She laid her down softly on the grass and heard the sound of thundering hooves approaching. Organa faced her foe with the might have seven blizzards swirling in her hands and readied herself for combat.

Myrcle saw Organa save Florie and her sudden stop. "What the hell is she doing?"

"Well, she isn't going to fight seven Black Riders on her own, now is she?" Velkin said as she ran toward Organa.

"By the Dawn!" Esvele shouted and followed behind Velkin. Myrcle shook his head and joined them as well.

The Black Riders reached the summit of the small hill and dismounted their horses, drawing blades made of metal black as an abyss. The woman's, however, was of silver and Blood Iron forged into the edges of the blade for the cleanest of cuts. The Black Riders began their approach, but the woman held up a hand and they all stopped on the spot. Organa stood in the vanguard line as the woman walked down the hill's slope. As the woman got closer, Esvele recognized her and saw that it was the same woman from the vision of the Slaughter of Turnmot.

She sheathed her blade, and held up her hands to show she carried no weapon. Slowly, she put her hands back down at her side and walked forward, stopping a few yards away from the companions. "Hello," the woman greeted them with a light and lovely voice.

"Who are you?" asked Organa sternly.

"I see you're a down-to-business type, and I understand that, but

I've no time to answer such feeble questions. You must come with me, Guardians."

"Like hell," Esvele scoffed. "We know who and what you are, Black Rider."

"Ah," the woman chuckled, "you like the name the locals gave us? Fine, my name is Merith, also known as—"

Myrcle interrupted her. "The Will of the Flame," he said and spat upon the ground.

"You know me, sir?"

"I know enough about the Menitheal Dynasty's lackeys to know you're the worst of them all."

"Do you now?" the woman laughed. "I promise you, Guardians, I bear you no ill will. But only if you come with me willingly. Let's not make a fuss over nothing, all right?"

"'No ill will,'" Organa laughed back at her. "You shot my friend out of the sky and almost killed her, and we are not 'Guardians.'" Organa felt her rage boiling inside her and heard that sweet melody of vengeance in her head, but she would not let it get to her.

"And Mortic will be reprimanded for such violence," she promised. "As for your title, you will earn it one day if you have the power and determination to seek such things. Now please come with me to Valistar and I shall explain everything on the way. We have spare horses you may use so you do not have to walk like the runts." She gave a courteous bow to them and motioned her head up the hill back toward the other Black Riders. They watched as one of the riders took their blade out and shoved the one called Mortic to the ground. Another one of the Black Riders took out their Night Shard and removed Mortic's helmet, revealing a scarred and death-like face, with pale eyes and hair as white as snow. The Black Rider looked at Merith, and she gave a nod back. With a single swift and heavy stroke, Mortic's head was removed from his body and rolled down the hillside to Merith's feet. She took it in her hand and held it up by the hair toward the companions.

"This is the price all pay for insubordination."

As she finished, the head let out a shriek of horrible and grotesque sounds from its mouth, pouring blood onto the green grass and sending a tidal wave of disgust and fear down the companions' spines. She laughed lightly and tossed the head back to the other Black Riders. One of them caught it with ease and placed it back on the still-kneeling body. The rider spoke an ancient language, one that the old ears of Esvele, Velkin, and Myrcle could recognize, and a flash of green flame bolted from her fingertips and around the scar of where the Mortic's head once was. With another shriek of abominable sounds, the Black Rider stood and placed his helmet back on his once-severed head. "See," Merith turned back toward them, "good as new. Now you will accompany me to Valistar."

"You're monsters," Organa murmured in horror.

Merith walked forward, and the ones she sought backed away from her. "'Monsters'?" she asked. "The veritable monsters are those who would force this chaos of death and rebirth upon the living. Freedom from death, from the Balance of Chaos, is a gift, my dear, one of which you and your friends may partake. But only if you come with me to Valistar."

Esvele stood in front of Organa. "You're not taking her or any of us with you to that place, dead or alive."

"We'd prefer alive, but if you insist, my Lady will resurrect you, willing or unwilling, back to this plane." Merith motioned to her Black Riders, and they descended the slope of the hill. The ring of their blades being unsheathed rang in the companions' ears, and they readied themselves for battle. The cloaks of the Black Riders burst into green and purple flames, burning away as ashes off of their backs and flowing into their armor, lighting them ablaze with more dark flames.

Mortic bolted for the closest target, Esvele, and drew his blade through the air three times. Esvele ducked under the blade of the first attack, and the second barely missed her chest as she moved to the side, away from the strike aimed at her heart. The third, however, struck her left forearm and left a gash on her skin. Esvele sneered at the pain and moved back from the Black Rider with her staff ready.

Myrcle reacted to this as any friend would and sent a spiral of flames from his staff. Five rays of flame were sent directly into the Black Riders' chests, each hitting their mark, and launched him across the landscape. Mortic slid across the grass and stood when Esvele, who was now right above him, said something in an ancient language, and the rider's arms and shoulders caught fire instantly, sending him screaming back up the hillside for a moment, trying to dispel the flames.

Organa held up her right hand and formed a gust of freezing cold, harsh, icy wind blowing toward the riders. The shards of ice hurtling forward cut the parts of the Black Rider's bodies where only leather protected them, plunging deep into their skin and then bursting, sending rains of blood all around their bodies. Organa sprinted over to Esvele and placed a hand on her gashed arm, and sang a light melody that healed her wounds.

One of the Black Riders stepped forward and sliced her own hand with her Blood Iron Blade. From around her armor, the flames gravitated toward the deep cut in her palm and created a great ball of green and purple flames, which she sent forth at the companions. Esvele and Organa barely escaped the inferno, but Myrcle, Velkin, and Florie were caught in the flames, sending them flying across the battlefield. Florie ended up on top of a boulder sticking out of the side of a hill, with Myrcle landing near her.

Velkin hit the grass near the feet of another Black Rider, who raised their sword high and made two strikes against her. The first swing sliced across her back, leaving a gash that seared with pain as she rolled out of the way of the second one, kicking back at the Black Rider and throwing him prone onto the ground. Summoning her holy blade, the Paladin of Calikan plunged it into the Black Rider's chest. The rider screamed in pain as light and holy powers burned through her body and the darkness that enveloped her soul was banished.

Velkin's breath was stolen as she looked from the corpse to her blade. Perhaps Calakin's grace had not left her as she thought...even after all she had done.

One of the Black Riders walked toward Organa and Esvele and struck the Kalishtani with his blade across her chest, slashing her and cutting her deeply. Organa grabbed the arm of the Black Rider, but as she did, the flames that coiled around his armor burned her hands, and she recoiled in pain. With his hand, he grabbed her by the neck and hoisted her into the air, readying to plunge his blade into her chest. Then six large, thorned vines grew from the earth beneath his feet and pulled him to the ground, forcing him to release Organa from his grip and drop her to the ground.

The other two Black Riders saw their comrade's distress; held out their hands, sending forth green and purple flames to the vines which held him. Tearing the vines, the knight jumped to his feet. The one on his right then took his Blood Iron blade and went to attack Organa, but missed his strike.

A tangle of air wrapped itself around the crimson edge as Esvele pulled it back and out of his hand.

Mortic finally subdued Esvele's flames and ran at Myrcle with his blade, making three strikes at his torso. Slice after slice, he only cut the air around Myrcle, whose own dexterity surprised him. He struck Mortic with his right fist in the knight's abdomen and again on his head, leaving him on the ground gasping for air. Forgetting for a moment the battle around him, Myrcle smiled with pride and barely heard the dark knight coming behind him with their Night Shard.

Oh, fuck, he thought, and he dodged the thrust meant to pierce his heart.

Myrcle then turned to the three Black Riders in front of Organa and Esvele and entered his friends' minds.

Move—now!

Myrcle gathered threads of emerald flame into his hands that he unleashed in a river of ruin.

You will never escape your past, Oraleus. the Dark One whispered to him as sorrow corrupted his threads. *Your father's death will forever be your doing.*

Myrcle drew more and more until the inferno melted away the earth in its wake down to the stone. The rocks shattered and flattened into a lake of fire that enveloped one of the Black Riders, devouring him.

Organa skidded across the torn hillside, breath sharp in her throat as she dropped beside Esvele. The wound carved across EV's chest gaped like a second mouth; heat pulsed up through Organa's palm as she pressed it down and let her melody spill into the tear. Light hummed through her touch—silver strands knitting beneath blood—until Esvele's breath steadied.

A chill prickled the back of Organa's neck.

Merith stood only yards away, still as a shrine statue, her amethyst eyes cutting through the drifting smoke and fixing on Organa with a predatory calm. The air tightened around them—not wind, but attention.

The sorceress turned her head as the Black Rider's body, flung aside by Myrcle's earlier flare, twitched in the dirt near Florie. Merith whispered a single word in Vodiran—hard consonants scraping like bone dragged over stone. The world recoiled.

The knight's corpse arched upright as if yanked by invisible strings. Black sinew snapped back into place. Her helm clattered to the ground as she snatched up her blade and charged at Florie, each step kicking up dust and cold ash.

Florie barely had time to rise to one knee. The Rider's shadow swallowed her. But the killing arc never fell.

Instead, Florie caught the knight's wrist with both hands, twisted with a grunt through gritted teeth, and drove the Rider's own sword up beneath the hinge of her jaw. The blade punched through with a wet, meaty crack. A fountain of black blood erupted, splashing hot against Florie's chest and steaming in the cold air. The Rider gargled—a rattling hiss that scraped Florie's eardrums— and collapsed, rolling bonelessly down the slope, leaving a trail like spilled ink behind her.

Florie staggered upright, swaying, her breath ragged. She ripped a dagger from her belt with her clean hand.

The blade cut the air with a shrill whistle.

Mortic jerked back too late. The dagger kissed his neck, parting skin. A thin line of red welled beneath the smear of ash on his throat.

Florie met his gaze with a look that dared him to try again.

Behind them, Merith's eyes glowed faintly never once breaking that soul-carving stare.

Esvele saw Mortic stand and turn to attack Myrcle, thinking the dagger had come from him, and slash Myrcle along his spine, leaving a deep and bloody cut. Myrcle fell to the ground screaming in pain. Esvele saw a smile creep across Mortic's dead face as he removed his helmet. He turned his blade upside down, ready to plunge it into Myrcle. Reaching high into the sky, Esvele took hold of the very pieces of creation that held the clouds together above them and called down hundreds of bolts of lightning into Mortic's chest watching as his armor smoked and his body burned black as he was cooked within. His blade dropped from his hand, piercing the ground near Myrcle, and he fell to his knees, then to the ground, dead.

Myrcle gasped on the ground, and Organa ran to him, leaving a brown dirty streak in the green grass. Merith's shadow loomed over them as she descended the hillside. A sudden blow to the dark commander's shoulder nearly toppled her. Velkin's bright armor *clanked* against the death knight as she drew her holy blade. The *ping* and shrill clash of the swords echoed across the rolling hills.

Esvele's fingertips touched the stark strands of air within the Flux and wove them with the wrath of the waves from the deep sea, and the crackle of Myrcle's river of flame, spinning a storm around herself, and unleashing barrage of jagged lightning.

Instead of hitting her, the bolts met a wall in Merith's hand and sent flashing streaks all around her and into the sky; scorching the earth nearby and creating loud cracks of thunder. Esvele began to levitate and move toward her foe. As she did, Merith redirected the spell at Myrcle and Organa, who both screamed in pain as the electricity coursed through them and singed their skin. At first, Esvele continued to use her spell, the screams of her closest friend and her old student unable to pierce the thunder that she conjured. But, Velkin shouted at Esvele to stop, and she turned her head to see her spell being used against her own, and instantly stopped. The Dark Song in her head faded, and she fell to the ground. Velkin ran to Myrcle and Organa, their wounds severe, and sang a song of healing as Organa had, but could not mend their wounds completely.

Merith smiled and walked back up the hill toward her horse, but then turned around. "Oh, I almost forgot," she laughed to herself. She lifted her hand from underneath her cloak and whispered a spell that echoed in all of their ears with a thousand voices in her dark and ancient tongue. This time the words singed their ears, and dark flames sprang to life around the corpses of the Black Riders and her hands. The wounds on them mended themselves perfectly as the words echoed through their bodies and the Black Riders rose to their feet, one by one, alive once more. "Seize them."

Her minions moved forward toward each of them, and Myrcle shouted to Esvele, who ran over to him swiftly, and called for Florie, who flew to his side. They all took his hand and disappeared in a radiant flash.

Itheca

Rain fell on their faces as they lay on the wet grass. A loud crack of thunder and a flash of white lightning across the sky woke Organa from her sleep. The rain falling into her eyes made it hard to see in the evening dusk. She used her hands to wipe the water from her eyes to see better, looking for the others. Myrcle lay directly in front of her on the wet grass with Esvele on the other side of him. Florie was to her right, just then waking up, with Velkin on the other side of her. Another loud crack of thunder roared across the sky, and a great chain of lightning gleamed in the clouds.

Myrcle came to shortly after Florie, wildly jerking about for a moment with fear in his eyes. Organa calmed him by placing her hands on his shoulders and giving him kind words of reassurance. Florie helped Velkin to her feet as the rain clinked against her silver and lapis armor. Esvele was the last to awake, holding her hands to her head as a searing headache began.

The storm above washed out most of the light from the setting sun, but a small glimmer crept around a chain of gigantic mountains at the top of the God's Way. Organa turned back toward her friends and saw, in the distance, a small town near the plateau. A great clock tower loomed in its skyline, ever watchful over the town of Itheca.

Organa looked for the Black Riders, but before she could get a good look around the area, Myrcle grabbed her hand and looked her dead in the eyes, "We have to hide now!" He repeated himself to the others and they made their way to Itheca. Through the deluge and the sticky mud, they ran across the plains and, after an hour, arrived at the gates of the City of Thieves. Velkin went to the door that was cut into the left of the two great steel doors that served as the only way to pass through the solid walls of stone and the guards who kept watch during the night, the majority of them elves bearing the crest of the Menitheal Dynasty.

A young Drakeman sentry came to the door and slid back a metal slit where his eyes and teal and light blue scales were the only things visible. He shouted over the thunder, "Who are you? What business brings you to Itheca?"

Velkin cleared her throat as a few violet tangles of night threads enveloped her voice in a strange accent. "We are travelers from the northern city of Nefis, on our way to the capital to see my family on the south side of the city. We wish only to stay the night somewhere out of this dreadful rain."

"Do you have papers?"

Velkin kept her composure. "What do you mean, dearie?"

"Your Travelers papers, of course. If you're from Nefis, you would have had to cross the Untier's Passage, which you would need papers to get through," the guard explained in a suspicious tone.

"Oh, yes," Velkin lied. "I know exactly what you mean, silly me. My friend 'ere," she paused for a moment, "Octavia, has them," and she pulled Esvele forward toward the guard who opened another slit in the door and held out an armored hand, waiting for the papers. Esvele smiled nervously and rummaged through her satchel, leaning her staff against the door of the gate. Moving around books and components for spells and potions, she revealed a long sheet of parchment. Esvele quickly glided her hand over the parchment without the sentry taking notice and placed it in his hand, with her voice not her own as well, more high-pitched and cloud-like. "Here you go, sir."

The Drakemen pulled the parchment through, and both of the slits closed.

"What did you do?" asked Florie.

"I enchanted the parchment to look like verification papers, made-up names and all," she said nervously, but, with a sudden shift, turned to Velkin. "Octavia?"

"Listen, it was the best I could come up with on the spot," she whispered back.

"Oi," the sentry shouted as the eye slit opened, and the words *Oh shit* came to Velkin's mind. "Open the gate," the Drakeman shouted and passed the parchment back through a slit, "Welcome to Itheca. Don't make any trouble now."

"Oh," Myrcle imitated an old man's voice, "The youngins here are the definition of trouble, sir, but I'll keep 'em in line," he chuckled. The companions walked through the great steel gates of Itheca and onto a cobblestone street where a small river of rainwater trailed down toward the gates. Esvele turned and could see the Drakemen from where she was clearly. A tall and slightly broad Drakemen wore leather armor with metal shoulder guards and leather straps that crossed over one another down his scaled arms. He wore a white cloth shirt under a red, sleeveless long coat with no hood, showing the tips of his crown of horns upon his head. His hands were wrapped with leather and metal gauntlets, and on his back was a longbow with a quiver of arrows, and a long sword hung at his side. His eyes were a cold crystal blue, and they gleamed through the night.

A hand settled on her shoulder, and Esvele turned to see Organa looking at her. "You all right? We're going to catch a cold if we don't get out of this rain."

"Yeah, I'm good," Esvele smiled and turned to see the Drakemen one last time, but he was gone.

The companions walked for close to another half hour before finally seeing somewhere to stay, the Merry Night Inn. Myrcle led them in. When they entered, they saw a long bar where at least twenty people sat, laughing and drinking away. Multiple tables with guests sitting around them had bottles of wine and plates of bread, cheese, and meats. A group of bards played music in a corner where people were dancing with one another. A tall podium waited for the House Master and, as he placed some dirty plates, goblets, and mugs on the extended shelf of a window, he opened a large ledger book.

"So," the man's deep voice bellowed, "what can I do fer ye?"

"We are in need of a room to stay in for the night."

"Aye, my good sir," he chuckled, "I can do that for you. A larger room for all of you, I assume?"

"Yes, please," Myrcle smiled.

"Let me go get the key, one moment. And it'll be seven silver for the night."

"Well," Esvele began, "this is going well."

"We need to keep low. Organa and Esvele, keep cool. Velkin, don't smite anyone. Florie, hands off other people's things."

Organa giggled a little. "I'm always cool."

"Sure." Esvele's eyes rolled back, and she smiled at her old student.

"I don't smite people," Velkin corrected and then thought for a moment, "Well, rarely."

"I know," Myrcle assured her, "just clarifying. Oh, and Velkin, you're paying."

"What," Velkin laughed it off and then saw the owner returning, "Oh fine." She pulled out the money, trading it for the key.

"I don't steal things." Florie paused. "Anymore," she clarified under her breath.

The House Master returned with a large hoop that had at least a hundred keys on it. "'ere you go. Feel free to take your t'ings upstairs and come back down for some supper."

"Thank you." Myrcle turned and took a key from the man's hand. Myrcle handed the key to Esvele, whispering, "Take them upstairs and put our things in the room. I'm going to enchant the building so they can't track us."

"They can do that?" Organa asked.

"You know this is a private conversation," Myrcle laughed.

"Oh well," she shrugged, "but how can they track us?"

"We flashed in front of them, and magic always leaves traces, either visual or in the Flux. Weave Oracles can read such things. I'll explain more when you come back from the room, and I'm done here. While you're up there, knock on Bendrit's door. Wake that crazy old man."

Esvele and the others moved around him and up a winding staircase in the back. Myrcle walked out the door of the Merry Night and began his enchantments. As he focused his power, he heard someone walk up behind him, their boots clopping on the cobblestone street. "May I help you?" Myrcle asked the figure, not turning to see them. Before he could ask again, a cloth sack fell swiftly over his face, and a portal of black and red light closed just as quickly as it opened as the stranger took him from the inn.

Esvele unlocked the door of their room to find four neatly made beds and a pile of wood in the fireplace. She lit a match and ignited the wood. A warm rush of heat filled the room, and each of them went to the room's restroom and changed out of their soaking wet clothes. Esvele now wore a nice blue doublet and black slacks. Around her shoulders, she wrapped a white cloak around herself for more warmth. Her red hair contrasted well with her outfit. She turned as Organa emerged in her new clothes. Instead of the flower dress, she wore a black top and skirt that separated at her abdomen. Long sleeves that revealed her shoulders and fell toward the floor were stitched with designs of green and golden vines. Her tall black boots were covered, save for the very bottoms of the shoes, by the black skirt, which Esvele noticed had more stitched vines with thorns.

"Is it weird that I am not your mother and yet I am disturbed by your clothing? However, you do look absolutely outstanding," Esvele said in amazement.

"Really?" Organa smiled and looked down at herself. "I bought this a while back, before Brok and I met you at Turnmot," Organa began, but paused. She smiled. "Brok liked it and said I looked like a queen."

Esvele walked to Organa, seeing the sadness building in her eyes. "Hey, do you want to talk about it? It helps."

"I just miss him," Organa said as she cried into her shoulder.

"I do too," Esvele wrapped her arms around her. "I remember the two of you training in the courtyard of the Silver Fountain. You were quite the spitfire of ice and cold, and his strength was beyond comparison. Once, you nearly lost to him, although I would not be surprised if he always let you win," Esvele smiled.

"I still blame myself." Organa cleared her throat and raised her head from Esvele's shoulder. "I don't see how I can't."

"It will take longer than you realize. I am old as hell," Esvele laughed. "But I still blame myself for the Fall of Dremica." She sat on her bed and patted a spot beside her, and Organa placed herself at Esvele's side.

"But why?"

"Organa, when the Cataclysm came, it was without warning. Even though one man said he saw it many years before, we didn't prepare for it. The land was wrought with hellfire, blight, undead, demons, and all manner of dark creatures. After the Battle of Husieàkritae, when we saved you and found your brother, we had no choice but to flee. The battle was lost. I blame myself because I am a Far Seer.

I should have known something was coming. The Thread of Time is there in the Flux for me to riddle out, and I missed it. The Weave Oracles should have seen something while tracing magic through the kingdom. They should have seen the trail of dark magic, but they didn't. We both have lost battles. One day we will finally rest and see the ones we failed. Maybe we will receive forgiveness."

"That story you told at the campfire that night before… everything… was it true?"

"Yes, and no. When I described what happened in the city, that was true. But my time with the 'Warden of the Forest' was not. That never existed. You saw in your memory who I was and what I did. I was a teacher at the Silver Fountain, as was Myrcle. That's how we knew you and your…" Esvele stopped herself short.

"My brother," Organa finished for her.

Florie's shout broke their tension-filled moment. "I can't get this freaking shirt around my wings!"

"Hold on," Organa called back, and she rose from the bed and went to the restroom where Florie was struggling. Velkin came from the other restroom, where she had changed from her glorious plate armor into a nice dress without the amulet of Calakin around her neck. The top was like Organa's, but a crimson red instead. The dress covered her torso and met a black band that wrapped around the waist with a silver buckle. The swirling bottom was the same shade as the top and had a small slit that revealed her left leg and a long black leather boot that rose just above her knee.

"What is that?" Esvele laughed.

"Look, it's all I had. The Golden Queen has to look her best," she smiled back and struck a pose against the wall. "Maybe I'll woo one of the other members of the Conclave. Heel ol' boy," and she gave a seductive smile to Esvele. They laughed wildly and tried to catch their breath but were unsuccessful. Florie and Organa emerged from the latrine, and Florie's wings were poked through roughly cut holes in the brown leather top.

"I did my best," Organa laughed.

"Thank you," Florie laughed.

"All right, you all head downstairs, and I'll go get our rooms taken care of." Esvele rose from the bed and walked toward the door. The others followed her out, and they headed down to the main floor of the Merry Night Inn. Esvele walked down the hall and knocked on the third door on the right, and as the third knock hit, it swung open violently. A sack fell over her face, another portal of black and red light appeared and diminished, and she was gone.

Velkin walked over to Organa. "I know you might not want to talk about it, but how are you handling your memories?"

Organa gave a long and terrible pause but eventually spoke. "I... I'm coming to terms with them. It's kind of funny," she giggled nervously. "I'm kind of glad they are back."

"I would hope so," Velkin smiled and placed her hand in Organa's.

"Well, it's not that simple," Organa rose and pulled away. She paced for a moment. "I had been living a life where I had been raised in the Living City for twenty years before I left. Brok and I grew up there together. I can see the resemblance in the memory. Great fields of trees and hills from the top of the Silver Fountain were replaced with an endless forest and a far mountain range as we sat on a stool in a tall tower. I remember growing up with Gerith and him always being afraid of me." She laughed for a quick moment but then became solemn. "I am glad I know the truth, but I also wish I didn't. 'Cause I would some days rather remember him one way instead of two. But it's better to know both sides of a person than just the one you see—or saw—every day."

"Let's head down." Velkin stood and smiled, and she, Organa and Florie followed her down the stairs and into the lobby of the tavern.

Organa and the others looked around the main floor and saw no one. The people who were laughing at the bar were gone, the bards were nowhere to be seen, the House Master was gone, and there was no one anywhere. "Hello," Organa called out. As Florie took a seat at the table, Organa shot at her, "What are you doing?"

"Taking a seat. Everyone's gone, so we have the place to ourselves."

"Get up," Organa pulled her to her feet.

Velkin became uneasy and tried to head back up the stairs to get Esvele, but found a wall of power preventing passage. She placed her hand upon it to force her way through, but as her skin met the wall, a rush of electricity shot through her body. She seized violently as the others turned to see her fall unconscious down a few steps. Organa instantly readied herself for the attack, a chilly wind circling in her hands. Florie removed her daggers from the sheaths around her waist.

Six clouds of black and red smoke appeared on the far side of the inn's main floor. They wore red and black garb that wrapped around their torsos and tight cloth pants, with black boots that had a dimly glowing rune carved into their leather. A red piece of cloth covered them from the nose down past the neck, and a hood covered their heads, leaving only their red eyes and the skin of their upper cheeks visible. Two of them looked pale and cold, while the others were darker and more deeply burned.

None of them said a word, and as Organa spoke, a sack fell over her face and Florie's from behind them, and they were taken away from the Merry Night.

Children of the Crimson Moon

Myrcle opened his eyes and saw only darkness, with a small amount of light peeking through the cloth sack where a few small holes had been cut. The air was cold and damp, and an echoing drip sounded through the room every few seconds. He moved and felt tight bonds of rope on his hands, binding him to a pole. As he tried to move his feet, he felt the same bonds of rope around his lower legs. He tried to speak, but a piece of cloth was between his mouth and his tongue. Only a few grunts could escape.

"Quiet, dear," a deep male voice spoke. "Your strength is required." Myrcle's eyes closed, and he fell back into a dreamless sleep.

He must have slept for another day.

A scream of agony woke him at some point, and he saw someone standing at a tall table in the room, much like the person before but broader in the shoulders. He tried to say something again, but only a grunt escaped him.

The person turned to him and a warm voice, higher pitched than the last, asked, "Ah, awake again? Would you like something to eat? Drink?"

Myrcle gave no answer.

"I'll get you something." He stood and went back to the table, where Myrcle heard a clank as he set something down. The sound of pouring liquid was like music to his ears, as his throat was dry and his lips chapped. They turned back around, and something was in his hands. Lifting the bottom of the sack off him, he asked, "Thirsty?"

The man took Myrcle's gag from his mouth, but before Myrcle could speak, the edge of a bowl was pressed to Myrcle's lips, and a warm liquid met them, relieving the dryness. The taste was metallic and had a coppery flavor with a foul smell. Nevertheless, he drank his fill until he realized his mistake as a glint of torchlight in the room shimmered on his scarlet drink. Instantly, he coughed up everything, gasping for air in between.

"Xeris," the male voice had returned, and the man jerked away quickly, standing as straight as he could, "Leave us. Now." The man bowed respectfully and left the chamber without a sound.

A few hours passed.

Myrcle fell asleep once more.

When he woke, he found another figure in the room with him. He tried to see the best he could, but the light from a flickering torch in the cold room was not enough. Fear gripped him, and panic set in. The shadow of the figure who was in the room with him moved in front of the light from a tall table where she had been doing something and then knelt down in front of Myrcle. Her head cocked to the side, and Myrcle could feel a foul smile cross her face. She rose to her feet and kept looking down at Myrcle. He could feel another supercilious smile cross the woman's face and saw her reach behind her back for something. Her fingers grasped something, but what, Myrcle could not tell.

In an instant, with a swift move of her hand behind her back, a sharp pain shot through his left leg. The gag around his mouth muffled his scream as a shiver shot through his body and his breath left him. He sucked in as much air as he could and let it all out, screaming in agony; a cold sweat dripped down his brow and his head sagged. The hilt of a dagger glistened in the torchlight with its blade plunged deep into his leg. Staggered breaths in the cold, damp chamber turned to mist as he shuddered with each breath, and the shadow of the man who was with him in the chamber rose against the walls, cocking his head to the other side. He stepped forward quickly and removed the dagger from Myrcle's leg. Gasping for more air and grunting through the gag in his mouth, Myrcle held tight, and, for the first time in a long time, he prayed to the gods for mercy.

The man rose to his feet and walked back to the tall table.

Another figure entered the room from the right. The same voice as before shouted, "What are you doing, Xeris?"

"I was just having a little fun," she said back.

"You fool, you were not to harm any of them!"

"I don't know what came over me. I just felt her hand on my shoulder, pushing me to cut for him."

The male shadow placed his hands on her shoulders, and she mirrored him. "The Blood Mother's will is less known than anything in our world. Do not fall too far into your own bloodlust, Xeris." The man took the acolyte's hand in his own and then struck him with the other. "Now bind that wound and keep him healthy. The Blood Mother will see him and his friends soon." The man exited the room, and Xeris fussed with the strips of cloth on the table.

Myrcle felt a wave of fear crash over him like a tsunami. He knew now where he was and who he was with—the Children of the Crimson Moon.

A woman echoed down the long chamber that the man exited. "Don't worry," Xeris began as he walked over to him, "only the foulest get that treatment." He paused for a moment and lifted his leg, sending a spiral of pain through him, "I want to apologize Myrcle," a chill ran down his spine as he said his name, "The Blood Lust of the Children is legend and is hard to control." Myrcle was disgusted as the man went on. "But we are loyal followers of the Blood Mother, and we embrace the natural order of life and death. The Balance of Chaos must be respected." Xeris ran water from a bucket in his hands onto the stab. Myrcle jerked as the water cleansed his injury. Xeris finished binding his prisoner's wound and stood to his feet. "I am sorry I harmed you. May the Vengeance of the Blood Mother guide thee." Xeris walked back, dried his hands on a towel, and left the room.

Myrcle sat there for a few hours before he saw someone enter the chamber again, though he did not hear them come in. The figure looked like the man who had been there before.e "Hello dear friend, my name is Corvin, Crimson Priest of the Blood Mother of the Crimson Moon, and we've much work to do." He moved his right hand, placed it upon his head, and pulled off the cloth sack, revealing the room. The man's hood covered most of his head, besides some skin around the blood-red eyes. A piece of red cloth covered the bottom of his nose and fell down into the black and red tunic. His eyes gleamed in the light from the torch and reflected the flame almost perfectly.

"Your leg feels all right?" the man asked, with such articulation, yet the cloth over his mouth did not move. "Let's get you up." Corvin unbound Myrcle's feet and untied the knot that kept him against a tall pole in the room. The man slowly helped him stand and, to Myrcle's surprise, he felt no pain when he put pressure on his wounded leg. Myrcle looked around and saw the damp walls of a cave. A few small streams trickled down the sides, and a long corridor led further into the cold. Corvin smiled and laughed. "Ah, the medicine took quickly." Myrcle looked at the man with astonishment. "Let's get going. The Blood Mother wants to see you."

Myrcle walked with ease, despite having suffered a stab wound, through a long cave corridor. Dripping water echoed as they walked;

few torches lit their way. The cold air blew past his face, and Myrcle felt another shiver pass through him. He tried to move his hands through the bonds but could not break free. He thought of casting a spell but could not even get a small spark of flame to follow from the torches to his bonds or conjure a flame in his hands. "I wouldn't try to cast any spells, my friend," Corvin turned back to him and continued to walk backwards. Myrcle could feel him smile beneath the cloth over his face.

After about five minutes, they made it to an opening into a grand stone chamber, at least sixty feet across, filled with a mass of hooded figures. Chandeliers of torches mounted on the ceiling and walls gave light to the grand chamber. A foul smell, like that of decay, flooded Myrcle's nose. The man guided Myrcle through the silent crowd of the Children of the Crimson Moon. From the small amounts of skin revealed on their faces, Myrcle could see Drakemen, Hawkinas, Kalishtani, Elves, Humans, and even some of his people, Firbolgs. Every race was present in this cavern and in this insane cult.

At the head of the chamber, looming in front of a steaming pool, six tall figures clad in solid but fringed maroon robes stood above them. Their flesh clung to their bones, what little was left, gray, brown, and rotting. Eyeless sockets peered back at the congregation as they held their cold, dead hands high, dripping water onto the stone below, receiving the prayers and calls of the Children of the Crimson Moon. Unhinged, loose jaws slacked away as they murmured their own prayers into the realm of their patron.

Something caught his attention. Seven large poles stood near a pool of liquid that he could not see well enough to identify. As the crowd broke and they got closer to the poles, Myrcle could see Esvele's horns. He made grunts, trying to call out to her but could not form the words. Each of his companions slowly came into view. All of them were chained with their hands above their heads to the large poles, suspended in the air, hanging from their arms.

The man took him to a pole, locked strong iron chains around his rope bonds, and motioned with his head to the other Children behind Myrcle. They hoisted him up the pole. He could feel the gravity pulling him back to the ground, and he could now see the pool of liquid for what it was, blood. The smell of thick, hot, boiling blood filled his nose, and he tried to keep from breathing in the stench of death.

Organa came to and moved wildly as fear took her. The stench of the lake of blood filled her nose and caused her to gag. She moved her head back and forth as if moving would make the smell go away, but it was all for naught. Organa saw Esvele to her left, strung up just like her. She attempted to call out, but the gag in her mouth made it muted and unintelligible. She saw Myrcle on the other end, her eyes meeting his, with Florie in between them.

Velkin, who was on the other side of Esvele, was the next to wake from her sleep. She struggled for a few moments, trying to break free of her bonds, and saw the hundreds of cultists in the chamber gathered around her and her friends before the crimson lake.

Esvele woke after her and did the same as Velkin, attempting to break from her bonds. She saw Florie, just then waking up and already struggling, trying to unfurl her wings, but bindings around her chest restrained holding them back. She tried to cast a spell in her hands, but the magic did not reach this hell.

The sound of drums echoed through the cave. A small boom far away that then grew with a mighty crescendo into a roaring and pompous thunder that surrounded every space of the chamber. The Children of the Crimson Moon recited burning words in a language that only Esvele knew, Flame Speech, the language of the Flame Lands.

"Our mother, who comes in blood, delivers us into your presence. Come

to us, your Children."

An endless booming of drums echoed around them, yet there was a silence with them—the silence of death and nothingness that filled the chamber. The drums grew in intensity, and their booming was never-ending. Eventually, a voice emerged from the crowd. A female's song took flight in the chamber, singing different words.

"Sweet Mother of Vengeance, come to your Children. Guide us with your bloodlust. Show us the way into your embrace."

Eventually, more songs from around the chamber came from multiple voices, singing in unison. The companions continued trying to break free of their bonds. Within moments of the song truly taking flight, many voices becoming one, the crimson lake boiled as the Crimson Priest sent his incantation into the pool below.

A great chain of black iron shot from the pool of blood into the ceiling, penetrating the rock and taking hold of the material plane. Another erupted from the crimson lake and took hold in the chamber. Another, and another, until seven chains had grasped the realm in which the Children of the Crimson Moon had prepared. Though they were not part of a mechanical system of pulleys and other machinery, they penetrated further into the rock, moving like the chains of a drawbridge and raising something from the lake. Then, the song changed. Esvele heard unfamiliar words of dark and twisted vengeance.

"Mother of Vengeance, come to us, *your Children for their souls are prepared for you!"*

They sang repeatedly and loudly. Esvele moved on her pole, trying to break free again, but could not. She twisted her fingers, but once again, magic did not flow this deep unless of a dark nature conjured it. The chanting went on and on as fear grew in the companions' hearts and minds.

The chains that were digging up into the earth of Lorial suddenly slowed, and a small black shape emerged from the boiling blood. A large metal platform with runes of red glowing liquid carved into its foundations rose. Long, deadly spikes along the edges barely missed the outskirts of the pit where the pool boiled. A single empty throne in the center of the platform became clear, with more runes of death and decay inscribed upon it. The platform was now fully brought into their world and hung suspended over the crimson lake. Darkness crept into the room as the torches each died out and the song did the same. She was here.

A flash of red, white, and black flames erupted in front of the throne on the platform, filling the room with radiant yet dark light. A wave of heat washed over the companions as the flames appeared and a figure emerged. She was tall, perhaps seven feet, and the crown upon her head was not of metal or craftsmanship of mortal hands, but something like bronze or brass wrapped in shifting shadows. The flashing crown overtook the light throughout the entire chamber. Rising up and bending back toward the lake, six horns curled inward and were a deep shade of red at the top, but black as a starless night the closer they got to her raven hair. Two more rested above her brow, curling inward, forming a spiral. Her eyes were shiny silver, like a polished sword, and dark shadows flowed from under her eyelids.

Sharp teeth that met perfectly revealed themselves as a foul grimace came across her face. Her lips dripped blood onto the platform. Trails of blood flowed down her chin and neck. Wrapped around her neck was a large blood diamond that pulsed with dark energy. From where her shoulders and neck met, a black collar rose, adorned with more chains and dark runes carved into a material resembling leather but crafted from human skin. A pulsing rune rested upon her chest, the symbol of her Children, the Crest of Vengeance. It was a shadowglass medallion with a skull carved into it; the eyes were made of blood diamonds.

Seven blades were carved around the skull, each holding another diamond in the hilt. The woman had long chains where the sleeves of her dress would have been, and they coiled around her arms like serpents, dangling a few inches below her fingertips and completing themselves with metal points. The right arm's chain led to a hook covered in smaller thorns, while the left led to a blade with more runes carved into its metal. Four large spines had talons on the end that could impale a man with ease emerged from her back, curling in like the legs of a spider.

She walked forward toward the edge of the platform, and her children fell to their feet and worshiped their goddess. She smiled to reveal fangs for teeth, and her eyes washed over the cave's chamber with rage burning in them. The unending fire that was ever-present in her eyes grew, and she laughed. Her laughter was like that of a siren, beautiful in every way and song-like in their ears, yet there was death within her voice, a dark brooding evil behind the seductive call.

The Crimson Priest retreated from his goddess but held his hands to keep her visage intact. "Blood Mother, we have brought those whom you wished summoned," said the man from the chamber where Myrcle had been held.

"My child, you have done well. Has your bloodlust remained strong?"

"Yes, *Mother*, I have done deeds in your name and read the Rite of Vengeance to those who your Web of Fate destined me to free."

"Most wonderful," the foul woman smiled. She looked around the chamber to the other Children, "Blessed is our vengeance—true and beyond measure."

Her children responded in her dark language, "Blessed be your will, our Mother of Truth. Seeker of Balance. Your children await your sermon."

"I have gazed into the Web of Fate, my children, and I have seen the design of the Great Dawn," she said in the common tongue. "Those who have rites to perform, leave from this place and spread our Gift to those who fate has destined. Those without Rites shall follow your Crimson Priest to the ends of time, for the Great Cleansing is nigh. The Second Cataclysm is nigh!"

Around a hundred children rose to their feet and spoke to their Mother, "We shall spread the Gift of Freedom, and all who fate has destined shall see. We will free them from their prison." And they bowed to their goddess, leaving the chamber, yet still at least a hundred more remained.

"Arise my Children and hear my sermon," the Blood Mother spoke, "I have seen the fate that will come to us all, mortals and gods, and we shall await the moment when we can give the Gift of Freedom to who the Greater Gods decree."

"Hail to the Shadow Monarch, the Formless One, the Dark One, the Shade of Perfection, who blesses us with its Gift! Hail Arratir, the Creator, The One, They Who Walks upon the Dawn, who breathes life into us! Hail the Pantheon of Dawn, who guard the Shining One's creation! Hail the Blood Mother, the Mother of Fate, who brings balance to the worlds!" the Children said in unison. Repeating their phrase three times until the Blood Mother raised her hands, and then they ceased.

"The Web of Fate has revealed to me its instruments in the coming times." The Blood Mother stretched out her wretched arms toward the companions upon the poles. "They are the Shadow's instruments who shall bring the Final Form of Creation. They will aid it in its conquest of this world and shall prepare a place for its disciples in the Void. You shall be the Fist and the Blades of Shadows, my children, revealing the Gift of Freedom to all who have strayed from the Final

Form of Creation." A roar of shouts of glee and joy filled the chamber but was short-lived as the Blood Mother raised her hands to calm them. "Orcus," she commanded, "take them down and remove their bonds; they are not enemies of ours." With the help of the other Children, he released the ropes holding them up against the poles, and lowered them to the cold floor. They took the companions' hands from the hooks and cut the bindings with blades that were strapped to their waists. The gags were removed, and they stood in horror and shock for a moment. Trying to come to terms with everything they observed. They simply stood there, and the children awaited a word or sign from them. The Blood Mother awaited them as well, and a rumble in the ground near them sounded as the pool boiled again as black steps arose from within the pit for them to approach her.

Myrcle spoke first, but Esvele interjected, "Greetings, Mother of Vengeance." Her companion she silenced gave her a confused look and began to speak again, but she held up a hand to stop him. *What are you doing?* Myrcle's voice entered her head. *Trust me*, she thought and approached the Blood Mother. "I am Esvele, of the Silver Fountain. These are my friends, Myrcle, Florie, Organa-"

The Blood Mother interrupted, "And Velkin. I know who you are. You who hold the blade at the throat of destined death." The goddess gave the paladin a sinister look. She broke her gaze from the noble knight to the others. "I am the Mother of Fate, the Mother of Vengeance."

"What is it that you want with us?" Myrcle asked.

"What we all desire. Freedom. From this doomed, false existence. And you will be our champions."

"Champions of what?"

The Blood Mother nodded her head. She raised her voice. "Return to your duties my Children, I must speak with my champions alone."

Her Children left through the many tunnels that centered on the room.

"Come closer, my children."

"I think I am good where I am," Esvele reassured her. The Blood Mother laughed her siren laugh and motioned at the ground. The rocks moved like the waves of the sea and brought them to her platform upon an ocean of rock and stone, landing stably. "Okay then," Esvele blinked.

"Few can say no to a goddess," the Blood Mother smiled as she sat on her throne.

"You called us champions. What do you mean?" Organa asked as Myrcle was getting ready to pose the same question.

"Exactly what the name implies, dears. You will be my hands and exert my will. Champions of Perfection. A form that none can detest. The true form from which this universe was derived." The Blood Mother turned back to her dark throne. "We serve the Light and the Dark. Giving our gift of freedom to those whose fate is written, but you, all of you, have no such thread in my web. I have searched each strand and found nothing. Your fates are unwritten."

"If our fates are unwritten, then our own chaos should disgust you," Organa suggested.

"I can never hate any life," the Blood Mother sighed. "All life is sacred, but it must come to an end. Eventually, yours shall too. May it be tomorrow, three seconds from now, or in Eternity's War."

"The what?" Myrcle squinted.

"The Last War and the First War. When the forces the Dawn and Void clash in one final battle against each other. One will triumph and bring about the perfect order, or neither shall. This is written on the Web of Fate. Comprised within eleven strands of destiny and woven in my grand tapestry of time itself. I have seen the end of all things, and at its center lies you and the one you betrayed."

Esvele began to walk forward, taking a deep breath as she pulled her hand back, but the steady arm of Myrcle held her back as he approached the lesser goddess. "We didn't betray him."

"He doesn't see it that way," she said from her seat of power. "For four hundred years, he's re-lived that moment. When the golden chains burned, his corrupted form was revealed. When the darkness of his prison overtook him, his eyes just opened as he saw your faces when the eternal shackles clasped his wrists and bound him in an endless cycle of torment." Organa turned away from the mother as she spoke. "You cannot run from him. There is no place on this earth where he will not find you."

"He's locked away," Florie stepped forward.

"For now," she corrected. "The Cult of Blighted Souls seeks the return of their savior. But he would see this world burn to get his revenge. I've heard his calls from his prison. His cries for release, his hatred flowing through him as his own blood does with rage and fire to consume it all. "This cannot be. So I task you with this: prevent the arrival of his Sepulcher, banish him to the outer reaches of the Deep, and safeguard the well-being of this universe."

"You spread death," Esvele interjected. "Why would you want to 'safeguard' anything?"

"Because there is a balance to be held in check, Daughter."

"I am not your daughter," Esvele's eyes sharpened.

"You are of the Flame Lands, born of the Infernal Lords' blood; you are mine by right."

"What balance?" Myrcle cut between them.

"There is the Balance of Chaos you know for your tainted magic. But there is another far older and far more delicate. The Balance of Chaos in the universe. Dawn and Void, Deep and Sky—only one can be on top for so long before the scales begin to tip in one direction. Too much, and all of creation can be undone with the simple lighting of a flame."

"But the Dawn has prevailed since the Cataclysm."

The Blood Mother chuckled, "If you think that the Darkness didn't win when Dremica fell, you've been lying to yourself for quite a while." Myrcle looked back to Esvele and then to Velkin, who instantly looked away.

"You said we were to be your champions, so why not one of your own 'Children'?" Organa asked.

"Because they are not and cannot be Magiqas." They each looked at one another with confusion, but the Blood Mother continued, "I am a goddess. I know much that many cannot see, and I have seen more than I wish."

"Don't you need us to do something?" Velkin asked. "Prove ourselves first."

"We have not the time for simple matters. A darkness is coming, and we must stop it."

"Why? Why are you helping us?"

"Ugh," the Blood Mother sighed, "My dear, I am a Lesser God. I help contribute to the Balance of Chaos, keeping the flow of life and death constant and in check. This darkness is destroying the balance, and I must correct it." She stood from her throne, and the tips of the four spines on her back glowed, and with a shot of purple light, a great web of silks made of time formed between the two great columns of the room. They all watched as the web moved and shifted into clear pictures of the heavens above them.

Stars died in an instant of vast glowing radiance and then collapsed into nothingness. The inescapable maw of the Void ripped apart worlds and galaxies alike, crushing them in the force of darkness there. In that darkness, a figure, veiled in shadows and black smoke, stood at the top of a grand spire, watching as the universe died with outstretched hands, exuding a terrible ruin of immolation that devoured everything in red and white flames. The companions watched in horror, and expressions of disbelief crossed each of their faces. Organa felt tears in her eyes. As some worlds fell into that dark maw, she could hear the screams of men, women, and children being devoured by that darkness. "This is what I have seen, and I believe you can help avert it."

"How can we stop him? He is the Shadowlight." Esvele asked. "What chance do we have?"

"You mortals never pay enough attention," she laughed. "The name 'Shadowlight' is not just shadow, is it? A child born of darkness and *light*. The prophecy from many years ago assumed darkness as it came first in the name, but where darkness, there is also light. He has a choice, and he will make it one day. Because Fate wills it so. He can turn from the shadow and walk the line between light and dark to bring about the new era."

"He's not a god," Organa said.

"Not yet." She held up a finger. "But he could be."

"Then how will we stop him?"

"I do not know. There are only a few things that anyone can do to stifle the power growing within him. His rage is his fuel. If he is unleashed upon Lorial, he will burn it all. Using the negative energies of death to tear apart reality and bring forth the legions of the Void. The second Cataclysm will begin."

"People die every day, so why hasn't the Void broken through yet?"

"A concentration of such energy must be on a vast scale to allow the death to seep into the fabric of the universe. Only then can one tear open the schisms and create a bridge for a brief moment. But this will leave the caster vulnerable, as it takes an extraordinary amount of power to open these ley-lines."

"If," Myrcle looked up at her, "We are able to stop him from being freed, we first need a way into Valistar."

"Florie here should be able to help you with such things as she mentioned before," the Blood Mother nodded at the Hawkina.

"Can you not send us there yourself?" asked Velkin.

"Not at this time. Something is blocking my power there. I cannot even contact the chapter of my Children in the city. You will need help. Seek them out when you arrive; they will have ways into the Citadel and into the Xurinal."

"Do you really think we have a chance?" Esvele asked.

"What have I been saying for the last ten minutes?" she laughed. "Kneel, champions, and receive my blessing. Though it is the blessing of a lesser power, it will aid you on your journey, be it in the city or beyond." They each bowed their heads slowly, thinking it through, with Esvele questioning for the longest but agreeing. One by one, the Blood Mother walked to them and kissed them. The taste of thick blood filled their mouths as the Blood Mother bestowed her blessing upon them and Organa, who was still asleep. "Corvin, take them to the surface and help them in this venture of theirs. We will meet again, children. May my blessing be of great use and help in this quest to save all." With the surrounding heat of the flames, they arrived back in their rooms at the Merry Night Inn.

* * *

Morning came not too long after their arrival back in their room, and Myrcle was the first to wake.

Nightmare or real? he asked himself.

He looked around the room for anything that could give him a clear tell of reality or whether he needed to lay off the intoxicating drinks. Esvele and Velkin were all asleep in their beds, and Florie

235

was up in the rafters, lying on one of the beams. Each of them was wearing the clothing that they originally had and not like what was worn in that dream or potential reality. He sat up and placed a hand upon his head, feeling a slight pain when he held it there and jerked his hand back to see what was wrong; what he saw struck him with fear. A symbol had been carved into his hand at least a few days ago, as the scarring was semi-healed and had formed a layer of skin over the wound. A great circle with three inner circles covered in runes and symbols he did not recognize. In the center was a skull, just like the one in the nightmare he had, though now he questioned his conclusion. The runes carved into his hand were articulate and clear, even though he did not know the language, and he was in a state of fear. His curious mind found them stunningly accurate and beautiful.

A creak of wood outside the room caught his attention, then another, and another, slowly getting closer. Myrcle stood from the bed, walked over to Esvele, and shook her shoulders to wake her. She made a grunting noise as she rolled onto her shoulder and over her hand, then jumped in pain as she shot up from the bed and held out her hand to see the painful spot. The same symbol and runes were carved into her hand as well, with a different rune above the skull. But Myrcle had no time to examine it completely as she stood.

Another *creak* sounded near the door this time. Myrcle now made his way toward Velkin, where he shook her like Esvele, who was now poking at Florie on the rafters to wake her. The Hawkina fell from the rafter and caught it with her foot on the wooden beam she had slept on. She looked at her black and silver feathered hand that stung with pain.

"What the hell-" she began, but Esvele shushed her.

Florie saw Velkin already up and making her way toward Organa, who was still sound asleep. Velkin had her holy blade drawn and ready to strike as the doorknob of their room jiggled. She felt a stinging sensation in her left hand but did not bother to look at the source. The paladin removed her hand from the blade and reached for Organa as a *click* echoed in the room and the door was unlocked. The doorknob twisted, and the click of the door opening and the creaking of its swaying motion woke Organa, who felt a jolt of pain in her right hand, which she held to see what was causing it. She found a symbol carved into her hand as the door swung open, revealing a tall blue Drakemen in its frame. Organa raised her hand and enveloped him in a winter wind, surrounding him from his waist down in a cold column of ice.

The man sighed and spoke, "Good morning to you all as well." His voice was a very smooth baritone, and his crystal blue eyes shone lightly as he walked forward into the room. Velkin went to strike, holding her blade in a way that would remove his head, but he held up his hands and shouted, "Wait, wait, wait!"

The paladin stopped just before his arms and growled, "Who are you?"

"My name is Talos."

"And what do you want, 'Talos'?" Esvele sneered.

"I was sent to retrieve you for the King of Thieves."

Velkin lowered her blade, and the companions got a good look at their guest. He was the same sentry at the gate the night they arrived. His attire and weaponry were the same except for the green shirt he now wore with his red coat. Light blue scales on his body brought out the colors of his clothes and showed a very weird amount of contrast to the scheme. A hand stretched forward to shake Velkin's, who did not receive it.

"Look, I know you do not know me, but I was sent by the King of Thieves, honestly."

"Oh, shut it, Talos," Florie called out from the rafters.

"Necros? Is that you?" the Drakemen said with wonder and excitement.

Florie descended from her perch and landed in front of her friends. "You and I both know neither of us works for him anymore. So come off it and spill."

"It's been so long! How are you, buddy?" Talos smiled as he recognized the rogue.

"You two know each other," Myrcle asked.

Florie sighed and turned to him. "Yes. We worked a few contracts together for the King."

"'A few?' We did almost every contract we got together. My brawn and her mind worked like bread and butter—we were flawless," Talos explained.

"Shut it, please," Florie turned back to him. "Spill it now."

"I don't exactly work with him anymore. I can't believe I didn't recognize you the other night. Must've been the dark."

"Must've," she replied, annoyed.

"I made a deal with the King of Thieves after you left the Silver Hand. I said I would owe him one last contract if he allowed me to leave the Silver Hand, as you did."

"And he wants to see us? That's the contract?"

"No, the contract is much worse. I told him about you all entering the city a few weeks ago."

"Wait, wait, wait, wait," Myrcle interrupted, "'A few weeks?'"

"Yeah, you all have been making quite the ruckus. A few bar fights. there was a murder in the outskirts of town that people think that one did," he said, pointing to Esvele. "The King of Thieves almost recruited her the other night via Jorman a few days ago while she was in the market, but Jorman never came back so we assumed it didn't go well. The Black Riders arrived and started looking for you all. I had to move you from place to place all through the city as the barkeeps ratted you out to their leading bitch."

The companions looked around at each other with completely confused expressions, mixed with massive amounts of worry. "Any of you remember any of what he's talking about?" Esvele asked. Each of them shook their head. "Shit."

The Undercroft

They all stood there for a moment as Myrcle tried to sift through their memories, channeling a spell through their minds as he placed his hands on their temples. He went around to each of them, and every time the memory stopped after the flames of the Blood Mother surrounded them and they landed here in their room. Their guest tried to ask questions, but Esvele shushed him each time without fail.

"Your memories are all intact." Myrcle twitched as he ran through Florie's mind. "There's no trace of Night Threads or any psychic imprints." Myrcle opened his eyes and let go of Florie, rising to his feet. "I have no bleeding idea," he said through staggered breaths.

"How do you all not remember any of this?" Talos asked.

"I have no idea," Myrcle replied worriedly, and began pacing the room. He stayed silent for a while as he walked from one end of the room to the other. Millions of theories ran through his head as he thought of every possibility. He knew that memories could be scrambled or affected. It was not magical, as magic leaves traces, which is why the Black Riders found them here in Itheca. It could not have been by a Mind Feeder because they only lived in the depths of the deepest caves of Lorial or a Memory Worm as they both have been extinct since the Cataclysm due to their primary home being the forest of Dremica. Every likely scenario filled his head, but he could not reason how this had happened. Then it hit him: the symbol. He looked at his hand and then walked to Esvele. "What does this say? You speak Flame Tongue, do you not?"

"Yeah, give me a second." She took his hand in hers, examined the runes closely, and tried to make out the text. It took her a few seconds, but she began to read aloud. *"Upon this being, a task has been set by the Goddess of Vengeance. Their life shall be charged with its completion, and until such a moment, they will be under her watchful eye. Go forth, Sage."* She pointed to the more defined title above the skull. "These are Title Runes, placements of stature used in Flame Tongue to discern the elite from the weak." She took out her hand and read her own, *"The Summoner."*

Then went to each of the others, Florie's reading, *"The Hidden One."*

Velkin's, *"The Sharpened Blade."*

Organa's reading, *"The Light."*

"Myrcle is a sorcerer and thus is *'The Sage',*" Esvele began. "Florie you are a thief and rogue, so you are 'The Hidden One', Velkin, yours is weird, *'The Sharpened Blade',* means two things: either a great warrior or a shadow that follows. Both are true, as you are truly a masterful swordswoman, and the shadow that follows you turned from its ways before we came along. I am *'The Summoner'* because, let's be honest, I am quite the bitch and stubborn and my magic is clearly superior." And Organa, you're *'The Light'* because it's true. You bring joy and life wherever you go. These are the roles we are to play. As for what task we're a part of, I have no clue."

"You're supposed to be a part of the contract with me," Talos said, raising his hand, "which we best get goin' on, as the bartender caught wind of who you all were and sent others for the Black Riders about five minutes ago. Cloak yourselves and go out the window. I'll meet you in the alley below."

"Wait," Esvele caught them all as they packed swiftly. "How can we trust you?"

"I saved your asses at least twice now. You owe me. What that is exactly, I do not know as of yet. Nevertheless, you are just going to have to if you want to leave this tavern without chains."

They both looked at each other for a moment, and then she resumed packing as he left the room and went down the stairs to distract the owner of the tavern. After they had packed, Florie slowly opened the window and looked around. Dawn was just a few moments away, and the cold air brushed her cheek. No one was out walking around except three guards on the street next to the alleyway they were aiming for. She held up her hand as a signal to stop and wait, and after a few moments she slipped out the window, down a length of rope, and into the dark alley. One at a time, the others followed her, and, eventually and surprisingly, they made it out of the tavern without a sound. A stack of barrels nearby served as cover from the street as they waited for Talos. About ten minutes passed as they waited anxiously. The sunlight of the Dawn was now peeking over the Gods Way and into the town. Rays of light hit the top of the walls of the tavern, and they waited for another ten minutes for their guide.

"We need to leave now, Myrcle," Esvele whispered to him.

"Just a little longer."

"We can't trust him."

"We can," Florie corrected her. "When Talos accepts a contract, he'll die before he fails."

As she finished, who should appear around the wall of barrels but Talos, and he looked at his old friend. "This bunch must have buttered you up a lot 'cause you never would have said that when we were in the Silver Hand."

"Shut it," Florie slapped his arm.

"Come on, you all, we need to get to the Undercroft."

They followed him down the back alleyway and toward the street. Talos peeked his head out first and then walked out onto the road. He looked closely with his thief's eyes before motioning for the others to cross over to the next alley. They darted across and traced his steps through the maze of buildings. A Black Rider was commanding a group of guards to search the tavern in which they were sleeping. He trotted along with his horse, but they slipped past him. Talos led them through the labyrinth to a stone building on the far side of Itheca. It was well kept, and its walls looked like they had just been redone. The room was consumed by the smells of food and pipeweed, with a hint of fresh paint lingering under it all. Laughter, cheers, and songs followed behind the scents within, even though it was barely midday. A sign dangled out front with a mug topped with brown bubbles of ale and a goblet with a red waterfall of wine down its sides leading to a plate of food, The Undercroft.

Talos opened the door and let them enter first. At least thirty tables stood around the main floor and two separate bars with some people of the town sitting near them on tall stools, either waiting for drinks or quenching their thirst. The entire building was made of thick and sturdy wood and was decorated with fine silver on both sides of the main floor. One side had a golden crown painted above the bar, and the other, a skull with ruby eyes, the same as the Children of the Crimson Moon crest. Suddenly, a foul odor of unclean people, beer, and some other unrecognizable scent filled the companions' noses. A large staircase ascended to the second and third levels of the tavern. Some of the patrons' laughter filled the hall, and others were arguing so loudly it almost overtook the others.

"What is this place?" Myrcle asked.

"Can you not read?" Talos replied with a laugh. "This is the Undercroft. Where the King of Thieves controls Itheca."

"And why is it split? What are the two signatures for?" Esvele asked over the roaring commotion.

"The right is for the King of Thieves, and the left is for the Children," Florie answered before Talos could.

"The Children drink?" Organa raised an eyebrow.

"No, but their contractors do."

"What a charming location," Myrcle smiled with unease.

"Come on, let me buy you all a drink before we head into the Undercroft."

"This is the Undercroft," Esvele rolled her eyes. "The sign outside said as much if you read it."

"We're thieves," Talos said, smiling at her cheekily, "not idiots."

"I doubt that," she smiled back the same.

Talos led them to a table and then went toward the bar with the painted crown. He ordered them ales and then made his way back toward the table with a tray, placing them in front of his guests. He went back and returned with food for them as well.

"You paid for this, right?" Esvele sneered.

"Someone did," Talos grinned back. "We're thieves."

"You don't look like the stealthiest thief," Myrcle pointed out, eyeing his weapons and slightly larger build.

"A thief is only as good as his tools. Stealth is good, yes, but kicking ass, taking shit works just as well. I normally get sent on collections, people who owe something to the King."

"He still does that?" Velkin asked.

"I know you from somewhere, don't I?"

"Fort Belidon," Velkin said as she palmed her forehead.

"You were there! Man, I was just starting my career back then." Florie gave a giddy smile. "You were good with that sword, I remember," she recalled.

"I knew I recognized you back in the room, just couldn't place it. Wow, the Velkin the Golden herself." Talos shook his head in disbelief.

"Anyone want to fill us in?" Organa asked.

Velkin's demeanor changed as she sat up tall and retold the tale. She and the King of Thieves once led a small team of nine to Fort Belidon, a grand armory for the Menitheal Dynasty. Their team comprised the King, Velkin, Talos, Florie, and five other skilled mountebanks. Together, they pulled off the greatest and most dangerous heist in history. They stole seventy-two thousand gold worth of weapons, armor, and secrets—all sold to the highest bidder. While they were smuggling out the last of the weapons, a guard found a body, and a fight broke out. The king and the others left on the ship while Velkin held them off.

Florie recounted seeing Velkin use her blade to cut down at least thirty men before a white flash of light burst from the mouth of the cave and they never saw her again. Until Talos had caught wind of a Golden Queen rising in the west again. It rather outraged the King of Thieves that someone would challenge him, so he sent Talos to retrieve them for the King so that he might make an example of a false king. When Talos had finally tracked down the convoy in the Deadlands near the western coast, he spent the last few weeks ravaging the locals of the desert, headed to the Golden Queen's current camp, and was caught by some guards around the convoy and taken prisoner. He traveled with them for three weeks on foot across the Deadlands and then met up with another convoy in Desert Guard, the furthest west civilized city of Rethial. After that, they traveled as one huge convoy, at least thirty wagons of stolen goods, from Desert Guard to Rento, and rested for a few days. By "resting," Talos meant heavy interrogation. From there, they traveled across the plains to Crais and then to River's Edge. After around three months of walking and little sleep, Talos explained that he'd almost gone mad and nearly died once or twice before they brought him before the Golden Queen.

He and the others were astonished when they met her at Mount Doloroth. They couldn't believe it at first, but there was no mistaking her height or the way she wielded a blade. She then explained that after the debacle she had fed him and nursed him back to health over the next two years. He did some work for her as well. They then rode together to Turnmot and over Leviathan's Crossing and down to Itheca, where she met her old friend, the King of Thieves.

"What's this king's name anyway?" Organa asked rather loudly, catching the attention of some people around them.

Talos grabbed her so fast she could have sworn he cut the air. The others at the table drew their weapons. "Never ask that again."

"Put her down or I swear I will remove your organs in alphabetical order," Esvele threatened with a spark lighting in her eyes, as well as her fingers.

"Which alphabet?" he winked at her. Talos then let go of the black collar of Organa's clothes, and they resumed tolerating each other's company once more.

After a few silent seconds, Velkin continued the story. The King of Thieves was very surprised to see Talos alive since the other spies and assassins he sent all came back as heads in boxes. Velkin's companions looked at her with disbelief, slight confusion, and a dash of horror.

She looked back at them and shrugged her shoulders. "Look, I had a reputation to keep." Another few silent seconds passed, and she went on again, concluding her story.

After they had met with the King of Thieves, who had sworn to execute the Golden Queen a very long time ago, Velkin made a bargain. If she paid him ten percent of her profits, she could continue as the Golden Queen and help keep the western part of Rethial in line. After a fairly heated debate, she whittled the King down to seven percent, and the next morning she and her guard left for Mount Doloroth. Just a few days later, Organa and the rest showed up.

"Well, that was quite the story," Florie began.

"No, no, no, no, no," Velkin smiled, "I forgot about you."

"Can we not?" Florie begged.

"Someone decided, 'Hey, let's steal from the second most powerful part of the Conclave of Daggers. Sounds like a great idea!' She followed us for about an hour, and as we reached the city gates, she attempted to rob us blind. As you know, she failed and was placed in my custody."

"You got caught." Talos was very surprised. "Impossible!"

"Clearly not," Velkin laughed into her mug of ale.

"Listen, I almost had you, but that stupid goblin shithead Witherspoon caught me right as I flew down and shot me out of the sky," Florie defended herself.

"Hang on! Did you say, Witherspoon?" Organa asked.

"Yeah, he's a tricksy little Goblin bastard!"

"We met him in the Forest of Bravica."

"So that's where he ran off to," Velkin said, shaking her head.

"I kind of liked him," Organa said with a shrug.

"He's a piece of dragon shit." Florie rolled her eyes.

Esvele nearly fell back, leaning on her seat so hard. "Thank you! Someone gets it!"

The group laughed for a moment, and then Organa remembered something. "You said you opened a Wishing Chest once. What was in yours?"

Silence crept over the table, and Esvele did not answer for quite some time. Organa began a new conversation with Talos about the King of Thieves, but Esvele interjected solemnly, "Hope."

"'Hope'?" Organa asked.

"I met Witherspoon a long time ago, in the days of Dremica. The first and last time I saw him until the day before Mount Doloroth," Esvele explained. It reminded Organa once again of that night, and she said a prayer in her mind, thinking of Brok. "I was on my way to the Silver Fountain, just after being named a master. I was on the main road there, getting ready to enter the forest, when I heard a cry for help nearby. My horse took me there with great haste, and I came upon a small cottage, no bigger than a few of my own horses put together. A few humans were terrorizing a family of Goblins, Witherspoon's family. I rushed to their aid and sent the criminals through a portal to a nearby town. Witherspoon offered me a chest for free. He wasn't as mad as he is now; he still had some sense in him, at least. I opened my chest and found a scroll. I took it and read it—a prophecy."

"What kind?" Myrcle inquired.

"The Symphony of Light," she said with a small smile, and then continued, "the coming of the New Dawn. That one day the Destined Flame would devour the world of the heavens and the Great Beacon. All life would end in an instant, and darkness would have won. But from that very darkness, a light shall spring from the shadows."

"That doesn't sound too bad." Florie smiled at her and held out a hand across the table, taking a few of Esvele's fingers in her own, which, to everyone's surprise, Esvele allowed.

"Not at all," EV said with slight pain, "but I thought about that, that one day this would all be gone. When the Cataclysm came, I was sure it was what was foretold." Esvele stopped and sat in silence for a moment. Myrcle took her other hand as well, and Organa moved behind her, ready to help her through that moment of sad memories. "And yet here we are," she cried lightly as a few tears escaped her eyes, "alive, well, and nearly insane." Esvele took a huge drink and set her mug down on the table. Organa wrapped her arms around her neck and squeezed. Myrcle and Florie grasped her hands to help her.

"All right, no more depressing things. Let's get down to business." Esvele sat up and took another drink.

The others found their seats again and talked for a few moments about everything except business. Finally, after they had finished a few more drinks and were well on their way to being considered drunk, a server removed the last of their mugs and Talos stood and walked to the person at the bar. They spoke for a few brief moments. Then the companions saw him point with his thumb over his shoulder at their table. The bartender nodded and reached below the countertop, handing a bronze key to Talos.

He walked over to the table and bent over it, looking at his new companions. "All right, time to meet the King of Thieves."

The Conclave of Daggers

The group stood from their table and followed Talos down the middle of the Undercroft tavern. They kept close to him and walked down a staircase that they didn't see before due to the density of people in the room. After descending for a few minutes, they eventually reached the lowest basement floor after passing at least six others. Each floor was barred by an iron gate and had three locks: a key lock, a cryptex of seven letters (sometimes five or six on certain gates), and a final lock that looked like it required some sort of spell to lift an enchantment. Some of those rooms were lit with torches, others with floating orbs of light. One of them even had a tall statue, much taller than the room it stood in, of a woman holding a basin of green, purple, and white fire.

She wore no shoes, and the stone toes of her feet were carved into the base. Its manner was of a woman in a stone gown and long wimple, made of stone like the rest of her, but Velkin could have sworn the stone was moving like white holy cloth stirring in a breeze from the old days of the East. She stopped for a moment and thought to herself, staring at the statue, wishing to return to a vastly simpler time, thinking about what was to come when they reached Valistar, and what could come after.

It will all be over soon, she thought to herself, and she released a sweet breath of relief, but she could feel a terror looming in her mind behind such solace.

A hand reached forward from her right, down toward the stairs, and grasped her forearm. "You all right, V?" Organa asked.

It stunned Velkin for a moment, as she had never heard anyone call her any nickname throughout her long years on Lorial. She simply stared, confused, at the child, her emerald-green eyes gleaming in the torchlight. "Sorry?" she asked.

"Are you all right?"

"No, the other thing—'V'?"

"Oh, sorry, didn't mean to freak you out," she giggled. "Just easier than saying Velkin, but if you don't like it, I'll use your full name."

Velkin paused for a moment and then shook her head and blinked her eyes quickly like waking from a daydream, "Oh, no, no, it's quite all right," she smiled at Organa to reassure her, "Just never had a nickname is all."

"Well, maybe you'll get used to it," she smiled back.

Esvele's voice called to them from farther down the stairs, "You two coming or what?"

"Yeah, we'll be right there," Organa shouted back. She turned to Velkin. "Come on."

"Wait," Velkin pulled Organa back.

"What's wrong?"

"I just wondered, what would you do to have the one you loved back?"

"I'd do whatever it took to get Brok back." Organa's joy subsided.

"What about Kyriel?" Velkin cautiously asked.

"Look, I haven't forgotten that you and the others stole my memories," she began, "and I can't pretend like it doesn't hurt knowing that you all betrayed me. But you, Myrcle, and Esvele are all I have left. I wouldn't trade anything for any of you. Even though you betrayed me."

"How can you say such a thing?"

"Because I choose to. I don't think I'll ever truly forgive myself for what happened at Mount Doloroth that night, but I can live with the fact that I know Brok is in the Dawn Eternal, just waiting with his arms open for me, you, and the others. Forgiveness is a choice we must all make. Even though you and the others took from me what would be considered by many, sacred, you did it to save me. I wouldn't be alive today had it not been for what you all had done, and that is the truth. No matter whether I like it or not or still hold some grudge against any of you, what matters is what is behind all the feelings, that you all did for me was out of love."

"Thank you, Organa." Velkin hugged her. To her amazement, Organa hugged her back, and they shared a tender moment, which was only ruined by Esvele marching back up the stairs.

"We have a job, you know. Let's go."

"Come on," Organa smiled at Velkin, and they walked down the stairs and toward the Conclave of Daggers, all the while Velkin thought of the future to come.

Two large doors of black steel, with bolts lining the rims of the metal, rested on the stone floor of the damp underground. On each of the doors was a carving of a golden crown with ancient runes spelled out around the band. Myrcle tried to decipher them but could not recognize the language. Esvele and Velkin attempted to do the same, also to no avail.

"I wouldn't bother trying to read that, love," Talos said, eyeing Esvele. "It's written in the Sharptongue; only those who work for one of the Conclave of Daggers can read it."

Esvele turned to Myrcle and, with a slight fury in her eyes, asked him, "Did he just call me 'love'?"

"I believe he did, my dear."

The fury that was barely there before in Esvele's eyes became engorged in an instant as she turned from Myrcle. In her fury, the ground rumbled, and the others could feel the quake in the stone. A flurry of soil-covered roots shot through the floor and wrapped around Talos like the arms of an octopus from the depths of the seas and lakes. They coiled around his arms and legs and threw him against the wall, causing it to give, and cracks appeared around the walls, webbing like broken glass. Esvele held out a hand to keep him in place with the roots of the underground and began to walk slowly toward him, mocking him as she walked. "If you ever presume to call me your 'love' again, I will be much less kind."

"Oy, put me down, you devil," he shouted back with a poor choice of words.

"'Devil?'"

"Oh dear," Myrcle backed the others away.

"All right." Esvele walked toward one of the roots and pressed her hand to it. In an instant, the roots became imbued with electrical energy that shot through them and channeled into Talos. A searing pain flowed through his body and caused him to seize violently as Esvele poured her power through her magic, all the while hearing an all-too-familiar melody in her head.

A firm hand gripped her shoulder tightly as someone out of her line of sight attempted to pull back on her, to no avail. Esvele continued to thrust more and more volts into Talos' body through the vines that bound him against the wall. Another hand took her other shoulder with greater strength, and this time she was moved slightly backward, but she resisted enough to maintain her balance and concentration on the Drakemen. Finally, a splintering of wood sounded through the tunnel from Velkin's blade. The electricity flowing through her spell was released in an instant explosion that was absorbed by the paladin's blade.

The blue bolts froze in time and then retreated back into her blade, crackling and flashing as they were pulled into the metal. The runes that were carved along the middle of the blade glowed with a blue radiance and illuminated its fine detail and legibility. Organa tried to read the runes but was distracted by Esvele plummeting to her knees on the cold floor and the loud *thud* of Talos hitting as well. She knelt down beside her old teacher and held her head up, as she was in a loopy state and weak from the power that left her. Myrcle had gone over Talos with his golden palms to try to mend his wounds from the dark magic. The radiance passed over Talos' blue, scaled chest and forehead, passing the light into his body. The burns along his skin were healed and reverted back to healthy flesh, and life flowed through him completely once more until he awoke from his unconsciousness.

He wheezed as he opened his eyes, taking a few moments to cough and catch his breath. "What the fuck did she do that for? Cause I'm not going to lie, it hurt, but it was hot."

Myrcle dropped Talos' head faster than a fiery orb of fire. The back of his head banged against the floor, and Talos gave a grunt. Myrcle smiled uncomfortably at him and walked away quickly.

Velkin was breathing heavily from the tension of the moment and sheathed her blade upon her back as Organa rejuvenated Esvele with healing energy. Esvele continued to mutter, "I'm sorry," repeatedly. She knew she had lost herself to the Dark Song, just for a moment, but, even then, it could have laid the whole city block low.

"You all and your magic need some tuning," Florie said, wide-eyed at the display.

"I agree," another voice spoke from the great door. Each of the companions jumped with anticipation and either readied a spell or a weapon for attack. The red eyes through the slats narrowed, and an unimpressed voice continued, "You really think that weapons and spells are going to get you through this door?"

Velkin sheathed her blade once again. "Sorry, you just startled us."

"That was quite the light show, though. A real interesting moment, especially since there hasn't been a Magiqas born in quite some time," the person behind the slit raised their eyebrow.

It did not surprise the others that someone recognized the effects of the Dark Song, and, truthfully, it had been quite some time since anyone had seen such a display of power. Even though Esvele's was not the grandest compared to some other substantial incidents of such power. Myrcle remembered a tale his father had told him when he had first found out about his son's powers. In Balinor, there was a Guardian of Lorial battling an ancient enemy of shadow, flesh, and bone. To push back the darkness that was invading the south, the Guardian willingly gave in to the Dark Song, allowing the deceptive melody to enthrall him, yet not entirely losing himself. For a brief moment, he could coexist with the Dark Song, letting it fuel him but not overtake him. But so much power being contained at one time within a single being cannot be done. The power surged through him, making him catatonic and razing the city to the ground in a matter of a few brief and blinding moments.

"So, Talos," the voice from behind the door began, "these the ones you were talkin' 'bout?"

Talos coughed for a moment and cleared his throat as he stood to his feet. He gave another grunt, as his body was still sore from the shocking encounter with his new crewmate. "Yeah, this is them."

The red eyes looked around at the others, and someone caught their attention. "Florie Nightingale?"

"Oh sweet gods," Florie grunted back.

"I thought you were dead," the voice shouted through, "It's me, Natalia!"

"Natalia," Florie shouted back in surprise, "I thought you were dead!"

"I guess we're both ghosts then." They laughed, and a dozen clicks and thousands more ticks sounded behind the door. Eventually, the sounds ceased, and the doors opened. An orange glow shone through as the decorated doors opened and a tiny figure emerged from within their boundaries. A grassy, green-skinned young woman stepped forward, a Kalishtani like Esvele. Two purple horns twisted down and outward like those of a ram. On her right horn a specially fashioned golden tip with a small string of green, hazel, and blue gems dangling from it. However, her red eyes drew attention away from her jewelry. The red was not just in the pupil, but the entire eye was like that of a glowing inferno. She wore a jacket that was mainly red with decorations of gold and silver all over it in twisting spirals. She wore a white cloth shirt with leather straps across her chest, abdomen, and waist, each of them equipped with two sheaths holding daggers. From what they could see, each set had different colored metal pommels. The top two were made of pure silver, signifying simple metal blades attached. A burning red metal was forged into the pommel of the daggers located in the sheaths bound to her abdomen. The last two were made of gold and decorated with swirling silver symbols. A black leather belt wrapped around her waist and, once again, two more daggers shimmered in the torchlight encased by leather. The last two pommels were made of a black material—shadowglass, a dark metal that rotted the skin with decay and necrosis. The two blades hung at the sides of the Kalishtani's brown pants, which were tucked into the black leather boots she wore. Three red leather straps met a round buckle on each side of the shoes.

A wide smile and open arms from the four-foot-three Kalishtani filled the doorway. "Bring it here, you little shit!"

Florie eyed her and begrudgingly walked forward with a slightly noticeable fake smile and pushed through the awkwardness of the hug. After they let go of one another, the young girl spoke, "How have you been?"

"It's been going," Florie replied.

"Well, it's good to have you back. Come on in, you all. Welcome to the Conclave of Daggers."

The group followed her into a gigantic room full of torchlight. It was bustling with people. In the center of the room was a massive circle of stone with four thrones upon it, each of them pointing in a cardinal direction. The Northern one was made of white marble, solid and pure, easily the most beautiful and mesmerizing of the seats of power. The West was made of silver, gold, and other metals compiled into its details, making it the grandest of the thrones. The East was a mass creation of what many people referred to as bloodstone or blood iron, with large metal spikes of Blood Iron sticking out from the back of the throne like the spines of a porcupine. The South was created from blue marble and from waves of the ocean that seemed to drown a green-colored metal, painted to look like the bounty of the seas.

Each throne represented a form of contract in the world of thieves. The marble from the North showed respect to the bounties of the Wild Hunt, an order of warriors primarily from Menagerie led by the Prime Alpha. Western contracts were the theft of precious jewels or metals of value, whose allegiances were given to the Golden Queen, giving themselves the title of the Golden Army. From the East were the assassins of common and powerful people alike, which the Crimson Priest held, the mortal leader of the Children of the Crimson Moon. Finally, from the South came the pirates—the scallywags of the sea who raided and pillaged the isles and continents around Lorial. They were the most deplorable and unlawful, as was the way of the Siren's Heralds. If only their leader, the Master of

Seas, would make them behave, there might be less murder in the Old Sea.

On the far side of the great room were at least fifty tables, some of them occupied and some not. However, each of the tables was marked with sigils like the bar upstairs. Some were marked with the same golden crown or ruby-eyed skull, whereas two new symbols appeared. One symbol, a mermaid with a scimitar blade in one hand and a harp in the other, was the crest of the Siren's Heralds. The other was of two spears crossed over one another with a large skull and antlers of a buck with two daggers plunged into the bones of the forehead. Black liquid dripped from the eye sockets and nose of the figure.

The people at these tables held wooden mugs in their hands and food on large plates that sat on the tall and short tables for the varied-sized people in the tavern section. Halflings, Kalishtani, Orcs, Humans, Elves, and all manner of folk were around the place. Laughter had been filling the room, and as the people saw Talos, they cheered for him. But when Florie came out from behind him, the cheering grew drastically. Some who knew her rushed to her side, welcoming her with handshakes and a rare few with hugs. Those who sat at the tables belonging to the Children of the Crimson Moon remained seated and either scoffed at the reunion or eyed them with confusion, as they did not understand the celebration of one's return.

Natalia backed the ones who gathered around them, away from Florie and Talos. Esvele, Organa, and Myrcle walked far behind them, noticing the crowd was finally dispersed.

"I thought the saying was 'no honor among thieves'?" Esvele asked."I thought the saying was 'no honor among thieves'?" Esvele asked.

"Did you see the thrones? Clearly, there is a sense of honor among thieves," Organa smiled with a surprised expression.

"Isn't one of those yours?" Myrcle paused and smiled as he bowed. "Your Grace."

Velkin slapped the top of his head. "Get up," she laughed.

"Forgive me, your majesty, I did not mean to offend you," he said with a smirk.

"You're about to really annoy me if you don't quit that shit right now."

"All right," Myrcle laughed, "all right."

Florie and Talos had walked back to their companions by now. "Enjoy your reunion?" Esvele asked.

"'Reunion'?" Florie scoffed, and her eyes narrowed. "I was waiting for someone to stab me in the chest. I owe them a lot of money."

"So do I," Talos nervously laughed and rubbed the back of his neck.

Natalia was quick to join them. "So, what do you think of the Conclave of Daggers? Is it all you remember?"

"Nothing has really changed," Florie remarked, "just a little brighter, though. Used to be very gloomy."

"Yeah, when I got a hold of it all, I wasn't much for the looming darkness and all that."

"When you 'got a hold' of it?"

"Oh yeah, I guess a lot has changed. I'm the Queen of Thieves!"

A Song of Power

Florie's eyes were as wide as the Element Moons. She continued to glance back and forth between Talos and Natalia. Her old, now-royal friend just stood there with a wide smile and open arms. Florie then walked over to Talos, rejecting Natalia's offer. As she got closer to Talos, she simply stared at him with a dead-eyed glare. A *crack* of a whip sounded loudly through the Conclave as Florie's hand contacted Talos' blue scaly skin. Another crack sounded as Velkin hit him again, the force from Florie's attack having pushed him her way, and a loud thud followed as Esvele struck him harder than either of them in the abdomen, sending him to the ground, gasping for air.

The others looked at Esvele in confusion, and she simply laughed. "Can I do that again? I've wanted to do that since I met him!"

"Behave," Myrcle rolled his eyes and held out his arm to help Talos to his feet.

Florie turned back to Natalia, who was still smiling but had already lowered her arms. "You're the 'Queen of Thieves'?"

"Yeah, for about two weeks so far. Ah, hey, no one has tried to kill me yet," she said with a naive smile. "Well," she paused for a moment and counted on her fingers, "well, no one has tried to assassinate me and made it past the Undercroft. And I think that counts as doing pretty good so far."

"Okay," Velkin began, "it's great you're Queen now, but where is Likan?"

"He's dead," Natalia said simply. "Been dead for a bit now—by that I mean two weeks—and the throne was up for grabs. Complete the tests and you're the new King of Thieves, except I am the first Queen of Thieves, so I get bonus points for ambiance… I think that's the right word; I honestly don't know, but you get the point."

"Okay, why didn't you say anything?" Florie asked Talos with a glare in her eyes.

"Hey, I said I didn't exactly work for him anymore."

"You could have mentioned a shift in leadership," Florie shook her head and then looked back over at Natalia, "No offense, I just meant in general."

"None taken."

"But seriously, why didn't you say anything?"

"Because we don't know just who might be listening."

"Speaking of which," Natalia moved between Florie and Talos, standing level with Florie's shoulders and Talos' lower stomach. "We'd best head to my place."

"You mean your royal chambers?" Velkin laughed at her.

"Oh, they aren't that lavish."

Natalia guided them to her private quarters, past the many tables of patrons, many giving her nods of respect, and down a long hallway to mahogany double doors with silver decorations of swirls and golden crowns for knobs. Where the two doors met was a massive arcane lock made of platinum and a series of runes on rotating spindles that created a passcode when aligned correctly. Natalia stood directly in front of the lock to hide her combination as she cast seven different spells of contrasting types to spin the locks on the door. After a brief moment, the lock clicked, and each spindle levitated. With the final casting of a spell, the locks dissipated into particles of sand and scattered into the air.

Natalia pushed on the golden knobs and opened the grand doors to reveal a vast and radiant golden glow that almost blinded the companions. Torches lined the walls, illuminating the treasures of the room and creating a blinding glare. As their vision returned, mountains of gold, silver, jewels, and precious things of mortal desire that almost completely filled the room came into view. Only a small amount of space was truly available for walking that wasn't covered in her spoils. Among her riches, Myrcle spotted a few tomes that he went to reach for but was caught by EV's hand and a smiling glare. He smiled at her and shrugged, continuing to admire the room's contents. A few chests rested, overflowing with emeralds, sapphires, diamonds, amethysts, and every precious stone imaginable. Natalia led them past a pit in the center of the room where a roaring fire heated the area and couches were carved into the floor, covered with soft pillows and furry animal skins that were unbelievably soft to the touch of Organa's hand as she grasped the pelts. Talos pulled her up out of the pit and kept her walking forward with them until they reached the far end of the room. A large bed with columns of gold-decorated stone rose up above the frame, with fine silks that draped down. A majority were white, but some of them were colored in blues and greens.

A figure moved on the bed's red sheets. "Is that you, my Little Devil?" As he stood and pulled back the drapes, another Kalishtani man of almost the same size as Natalia revealed himself. "And who are these you've dragged into our cesspool?" He wore a long red robe like Natalia's that trailed far behind him on the cold floor. His feet were covered in soft shoes of animal pelts, like those in the pit. Long black hair with blue highlights hung from his head with a small bun at the top that sat neatly between two horns that curved back and upward toward the ceiling. Two golden hazel eyes stared at them as he descended a small flight of stairs, placed his hand on Natalia's shoulder, and gave her a kiss on her lips, which she seemed to be confused by but very open to the affection.

"Ah," Natalia stuttered as her partner pulled away from her, "I forgot you were here, Mal-Mel-…."

"David," he sneered and walked right past her in a huff, but stopped as he sideswiped Esvele. "Well, well, well," he said as he eyed her. "Come find me at the Gaffer's Brothel if you get lonely." He winked at her and walked on, not seeing her look of disgust as he turned away.

"Yeah….sorry. I forgot he was here," Natalia nervously laughed.

"Clearly," Esvele smiled uncomfortably.

Natalia walked over to the bed and took a seat, snapping her fingers as she did, bringing a nice cool breeze into the room, rolling up the drapes of the beds onto the canopy above her, and putting out a few of the torches in the room to regulate its temperature. "So, what brings you to my city?"

"First of all, how did this become your city?" Velkin asked with great confusion.

"I told you, I won the mantle when the last king died."

"Yes, but how did he die?"

"No one knows. He was here one day, and then his body was in the sewers the next. Our apothecaries determined it wasn't by blade, weapon, or poison, nor was it natural causes. It was like he was there, his soul I mean, and then he wasn't. Just gone," she shrugged as she finished.

"Just like that?"

"Just like that," Natalia concluded with a nod of her head.

"Did you bury him? Properly?"

"Of course." Natalia laughed for a moment. "We're not savages, and you still have a seat of power among us, you know, Golden Queen."

She paused for a moment and then struck her palm against her face. "Good gods, I totally forgot," she shouted. "There's a meeting today!"

"Seriously?" Velkin sighed with annoyance.

"Yeah, sorry. I sent a messenger a while back, but she came back—which was odd at first glance, as your gang doesn't normally do that. Anyway, she came back to inform me of what she described as a blasted heap of trees, ash, bones, and all sorts of manner of death and destruction. Whoever caused that, I'd fuckin' love to meet them and get a taste of it. I am positive it would be spectacular. Better than the light show out at the doors a bit ago, eh, tall one?" She winked at Esvele.

"I am sure you wouldn't," Organa replied as her memories played in her head once more on that fatal night. Her guilt swelled, and her rage toward herself grew, but a firm hand from Myrcle took her attention, and she was taken from that place of grief immediately. She smiled at her friend and saw Natalia's grin disappear.

"Oh," Natalia gasped, "I'm so sorry." Natalia took a moment, and then it hit her. "Wait…you might want this then." She jumped from the bed and ran over to one of the many mountains of her spoils and rummaged through its deepest burrows and pulled forth a leather strap with a crescent moon buckle upon it. "I believe this might belong to you, dearie," she said as she placed it in Organa's hands.

Organa could not hold herself upright as she took the strap of leather in her hand, and a fountain of tears ran down her face. It was charred in some spots, and the smell of smoke still clung to it, but she did not care because it was his. Her tears soaked the leather and ran down its burnt passages. A soft hand fell upon her shoulder as Esvele knelt down beside her. In her arms, Esvele cradled the crying girl and held on tight as she seemed to fight back, but eventually succumbed to her embrace.

Florie could see Natalia's confusion and sympathy and pulled her aside to recount the story of the events on the slopes of Mount Doloroth. Talos overheard the telling of Brok's death, and he remembered seeing in the distance two great towers of smoke from the mountain and its twin off to the west of its snowy side some time ago.

A few minutes passed in the royal room as the others gave Organa time to grieve. But Myrcle knew they had a job to do and so he asked Natalia, "Have you seen an old man who goes by the name of Bendrit in these parts? He was meant to meet us at the Morning Glory in Valistar, and I would very much like to speak to him if he is still here."

"I haven't heard of or seen anybody like that," Natalia said, shaking her head. "What kind of 'job' do you have?"

"Our business is our own, my little friend."

Natalia gave a respectful nod and walked toward her old friend. "I'll leave you all to it," she whispered to Florie, then walked toward the exit, but stopped as she reached the doors and turned about, "Oi, Velkin, come on, you have a throne to sit on."

Organa had calmed down now, and Esvele helped her to her feet, still holding onto her. Talos walked behind the grunting Velkin toward the door as Florie and Myrcle waited for Organa to completely collect herself. Esvele continued to hold on to her pupil and comfort her for another few moments before Organa came around. Myrcle and Esvele walked behind Organa as they left the chambers of the new Queen of Thieves.

When they entered the great space, they saw many more people in the room than before, and more were pouring in through portals of red and white swirling vortices. Children of the Crimson Moon, Siren's Heralds, Golden Soldiers, and Wild Hunters filled the room, wearing different regalia that set them apart from one another with easy distinctions. Three of the members, however, stood out among the rest. One of them was a tall Elf dressed in red, black, and white robes, with a circle of Blood Iron upon his head. Long dark hair flowed over his dark skin, and his golden eyes glared into the room.

An Ishtari woman—her skin sky-blue—wore white and gray wolf skins and furs, with a large spear strapped to her back, and she wore a crown as well. This one was more complex in terms of decoration compared to the others as it was made of white and gray marble with the small skull of a young ram mounted to the middle of the crown with eyes of pure emerald. Her mark of royalty sat upon fiery red hair that transitioned into white strands.

The last of the distinct figures was a Human man in a long black coat and short blue hair like that of the sea. His hair was slightly longer on top and fuzzy, yet well-groomed at the same time. As he turned around and faced the center of the room where his throne was, they could see the white cloth shirt and tanned skin from many days at sea. Upon his face was a long tattoo of a mermaid holding a trident in her left hand that started with the tail near the bottom of his right jawline, tangled up and onto his cheek where the trident was, and then twisted around his eye and rested just above his right eyebrow, where a teal-skinned woman with red hair rested her head with a wicked smile. Upon his head was a crown made of dark and light wood, set with many precious gems and rimmed with gleaming metals.

Natalia worked her way through the crowd and stood before the four thrones, holding her hands in the air, quickly silencing all those in the room. Everyone's eyes were now fixed upon her as the air between her hands vibrated and a few shots of lightning flashed in her palms. As the lightning gained more energy and became more violent, a few bolts escaped and struck the walls, causing great claps of thunder to consume the sound in the room, and with a final crack of bright light and immense sound, the crown of the Queen of Thieves appeared. It was a collection of Blood Iron, precious gems, metals, and blue and white marble, all merged into one twisting, beautiful headpiece. Upon each of the cardinal directions was the shape of three daggers. The shape showed two daggers pointed downward, with hilts made of gold and pommels of amethyst, which joined with a blue marble hilt leading to a white marble blade pointing upward.

She placed the symbol of her reign upon her head and spoke to the people.

"Hello, all," she said, her voice echoing in the room. "This is my first Conclave of Daggers, so please don't try to kill me." Her audience responded with some laughter. "This meeting was called for a dark reason, though. For many years now, the Menitheal Dynasty has ruled as tyrants. When the Lady Magis and the Soulflame King took the Crystal Thrones, they began this reign of terror."

Her audience responded with shouts of accusation and disgust toward the monarchs. Natalia held her hands up once more to calm them, and they complied.

"Now, I have called the Conclave of Daggers today to answer the threat that they have posed and will continue to pose if nothing is done to stop them. Information has passed from the previous King of Thieves' ears to my own, and I have heard the whispers loud and clear. Rumor has spread that the Guardians of Lorial have returned, and the 'Soulflame King' and 'Lady Magis' fear this. For if their power is as great as it was in the days of old, they will fall swiftly."

Her audience responded with shouts of joy and proclamations of "Down with the Tyrants!"

She quelled them once more. "And so, I present to us a solution. We must bring them down before their 'Valiant Inquisitors' or, as we call them, 'Black Riders' are sent to dismantle what we have worked hard for. Now, Prime Alpha, do you heed the call of the Queen of Thieves?"

The woman in the white and gray furs stepped forward from the crowd, her raspy and strong voice calling out, "I honor the call of the Queen of Thieves." Natalia nodded her head as the Prime Alpha walked up the stairs and sat on her marble throne.

"Will the Crimson Priest heed the call of the Queen of Thieves?"

The Elven man stood tall among the crowd and walked forward, bowing respectfully. "I will honor the call of the Queen of Thieves," and he took his seat of power.

"Will the Golden Queen heed the call of the Queen of Thieves?"

Velkin stepped forward bearing no crown of power and dressed in the armor she had been wearing almost every second they were with her and bowed as the Crimson Priest did, "The Golden Queen shall honor the call, even if it is without the proper attire." She got a pleasant laugh from the crowd as she ascended to her throne.

"Will the Master of the Seas heed the call of the Queen of Thieves?"

The man with the mermaid tattoo stepped forward, his black coat dragging against the floor. "We are the people of the sea. Ours is the back that carries grain and sustenance to the other lands of Lorial. I have sent forty ships into the Far Lands since I inherited my crown to look for better places for those who have little to live and thrive. The Master of the Seas will gladly honor the call to bring the fuckers down and let them choke on their own blood."

Shouts of agreement filled the chamber, and a roar of war cries followed them. Natalia raised her hands a final time and shouted at her subjects to calm themselves.

After they all regained their composure, she spoke, "I told you I was going to be different from the Kings before me. We have never had a Queen of Thieves, and I am going to make sure that, as the first, I leave a mark of confidence and peace upon my tomb when I die. We will bring them down! We will raise the lowest person to the highest and topple the oppression of our monarchs! But we will do so with as little bloodshed as we can!"

The Master of the Seas gave her a disapproving look and then nodded respectfully and took his seat upon his throne.

"The Conclave of Daggers has begun. Now we will deliberate our future as one," Natalia proclaimed. She held out her hand over the stone stairs that walked up to the circle of power, and the floor rumbled. Brick after brick shot up and formed a ramp only a few feet long that led to a currently assembled throne of iron and steel. Natalia sat upon her throne, and the bricks then pulled her closer like the waves of the ocean. "So, let's get this party started," she smiled.

The Prime Alpha rose to her feet and walked to the center of the circle and spoke to her superior, "What is the news you have heard from your predecessor?"

"That there is a darkness seeping into the Dynasty like none on this earth, that the Guardians of Lorial are returning to free us from its grasp, and that we have one chance to stop it."

"Pray tell," asked Velkin.

"All of you are familiar with the Cataclysm, there is no doubt, but my question concerns this, not—"

Velkin interrupted, "I know you're the Queen of Thieves and all now, but please, please, speak clearly so we might all understand."

Natalia laughed. "Sorry, just got a little too into it, I guess. Anyway, what do you know of the Shadowlight?"

As the words echoed through the hall, Organa and her companions shuddered at the mention, and the Children of the Crimson Moon were affected as well. She thought about her brother for a moment, and she felt anguish fill her heart, but she pushed it aside and forced herself to regain balance.

The Crimson Priest stood from his throne and took the center of the rulers' platform. "Many know of the Children's knowledge of the past, as it is our duty as weavers of fate and destiny," his low voice called out around the room. "I, and others in the Crimson Council, have known of this prophecy, and we have determined, many times over, that such a prediction is folly. There never was, nor can be, a 'Shadowlight.'"

"You're wrong," Velkin said, clearly agitated. "He exists," she continued as she reached the center of the circle of rulers. "Many know who I am and how long I have lived. You know my story and what I have seen. Some of you even know what I've done to try to set those wrongs from ages past right. Now I stand before you to tell you that the Shadowlight exists. But with the grace and power of the gods, we could contain him within a Sepulcher."

A gasp of horror came from some members of the crowd, and Organa noticed some of them could not look at Velkin while others were confused by the name of the object spoken. "The Cataclysm came when Vexian agreed. We all know this story of when he became Golgorot." Many nodded in agreement. "Respectfully, my brother," she turned to the Crimson Priest, "I must disagree. The Shadowlight is very much alive, and he is coming back."

The Crimson Priest gave a glare of frustration as he backed away from her. It was quickly subdued with a single motion, touching the tips of his fingers to a pyramid's tip and taking a deep breath. "It is said that the Shadowlight will become the vessel of darkness. That they will bring about another Cataclysm. But this time, it shall ravage the world and leave a hole in the fabric of reality, letting the Void pierce its prison and into our universe. I have a contact in Castle Black Rose who has told me exactly this: 'It is their ambition to open an object beneath the Xurinal before the end of the year.' My contact looked into the object they spoke of, and I have not heard from them since. But another path has opened to us. Come forth, friends of Florie."

They looked around at each other and, though they had no choice, they complied and ascended to the platform. The crowd of people examined each of them—Organa, Myrcle, Talos, Florie, and Esvele, closely noticing all they could about the strangers in front of them.

Natalia continued on. "It is my understanding, Golden Queen, that these are your companions you have been traveling with?"

Velkin concluded Natalia's reasoning and stepped forth. "I met them at Mount Doloroth, where a vast accident swept across my camp and killed many, if not all, of my people." A roar of confusion and horror swept through the room from rulers and common alike. Organa sank into herself as the sea of sound grew louder, leaving her standing at the brink of an oblivion of guilt.

But the voice of Natalia was like a hand pulling her from her impending doom. "Florie, the one whom you know, has recounted the story to me of the incident on Mount Doloroth, and I trust her implicitly."

Organa was relieved of her guilt, and she found a strange sense of peace upon focusing on what she might be able to do to help them all there, and she spoke out of turn, "I am Organa Evenstar, and I am the last of the Starlight Dynasty." As the words left her mouth, she realized what she had done, and Myrcle and Esvele instantly shielded her with themselves.

A great commotion rose as some shouted, "Praise the Gods," and others shouted, "Liar!" The negative was in the majority.

Organa could feel all the eyes in the room forcing themselves upon her. The rulers in the circle came forward, but Velkin placed herself as a sturdy wall between them and Organa.

Natalia jolted up from her throne and shouted with a booming voice that she projected from a spell. The room fell quiet instantly and turned to her. She walked toward the center of the circle to see her subjects clearly. "Hear me loud and clear, if what she says is true, although highly doubtful, she will prove herself."

"There is no way that she is the last Child of Starlight. The

Cataclysm nearly swallowed most of Dremica and her 'family' along with it," the Crimson Priest mocked.

Natalia turned with rage, and her eyes of flame returned to her as she scolded the lord. "You will remember, Corvin, that I know of the contact you had between them and the Blood Mother. They have the Blessing of Vengeance, as you should well know." As the words of their blessing left Natalia's mouth, the burning red symbols that had been cut into their shoulder glowed beneath their clothes, and each of them revealed the symbol.

Myrcle thought to himself about how the events in that cave were now confirmed to be not of nightmares but reality, and fear filled him. He rubbed his hand over where he thought he had only dreamed of a wound by a large blade, and he found a small, raised area of rough, healed skin where the blade had pierced his leg, now formed and revealed.

Corvin had backed up toward the throne of Blood Iron and, as the companions examined him, he looked nothing like the one they saw in the cave. He spoke again. "I was charged with aiding these 'Champions of Eternity' as the Blood Mother has deemed them. Forgive me for my attempt at deceit, my Queen, but I did not want the nature of the sacred mission we had been given revealed."

"What he says is true," Velkin concurred. "My friends and I were taken to Salvation and have met with the Blood Mother. We have been tasked with the destruction of the darkness that you, my Queen, have heard of." She hesitated for a moment and then revealed the dark truth. "Myrcle," she paused again, "give me the scroll of the Xurinal." With reluctance, Myrcle took from his bag the scroll given to him by Malorian and he placed it in Velkin's hand. She took it and unraveled it, showing it to the Conclave of Daggers and then to the Queen of Thieves. Each of them glanced at one another with fear in their eyes.

"A Sepulcher," the Master of the Seas asked. Velkin nodded and confirmed his suspicion. She could see a great wave of fear come over his and the other faces in the room. Silence filled the now-overwhelming tomb. The voice of the Master of the Seas broke this silence soon after it settled. "How was this placed there?"

"I've no idea," Velkin replied. "My best guess is that it was summoned there by the Enemy."

"'Enemy'," the Master of the Seas laughed back bounteously, "What enemy are they?"

"I know that many of you have heard the stories about how the Fall of the Silver Kingdom occurred," Velkin explained, and as she did, the room fell silent with joy and any resemblance of happiness. "That is a true tale. I know this is not going to be easy to accept; however, without a doubt, I can tell you the Cult of Blighted Souls were, and still are, *the enemy*, then and now."

There was no immediate response until the booming laughter of the Master of the Seas broke the silence, and others soon followed after him. This remark was not in disbelief that the Enemy never existed, but all people of Lorial knew that the Cult of Blighted Souls died with Dremica.

The room became so full of noise that Natalia's voice was barely heard above it—until her third call, which was as loud as a cannon: "Shut—it!" She drove any sound that was there out and into the night sky outside the Conclave of Daggers and through the Undercroft.

"It had to have been before Valistar was built, or placed during the process of its construction," said the Crimson Priest.

"Does your chapter of Children in Valistar know anything about this?" Natalia asked.

"Sadly, as the Champions know, we have not had contact with the Valisterian chapter for quite some time. Many spies have been sent into that city, and each of them has yet to return over the years."

The Prime Alpha of the Wild Hunt took the center once more and proclaimed, "If there is a Sepulcher beneath the great pyramid, then we must strike and cast it into the seas to be forgotten. Let it disappear into the Far Lands if we must."

The crowd gave shouts of agreement and mockery. "Destroy it," one shouted, "Let it sink into the abyss."

Organa could feel the weight of the thought of her brother being lost under the crashing waves of the Old Sea. She heard their cries of retribution and fear, but another voice broke through it like thunder. "No," Myrcle shouted. The crowd grew quiet as they tried to recognize the stranger who would dare speak in the Conclave of Daggers.

The Prime Alpha walked over to him and jerked him by the shoulder, pulling him away from the center of the Conclave of Daggers. "Who are you that would speak as one of us in a position of power?" She asked with great anger and disgust.

"I am Myrcle of Dremica, and I am one of many who stand here with me, who were charged with the protection of Organa Evenstar. We cannot lose the Sepulcher to the waves of the Old Sea."

"You are bold to take such a tone with us, boy," she sneered back.

"'Boy,'" Myrcle's tone became enraged, "I have lived far longer than any in this room, save for Velkin, your Golden Queen. I saw stars die in the night, I saw the Fire in Heaven, I heard the cracking of the earth beneath the cities of Dremica, I saw the legions of fell, eldritch creatures of darkness and shadow, bone and flesh, and nightmares come to life before my very eyes. We," he pointed to Velkin, Esvele, and Organa, "have seen and lived through more than any should in a single lifetime. Those of you who are of the blood of Dremica, and I assume many of you are of such, know the stories your grandparents and maybe parents told you about the Cataclysm. The horrors that crept from the shadows of the darkest depths of the Void, I hope you never see. But if we lose the Sepulcher, we will have lost an artifact that contains a dangerous foe to the crushing oppression of the sea."

"And what is it that this prison contains, oh mighty ancient one?" the Master of the Seas mocked him and laughed.

"Death, destruction, malice, cruelty, evil, darkness, pain, and suffering beyond any measure of comprehension for a weak-minded sea rat," he shot back.

Another moment of silence crossed the chamber that was suddenly broken by a sea of laughter from the many thieves and other lords of the Conclave of Daggers, and like the sea, it crushed over the companions without remorse. Esvele sighed and shook her head. Velkin spoke with the other monarchs. Florie sat next to Organa on the stairs, trying to muffle her amusement. Talos was laughing as well, for he had not seen the things they did and found them wildly beyond what reality could bring. All the while, Myrcle heard a malicious and grim melody in his head.

Voices filled the room of shouting monarchs and others, screaming about the lies or truths spoken tonight. Many times over, Organa heard foul remarks to Velkin and Myrcle, and though she wished to silence them all, and she heard darkness creep into her mind, she held tight to the feathered hand that placed itself on her shoulder.

Esvele stood to her feet and thrust her hands deep into the foundation of the earth, and from within the dirt came a rumbling like an earthquake. Bursting through the floor, seven large roots of massive proportions broke through the stone and crawled along what was still intact, like worms. People ran from them in terror, and others were stunned by this display of power. Her annoyance with their petty squabbles had enraged her, and she could not listen to their denial of the truth anymore, but she knew how to get their attention.

Her creations stopped moving, and she removed her hands from the floor, which was now cratered where she had cast her spell, and she shouted at those in the Conclave of Daggers, "Idiots! Imbeciles! You would refuse the truth if it were a snake and had its fangs locked into your neck!"

No one blinked or breathed.

"Darkness has been descending upon Rethial through the ages, and what has the Conclave of Daggers done? Nothing! You have focused your minds on material pieces of metal and stone that will not help any in the long run! Eventually, The Void calls to all, through magic like us, through malice like the Wild Hunt, duty like the Children, gold and gems like the Golden Queen, or the sea for you, Master. None of this matters. She," Esvele pointed at Organa, "is exactly who she claims to be, as am I, Myrcle, Velkin, and all the others who lived through the horrors of those few days when the world was ripped asunder. You were told stories by your great-grandparents, their children, and your mother and father of the Cataclysm. Though they hold truth within them, no one can show you like I can the truth of the Fall of the Silver Kingdom."

With a wave of her hands, Esvele conjured a mist that circled above where the monarchs sat. Colors appeared within flashes of purple, red, green, and white, light that then formed themselves into images made of the vapor. Shadows crossed close to the edge of the spell, and then voices pierced through like a crack of thunder. The images came into focus, and a city ablaze with flashes of light shone darkly in the night sky from her memory. Monstrous creatures revealed themselves from beyond the edges of the mist, and the people of Lorial who were being chased were either captured and mutilated or eaten by the beasts. Horror filled the room as everyone saw the memories, and Organa could see Esvele trying to hold herself together. A familiar voice echoed from that orb of dreams and called out in a thousand voices, *Come forth, Guardians and despair, for I am the night!* Through the orb, she saw a clear image of her brother there in the Xurinal of the Fallen Kingdom; and sorrow filled her.

The image then vanished as the ring of a blade from its sheath was drawn. The Master of the Seas raised his hand, and a dagger of sharp, blue glass in hand came down on her and into her shoulder. "You show nothing but lies and would dare use the Great Tragedy to win us over, you foul, fiendish whore."

The light in the room diminished quickly. Torches receded their flames in quivering fear and began gathering in the grand center of the Conclave of Daggers. Laughter from all parties died as the light from the torches moved through the air like the tendrils of a great leviathan of the seas, or across the floor like serpents that crawled up the stairs toward the epicenter. A dark light of maleficence grew from that place and every eye in the Conclave of Daggers was on Myrcle.

His clothes had become slightly shredded as small flames had burnt them in some places. His robes were torn and battered unlike they had been, and he was silent as the grave. A god's gaze, burning and blinding, was how his own eyes felt to those who met them. A foul grimace of enjoyment from the power replaced what was once his smiling face, and it grew as the melody of the Dark Song echoed in his mind. The ground beneath him cracked and gave way to the immense weight of the power he was harboring inside him, eventually shattering like glass and leaving an explosion of green, white, and purple flames in its wake. The monarch and his companions were sent flying across the room and against the walls.

Golden light surrounded them as Velkin created a ward of protection around the ones near her, being Esvele, Organa, Natalia, Florie, and the Prime Alpha, but the Master of the Seas was instantly incinerated by Myrcle's immolation and reduced to smithereens. The Crimson Priest mirrored Velkin's spell with his own Blood Ward and could safeguard himself, a few Children near his throne, and Talos. With each impact against the wall, however, shock waves of substantial proportions were sent through the foundations of the Undercroft like a large tremor of an earthquake. The patrons who ignored the warning soon shared the same fate as the Master of the Seas below as the flames of Myrcle's magic burst through the doors of the Conclave of Daggers and filled the Undercroft, killing all inside and sending the building up in a vast explosion of flames and shrapnel that pierced nearby buildings and the people of Itheca. Myrcle's writhing flames erupted, releasing a cloud of embers and a shock wave that ignited the barrels of oil and alcohol, leveling two houses near the Undercroft and greatly damaging others close to it.

Organa looked upon the destruction from Myrcle's magic and saw that any who were not in a Ward of Dawn, or another powerful spell of protection, were reduced to nothing but ash or shadows cast against the very slim amount of what was once walls in the Conclave. She saw endless slopes of rubble that now sat in the place where the Undercroft and other buildings once stood, piled at least sixty feet above them. Where the Conclave of Daggers' thrones once stood was now a spiraling cyclone of bricks, stone, metal, and ash around its epicenter. The floor near that area was cracked and shattered, lingering as if time or gravity had no effect on them, and the destruction crept through the remaining ground or bedrock of the earth, able to cut it like a blade through silk. At the center of this crater was Myrcle, levitating above the ground and pulling all the power into his body before releasing erratic waves of energy. It launched clouds of dust and debris with the escaping power. The Dark Song had a firm grip upon his mind, and the companions could hear the screams of the people in the city as giant bolts of lightning thrust themselves from the heavens and the clouds grew darker and darker, shutting out the light of the evening sun and surrounding the city in darkness.

Esvele pushed forward to get to her friend. The waves of magic shoved her back every few seconds, but she remained diligent, driving herself against them to balance the equation. Her boots dug deep into the earth, and she held her arm in front of her like a shield, using her other hand to create a ward of radiant light to guard her against the darkness as she progressed.

Velkin thrust her blade into the dirt and wrapped her hands around the hilt. She shouted arcane words of protection, and a golden shield of light like Esvele's erupted from the pommel and created a dome around her, Florie, Natalia, Organa, and the Prime Alpha.

Corvin opened his eyes to the horror that surrounded him. Talos and the few Children he had saved with his spell lay beside him, unconscious from the blast. He gazed at the scene before him. Myrcle was exuding raw magic, and the Kalishtani woman was about to kill herself trying to get close to him. He remembered his duty to the Blood Mother and took out a dagger from his side and slit his hand. A deep valley with a river of blood appeared as he drew back the blade from his skin. He looked upon the Kalishtani and uttered arcane dark words, and the blood in his hand began to writhe and boil, creating a few towers of steam from that place. The pain Corvin felt throughout him stung deeply, although it quickly subsided. He walked over to Talos and each of his Children, drawing a symbol of blood upon their foreheads and speaking in an ancient tongue. Their senses came to them as he finished his words, and Talos jolted about, looking for Esvele. He saw her only a few yards away, standing in front of Myrcle.

"Myrcle!" she shouted with no verbal reply, yet a burst of magical energy pushed her a few inches back, but she stood against it vigilantly. Myrcle stood there vacant of himself, and the Dark Song controlled every action. She shouted to him once more, "Myrcle," and this time she saw his head move. His eyes were no longer full of life, for rage had replaced it, and a dark fire burned there too. Those dark eyes glared back at her with contempt, and a thrusting hand motion sent a stream of purple, green, and white flames her way, surrounding her and wrapping around her wrists like chains. She was pulled to the ground with the flames burning her skin heavily. She screamed out in pain, and that scream echoed throughout all of Itheca and melded into the others around the city. Talos saw this and bolted from the ground, drawing his bow to line up a shot, but as he reached for an arrow from the quiver, Myrcle twinned his spell, and flames coiled around him as well.

"We have to do something," Organa shouted to Velkin.

"I can't drop this field. If I do, we'll be killed."

"If we don't do anything, we'll be killed." Organa thought for a moment, and then an idea came to her. She turned back toward her friend, saying, "Florie." Organa turned to her friend and found her still out on the ground. She rushed to her and gave her a few taps on the face, waking her up slowly and bringing her back. "Hey," she said as she got Florie's attention, "Hey, it's all right. I know you just woke up, but how's your aim?"

"Fair," she grunted.

"Good, 'cause I need you to create a distraction. Throw a blade over near the other end of the crater and get Myrcle's attention."

"'Crater'?" Florie's eyes went wide as she looked around and cut Organa off.

"Yes, a crater, but we don't have time to explain right now, so distract him while I free EV and Talos." Florie nodded her head in agreement, and Velkin let down the barrier for a brief moment between waves of pulsating energy. The two shot out toward the cover of the remaining pillars of what used to be a wall. Myrcle's rage was circling faster around him now and every few moments, he would send forth a serpent of flames that crawled up through the rubble, winding in the chaos like a snake among the grass. As these beasts of living flame reached the precipice of the crater, they then spread that rage upon stone, wood, metal, and flesh. Organa saw one of these flaming beasts and left her place of cover. She stretched forth her arms, calling upon the Flux, and cast a spell underneath her foe, creating a cascade of water that snuffed out its flames with ease, splashing around the area and creating a column of steam above where it once wreathed. As she turned to her right, she saw Esvele lying on the ground with the flames still holding tight to her, as well as Talos across the crater. With a single thought, more water appeared, and the flames diminished from around her friend and a new companion.

Myrcle twisted his head, with a cracking sound echoing over the air like some dead thing. He looked to Organa, and as he did, Esvele truly came into view, and his vision restored itself as if he were back in control of himself once more, but his power overtook him again, and he cast a dark spell her way. He extended his hand toward the heavens of the dark sky, causing the lightning in the cloud to sound chaotically and then strike the ground near Organa. She held up a ward to protect herself but was not fast enough before the bolt touched the earth and sent her flying across the way.

Florie revealed herself, throwing two daggers at Myrcle. One bounced off of one of the circling stones with a *clink*. The other did not make it far enough to strike him. His head turned again with a painful cracking sound, and he cast the same spell again that he had at Organa, calling forth the lightning from the clouds and striking the ground near her and sending her hurtling into the rubble of the crater.

Velkin watched with fear as she held her Ward of Dawn to protect those within, and two of the living flames rushed across the earth toward her, leaving a scorching trail behind them. They thrust themselves into the Ward, creating swirling kaleidoscopes of colorful flames. The ward gave slightly, and then some small holes burned through and scalded the flesh of Natalia, who was in a state of pure shock from the display of power before her. As Velkin noticed holes being burrowed into her ward, she recalled the shield into her blade and then glowed with a powerful radiance of light. She swung and plunged the sword into the flaming flesh, causing a scream of pain from within itself and an uncomfortable reaction from Myrcle as if the blade pierced him as well. Velkin saw his hand cling to his lower chest as blood colored his clothes.

Esvele and Talos arrived shortly after. Talos looked around the scene and saw the desolation of Myrcle, his home, and his friends. But he saw Esvele there as well, among the rubble at the base of the crater. Myrcle floated in the middle, his magic swirling around him faster than before and still in control of him. His eyes shifted their way, and seven serpents of living flame formed from his immolation. Each of them reared their heads back and thrust themselves across the earth, burning away at the rock and dirt until they stopped just short of Talos and Esvele. They thrashed about erratically and then diminished like a dying light into a single point in the middle of Esvele's hands, which she now held with great power as her magic flowed through her without resistance. She took the flames Myrcle had conjured and, with a piercing scream, she hurled them back at him, meeting his bursts of energy and crashing through them like an explosion through walls of stone. As the flames struck the barrier Myrcle had made around himself, a loud concussive sound erupted from the impact, but his barrier was still intact, with a foul grimace of darkness crossing his face. She drew back a hand and, from the ground, an earthquake sounded as the rock burst awake with vitality and shot itself through the bedrock, meeting Myrcle's shield once more with another concussive blast. Esvele fell to her knees, staggered from the amount of power flowing through her. All the while, Myrcle was relishing his.

Myrcle sneered at her feeble attempts to attack him, and he conjured a wave of fire, taller than the crater, and stretching almost to the rooftops of the few remaining buildings of the city. The crest of the waves gave birth to more serpents of living flame that consumed all in their path. Velkin ran to Esvele and Talos, holding her hand up as if there was a star within her palm, and all the others in the crater were instantly pulled into the Ward of Dawn that she now produced as she thrust her blade into the bedrock, cracking the foundations and pulling the energy from her own life force to fuel the spell once more. The great wave of molten rock and fire came crashing down upon them, hardening like ice as Organa reinforced the barrier with her powers, and the wave became like glass. Esvele thrust her hand forward, creating a swift and violent gust of air that shattered the dome and the Ward of Dawn. Velkin fell to the ground, unconscious of this blow to her life force, but alive.

"We have to stop this somehow. His power will tear him apart, and Itheca will be nothing but vast rubble of ash and dust," the Crimson Priest shouted. A swirling cyclone formed around the crater and climbed up into the sky. "We have to do this now. Take my hand!"

"What are you going to do?" Esvele asked with a heavy breath.

"We have to kill him before it is too late!"

"No!" she shouted back at Corvin and turned to Myrcle and rushed for him.

"Esvele, stop!" Organa shouted. This scene was all too familiar to her. But she did not heed her warning.

Esvele stopped at the brink of Myrcle's shield, composed of rock, metal, wood, gems, dust, and energy. His foul smile made her heart boil with rage. "You give him back!" The crater immediately fell silent and motionless as all harsh wind, whirling rocks, and flames died. The sound that came from Myrcle's mouth was that of thousands of voices laughing in different intensities, pitches, intentions, and forms of malice. Those voices shook the earth, and the whirling powers of Myrcle moved faster than any eyes could follow.

From within his shield, Myrcle emitted a bright and blinding light as his laughter continued. "Give him back," Esvele pleaded once more. "Please, Myrcle, come back; this isn't you! You are kind, not destructive, and dark! Come—back!" As she shouted the last time, an eruption of energy like thunder, but louder than any heard in the current age, boomed across the city and traveled along the ground, leveling some forests near Itheca and collapsing buildings. Great rockslides, avalanches, and other disasters wreaked havoc across the King's Isle.

Be free, something called to him in his mind. He could not hold it back; a final burst of energy erupted from his veins in a twister of blistering, chromatic heat. Myrcle screamed out as he drew the flames back within him and redirected them into the sky. A vast display of colorful explosions in the clouds above *boomed* as thunder below before he fell to the ground, unconscious. A pale gray coat of ruin enveloped the broken center of the city as life, drifting snow, ash, and dust descended from the sky.

The Desolation of Itheca

The ash had barely begun to settle as the deafening sound of the wave of energy subsided, leaving a slight ring in their ears. Velkin still lay on the ground, unconscious. The others looked around as their sight returned to them. Organa sat on her knees near Esvele, and together they created beams of pure light in their palms and sent them down upon Myrcle's body. Life flowed through him as their rays graced him with their power. He was stabilized but severely drained of the energy needed to stand or even open his eyes.

Natalia looked around at what was once her home, her place of ruling, where her friends would come to commune and be merry. It was now entirely gone. She tried to look around the crater for any trace of her chambers and precious material things but was unsuccessful. She slipped her hands into the cracks and nooks in the rubble, still unable to find what she needed. Natalia saw the others pulling Myrcle from the crater he had formed when he fell to the ground. She got to her feet, rushed across her home, drew forth two daggers of ethereal energy from the world around her, and launched herself into the air to attack.

An arrow struck her ankle, and she hit the ground with a scream as the shaft snapped and plunged the head of the weapon farther into her flesh. The daggers dissipated the moment her concentration was broken, and she landed with a *thud*.

Talos slung his bow around himself and sprinted across the ruined crater to Natalia to check on her.

"Son of a bitch," Natalia gasped for air as the pain surged through her. "What the fuck, Talos? I could have you killed for that, you bastard."

"Can't let you go hurting my colleagues now, can I?" he smiled as he took a vial from a pouch at his side. Natalia squirmed with discomfort for a brief moment, then relaxed as the pain subsided and Talos removed the arrow from her ankle.

"'Colleagues,' huh? We should kill them right now; the world would be better for it."

"No," Talos quickly shot back.

"And why not?"

"Because," he said, pausing for a moment.

"What makes you like them so much already?"

Talos did not respond, only looking at the group of companions.

"They remind you of someone, don't they?" She stared at him as he bound her foot. He pulled the cloth straps tightly, and she flinched. Natalia placed a hand on him as he blankly stared at them. He shook his head, and he returned to himself before giving a sigh and continuing to heal his friend.

A thunder of hooves sounded from above and seemed to surround them as the echoes rolled through the crater of the Conclave of Daggers. Seven figures manifested at the gaping mouth of the beast Myrcle had created, and a woman dismounted her horse. A puff of black smoke enveloped her body, and then she reappeared at the bottom of the desolation.

Merith removed her helmet, and she smiled at them. "You should have been more careful if you wanted to avoid us, Guardians."

"Go now, or I will show you why you should run from us," Organa threatened.

"Oh, hush now, Organa, you mustn't be rude. Besides, someone wants to see you, quite desperately, I might add."

"Who?"

"This is not the place to discuss such matters. We don't want certain ears to hear the truth of your identity."

"I've already told those of the Conclave of Daggers. Many know me now."

"And look where they ended up," Merith gestured to the ash they moved with her feet, causing a minor storm of it to whirl around her. "Dead." She paused for a moment as the ashes settled but then began again. "I would very much like to have you all, but I will take the Evenstar."

"Like hell," Talos stepped in between them.

Merith smiled, "And who are you, my blue friend?"

"Talos Merine of Itheca, m'lady bitch." He gave a dishonorable bow and, as he did, a dagger shot up from his chest and a small ball dropped from his hand and burst with red smoke. Merith raised a hand, deflected the blade, and pulled the smoke from the air and into her hand. With a sweeping, swift motion, an eruption of red flames emerged from her hand and lit the crater ablaze. The companions moved out of the way of her flames, and they watched as a foul grin crept across her face.

"You really think it wise to cross magic or blade with me, boy?" She glared at Talos.

"Any day, anywhere, dollface."

Rage crashed down upon her, and she drew the blade across the leather over her palm, igniting it in purple flames. The blade too shimmered like the stars of the night sky above.

Talos drew his bow and unlatched the buckle on his broadsword as he drew an arrow from the quiver on his back.

"Talos, don't be a fool," Natalia shouted to him.

"No," Merith corrected him, "let him learn, dear."

A whistling sound shot through the air as those last words left Merith's mouth. The arrow struck the right corner of her mouth, gashing her face. She fell to the ground with a scream, and blood fell from her mouth in a scarlet waterfall. He then threw another glass ball of red smoke to cover their escape as they clambered up the other side of the crater.

The other Black Riders took the form of black smoke and appeared below with their commander, who was writhing in pain from the wound. Talos threw Myrcle on his back with ease, and Velkin picked up Natalia. Organa, Florie, and Esvele climbed behind them to defend them if the Black Riders chose to advance.

The Black Riders manifested behind them as they climbed. Organa felt a surge of energy flow through her, and from her hands came a winter storm of ice and snow that cut like glass on the assailants' open skin. She then commanded the storm to surround them in an arena of winter, and it complied with great ferocity as the winds blew harder and harder, swirling around the floor of the crater and up into the sky, forming a cyclone of blistering cold.

Esvele recognized the burning eyes of Corvin and launched seven magic swirls of lightning from her hand that spun around one another at speeds faster than the eyes of mortals could perceive. Forming a blade like that at the tip of a spear, full of crackling and chaotic thunder, the spell struck Mortic and threw him to the ground. Electricity surged through his armor, and his body seized from the shocking jolts. After a few moments, he stood again; rage fueled him.

Mortic raised his left hand, and with the other he drew his blade, slicing through the leather of the clawed gauntlets and gashing the skin. As the blade was coated in crimson, it ignited into a foul-smelling green flame. With a battle cry, he sprang forward across the rubble and leaped into the air. Mortic's body became like many wisps of smoke, and he flowed gracefully through the air. He pointed his blade down to strike and plunged it into the flesh of the crater as Esvele moved just in time to dodge. He swung three more times: once at her head and missed, then a thrust at her chest and missed again, and finally a slash across her shoulder that found its mark. A deep slice opened in her shoulder, and Mortic smiled with glee—but that grimace was soon gone when a dagger cut behind his knees. Florie slid into the rubble behind Mortic and sliced clean through the rings of armor around his legs and deep into the skin. Mortic fell to the ground with a shout of pain. As Florie turned about, she unfurled her black wings and took to the night sky. She dove directly onto Mortic's shoulders and dug her talons into him, taking him with her into the night. Her wings carried her to the outer ring of the crater. She then reached down and slid the dagger's blade across his throat, and a black substance gushed forth. His eyes rolled into the back of his head as his body jerked. Florie released him and watched as he fell before being impaled by the stones below.

Unfortunately, the companions had bested the Riders before, and they knew of Merith's magic. They watched as she stood to her feet and a vast web of green and purple flames shot forth from her fingertips. Her eyes turned deathly white, and her mouth emitted a dark, shrill scream like a banshee. Black threads of the darkest shadows crept from the few places unlit by Myrcle's fire. She guided the streams of undeath through his corpse, snapping the bones back into place and restarting his heart with false life. He rose once again, a pawn of darkness.

Merith's scream ceased.

Her prideful smile gleamed at her prey. "We can continue to play this stupid game of cat and mouse, in which you will always find defeat, or you will come with us willingly. Your mother wants to see you." As she spoke, a rippling waterfall of blood poured from her arrow-cut mouth, garbling her speech, yet a clear, clawed finger pointed at Organa.

"What did you say?" Organa asked with a staggering breath.

"Your mother wants to see you, Organa. She has missed you terribly. She knows your memories have returned and wishes to reunite with her lost daughter. Won't you see her?" Organa felt compelled to follow Merith as the dark sorceress's charm took hold. She walked forward, disregarding the shouts of her friends. Her feet slowly skidded across the rubble as she made her way down into the crater like a marionette. Esvele continued to call out, but Organa could not resist the commanding voice of Merith. "Won't you see her?" she repeated as Organa got closer.

Talos laid Myrcle upon the rubble of the crater and drew his bow and an arrow from the quiver on his back. He whispered a spell under his breath, and the arrowhead caught a blue and yellow flame that sparked sporadically. The arrow cut through the air at the speed of a shooting star and pierced Merith's knee, driving directly through the bone.

Merith's scream pierced the night as the arrow struck home. Organa fell to the ground, limp, as Merith's concentration was broken. The other Black Riders surrounded their commander with blades and magic, ready to strike at those who would harm her again. A few of them appeared beside Organa and hoisted her up, dragging her forward.

Organa shook her head as she came to and found the three Black Riders shielding their commander while the others held her with a deathly grip. Organa could hear something in her mind as she cast another spell—a new song that she could not place—but she had no time to examine it before she transformed her arms into blocks of freezing ice that spread across the armor of her captors. As they noticed the expansion of winter on their bodies, their arms shattered into shards of ice as Organa pulled back against them and cracked the foundations of their bodies. The two Black Riders gave no expression but an annoyed glare as they turned back toward Organa. She pulled herself across the dirt away from them and met Esvele's knees, who reached out a hand and helped her up to her feet. "How are we going to beat them?" she asked.

"We did it before," Esvele smirked nervously.

"Yeah, but then we fled."

"Fair point," Esvele nodded.

"Harmonizing," Organa said.

"What?"

"Harmonize with me. We'll cast the same spell and make it—"

Esvele cut her off. "Yeah, I know what it is; I just couldn't hear you. And I don't think it's a good idea; that much power could trigger the Dark Song to take hold."

"It won't because I won't let it. I've already lost enough to it; I can't lose more."

Esvele looked at the Black Riders, who were now separating from their commander, and she gave in. "All right, but we have to be careful."

"Let's not fuck this up." Organa took a deep breath.

Organa and Esvele acted as one and cast a spell together to surpass its normal output of energy. Their hands were placed a few inches from one another. Small coils of magic pulsed between them. Esvele took the strands of fire from Myrcle's ruin, and Organa grasped the threads of air from the scorched winds around them. They concentrated on each thread, interlacing them at the finest point, and the melody of the Dark Song stirred.

You are a failure... the Dark One whispered to Esvele. *The one whom you loved as your own daughter despises you. She only stays so that she may ascend to higher power and cast you down.*

Brok's death will forever stain your hands... the Shadow sang to Organa. *You will never be rid of the guilt. It will fester in you like plague until it consumes you entirely. There will be no escape for you, unless you give in to the power we offer and free yourself. It waits at your fingertips.*

The weaves of their spell became unstable with each passing word of the Betrayer. Lashes of air refined themselves into blades sharper than castle-forged steel, jutting out like spears. The flames shaped themselves into infernal beasts of ruin that hissed with the Dark One's own hatred. A cyclone spun up around them, grasping even the largest stones and throwing them up into the sky like lakeside pebbles.

A Black Rider approached with their blade drawn, braving and dodging through the slashing tempest.

Velkin bolted and summoned her holy blade to her hand in a tangle of golden and black threads. As the Black Rider was about to strike, Velkin's gleaming sword shattered the Blood Iron cutlass and smote the enemy to its ruin upon the crater's floor. A hum of magic filled her ears as she saw Organa and Esvele glowing with the radiance of their affinity and dove behind a patch of rubble.

You will destroy them all... the Shadow's chorus smiled through its prophecy as it turned its foul gaze upon Esvele. *You will turn to us when your heart is ripped out.* Then it looked upon Organa. *And you have always been ours—just as your brother is now—and you shall herald the Silence into all worlds. Taste of the power we offer you in the freedom of the Void.*

Esvele and Organa's breath was stolen from them as the Flux surged through their bodies. Every thread thickened to the size of a great tree trunk and spun high into the black above. The clouds rolled with the thunder of a hurricane as flashes of every color imaginable ignited them. The very air seemed to electrify and scream as the wrath of the heavens welled up with the power of untempered Flux weaving.

Then, it all came crashing down.

Every lance of light shot from the night above, and darkness had no place to hide. A cascade of thunderbolts like a tapestry of ruin unfurled from the clouds and erupted around the crater and across the city of Itheca. The Black Riders tried to flee, but even the dark magic that gave them their unholy speed could not save them. In the blink of an eye, every one of the death knights was turned to ash, save for Merith.

Her outstretched hands held a ward of flame around her with every ounce of strength she could muster. Still, holes darted through her barrier as lashes of heavenly fire jolted through her body, yet she held firm with an unnatural strength.

"Organa," Esvele shouted through the hurricane. "Let go! We have to let go, now!"

"I can't!" she screamed back as the pain of the raw Flux flooded through her.

Velkin peeked over her rubble to see the threads thickening even more as they called upon more power. She took a deep breath and leaped over the ruin, rushing towards them. A bolt of lightning shot down right next to her, arching across her armor and throwing her to the ground.

"*Aven torvent!i*" A voice called from across the crater. It was Myrcle. He was singing. "*Asor'Nevrai tu li'aman!*"

Esvele knew those words—the Song of Silver they would sing at Consecration each year at the Silver Fountain—and she joined him in singing.

"*Veshir qal'mi ac roventi!*"

Organa recognized the words too. Even though she could barely remember them, she joined when she could.

"Sol'mar reventiri... am... ashir!"

The storm's rage unraveled with each word as the Dark Song was slowly drowned out.

Organa and Esvele's spell ended, and they fell to their knees.

Merith released her ward.

"My turn." She grimaced.

Before they could realize the movement, Merith had disappeared in a wisp of black threads and then reappeared behind them, slicing through any barrier they could conjure and gashing at them with her blade. She transported herself again to Myrcle and attempted to strike him with a meager flame.

Natalia saw Myrcle's fate as it rushed to meet him. With a quick throw, she summoned a blue dagger and loosed it at the dark knight. The blue blade soared through the air across the crater to pierce the Black Commander's spine, but the shadows claimed the corrupted knight once more. The blade and the knight disappeared, then suddenly manifested behind Natalia. Merith held the hilt of the magical cutlass, redirecting the knife into the Queen's chest. It pierced just a few inches from the heart, and a fountain of blood came pouring from the mouth of the Queen of Thieves.

Florie's heart stopped as all the air left her lungs. Her wings took her up the side of the crater, and she flew to her old friend, but not in time. With a smug grin, Merith dispelled Natalia's dagger and used her flames to shift across reality once more; this time manifesting in front of Organa.

Merith seized Organa's arm as she shifted through the planes once more. But as the dark knight materialized, Velkin's blade rose to meet her and found her hand from the wrist up still gripping Organa. Merith left the crater with a wild cry of agony, her darkness consuming her and slipping her back to the courts of her masters.

Talos heard his name from behind him and turned to see Myrcle reaching up at the night. He crawled over the rubble and saw Myrcle's eyes barely open. He was muttering something indiscernible save for a few words: "Bring them… me."

Talos asked what he needed, and his hand was fluttering about toward the others. Talos sprang up and ran down to Esvele, grabbing her by the shoulder. She jerked back as she thought he was one of the Black Riders, and he shouted to her, "Myrcle needs you!" Esvele and the others ran for their friend.

In her last few breaths, the Queen rasped through the blood in her throat. Her grip on Florie's arm became painful, and she pulled her in. "The Baron—take it." Florie held her close and wept over her as Natalia died. Organa waited for a brief moment before hearing Esvele cry out for them. Florie, instead of standing alone, stood with Natalia's body on her back and made her way to her companions.

Myrcle held up his hand, still far from his full power but alive. "Take us to Vergeht."

"No," Florie corrected, "We must go to the Red Baron."

"Where?" Organa asked.

"The Red Baron, the Queen of Thieves' ship. It will take us to Valistar so Talos can get us inside."

"More Black Riders might be there, Florie," Esvele worried.

"I doubt it; if they are, I'll kill every last one of them."

"I don't know where it is; I can't take us there," Esvele said, shaking her head.

"Can you see it through my mind?" Talos asked. "Some magic thingy to look into it?"

"Maybe?" Esvele shrugged.

"You know, for smart people of years gone by, you are all very stupid in the current age," Talos laughed. They all stared at him with serious expressions, and he ceased his amusement. "Sorry," he gave another light laugh, but out of nervousness, "Trying to lighten the mood."

Esvele placed her hands on his temples and looked into his mind, seeing memories of himself, Natalia, and Florie completing contracts. Memories of a ship with crimson sails and many merry times flooded her mind. But there was something else she found in his thoughts: a warmth that fluttered in her heart every time she looked into his eyes and saw her face.

Esvele pulled her hands back. "I should have it now." She tried to shake the feeling, but she could still feel her heart beat.

The light of Esvele's spell surrounded them, and they felt a vast warmth as they were transported to the location within Talos' mind. Sorrow swept over Florie as they left, and Organa held her close.

The Queen of Thieves

When they arrived, they were met with golden torchlight down the hall of a cave corridor. The roof was low by a few inches, forcing Myrcle and Talos to hunch to fit properly. It was just wide enough for Florie and Organa, the smallest of the group, to stand side by side with only a couple of inches to spare. Florie looked around at the tunnel she had been in with her friends. Talos recognized the walls as well, though even for him, like Florie, it had been quite some time since he, Natalia, and Florie had been working for the prior King of Thieves. He remembered their contract in Menagerie: the theft of a majestic rune blade said to have been created in an ancient forge on the Isle of Twilight, long since lost to the sea during the Cataclysm. That was the last time he had seen Florie. After that failure and their flight from the authorities, they had been separated by a winter storm and presumed dead. He could not believe he was about to get back on that ship and possibly sail, yet again, to his death.

The darkness hid from the torches, which ignited to life as the companions followed Talos through the damp cave. Florie stuck to Organa's side and held her hand for comfort. Myrcle could barely stand but pushed through, using Esvele as a crutch to lean on. Eventually, they came to a vast and wide expanse of an underground sea. Sand lined the rocky shore, and small waves crested in the distance, creating a calming echo against the walls of the cave. Myrcle thought to himself how he missed the sound of the ocean, and even though they were about to depart into the Red Sea, it was still the sea, and that is all that mattered to him. He remembered the tossing and turning of his father's boat. Those days out in the Old Sea, where the waves were fifty feet high, and he could feel his stomach fluttering wildly as the ship soared down over the waves. Those vast and endless depths with marvelous creatures beyond comparison to anything else on Lorial. He longed to be there—not just on the sea, but with his mother, father, and sister. A family once more.

Esvele's eyes widened as the flames of the torches ignited with each step closer toward the ship, and it revealed its grandeur to them. A great ship with red boarding that darkened to black as it neared the water. The far-off dim light of dawn shone down the long channel that led out to the Red Sea and illuminated the sails that were streaked with colored silks. Swirls of blue, red, green, gold, and silver were stitched into the sails, and their masts were made of pristine white wood. A great ship's wheel of mahogany and golden accents sat where two grand staircases joined on an extended platform above the door to the captain's cabin. Five statues, each representing one of the lords in the Conclave of Daggers, sat upon the three enormous walls that encapsulated the balcony of the helm. Along the sides of the ship were gun ports for the cannons made of pure silver and carved with magic runes to keep them from combusting their glamorous stature. She was built for silent running and smuggling, but the lines of cannon ports along her sides ensured she was ready for battle.

"So," Talos said as they boarded their mighty vessel, "I can get you into Valistar, but first, we need to give Natalia the proper send-off of a Queen of Thieves."

"How do we do that?" Organa asked.

"A proper burial."

"I'll go back and get her body," Esvele said with a grunt as she set Myrcle down on a bench on the deck.

"You can't," Myrcle sighed, "Merith will expect us to come back for something. It's too great a risk."

"We don't need her body," Florie corrected.

"Why not?"

"Every King or Queen of Thieves, of which Natalia was the first Queen, is coronated with a unique crown upon the completion of the Tasks of Masters. We stored every crown on this vessel in the captain's cabin. "That's where the crown was summoned from during the Conclave."

Talos opened the double doors to the room and saw a grand sight of luxury with pristine bedding, furniture, and all manner of other comforts of home at sea one could need, and in the back was an extensive wardrobe. A large lock marked with ever-changing blue runes glowed on the front of the cupboard. Its key was a word, and only that word could open this lock, but as Talos knew, only one person knew the password to the lock, the Queen of Thieves.

Talos shouted to the others on deck, and Florie came in first. "By the Dawn, she actually remembered to put a lock on something." Florie laughed, but there was sorrow there.

"I'm sorry?" Esvele asked.

Florie had a few tears in her eyes as she turned around with a gleaming smile on her face. "For a magnificent lock pick, smith, and other things, she sucked at locking doors or putting locks on important things."

Talos laughed and shook his head. "You remember that time when we were in that blistering heat a long while back in the west? What was the name of that shit-hole?"

"Hell if I remember," Florie laughed again. "Anyway, we were doing a job, the three of us, and we had completed it, treasure and all. We stayed in the best place you could as a thief—plain sight—and Natalia forgot to lock our room door. That night, some lesser thieves belonging to the Golden King at that time broke into our room and stole our stolen treasure from us while we slept. We were so mad, and so was our employer. We were on the run for seven weeks before we could return to Itheca."

"Sounds like you all were not the greatest thieves," Myrcle said as he hobbled into the room. The laughter grew for some time as they enjoyed their revelry in old memories. "How the hell are you going to get it open?"

"Florie," Talos eyed her, "do you know? Cause I sure as hell don't."

"I've got no clue," she thought for a moment, trying to recall anything that could have been a key to the riddle of the lock. Her mind poured through old memories that passed swiftly from one to another. Nothing stood out as she sifted through her mind until she realized it. "Red Baron," she said softly.

"What?" Organa asked.

"Red Baron, that's what Natalia called this," she gestured around the boat.

"That's not the ship's name," Talos said. "It's always been the King's Gambit."

"Yeah, but times change, names change, oh well, we still need to get that lock open."

"So, she re-named it, but why Red Baron?" Organa asked.

"The only thing I can think of is her." Florie stopped and froze as she realized the password. "I hate her so, so, so, much."

"What is the password?" Talos asked.

"Me." Florie shook her head and laughed, and as she said the word, the lock clicked and dissolved like grains of sand in the wind, opening the wardrobe and revealing at least seventy crowns. Some were gold, others platinum, and many were bejeweled with stones of great value.

"How was the password 'me'?" Talos looked at her with confusion.

"Red Baron is what she called herself when she first made a name for herself in the Conclave of Daggers," Florie laughed. "She would be egotistical enough to make the password her."

"Which crown is hers?" Organa asked, peering over the many.

"This one," Talos said as he reached down to the next-to-last slot available, "Each crown is arranged in the order of the Kings—and now Queens—predicted by the Weave Oracles of the Children of the Crimson Moon."

"Who has previously been wrong in almost every scenario?" Esvele interjected.

"Well," Florie said, "maybe they got this right?"

"Let's give Natalia a proper goodbye." Talos took the crown in hand and walked across the captain's cabin. The others followed behind him as he walked toward the bow of the ship. A long stair extended on the spine of a great black, silver, and gold-designed dragon. Seven horns made of iron crowned its head. The furthest on the left was more rusted than the others, and its siblings, which were staggered by age and size, retained more of their original gleam as they moved closer to the middle where one final slot in the crown of horns was.

"What is this?" Myrcle asked, surprised by his lack of knowledge.

"The Beggar's Cowl," Florie sorrowfully answered, "EvEvery ninth crown was melted down and molded into a horn to place upon the dragon's head. A symbol of their mastery in thievery, so that they may ride upon the head of a dragon, and the beast would never know. Now Natalia can rest upon the dragon forever, and she'll go down in the annals of the Conclave of Daggers as the most courageous Queen of Thieves, as well as the first."

"Myrcle," Talos nodded over to his right at a small fire with a stone cylindrical mold on top, "I know you probably don't feel like doing magic right now, but could you give us a light?"

With a snap of his fingers, Myrcle conjured a small bonfire beneath the miniature forge. Talos walked over to it with the crown in his hand to a stone cylinder cut for the ring of Natalia's unique crown. Laying the royal piece within as it heated up and with a little more coaxing from Myrcle, the crown melted down and funneled through four spouts and into a mold in the center. A few moments passed, and a bubble formed from the molten gold in the middle, along with four whole gems that, for some reason, did not melt.

Using pincers, Talos reached into the mold, removed the jewels from within, and placed them on a wooden slab nearby to cool. A bubble burst at the surface, and the mold began to set as Talos removed it from the heat.

"A little help, Organa?" Talos asked.

Organa's hands trembled as she began to reach for the Flux, but she did anyway, and gathered air and water to form a cold rush of air that surrounded the mold; sprouting small patches of ice upon it. The mold was finally set with Organa's help. Talos took a small hammer and gently tapped a nail into a groove on its top, and the stone split down the middle. The mold revealed a glittering golden horn unlike the others in the Beggar's Cowl.

"Gold would be the only thing she'd accept to be remembered by." A light laugh echoed through the tunnel of the cave. Talos picked up the horn and walked over to the dragon, placing it in the slot among the others in the Beggar's Cowl. Florie and Talos both teared up, Talos becoming vocal first and Florie soon after. They clung to one another, and Esvele felt some shame over misjudging him. The two old friends held each other and mourned the passing of Natalia, the Queen of Thieves.

Sailing to Valistar

After Florie and Talos took their time to mourn Natalia's passing, Organa levitated the stones from her crown, took two gems for each of them, and formed necklaces for the old friends of the queen. Talos' was red and green, while Florie inherited blue and white.

Talos took command of his crew, instructing them around the ship on how to ready it for sail. The Red Baron sailed into the Red Sea and along the coast of Rethial toward Valistar to uncover the truth of the dark matters.

The Red Sea was named for the color of its waters. Balinor was a red waste, save for a rare oasis somewhere in its vast desert. On the windiest days, the sea would erode sand, dirt, and clay from the western coast, and great storms of dust would blow the grains into the ocean. So great was the volume of minerals that it turned the sea red, thus giving it its name.

It was Veraelia the Vast who sailed across the Olde Sea to all the lands of Lorial on her great expedition nearly a thousand years ago, after the Lux helped her build a mighty vessel, the Dawn Treader. The ship was said to have the power to sail upon the beams of light from the sunrise and travel faster than the blink of an eye, emitting a great green flash whenever she sailed off.

Talos was at the helm, steering the Red Baron down the tunnel that led into the Red Sea. Esvele sat on a bench near the helm with a book in hand, containing spells, wards, and other arcane arts. As the bow of the ship cleared the mouth of the cave, light blinded its passengers for a moment. When their sight cleared, they saw the vast, clear waters glowing a light teal beneath the radiant sun as light crept across the rippling sea. Behind them was a great green forest with the tip of Mount Doloroth still peeking above the treetops, and beyond it rose the great plateau of the God's Way, its cliffs standing alongside the Veiled Mountains. Yet, looming above and stretching high into the clouds, a great shadow grew and passed over them as the wind picked up. A column of smoke a few thousand feet high rose from where the trees and the God's Way met, where Itheca rested in the shade of the plateau.

Myrcle dared not look upon any sign of what his power had wrought. The thought of him having done what he had done was too terrible for him to contemplate. Shame filled him, and a melody sounded in his head as he sank into his disgust and hatred, forcing his will upon the sea and causing it to writhe and roil around the Red Baron. A quick hand slipped into his left, and he opened his eyes to see Florie there, holding him back from his temptation.

"The Dark Song calls so greatly to Magiqas; sometimes it would be simpler if we could just give in," Myrcle said with a grim face.

"I hate that such power is brought to you, Esvele, and Organa, because when you really think about it, as long as Talos and I are with you, we'll never be safe. No one is safe around Magiqas." Florie Said.

Myrcle felt a sea of guilt wash over him much greater than the one he already was drowning in, but she spoke again.

"But no one is safe, ever. We are just small specks in a wild world and an even wilder universe that is full of dark, dangerous beasts beyond our imagination. Who knows what's beyond that blue sky?

All we can do is push on and through our mistakes and our faults. Make a choice to help whom we can along the way. Always make amends for your wrongs so that we can."

She smiled at him, raised his hand, and gave it a pat.

He no longer heard the Dark Song in his mind, but instead, all was quiet, and the music of the crashing waves filled him instead. The night before, he thought of his deed and feared what he couldn't control. He knew that she was right. Perhaps one day, if they were lucky, the Curse of the Magiqas would be resolved and the Dark Song would no longer trouble him and his people, as it had since the Shadow Monarch first composed it many eons ago.

Talos set the course for Valistar and turned to Esvele. "So, this 'Merith' bitch—who is she, where is she, and can she die?"

Instead of Esvele, Velkin answered, "Merith is a Valiant Soul, one of the leaders of the Flames of the Sphinx. It is the highest commanding position given other than the king and queen. She is a dark and vile beast of shadow and death. A heavenly sword such as mine could dispatch her from immortality and cast her back into the Void."

"Why?" he asked with a shrug. "My arrows hurt her."

"Yes, you can hurt her, you can kill her, but she will come back every time. She is like a Shade Binder, if you know of such creatures, yet there haven't been any since the Three Days. Her life is tied to an object or a person."

"I don't think you understand how mortality works, old-timer."

Velkin's eyes flashed bright green as she tightened her fist around Talos' throat with such force he was lifted a few inches off the deck. "You have no idea the burden immortality brings."

"Let him go," Myrcle commanded. The air stiffened as Velkin contemplated her choice. But she dropped him. Myrcle allowed the air to settle and continued with what Velkin had begun explaining. "Magiqas are gifted, or in some eyes, burdened with long life. Still able to die, but not of old age. If you led a simple life, you could live forever until the universe came to its crashing end. Those who serve the Pantheon of Dawn are blessed with long life as well, that we may help purge the world of vice and sin and the influences of the Void."

"Then why didn't you stop the Cataclysm?" Florie asked.

A long pause of stale, dead silence washed over them; not even the waves were audible. Velkin shot from her seat in such a rage that she picked Florie up by the throat with ease. With her other hand—her sword vanishing quickly—she restrained one of Florie's wings. Florie's eyes were alight with fear, and Velkin's grip became like shackles of iron, tighter than any Florie had ever been held in before.

"You dare?" Velkin furiously whispered. Her eyes were burning with rage, and then she placed Florie down on the floor. "I did everything to stop the Cataclysm. I lost my husband and two sons. I lost more than you could know. I will not suffer the infernal slights of a half-wit such as yourself on matters you could barely comprehend. Do—not—test—me."

"Velkin, stop!" Organa shouted. "The last thing we need is to be fighting one another right now. We are at the door of a great evil that we don't even know how to stop. The Lord and Lady Menitheal are looking for us, and according to Merith, my mother is alive." Organa's face lit up, but her excitement turned to confusion.

"She can't be," Esvele said, shaking her head. "Bendrit said that she died in Dremica when the city fell. Merith is just trying to get you to come willingly with them."

"But what if she is alive, held as a hostage? We have to save her."

"Organa, trust me, please, Merith was lying," Esvele pleaded.

"But I have to try. I have to find her. She would be all I have, because Kyriel is gone," Organa shouted. Her words echoed over the Red Sea, passed far over the waves of the nearby horizon. "I have done my best to forgive you three for what you did to me. I understand why you did what you did, but this is a chance to have my family back. He was imprisoned forever because of a role they forced him to play."

"Organa," Myrcle began, but she cut him off.

"Please don't," she shot back, "I have to."

Esvele walked over to Organa and wrapped her arms around her. "Oh, my sweet girl," she whispered, hugging her close. "I understand your pain more than anyone here. My family was ripped from me as well, but you have to realize Merith was lying to you. But while we are in Valistar, we will keep an ear close to the ground and our eyes within the shadowy places for any signs or mentions of the mother of a Starlight Child." A smile appeared on her student's face, and Organa nodded in agreement.

"This is the most dysfunctional group of broken people I have ever set eyes on," Talos laughed to break the tension, but found only blank stares in his wake. "Sorry, poor taste." Esvele nodded at him with a fake smile, and she walked Organa onto the deck of the ship, where they sat to talk for quite some time. Florie was rubbing her wing from Velkin's firm grip. Although she did not receive it until later that night, Velkin offered an apology, and they had an understanding. "So, how do we get past Merith?" Florie sighed.

"I don't know," Velkin shook her head, "We will need your help to get into the city, someone's help to harbor fugitives of the crown, a way into the Xurinal without being detected, someone who can access Castle Black Rose, and then a way to open the Sepulcher without destroying a city with a population of over three-million people, all while avoiding her."

"Sounds like we're fucked." Talos threw up his hands.

"You know, I actually agree with you on something." Esvele smirked.

"You said, 'open the Sepulcher,'" Myrcle questioned. "What do you mean?"

"Myrcle, we have to do what is right." Velkin's sad eyes locked onto his.

"Which is?" His breath caught in his throat.

"Kyriel must die." Velkin stood valiantly.

"Excuse me?" Organa interjected.

"Organa," Velkin began.

"No," Organa shouted back, "you are not killing my brother."

"Organa," Velkin tried again.

"You—will not—kill—my brother!" As Organa shouted, she held back her hate and fear, refusing the dark and vengeful melody in her head, but it took all her strength.

"Your brother is a beast of darkness—a herald of death and destruction that could raze Lorial to its foundations."

"Velkin is right," Esvele closed her eyes. Organa turned to her old teacher, and she could not believe what she was hearing. "Organa, I know you and your brother never asked to be a part of anything like this. You and Kyriel were meant to be rulers and prominent leaders of the Silver Kingdom. The Prophecy of Shadows foretold of the Shadowlight's rise and the destruction they would bring. Show her Myrcle."

Myrcle looked at Esvele with uncertain eyes and unlatched his satchel. An old and dense tome, covered in Stellevarian runes and bound in white wood with a spine of decorated gold, bore a central symbol made of silver. Four arches in the shape of crescent moons—two vertical and two horizontal—and two streams of twisting light lay parallel beside each other: the Arches of Creation.

Hovering his hand over the ancient seal of the gods, Myrcle spoke in that old tongue, "Veritas, the first star, grant us thine wisdom," and two locks, one of white metal and another of shadowglass, clicked.

Myrcle peeled back the heavy cover and opened it to the first page. The dust had gathered on the paper where it was concealed for so long without consultation, twinkling almost like stars in the light of the sun. Myrcle shuddered as he opened his eyes and gazed upon the ancient manuscript, letting out a terrible groan as a single tear escaped his solitude. Esvele's right hand caressed the pages and, without saying a word, told Myrcle it would be all right. She took the book from his hands. With her other hand, she cupped his face, wiping away the tear of her lifelong companion.

Page after page, Esvele searched for the passage she needed. Passing chapters, Organa could glimpse the titles of *Elder Truths*, *The First Song*, *Eyes of the Deep*, and others that only allowed certain words to be seen. Esvele stopped abruptly as she gazed at the chapter, *Songs of Sorrow*. Esvele's eyes welled with tears as she recalled all that had happened because of the very words on the page below.

But she steadied herself, cleared her throat, and recited the Prophecy of Shadows.

"This I sayeth unto thee, thou who wouldst heareth the Dark Song, heedeth mine own words, for the Cataclysm is nigh. Upon these words, beware, the one who walks in Light and Shadow is nigh. Darkness shall beest their burden and Light, their deliverance. Shadows will rise and fall upon the world. He who walks upon the Void cometh soon: the Herald of Hatred; the Vengeful Son of Sorrow; the Forgotten Brother; the Burning One; the Unending Flame of Chaos. Within his fire shall all things be devoured. This I sayeth unto thee: the Silver Kingdom will fall. Dremica will fall. Dremica will fall. Mine eyes have seen the coming of darkness and the coming of destruction; the coming of the Cataclysm. Fear the Dark Song, the Age of Shadows comes soon. The Days of Doom are upon thee. Yea, though I hearken toil and grief, sowing seeds of fear, there is still hope. Hope in the forsaken child of treachery, hope in the hands who wield the star-christened blade. Damnation is at hand. Salvation is Nigh. This I

sayeth unto thee, the Cataclysm is nigh."

Myrcle sighed as he pondered those words. "Many believed that the Shadowlight would be a fallen Lux, one of the ancient Celestials of the Dawn Eternal who went against Havithreal. Others believed it was to be the Fallen One, Maltheil, the brother of Havithreal. When we went to retrieve your brother from the bowels of the Xurinal of Husieàkritae and saw what Golgorot and his underlings had done, we had two choices: kill him or imprison him. I wish I had chosen differently than I had."

Organa simply looked at Esvele with a blank expression. The words she heard coming from Esvele were appalling. The thought of killing her brother was actually now on the table. "He is all I have."

"That, my dear, is not true," Myrcle shook his head. "We are your family."

"Why would I want a family that wants to murder my brother?"

"It would not be murder, dearie. It would be mercy—not only for him but also for the thousands of worlds that would fall under his tyranny."

"You suggest that he is pure evil, and you didn't even give him a moment to show what he would do with his power! He could have used it to save people!"

"That is exactly what he would think he was doing!" Myrcle shouted now with frustration. "He would be under the control of the Shadow Monarch, whose goal is to bring all into a grand eternal darkness. To make life and death indistinguishable and all thought the product of a single mind. Darkness will envelop all, and no one will be free. How else could the Dark Song fade, and evil be rooted out? Save the universe from free will."

Silence fell over them and the crashing waves upon one another as they sailed toward Valistar. The grand sails of the Red Baron were at full canvas, and the wind carried them swiftly over the sea. Organa pondered the words of Myrcle and thought to herself for a few brief moments. She attempted to speak, but the words would not exit her mouth, for she knew that her response would be unkind. Every thought of her brother that crossed her mind made her think of the agony he must be in. She wanted to save him, but maybe it was too late. She could barely imagine what darkness it contained within its Sepulcher. Nevertheless, she had to save him no matter what. She had a debt to repay. A life debt.

"Organa," Velkin said lightly to her, "you have to understand, Kyriel, he is not who we remember, who you remember. What you do remember of him is the wonderful boy he was. But when Golgorot took him and summoned the power of the Void into him, he was lost. Darkness that potent is impossible to reverse. Myrcle is right; it would be mercy because he would be free of that pain."

"Memory is pain, and I wish I never knew mine." Organa walked over to the starboard edge of the boat. She placed her hands on the railing and looked out upon the Red Sea, able to see the thin edge of the red, sandy wastes of Balinor.

Myrcle came to her side and placed his hand over hers. "Memory is life. We are nothing without it."

"I wish I never knew mine," she repeated, "Yet I am grateful for them as well. They remind me that this world wasn't always dark and deadly. Once, it was peaceful."

"I remember. I am a little older than you, though we are both ancient," Myrcle said with a soft laugh, stealing a grin from Organa as well. "I can see it in the distant sea of memory. The green hills roll before the lush green wood below the Silver Fountain. Tall, white, beautiful cliffs rose high above a clear blue shore where the sand mirrored the snows of the highest peaks. Vast expanses of vivacious flowers and grazing creatures in the light of the sun. The infinite glory that shone above us all when the Element Moons danced among so many stars, only Havithreal could know each name, both seen and unseen splendors of blue, red, white, green, and golden radiance. A time of peace and plenty that turned to ashes before we had a chance to realize the grandeur of what we had."

"I can't see it all, you know," Organa sighed. "There are fragments, simple things that I can't recall. I can't remember the castle we grew up in, I can't remember the streets of Husieàkritae, I can't remember the sky without the Fire in Heaven burning above us. I feel like a stranger. A stranger in a strange land that I should know but I don't."

"Organa," Myrcle's heart sank. "When we removed your memories, we took so much in fear of what it might do should you discover what was happening. If what happened at Mount Doloroth had happened in the Living City, countless people would have died in the firestorm. The Dynasty would come after you and force you to do their bidding."

Organa rolled her eyes and sighed. "I know, Myrcle. I get it. But what if I never remember it all?"

"Then you were not meant to. As much as I hold to my adage, which I don't know if I have ever said aloud to anyone, 'free will above all else,' there are, sadly, things beyond our control."

"What if I need to one day and can't? What if there is a memory that can save Kyriel, and I can't show it to him?"

"Why are you asking this, Organa? There is something you're not telling me."

Organa took a very long pause before she shook her head. "I hear... or I think I hear... vengeance in my mind."

"You 'hear vengeance'?"

"I know it sounds insane, but the Dark Song calls to me through vengeance."

"The Dark Song is of the Void and calls to its host with the promise of their deepest desire. Yours was vengeance when you discovered our illusion of your past. Unless…" Myrcle eyed the waves. "It might not be your Dark Song."

"What?"

"We've told you that twins are connected far beyond the bounds of the material world. You remembered your past through the memory of your brother rather than one of your own, and then it all came flooding back in a single moment. Your brother's Dark Song being vengeance against us who imprisoned him may flow through you as well as your own. Perhaps the connection runs both ways? Your Dark Song did not show itself until after Mount Doloroth."

Organa's thoughts ran wild, and she feared what she might do. After all, she had killed someone close to her before when she lost herself to the Dark Song. What could hold her back from becoming a murderer of thousands? Her brother's power, being so far beyond hers, terrified her as she thought of the destruction that he could bring. "How do we know that it's his prison they'll be able to bring back?"

"Sepulchers need to be recharged with a Glass Key every four hundred years to keep the thing within them locked away. If they obtain the key, they will summon his prison back to this plane, and then they will free him."

"What will happen in the end—to Kyriel?"

"I think we both know the answer to that question, my dear," Myrcle said with guilt.

"Do you think there is a way? Maybe the gods will pardon him?"

"I do not know."

"He never asked to be a part of this. Neither did I. Why should his guilt be set in stone for action when no one knows if it's still him in there? What if the person we remember is gone forever?"

"If he is no longer there…" Myrcle began, then stopped as he pondered.

"Then what?"

"If he is no longer there, then he has already met the judgment of the Pantheon of Dawn—which makes him even more dangerous. If the Shadow Monarch obtained a vessel, and only his mind is within, that makes him mortal—and vulnerable He can be killed. Not by mortal weapons, I am sure, but by those of a Twilight Forge."

"That's… good news."

"Yes, yes, it is, dearie, and it also means we wouldn't be killing your brother."

A smile crept across Organa's face, and peace of mind swept over her.

Myrcle left her, but as he turned and took a step, she reached out and took his hand. "Myrcle," she asked, "I know this is a rather personal question, but… what is your Dark Song?"

"Power," he said. "Power enough to overthrow darkness and keep those I love from harm. Yet that very power always overtakes me."

She gave him a confused look that shifted into understanding before she wrapped her arms around him, her feet lifting a few inches as she enveloped his shoulders. Pulling back, she watched him bow, and she smiled at him and curtsied terribly.

"Maybe that will come back in time," he said as he rose and turned away.

"Maybe," she giggled—though Organa fell solemn quickly. "One last thing, Myrcle…"

"Yes?" he laughed as he turned back around and then saw her sadness veiling over her.

"Do you think Merith was telling the truth—about my mother being alive?"

"I wouldn't trust the words of a venomous snake, and neither should you."

"What if she isn't lying, though?"

"Then we will free her and reunite her with you, and we will have a beacon of hope with us as a new companion to help combat the darkness with the power of the gods at our side."

"Are they really gone?"

"I don't believe so, my dear. After all, where does Velkin draw her power, if not from the gods?"

"And my power? Where does it come from?"

"Think of your Balance of Chaos—the pull between the Dark Song and your strength. Keeping them in check, as you well know now, is harder than one might guess. But you have conquered it before, as a youth, I might add, which shows your connection to magic is stronger than you know. The gods gifted us with magic so that we might create and destroy, which is why our free will was given to us. Power is great in the line of the Starlight Dynasty. It always has been and forever shall be, which is why your brother being the Shadowlight frightens Velkin, Esvele, and me so much. The power of a Magiqas is so great that even the Wizards of Corthal cannot signify it with a single being or equation. Magic flows through our veins as our blood does—with such ease that we lose ourselves at the slightest cut, and it all comes pouring out."

"How do I keep that from happening?"

"You did it before, on the hill after the accident."

"You can say it like it is, Myrcle," she bluntly stated.

"After Brok's death," he corrected himself, "and as I said, at a very young age. Esvele nor I have done such things. She lost herself for a moment before we entered the Conclave of Daggers. I lost myself when I saw her, someone I love, get hurt."

Myrcle fell silent, thinking of all the lives he had ended with the great immolation that ripped through Itheca. A fear shadowed him like a great cloud, and in that moment, he questioned himself. The image of that simple strike against Esvele had sent him spiraling into his magic without restraint. The thought then crossed his mind: *does the Dark Song take such hold over us so greatly, or is it us that gives in too quickly?*

His thoughts were interrupted by a soft hand upon his. "I've been there," she sighed. "I know. I have been here before many times, my dear. This was not my first time losing myself to the Dark Song, and it won't be the last. As long as Magiqas can draw power from the realms of the material and beyond, the Dark Song will swim in the deepest reaches of our minds when we cast our spells and get too close to that dark abyss." Myrcle finally turned to speak with Velkin and Esvele about the plan once they reached Valistar. Organa followed him over to them.

Esvele sat on a bench watching Talos at the helm of the Red Baron, and he seemed to smile each time he caught her glancing his way. Florie leaned against the middle statue along the wall of the helm, reading a small note in her hand. Myrcle could see a few stains on the parchment where the light passed through the dark spots. All the while, Velkin leaned against the corner of the walls around the helm, peering over the scroll of the Xurinal. She was eyeing it so intently that Myrcle thought it might burst into flames from her scrying. He walked over to her and saw that instead of their usual color, her eyes were gray and clouded. Myrcle placed his hand upon her shoulder and was instantly taken into another state of mind and being.

* * *

Velkin stood at the precipice of a cliff cast in vibrant marble that slowly crumbled away into an endless oblivion. Darkness shrouded most of the area like rising smoke, and Myrcle could see the many statues of the Pantheon of Dawn, including the Betrayer. Velkin stood upon the brink of oblivion, its maw open to devour her into its darkness. Two figures behind her—no bigger than young adults—held her hands in theirs, and another figure was present as well, though Myrcle could not see it. He felt its presence; radiant yet abyssal, savior and destroyer.

As Myrcle deciphered the presence, he heard a voice in the air. "Are you okay?" echoed one of the younglings.

Velkin's voice replied, "I'm fine, sweetheart."

The other youth called out, "Where's dad?"

"I haven't found him yet."

"Where is he?"

"Somewhere in here, I guess."

"When will you find him?"

"One day, and then she'll deliver on her promise. We'll be a family again, just like we used to be. How's that sound?"

The one on the right responded first, "I don't like that voice; it's so mean to you."

"I know, but soon we won't have to worry about that anymore, and I'll find your father."

The younglings reached to hug her, but before they could, they dispersed into dust. Myrcle watched as Velkin plummeted to her knees and hit the floor, crying. She wept ceaselessly, loudly, and such cries echoed into the dark night of the world in which they both stood. Then thousands of voices sang together to Velkin as one.

"Why do you weep, my child?"

Velkin gave no response.

The voices beckoned again. "Why do you weep, my child? Are you frightened?"

"Yes, I am afraid."

"What is it that you fear?"

"I will never have my family back. I have served you my entire life, Great Sentinel, yet each time I have come to your place of wisdom, darkness has grown stronger."

"It is the darkness that festers in the Xurinal, my child. Until you have completed your task, the darkness will continue to grow and infect our place of worship. You cannot fail me. Unleash the shadow from within and cleanse the world of the First Sin."

As the voice echoed its last words from the pit, a brilliant light shone about the room and darkness retreated from it for a moment, then the darkness smothered it. Each of the statues rumbled and collapsed. The ceiling high above the pyramid fell upon Myrcle and Velkin. They were yanked back into reality.

* * *

Myrcle and Velkin's breath left them all at once as they were thrust back into the hold of the Red Baron. Her eyes darted wildly with fear until they found Myrcle, whose hand was still resting on her shoulder. Myrcle stood there silently, with only his breath making any noise, and even that was mostly covered by the sea. His friend had tears in her eyes, and he now knew what she was fighting for, but he was confused.

"Velkin," he began with a light whisper, but she cut him off.

"That was not meant for your eyes!" Velkin snarled.

"I know, and I'm sorry, but," he paused for a moment, "Velkin," he tried to find the right words, but he couldn't, and simply spoke, "They can't come back. No one can bring them back."

Organa and Esvele walked over to them.

"You know nothing of the limits of life and death," she snapped back at him.

"Everything okay?" Organa asked, worried as she approached.

"It's fine," Velkin shot back swiftly.

"Indeed," Myrcle confirmed with suspicion.

"Well, come on. We need to plan for Valistar—and how we're not going to die," Organa joked, trying to lighten the mood.

They walked over to the helm where Talos stood, tying a rope over a prong extending from the wheel to hold the course toward the city.

"All right," Esvele started, "we either figure this out, or we're fucked."

"Good start to the planning stage," Talos laughed. Esvele shot an annoyed look at him, as she always did. "I get the weird feeling you don't like me."

"Not right now, I don't." Esvele gave a fake grin.

"So, you like me sometimes." He gave a cocky smile.

"Don't get ahead of yourself," she said blankly.

"I think we should find the Chapter in Valistar for the Children of the Crimson Moon," Organa said as she walked over to them.

"What?" Esvele gave Organa a confused look.

"The Crimson Priest said he hadn't heard anything from them. The Blood Mother mentioned it as well; it has to mean something."

"There is nothing we need to worry about."

"What if they could help?"

"They wouldn't trust us," Myrcle explained.

"The Blood Mother named us her 'Champions of Eternity.'"

"And that means?" Talos asked.

"I've no idea, but it gives us standing with her and, therefore, standing with the leader of the Chapter in Valistar."Myrcle suggested.

"If they're still alive," Velkin said bluntly.

"Well, who has a better idea, then?"

"The information we need is the validity of the Sepulcher beneath the Xurinal; the easiest way to get any information would be the Western Obelisk," Myrcle said.

"And how are we going to do that?" Velkin asked.

"I could get in there," Florie interjected.

"How?"

"I could fly up to the bridges and sneak inside. Just tell me what to look for." Florie said.

"That might work to find what we need, but the problem still remains of how to stay hidden in the city. The Black Riders are looking for us. The Lady Magis and the Soulflame King are looking for us. Who knows? The other members of the Conclave of Daggers might look for us now after what happened to Itheca. Multiple people want us. How are we going to stay hidden in the biggest city in the world? On top of that, we do not know where Bendrit is, the strongest of us all." Organa said while counting on her fingers for each person in search of them.

"He'll be in contact soon," Myrcle assured her, "but you are right—we have to stay hidden."

"We'll reach the city tomorrow if the wind holds like this, so we'd better figure it out," Talos explained.

"What if something happened to Bendrit?" Florie asked. "What if they captured him?"

"Then it will be our job to set him free," Velkin stated.

"Great, just another thing to add to the list," sighed Esvele.

They sat quietly, deliberating on how to accomplish their goals for a while, and then Velkin figured it out. "We could play into Merith's claim."

"I thought paladins didn't drink?" Florie raised an eyebrow.

"I'm serious. If Merith was right about Organa's mother being alive, then we have a direct way into the Citadel and stand with the Lord and Lady."

"If she is alive somehow, she's a prisoner," Organa said, thinking back on her conversation with Myrcle.

"Think about it," Velkin began. "If the Menitheals have your mother, then we have an advantage. She is a sage of wisdom and power who could easily dispatch the Enemy with great prejudice. And when we find Bendrit, there will be two—and nothing could stand against us."

"If they had her, they'd kill her," Esvele barked.

"You're not understanding. We could free her quickly and overthrow them, finally bringing peace. All we need is the help of Bendrit and your mother," Velkin assured Organa, another green shimmer passing in front of her blue eyes.

"I want to believe she's alive, Velkin, but I don't want to cling to a false hope." The words cut through everyone as they left Organa's mouth. Neither Myrcle, Esvele, Florie, nor Velkin said a word.

The words from such a young child in his eyes surprised Talos. "Rough life?"

"You could say that," she said solemnly.

"We have the Glass Key; without it, they can't open the Sepulcher," Esvele quickly changed the subject.

"The darkness always wins," Velkin grunted. "They are always seven steps ahead of us. We have no chance."

Myrcle squinted and noticed the difference in Velkin, but before he could speak, the drakeman cut in. "Okay, calm down there, holy one," Talos said, rolling his eyes. "I know you still worship the Pantheon; it's written all over that golden get-up of yours, but some of us had to learn to live without them. Not all of us are all-powerful beings with the gods on our side. Florie and I are not Magiqas, royalty, or like you. How do we stand a chance?"

"He has a point," Florie agreed with him. "What can we do?"

"Whatever is necessary to ensure the safety of Lorial," Myrcle answered, "You may not be able to alter the world with ice or fire like Organa and me, or the power to call upon the gods for aid, or the command over nature that Esvele has, but we all have something together…loss. We have all lost and suffered under the tyranny of the Void, which has found its way into the hearts and minds of the Soulflame King and Lady Magis. And now we have another point of common ground: we have something to fight for—the people of Lorial."

"And each other," Organa added.

Talos looked at her in disbelief. "I barely know you four, and in the brief time I've been with you, my city was destroyed, one of my best friends was killed, and I've nearly died twice. You are a cataclysm of your own."

It was with those last four words that the rage within Velkin sparked in her eyes and erupted like a volcano. She moved with such ferocity that the others could not stop her. She grabbed Talos by his scaly blue neck and hoisted him into the air with one hand once again.

"Enough, Velkin." Myrcle thrust her against the wooden floor, which gave way under her, splintering planks into pieces. A bright shimmer appeared in Velkin's free hand that was overtaken quickly by flecks of shadow, and her holy sword manifested in her hand. With a swift descent, her blade penetrated the floor and gave her fortitude against the spell, breaking from Myrcle's influence. Florie rushed to strike the paladin with a dagger but met the blade of the longsword—once kept in Talos' sheath at his side, now wielded by Esvele. The loud ring of the blades echoed across the sea, and Velkin felt herself come back to her senses.

Velkin's sword diminished, and a look of horror came over her face. "I'm sorry," she said with a stutter. "I'm sorry," she repeated at least five more times.

The night came not too long after, and the stars above seemed so faint and dim. Velkin kept to herself all evening and most of the night in solitude in a cabin below deck; though she believed the brig was more appropriate for her actions, the few rays of light that shone through the square slits in the ceiling made it almost look like prison bars. A place she deserved more than anyone she had ever banished into the dark planes of reality. *I will safeguard the innocent, fight for the weak, and be a herald of light upon the world. I am a Servant of Dawn and wielder of starlight. I am the light in the darkness and the shield of the Silver Kingdom. I will never falter in my duties, and I will prevail over all evil. I am a Paladin of Dawn.*

The old vows ran through her mind, repeating themselves without end until a new thought entered her mind, though she was not sure if it was her own. *Why do you recite old falsities and noble words of a bygone age? Your faith has left you, and you've nothing to do but burn..*

"Get out of my head!" she screamed, and the room shook violently with her rage.

The sound of tumbling and a flutter took Velkin by surprise. She jolted from her position, summoning her blade to her side. A groan in the dark came with easy recognition: it was Myrcle. "What was that?" he trembled, small streams of tears falling from his eyes.

Velkin made her way over the scattered boxes of supplies Myrcle had knocked over during his descent and looked down at his feathered friend. "What are you doing down here?"

"Apparently giving myself a concussion," Myrcle said as a hand stretched out to aid him. He took Velkin's hand, and she pulled him to his feet. "Why are you down here?"

"I needed to be alone for a bit."

"Velkin," Myrcle began and then stopped.

"Yes?"

"What was that I saw in your mind? Where were you?"

"The Xurinal. The eyes of a paladin see more than just the mortal plane. Even here, I can see darkness as it wraps over the world." She walked over to the small round window and peered out through the porthole. She saw there in the distance, beyond the Red Sea, writhing shadows that slowly expanded over the little of land she could distinguish. Velkin explained all she could see to Myrcle behind her, and she said the words of old, "I am a Paladin of Dawn."

"I heard the voices in the Xurinal speaking to you."

"And what did you hear?"

"I heard the voice of the god Calikan speaking to you. I saw your children wishing for their father to be there as well. The darkness I saw reached from within the Xurinal's deep foundations…"

"Calikan has brought me there many times in recent years to show me the growing corruption and guide me."

"And who is this 'she' you told your sons would deliver?"

"Organa," Velkin said with a small smile. "She is so powerful she will deliver us from the darkness."

"One person could never keep such power."

"No one thought that the Shadowlight could hold its power, and look what we found out. Who knows what the limitations of magic are?"

"Velkin," Myrcle said, worried for her, "you're clinging to false hope. We can't change the past."

"Who is to say what I can and can't do?" she shouted back at him in rage. He jumped away from her. In his hand, she saw the shining light of a small fire.

"I'm sorry, Myrcle." Her face instantly changed to disgust and sorrow. She fell to her knees and wept ceaselessly. Myrcle knelt down to comfort his friend as she cried into his shoulders.

"Of course, you are, my dear."

"I don't feel like it."

"Velkin," Myrcle said as he walked closer and placed his hands on hers, "the trauma that we have lived through is more than many could bear in a single life. Everything we ever loved was ripped from us. I lost my students, and you lost a family. Esvele lost hers, and so did Organa. It is our duty to their memories to fight in their name and bring the light of the Dawn Eternal as close as we can to the world. To live is to suffer; such is the curse of mortality. In the suffering, there is peace, and truest of all friends are revealed in that darkness and brought to your side to aid you."

"Life is a prison. Suffering holds you against the rushing waters of grief and pain while you can't fight the eternal current of anguish," Velkin whispered under her breath.

"Only to those who feel lost. Those trapped alone in their minds. You are not alone, Velkin."

"Worlds will rise and fall, kingdoms will crumble into ashes, the sands of time will run out, and I will never have my children back or the one whom I love," she said as she burned a hole through the ship with her stare. "Leave me—please...I need to be alone."

"Velkin," he paused, "are you-"

"*Leave me!*"

Myrcle jumped and turned to go back up the stairs, allowing Velkin her solitude.

* * *

The night passed. The light of the sun rose and shone over the Red Sea's waves as Talos steered them north toward Valistar. It would be a few days upon the Red Sea and where it mixed with the Old Sea before they reached the shores of the City of Kings. Talos spent that time either steering the ship or crafting his masterful plan of getting the others into Valistar. He was ready to go back to Itheca, but what was there to go back to? The Conclave was gone, the Queen of Thieves was dead, and his home was destroyed. Though he had not decided to stay, he thought to himself about the possibility. He eyed one in the group, though she did not notice or, more than likely, did not feel the same way. She was stone cold, determined, and yet graceful, kind, and compassionate... at least he hoped she was. He had often thought of approaching her before, but it had only been a short time since he had met her.

That night he watched as her hair flowed like the waves of the Red Sea, the red flowing down her back and as beautiful as the sky above it. Esvele was always so beautiful to him. Even when she held him against the walls of stone in the Conclave. Her actions after had been worrying, but he had them coming, as he made an advance far before he should have.

Esvele's gray, foggy eyes peered into the future—or what she believed to be the future.

*　*　*

Five great dragons—each a different color: black, green, blue, red, and white—flew overhead to different scenes shrouded in darkness until the first unveiled itself: a golden-topped city where the Xurinal stood above almost all, save a great keep along the cliffs of the sea. A rumble beneath the streets, like an earthquake, shook the depths of the Lightless Maze, with its climax coming with the shattering of the holy temple from within by the breath of winter. Magnificent and terrible winds of the blizzard turned the very foundations of that place into crystal blue ice until the heat of a frenzied flame erupted from the origin of the snowstorm. An unadulterated, rageful, potent flame rushed over the land beyond the city like a tidal wave. The rushing fire burst across the hillside where Esvele stood, and it consumed her. Rather than a burning sensation across her body, she felt a piercing flame crawl inside her, where a blade of immolation, connected to the hand of a red-eyed figure consumed by rage, stood within the red sea.

Her pain didn't last long as she was taken to a new premonition: a sprawling temple of white wood covered in blooming flowers of every land across Lorial, sprouting from vines that held two colossal stone, rune-carved doors shut. A skyward mural along the ceiling, carved in silver, showed a terrible, misshapen creature of tendrils, eyes, teeth, and bone protruding from a tear between realities, ready to devour all creation. Two tall figures, one of white marble and the other of shadowglass, stood side-by-side, erupting what looked like beams of energy upon the ungainly beast. The mural stretched on, telling a story further, but before Esvele could comprehend its tale, a toxic fume burst through the ceiling from the mouth of the green beast. Her feet carried her as fast as they could, bringing her back to the massive doors guarded by the blossoms, and one stood out.

Without a second thought, Esvele plucked the flower from its stem and placed a petal on her tongue. A swift feeling spun the world around her as the light from beyond the two weighty doors opened and blinded her for a moment. Esvele looked back and could see the rest of the temple being eaten by a rapidly growing rot. Pustules of death grew along the walls, covering every surface as the dragon's blight spread further. The light beyond the door vanished as she ran from the besieging decay, emerging upon a war-torn battlefield that was once the Living City. Screams echoed far and wide, only to be overcome by the roars and shrill screeches of a demonic host.

Boom!

Crash!

Concussive explosions rang throughout the haven as falling stars rained down from the black, starless heavens, made clear by the lifeless foliage. Crushed, burnt, and popping wood gave way to the power of the green dragon as she landed in front of Esvele, snarling with her snaggled teeth. A crown of five red horns that turned white at their tips led down to a long face where purple eyes glistened with a strange beauty. The dragon's mouth opened, exuding a terrible breath that nearly killed Esvele the moment she took it in. Esvele could see the bloody sores of the poison writhing within the beast's mouth and further down its throat, ready to unleash a miasma of death.

Another *crash* caved in the top of the temple behind Esvele as the great blue dragon landed. Its face, more so the eyes, was very familiar, but she could not place its origin. The blue dragon reared back its head and opened its mouth, where crackling streaks of energy connected the sharp teeth like a spiderweb. It thrust its head forward and released a thunderstorm energized with flashing lightning. With the force of a hurricane, the green dragon's armor-like scales shattered like glass as her gargantuan body broke the massive trees. Revealing the starless night high above them.

A glimpse of hope broke through the night as twelve stars shone through the oppressive shadow above, growing in their grandeur with each second, moving with such speed that they were barely perceptible. Esvele's hope quickly ran out as the stars revealed themselves to be massive, burning red meteors that fell from the dark heavens. Engulfing the trees in red immolation, the fire spread like an infection in the body, devouring and killing as it went. Two figures stood about it all, butchering corpses upon a jagged rock stained by the blood and entrails of the innocent. A man in red robes, accented with gold patterns of fire, stood beside a woman with silver hair like his. Burning crimson eyes glowered over his domain as he reveled in the ecstasy of destruction. Behind him, his twin stood with timeless emerald eyes, but her pain was clear as she struggled to watch her home consumed by her brother's rage. Esvele called out to Organa, but the darkness consumed her, tearing her away from the vision of the future.

* * *

Esvele snapped back into the world with a rush of freezing wind as she dangled over the Red Sea. A column of air whirled around her, and she screamed as her eyes focused on the crimson water. Organa held her concentration intensely to keep the wind tunnel at the pace of the ship and, for a quick moment, Esvele felt herself fall toward the water. A yell from behind her echoed across the sea, and she was pulled high up into the sky before she fell again, this time toward the helm. Another twister of air caught her just seconds before she would have connected with the wood, and then she fell only a few inches onto the floor. Talos ran quickly to Esvele and helped her up, but she shoved him off and ran over to Organa, who was gripping her head and beating it.

"Stop, stop, stop, stop!" Organa screamed as she heard the Dark Song.

"Organa, listen to me. Listen—follow my voice back." Esvele pleaded.

Organa's sealed eyes flashed images in front of her of power and pain. A charred body and gurgling blood, screams of thousands, and death everywhere.

"Organa, come back! Please come back!"

The images became clearer and clearer as they passed by or dragged on in moments of agony. Shadows of evil beasts of flesh, bone, decay, and death ran through her mind as they slaughtered innocents. Her vision slowed almost completely and focused on a single dark form in front of a large black pyramid that gleamed like polished shadowglass. The figure was made of darkness, yet flowed and pulsed from bursts of light and radiance within it. *You are so weak, Esvele. You would have so much power, you do have so much power. You need only let it flow. Listen to the Dark Song, let it be a part of you, harness its melody and use it,* a voice echoed in Organa's mind, *a state of peace and in knowing we are the future.* The voice was dead and grave, and Organa turned to see the figure behind her. Her gaze met two pairs of eyes burning with red fire. The vision faded, and Organa's eyes traced the faces around her, wild as she screamed and returned to her friends.

"Organa," Esvele shook her.

"I saw," she gasped, "I saw Kyriel."

"What?" Myrcle asked.

"I saw Kyriel," she gasped for more air. "He was—he was—he was talking to Esvele." Myrcle gave his old friend a curious look. "He said to 'listen to the Dark Song'—that it was 'the future.'"

"He's free," Esvele trembled.

"No," Organa gasped again, "No. It was like I was seeing the past again. Like a memory."

"He never said that to me."

"Not yet," Velkin raised an eyebrow. "The Sepulcher rips apart your power, and your soul, over and over again. Putting that back together so many times could have given him more abilities."

"You think he developed Far Sight?" Myrcle asked.

"Is that even possible?" Talos asked. "I know very little about magic, but you can't just manifest powers."

"If you are a Magiqas, you can," Myrcle corrected him, "We are connected to the Flux of Magic, and the Balance of Chaos is so ever-shifting that when we release so much magic at one time when we regenerate, new powers can manifest."

"Magic is too confusing to keep track of," Talos sighed.

"How can she have Far Sight?" Florie asked.

"*She* doesn't, *he* does," Myrcle answered. "There must be some connection between the two of you."

"What else did you see?"

"A black pyramid. Glossy and huge. Esvele was in chains, and there were two pairs of burning purple eyes. Gurgling blood sounds, thousands of screams, monstrous eldritch beasts…"

Organa named off the moments from her vision, and Myrcle said, "The pyramid was the Sepulcher."

"I thought so," Organa nodded. "How are we going to stop him?"

"I don't know," Myrcle shook his head.

Talos walked over to the helm. "We'd better find out," he said, turning the wheel, "'cause we're not too far from Valistar."

A couple of days passed with much conversation about what the plan could be once they reached Valistar. Talos suggested that they use the old passageways and sneak into the Western Obelisk. But Florie admitted that such a feat would take over six months to properly plan. Velkin believed they should rally the people in a grand revolution against the Menitheal Dynasty. Myrcle disagreed; it would be effective in overthrowing them and that their mission should be done in secret to avoid unneeded chaos. Organa still believed that they should find the Chapter of the Children of the Crimson Moon in the city and use that as a base of operations before infiltrating Castle Black Rose. But Esvele advised against it as she did not trust them. Not to mention the Priest the Blood Mother mentioned to them had yet to reveal himself or contact them. Some arguments and choice words were exchanged, and Velkin and Myrcle had a long conversation on the second deck of the Red Baron. Talos continued to try to talk to Esvele, but a conversation that Organa slightly overheard blew up in his face when he made an advance on her.

Organa went to Esvele that night. "So, someone has the hots for you," she wiggled her eyebrows.

"No thanks," Esvele scoffed back. "He's egotistical and, by all means of the word, an idiot."

"Fair point," Organa laughed back.

After a moment, their laughter died down, and Esvele sat beside her old student. "How are you holding up?"

"Well," Organa said with a harsh breath, "one day at a time. How's that sound?"

"Out with it," Esvele raised an eyebrow.

"I'm getting scared more and more. I feel like I can't go a single moment without hearing the Dark Song in my head when I think about the possibility of my mother being alive if Merith wasn't lying, or when I look at my hands and see the burn scars from that night, or anytime I remember something."

"You're remembering more?" Esvele asked, turning toward her.

"Again, bits and pieces. Right now I can see the top of a mountain, a courtyard full of magical students, and my father's face," she said, smiling as the images flashed in front of her eyes—but it was quickly taken away by the thought of Kyriel. "His smile, his laugh echoing, our duels and adventures along the mountainside; everything is still a jumbled mess but when I see him, all I feel is anger and guilt."

"'Guilt'?"

Organa rose from her seat and paced back and forth. "I wasn't able to stop them from making him what he is now. I feel somewhat responsible for not helping sooner before Vexian took him and twisted him beyond anything we could have imagined. I should've known better. I should've seen." With each sentence, Organa's voice broke further until a stream of tears flowed down her cheek. Esvele leaped up to hug her, catching the young woman in her arms and holding her as she wept.

"You have no part in this. Neither of you should have ever been pulled into this in the first place," Esvele tried to calm her down.

"But if I had tried harder, I might have saved him."

"The same goes for us, love. If all of us had been a few seconds earlier, there is a chance that he could have been spared his fate. And there's also the chance that he would have been corrupted, anyway. No one will ever know the truth of the matter, but what we do know is that he is not the same and will unleash ultimate terror upon the world if he is allowed to escape."

"But he's suffering in there. Four hundred years, Esvele. Four hundred years in the dark and surrounded by nothingness."

"And that is where he must stay. If he doesn't, we will be damning the world to whatever power he can conjure."

"There has to be a way to save him," Organa's eyes twinkled with the slightest hint of hope. "Maybe I could convince him. I could change him back to who he used to be."

"I highly doubt that. And even if you could, what if he doesn't want to change?"

"Then I will make him change! He shouldn't be who he is now," Organa snapped at her old mentor.

"You are internalizing something that will tear you apart, Organa," Esvele pleaded with her. "Please do not fall into the trap of thinking you can fix him."

"Why are you so sure he can't be fixed? Why have you given up?" Esvele sputtered, trying to find something that would comfort Organa, but there was nothing. "I have to believe there is a chance to get him back. He's all I have left of my family."

"We could be your family Organa," Esvele sighed.

"Not like he could." Organa left the room and fell onto the softness of her cot as the sea rocked her into a dreamless sleep.

A red dawn rose over the mountains on the eastern shore of Rethial. The waters of the Red Sea lost their color and changed to a violet shade before eventually, the crystal-deep blue of the Old Sea consumed it. Talos stood at the helm of the Red Baron and steered the ship around the fjord that led into the Blue Markets of Valistar. Organa wondered that when she saw the city, it would be as Myrcle said it was. A living replica of Husieàkritae, with its marble-walled homes and the great citadel in all its majesty. The Xurinal a beacon of hope and gleaming light in the darkness on Lorial.

Esvele walked behind her and placed a hand on her shoulder. "Are you ready?"

"I don't know," Organa nervously sighed. "What if I can't handle seeing Husieàkritae? What if it reminds me too much of home? My mother? Father? My brother?"

"You are strong, Organa. One of the strongest Magiqas of your age. Your power is limitless, just like ours. But in that infinity, we must regulate ourselves and hold to our truths of love and compassion. Memory holds power over us, but we cannot let it overtake us. 'Forgive and forget' as the saying goes. "That is what must happen for one to conquer the Dark Song. I brought Myrcle back when he realized the destruction he was causing. I was brought back by the words of my oldest companion—you—"

Organa interrupted, "failed."

"No."

"Yes," she said sternly, "I let my power erupt from within me instead of controlling it at Mount Doloroth. When Myrcle tried to comfort me, I nearly turned his arm into solid ice and shattered it. I have lost myself twice now, and before I knew of my past, I never had it.

Sometimes I wonder if it would have been better to have met you and Myrcle again. Brok would still be alive."

"Organa," Esvele spoke but stopped herself. She did not know how to respond. She could feel Organa's shoulder quivering and felt the air around her get colder. "Organa," she finally spoke, "you're right." Organa looked at Esvele now. "You are right about everything. If we had not come to find you, Brok would still be alive." She could not think of what else to say. All she did was stand there and hold on to her student.

"I miss him, EV," Organa said as her eyes began to tear up. "I miss him so much."

"Me too," Esvele sighed.

"I forget you knew him too."

"I knew a different Brok, I think," she laughed. "I remember a Brok that was naïve and reckless; kind yet stern in moments of tension; proud but humble—a good man."

"No," Organa corrected her, "We knew the same person. He was just an idiot for the last half."

The two laughed for a brief moment and heard Talos shout out, "Valistar right ahead!"

Organa ran to the bow of the Red Baron and looked onward as the ship rounded the edge of the rocky shoal hiding the City of the Reborn.

The back of Castle Black Rose faced them, and along its spine was a great cascade of painted glass that swirled inward to form the crest of the Menitheal Dynasty. The Silver Spires rose high into the sky from the great hall of the castle, and the bridges that connected them spanned great distances. Myrcle's eyes were fixed on their goal, the Western Obelisk. Its peak was a large balcony with five stones so large that even at this distance a copper would have covered one of the boulders and there still would be a few centimeters left to spare. The orbs rotated around the apex, and a few soundless bolts of lightning flashed from within the observatory. The King's Pillar stood high to the north like a torch on the hillside behind the city, which dipped down into a river. Myrcle saw the Eastern Sunrise Tower and its golden top with sunlight-filled glyphs carved into the throat of the tower. The symbols burned with the dawn, gleamed like stars, yet were still gentle enough upon the eyes not to hurt when seen.

The Blue Markets held hundreds of docked ships. Most of their sails were white, but a few were colored green and red; a single purple sail stood out to Talos. The squawking of a seagull among the silks of the masts drew Organa's attention as she looked to the left and saw that the city stretched on for miles. But she saw something that made her heart flutter as well. The Cathedral of Dawn, the Xurinal, stood tall and proud among the buildings. A great pyramid of marble and chiseled stone, decorated with fine borders of precious gems and metals. It disgusted her, as if the building were more important to the people than the actual gods themselves.

The City of the Reborn gleamed in the rising sun like fire upon the cliff-side. The white marble that Organa remembered was not the source of the shimmer upon the city. Instead, the large, gold-lined roofs of the red-bricked structures. A gigantic wall, seventy feet high, stood guard around the city, and guard towers that stretched another thirty feet higher stood where the individual walls joined together. Small balconies that extended from doors held barrels of arrows and racks of longbows. Slits along the throat of the towers' expanse allowed them to see the barrels of cannons, ready to defend against any fleet or armada that dared sail to Valistar with violence on their mind.

The loud sound of a high, wobbly-pitched horn drew all the companions' attention as darkness moved across the field leading to Valistar. Bobbing black banners held by the Flames of the Sphinx came upon the city like a hurricane. Organa could barely make out the seven Black Riders leading their legions of soldiers as they got closer to the city.

"How are we going to survive in there?" Florie rightly asked as she walked up beside Organa.

"I've no idea," she answered.

III

The Gathering Shadow

"The sky was silent, Heaven still,
No angel's trumpet cried.
The Moons grew pale on every hill
And the stars themselves seemed blind.
No god nor saint nor whispered name
Could stay the endless flood,
And all that dwelt in silver flame
Were buried in their blood."
- The Songs of Sorrow
Gavrel Ul'Tar, Court Poet of Valistar
27 AC

City of the Reborn

They docked the Red Baron in the Blue Markets under the shade of the great walls and the cliffs above them. Talos and Myrcle pulled up the sails and Florie dropped the anchor. The water sloshed against the beams that held up the wooden dock. The Red Baron and the other ships rocked in the wake of boats going by. Myrcle took notice of at least eight galleons with dark-wood hulls and sails of red and purple silks. Cranes loading crates of grain, supplies, and other goods lowered their loads into the cargo hold of each ship. Raised voices giving commands echoed along the Blue Markets docks as the Red Baron got closer to the southern shore of Valistar. Castle Black Rose pierced the heavens like a blasphemous tower of mortal pride, making itself out to be a god. The shouts of dockmen calling out orders as they grappled the ship's side drew Organa's attention away from the gigantic castle on the coast. Triple-pronged hooks caught the railing of the Red Baron, pulling her to the side of the dock. A ramp raised up and fell, bridging the gap over the rippling water. Esvele's boots clopped against the wood as she descended to the moor. The others followed behind Esvele, making their way down the berth.

Esvele's boots clopped against the wood as she descended to the wharf. His quill surprised her; it was a Heltic's feather. It was tall and thin with a vein that was an ombre from top to bottom of a deep blue that shifted into a fiery and burning red and yellow. The birds were uncommonly rare, even before the Cataclysm, as they preferred solitude in high mountains or dense forests where game was plentiful and peace and quiet were common. An adventurer once told her that while he was on an errand for a local man in his town, he wandered into the Golden Forest of Dremica and came across a Heltic and its chicks. He had told her it was like its wings were made of pure fire when the sun shone upon them and that it, unlike many birds, allowed him to approach the nest. Although Esvele did not believe he would have had the chance before the Heltic attacked to even look at the nest, she wondered what such an experience would be like. Maybe she would, one day, before the Vitu'Lux left her. But she knew that wouldn't be too far off; her mortality was catching up to her.

She threw her somber thoughts aside and went to speak to the man, but before she could utter a word, he spoke in a gravelly voice, "Papers and identification, m'lady."

"I'm sorry?" She raised an eyebrow.

"Papers, please, m'lady," he repeated.

"Oh," Esvele gasped as if she knew what he was talking about. "Myrcle, could you please get the papers out of your bag? I forgot you had them." She turned her head and put emphasis on every other word. Myrcle was confused and, for some reason, did not understand what she was trying to explain to him, but then a voice entered his head: *Conjure up an illusion for me so we can dock, idiot.*

Myrcle suddenly understood. "Oh yes, sorry, I had trouble hearing you." He reached down into his satchel and, as he pulled his hand back out, wove Night and Earth together, forging papers. "Here you go, dearie," he said as he stretched his hand out to her with the fake papers in hand.

Esvele held up the papers for the old man to see and concentrated heavily to maintain the spell. He paid her no attention and instead pointed to the empty space on the podium. Esvele worried about keeping the spell intact as she set them down. There were seven in total; six of them were identification forms and the other was the paperwork for the Red Baron. Esvele set the papers down on the podium. The old man went to touch them, and each of the friends worried wildly as he went to inspect their information.

The old man wrapped his fingers around the edges of the first page, which stated Esvele's name as "Lady Vestenra of the Lonely Isle and Magistrate of Nefis." The old man instantly worried, his face went pale, and his voice quivered with fear, "Forgive me, Lady Magistrate," he said as his knees slowly sank to the wooden floorboard, "I did not realize you were coming this early for the Council of the Nine. Please have mercy, m'lady, have mercy." He cried and groveled at her boots. Many of the other people around had heard him say Esvele's "title," and everyone who did instantly fell before her, trembling. Even the stoic guards knelt in their heavy black metal armor, inverting their blades on the floor of the

Esvele, without turning so as not to be suspicious, sent a mental message to Myrcle: *What the hell?*

Myrcle responded, *Sorry*.

Esvele looked upon the people and saw them still in shock. She elevated her voice and commanded forward, "How dare you disrespect me in such a manner, all of you?" There were many whimpers among the subjects. "You are lucky I have had a lovely trip down and will spare you my wrath. *But* should I ever return to find such informality? I *should* have you imprisoned and hanged for this ignorance. However, I will spare my wrath." Esvele then strutted forward with her friends behind her, and the papers faded as her concentration broke. The companions straightened their postures and walked with pride behind their magistrate.

Esvele heard Myrcle enter her head, *Well, this might be easier than we thought.*

Esvele saw a thin Elven guard walking down the stone stairs leading up to two large, carved metal gates as the companions made their way toward the city. He wore no helmet, instead donning a golden circlet with a diamond-shaped sapphire in the center. A long white cloak, turned brown on the train, trailed down the stairs behind him. His clothes were made of fine leather and blue-colored fabric. Although he wore plain black slacks and black pointed shoes, his top was a deep-sea blue with golden buttons up to the neck that accented with silver lining as well as the cuffs at the ends of the sleeves. His head was buried in the paper clenched in his black-gloved hands, and she cleared her throat.

"I'm sorry, madam, but I am too terribly busy to have to deal with such trifling matters. Out of my way," he said without looking up from his paper.

"How dare you?" she said in a very posh voice.

The Elf raised his head at last. "Who are you?"

"M'lord, this is the Lady Magistrate of Nefis," a kneeling guard clarified for him as Esvele gave him a disapproving look. "My lady," he said as quickly bowed, "welcome to Valistar. We did not expect you so early for the Council of the Nine."

"I believe I can arrive whenever I want, Ser–" her voice trailed off.

"I am no Ser; I am Captain Markus, my lady, and I am in charge of the Blue Market Guard," he said as he rose. "If it pleases, m'lady, you do not seem quite dressed for such an occasion as the Council of the Nine."

"Do not presume to straighten yourself in my presence or question my dress, Captain!" Esvele shouted, enraged.

"Forgive me, m'lady. I meant no offense."

"Well, you have surely failed in such a venture. Furthermore, I wore this to disguise myself in case of pirates or other miscreants of the Old Sea. I assure you, Captain, I will speak to the Master of Arms about your incompetence."

"Forgive me, m'lady," Markus's voice trembled.

"Now, where will I find my transportation?" Markus raised himself again. "Did you not hear me, Captain?" and he corrected himself, returning to his bow.

"Within the city walls, m'lady, I will assure you a coach will be waiting to take you to the Citadel."

"It better be there when I enter the city. I dislike being kept waiting."

"Of course, m'lady."

Esvele and her friends walked onward up the stairs toward the entrance into Valistar. The people below on the docks stayed in their bowed positions until Esvele had ascended the staircase. Then they continued their day, but the fear would stay with them for days to come, knowing that the Lady Magistrate of Nefis was in the city. When the companions approached the gate, the guards were already kneeling, as they had heard the discord from the docks. A breeze kicked up Esvele's cloak, and she thought about how these people could believe she was nobility. Her black cloth, leather clothing, and ripped cloak gave every indication she was common, and frankly, she was in awe that they believed the fake paperwork. "I wish to enter the city. Open the gates immediately!"

"As you wish, m'lady."

The carved gate of silver and gold looked like the stars above, each with the trailing tails of comets behind them. A venture of such magnitude, the gate must have taken at least three years to carve to perfection. The walls of Valistar were made of sandstone, but red like clay. They saw great embrasures where many archers were looking down at the Lady Magistrate and, when Esvele's gaze met theirs, they instantly disappeared behind the defenses of the wall. A loud *clank* sounded as large horizontal columns, two in the front and two in the back, made of jade, moved back into the wall and out of large silver hoops that held the gate closed. They could hear the sounds of chains pulling the supports back and saw the gate opening into the city as the morning sunlight shone through the break in the gates.

Valistar was revealed to them in all its glory, and the flames they had seen from the ship in the fjord were not as bright, but still gleamed on the rooftops of the buildings. The buildings were made of red bricks and concrete, but there were many tents lining their edges, with people exchanging goods or coins for food, jewelry, and other items. Many people were rushing out of the street as they noticed a magnificent coach driven by a Kalishtani woman and drawn by four black horses wearing silver armor approaching. The woman wore purple cloth and leather clothing, and a long white cloak and golden circlet with an amethyst cut into an upside-down triangle. The coach itself was made of a dark wood and decorated with gold and silver accented pieces and curved doorknobs made of overlapping precious metals.

The woman who drove the coach walked down a small ladder onto the ground and made her way to them. Her cloak dusted the ground and flowed with the breeze from the sea. Her skin was dark gray, and her eyes were a bright emerald green like Organa's. Veins of gold and silver defined four horns pushing through her black hair. She wore the same outfit as Captain Markus, except her top was colored a deep purple, had silver buttons up to the neck, a golden embroidered collar, and cuffs along with silver buttons at the end of her sleeves.

She bowed and rose. "I am Miranda, captain of the Moon Guard of Valistar. I am at your service, Lady Magistrate. Welcome to Valistar."

"Thank you, Captain Miranda. I am glad there is one captain who has respect for the nobles of our land."

"Indeed, m'lady," she said with a smile. "It is very good to see you."

"Have we met before?"

"A very long time ago, I am afraid. I would be greatly surprised if you remembered me. I am from Nefis, and I met you when I was a child." The companions' hearts began to beat faster as fear gripped them. "But I was only a few years old at that time. All I really remember is that commanding voice you had, which is still impressive to this day, m'lady."

Esvele cleared her throat. "Sorry, had something stuck there, I'm afraid. Please excuse me," she nervously laughed. "I am sorry to say that I do not remember you, my dear."

"I didn't expect much. It was one of the last festivals we had in the city before my family fled."

"Ah, I see, well," Esvele paused, "I hate that you missed the others."

"Why?" Miranda laughed back. "Those things were truly dull affairs and celebrated the Old Gods."

"The 'Old Gods'?" Esvele asked.

"Yes, m'lady," her tone changed to a fairly loud whisper, though still quiet. "The Pantheon of Dawn, of course."

Her words stunned Myrcle and Esvele, but Esvele dared not react incorrectly. "Ah yes," she faked her approval, "The heathen gods of old. I rejoice every morning that we have finally cast them aside."

"As should we all," Miranda said with a smirk. "Now, if you would come with me, I will take you and your advisors to the Citadel, although only four of you would be able to fit in the coach, I am afraid. I can send for another if you wish, m'lady."

"No, not to worry. I need a few of my associates to gain some items and intel for me before they return. "Ava," Esvele said, pointing to Florie, "take Malika and Dimitri with you." She motioned to Velkin and Talos. "And get me the things I asked you for when we disembarked the ship."

Florie and Velkin understood, both giving graceful bows; however, Talos did not understand being called Dimitri. He began to speak, but a sneaky stomp on his foot from Myrcle caught his attention, and he shouted in pain and glared at the old wizard.

"What the hell was that for?" Talos asked.

Myrcle changed his voice to a deeper, bellowing sound. "Oh, I'm sorry, Dimitri, I must have lost my footing for a moment."

"Dimitri?" Talos asked.

"Yes, *you*, Dimitri," Myrcle tightened his gaze.

"But?"

"Dimitri?" Esvele asked, annoyed. "Did you take your tonic this morning?"

"What tonic?" Talos was still confused.

"Your memory tonic, you fool," Esvele laughed back.

"What are you talking about?" Talos' voice was now raised slightly. "I don't need a memory tonic."

Esvele turned back to Miranda. "Poor thing, was hit by a hoof a few months ago right in the head when he was bucked off his horse and has never had the same capacity since."I only stand him because I must, due to an arrangement I had with his mother."

"How tragic," Miranda scoffed. "I'm surprised you haven't just gone to a healer."

Esvele took this opportunity to scold Talos freely. "That's actually why we came down here so early. We heard there was a healer in the city who could help with his condition."

"I am sure there is, m'lady. If it pleases you, I think we should get you to the Citadel."

"Ah yes," Esvele shook her head.

"Malika, do be sure you get him healed up, won't you? And Ava, make sure he doesn't get out of hand."

"Yes, my lady," the two answered in unison, although Talos was still very obviously confused, as they dragged him to the side of the street toward an alleyway to find a healer.

"Come along now, Olena and Kester; we don't want to keep the Lord and Lady Menitheal waiting," Esvele said through a nervous smile.

Passed Through Fire

Velkin, Florie, and Talos watched as their friends boarded the coach and Miranda took the reins in hand before driving off toward the Citadel. A dust cloud was left in their wake as Miranda shouted to the people in the market streets to make way for them. Florie saw a few citizens spit on the ground as they passed by in the coach.

"Why did she call me Dimitri?" Talos asked rather loudly. Velkin slammed him against a nearby wall.

"You are really thick, apparently, and don't know when to lie," she whisper-shouted. "It was a decoy, a lie to make sure none of us were imprisoned, or worse, executed on the spot."

"Oh," he simply sighed.

"Gods, you're dull," Velkin pushed away from him.

"Okay." Florie stepped between them. "We need to figure out what we need to do."

"We should never have brought Talos. He's an accident waiting to happen."

"Shut up, V," Florie shot at her.

"'V'?" Talos asked.

"It doesn't matter. We need to focus. This city is a death trap. At any moment, we or the others could be found out and killed, so we keep our heads down and stay out of trouble. Got it?" Florie looked furiously at both of them. Velkin nodded her head, as did Talos. "Now," Florie collected herself, "We need to figure out what Esvele, Myrcle, and Organa need us to do. Velkin, can you use a message spell?"

"I can, but it takes a few minutes for me to cast."

"Okay, let's find somewhere to lie low that has room for you to cast it and we'll get in contact with them." Florie, Talos, and Velkin left the alleyway and entered the booming markets, where they could be easily lost in the crowd. Hundreds of people pushed past one another and traded with the merchants. Florie saw a few other Hawkinas as she pushed through the crowd. One was like her, black and silver, feathered and small. There were so few of them left, the tribes scattered in Menagerie many years ago when the Cataclysm ruptured the land. Many of her people died during that time when the refugees of Dremica came to the north. Food had become scarce and impossible to grow because the Darkness blocked out the sunlight, freezing the land into a winter waste.

Talos pushed through the crowd and peeled off to the side where there was room to breathe. Velkin and Florie followed him into a covered alleyway that was shaded. "Is this a good spot, Velkin?"

"No, I need somewhere quiet where I can concentrate."

"What do you suggest then?" Florie wondered.

"Is there a tavern we can get to where we can pay for a room?"

"I have no idea. I don't know this city that well."

Talos thought about the different routes he used to take to get goods, weapons, and other things he smuggled into the city before. Then one came to mind: "We could go to the Horseman's Blade?"

"No, Talos," Florie instantly disagreed.

"It's the only place that would be able to harbor us without some fancy name. I know Jerald. He'll be able to hook us up with a room."

"No, Talos," Florie repeated, "We can't go somewhere where the

Conclave has influence. They'll kill us the moment we step foot in their territory."

"I hate to say it, but almost no one survived what happened in Itheca. How would they know?"

"The Prime Alpha and Crimson Priest survived. They could be waiting there."

"If they are, Corvin is sworn to aid us for his patron. The Prime Alpha will understand. I hope," Velkin said as she pulled down her blue hood.

"It's too risky," Florie said, unnerved.

"It's our only option," Talos said, raising his hands.

"Wait, no, it's not," Florie's eyes gleamed. "Velkin, where is Bendrit's note?"

"Why?"

"Because he said he'd meet us somewhere, maybe he's still there."

"I highly doubt that," Velkin sighed. "He could have been captured or worse, killed, by now."

"Just let me see it." Florie held out her hand, irritated. Velkin reached into a pouch on her side and put her whole arm inside, feeling around for the piece of parchment. She continued to search but couldn't find it."Oh, let me look." Florie moved Velkin's arm aside, plunged her own down inside up to her shoulder, and instantly found a piece of parchment. She gave a confused look at Velkin, who did not really react, and Florie went ahead and removed the note. Talos noticed Velkin's hand shifting under her blue cloak. Florie stood back a bit, scanned the words, and found it. "'The Morning Glory Inn on the west side of the city'—that's where we need to go."

"Then let's go get him," Velkin said. "I only pray he's still there."

The trio set back into the roaring crowd and disappeared within the sea of people in the market. They walked for about ten minutes before Florie stopped as a screaming crowd drew her attention. Velkin and

Talos looked around wildly, calling out the fake name Esvele had given her, but she never acknowledged it.

The people around her were shouting, "Traitor! Rebel! Murderer!" and other titles at a man and a woman on their knees on a stone stage for the crowd's entertainment.

They were both naked, laid bare for all to see. A few of the people shouted at the woman, "Rebel Whore," and other derogatory names. Two executioners hefted large axes, their blades decorated with blue and red flames wrought from colored metals. A set of armored soldiers guarded the staircases of gray stone on each side of the stage. A couple of banners, like the ones carried by the legion on the hillside before the Black Riders found them on their journey to Itheca, were draped over wooden stilts that held them high for all to see. The people fell silent within seconds as a door opened from the side of the stage.

Florie recognized the figure. From a dark oak door, opening like the wings of a stage, stepped Merith. She was dressed like the other captains they had met but clad in all black save her white cloak. Instead of a simple gold or silver circlet, she wore nothing to signify her nobility, as all citizens of Rethial knew her either by her face or devilish reputation.

Velkin and Talos finally spotted her. They stopped, pulled their cloaks closer to hide from the Black Rider's eyes, and watched the coming carnage. Merith waved her hand and gave a nod to the guards at the stairs. One from each of the staircases turned on the spot and grabbed chopping blocks from the back corners. Florie wanted to look away but was too fueled by the rage she harbored for Merith. Florie felt her heart burn with rage, waiting for a moment to strike, to make her pay for what she did to Natalia. Velkin felt nothing, but she knew why. Talos simply readied a dagger to throw at Merith the moment she dared order these people's death. He knew Merith was no coward and would swing the sword herself, but he knew that she was drunk with power and would feed off the fear she instilled by simply giving the orders.

"Good people of Valistar. Loyalists of the Dynasty. Before you stand two insurrectionists. Those who would dare stand against the laws of our land, be warned, for this will be your fate." Her eyes focused on Velkin's blue cloak. A foul smile crept over her face. Florie and Talos' hearts were beating so fast they felt that they might lurch forward from the power or simply leave their bodies behind. Merith said nothing, turned back around to the prisoners, and walked to stand between them.

The morning sun hit her brow but seemed to flee from her eyes as they became so dark that they simply disappeared. Merith held out both hands, and her fingertips glowed with a white and green fire. The executioners stood back, as did the guards, and Florie could hear the crying from the two people on their knees. "Behold the fate you will have."

The trio could feel the dark eyes peering into their souls.

Five green and white tendrils of wispy flames shot forth from each of her hands and then slowed down to a creeping pace a few feet away from them. The magic coiled around the prisoners' necks and moved across their skin, burning their flesh. At first, their expressions were blank and painless; they made no sound nor flinched. Once the essence reached their faces, penetrating their eyes, mouths, and nostrils, they began to roar out in agony. The flames crawled inside, flowing through their veins like blood, radiating a foul light, burning their bodies from the inside out. Their pain was so great, and the sounds that they shouted were so terrible, they could not have been explained in mortal tongues. Those there for the morning's entertainment either gasped or averted their eyes from the sight until the screams of the dying ceased and the prisoners passed on into their eternity.

Florie, Talos, and Velkin were all too familiar with the smell of burnt bodies and the sights of death, but so as not to draw attention to themselves, they mirrored the rest of the crowd and turned away from the dying prisoners. When they finally looked back, the bodies were charred black and smoking. The flames flowed out of the corpses' mouths, noses, eyes, and ears like serpents slithering across the stage. They crawled up Merith's clothing before returning to her fingertips. Her eyes reverted to their original state.

"Go now," Merith said, her voice dark and echoing. "Return to your homes and lives. Go knowing that none can stand against the might of the Sphinx's power."

Rather than exit through the door she had entered, she conjured a column of swirling green and black fire. It coiled around her body, and she vanished—falling into the space between realities.

As the guards pushed people back, the executioners—who had only been there for show—picked up the bodies and tied ropes around the wrists to carry them for honorable burial. Others moved the costumes to the back of the stage, hanging them on one of the five large hooks jutting from the wall.

Florie tensed, ready to sneak onto the stage the moment the guards dispersed, but Velkin caught her wrist and stopped her. "I'll kill her," Velkin whispered, voice shaking with rage.

"I get the first cut," Florie snarled.

"I get to keep her head. We'll avenge Natalia," Talos said, eyes fixed on the departing dark knight.

"She's mine!" Velkin barked and shoved through the crowd. Panic rippled as she summoned her gleaming sword. Merith, who had not completely left the square, turned back. A wicked smile curved her lips, and she walked once more to the edge of her stage.

Velkin stood only a few feet below her. Guards rushed to surround her, but Merith lifted a clawed, gloved hand, signaling them to hold.

"Come up on stage," Merith invited through her dead smile. "Let's give them a show." Her gaze flicked to Florie and Talos. "Do you two want vengeance as well?"

"This is between you and me," Velkin growled. "I will give you justice."

She climbed the stairs to the right, passing the soldiers, never once breaking eye contact with Merith. The crowd held their breath as Merith drew a Blood Iron blade from her waist. Talos tightened his grip on Florie to prevent her from charging up the stage and slitting Merith's throat herself.

Velkin took a fighting stance, and Merith stood tall and proud, waiting for her to strike.

Silence settled—only the clank of boots and armor carried in the air as they circled one another.

Velkin struck first. Her blade collided with Merith's crimson sword in a harsh, grating ring. She backed away and shifted her stance. Merith smiled, savoring the suspense. Another brutal clash followed as Velkin brought her sword down in an overhead strike. A side strike came next, then another—then another. One blow missed as Merith slid beneath it, slashing a line across Velkin's armor before gracefully stepping back.

Florie saw the hatred twisting Velkin's features. Velkin screamed and rushed again—no longer striking at Merith's blade, but at Merith herself. The dark knight dodged each blow with effortless precision. Velkin's attacks grew wild, less tactical, driven entirely by fury.

She swung again and again—missing, striking air, or clashing against the crimson Blood Iron. Then Merith's blade flashed, cutting the top of Velkin's hand.

"You ought to give up," Merith said. "Rot away in the Raging Cells below the Citadel. Give in... or reveal your true self. Those are your options." She laughed. "You've gotten sloppy in your old age. No wonder people have lost faith in the old gods."

Velkin swung again and missed.

"Oh dear," Merith purred. "You're either worthless… or you're holding back. If it's the latter—let go."

Velkin's blade struck the stone stage. Merith stepped lightly aside.

"Let go, Velkin." Another dodge. "Let—go." Velkin's sword struck the wall behind her. "Show the world who you are!"

At last Velkin found her mark. The crunch of metal and spray of blood marked the blow as she sliced through the back of Merith's knee, cutting through greaves and leather. Merith dropped to one knee, smiling. "Good."

She reached back. A green flame wrapped her wound, sealing it instantly. She rose. "Again."

Velkin lunged, rage surging through her. She nearly pierced Merith's heart. Merith glided away with a laugh. Velkin struck again, aiming for the throat. This time, she nicked Merith—just enough to draw a line of blood down her neck.

From below, Florie saw the delight in Merith's face—the joy of toying with Velkin—and fought against Talos' arms, but he refused to let go.

Velkin struck a shoulder plate, and Merith smiled as another attack came her way. Each one got faster and faster as Velkin shouted loudly until eventually, a *crunch* sounded through the area and a flash of light from the impact glowed. Gasps of horror were heard, and Talos let Florie go. She exposed her wings, flying up onto the stage and beside Velkin.

The once-holy blade was lodged in Merith's chest. Velkin's eyes were wild, and she gazed into the eyes of the Black Rider. "Well done," Merith whispered. With her guarded hand, she pulled herself further on the blade toward Velkin. She placed her clawed hand on

Velkin's cheek as her last raspy and dead words fell from her lips, "Sister."

Florie watched as Merith fell limp and the light from the holy blade faded, its sterling metal rusting as a wispy shadow slithered across it. As Florie landed beside Velkin, though, the darkness found its way into the cut on Velkin's hand, unseen.

"V, let go," Florie whispered. The guards rustled in their armor and instantly ran up the stairs toward them. Florie removed Velkin's hand from her blade, and Merith's body dropped to the ground with a *clank*. As she hit the ground, her body quickly rotted, as if time had finally caught up with her. Merith's remains turned to ash and slowly swept away on the wind.

Velkin, Florie, and Talos ran as fast and as hard as they could away from the scene.

The Weave Oracle

As Esvele, Organa, and Myrcle entered the coach, they saw fine leather seats dyed red, and the walls were lined with soft wool dyed purple. Four small sconces with unlit black candles in them were bolted into the wool walls, and Esvele wondered why someone would put open flames inside a compartment with flammable wool. She stepped up onto the small set of stairs that led into the coach and took a seat on the fine cushions. Myrcle came in after and sat beside her, noticing that the colors clashed, though he wasn't completely focused on that just yet.

Miranda looked over at him as she climbed up to her seat to drive. "M'lord, is everything all right?"

Organa stuttered for a moment and then responded, "Oh yes, just not a fan of confined spaces, but I'll manage, thank you," she lied, and then climbed inside. She took a seat opposite Esvele and stayed silent. For a moment, Esvele thought about asking Organa what was wrong, but as her hand graced hers, the Thread of Time passed through her eyes.

* * *

Esvele saw scenes of carnage and mass fear across the city and the great wave that came to devour the people. Valistar was truly lit aflame now, and its buildings burned in the night. The Citadel was a shambled ruin of fallen stone and broken glass, and the Xurinal was no more. In its place stood a black pyramid, maybe twenty feet high. It was smooth and glassy, like Organa had said, but as Esvele marveled at the craftsmanship…but cracks webbed its surface. The ground around her rumbled and fractured, the pieces floating above the rubble of the Xurinal. Large chunks of the holy place lifted high in the sky and formed a protective dome around the Sepulcher. The rocks broke apart into small fractals that made a haze over the area. A dark, cloudy mist exited from the cracks in the Sepulcher and flew high up into the sky. The mist formed itself into a single, jagged purple-and-white crystal about one hundred and fifty feet in the air. More of the mist poured into it, and suddenly it burst into a million shards.

From the apex of the Sepulcher shot up a beam of blinding white light that spread out like a spider's web and then converged on a single point that flung the beam into the clouds above. The clouds rotated around the tower of energy and spiraled down over it. In a fraction of a second, the clouds receded, and an explosion of green, white, and purple fire erupted and sucked in the stars above. A bottomless abyss opened up, and the reality it shattered fell like rocks into a river and disappeared only a few moments after falling upward into the nothingness.

From out of the darkness rained white, flaming meteorites that crashed into the buildings, crumbling them or instantly pulverizing them from the force of the explosion. The craters left behind dug deep into the earth, and a faint light still burned from the impact. Esvele looked into one nearby and saw a long, dark, clawed hand made of shadows stretch forth from the depths of that abyss and dig deep into the ground to pull itself out, revealing seven heads with one burning eye each. The beast stood about ten feet tall, with seven tendrils that revealed seven more tentacles that slid through the rubble and caused it to decay instantly, losing any gleam it once had.

The land around it died and rotted away as it moved through the city before Esvele. Behind it came a horde of skinned humanoid figures that she recognized, the Soulless. They ran and slaughtered all in their path. Their clawed hands indiscriminately butchered men, women, and children.

A loud explosion from where the Xurinal had once stood caught Esvele's attention. She sent her sight to that place and saw the Sepulcher besieged by two streams of energy from separate entities. One was a man who wore a red satin robe and a crown upon his head, and the other was a woman whose dress was black as the void above, and she, too, bore a jagged crown. From their hands came the power of death and decay; there stood another figure that manifested as a shadow. Its darkness consumed the light around it, devouring it like a whirlpool of the Old Sea. The shadow reached behind its head and summoned a blade made of starlight, and a radiance flowed about it. The blade was pointed toward the Sepulcher and then dove deep into the ground and webbed the stone around the one who bore the blade. From the blade, white light erupted, cracking the Sepulcher's foundations. A flash of light erupted, and only the three figures and Esvele managed to remain standing within sixty feet of it. The building crumbled into molecules of dust as if time had been turned backward, and a blasted waste was left in its wake. As the dust settled, a new entity floated above the ruins of the Sepulcher.

* * *

Esvele was thrust back to reality with Myrcle and Organa calling her true name softly. A cold sweat was dripping down her head, and her clothes were wet from these few moments. Her eyes darted back and forth rapidly, and her hearing came back slowly.

"EV," Organa whispered, and Esvele's eyes finally focused on her. "Are you okay?"

"It fell," Esvele said.

"What did?" Myrcle asked.

"Everything." She recounted her vision to them.

"By the Dawn," Myrcle's eyes shifted with fear.

"I fought him," Organa said, her voice quivering with anxiety. "I died."

"It was just a vision. None of it may come to pass," Esvele reassured her.

"Or all of it could."

"No one knows for sure," Myrcle interjected, "but what I do know is that if Kyriel is set free, it will mean the end of all things."

The three of them fell quiet, and Esvele watched through the decorated glass window as they pulled away in the coach. Her sight of the others diminished, and, for the first time in ages, she prayed to Havithreal.

Lady of Light, Mother of Creation, watch over them. Be their beacon of hope and guide them back to us. Allow the darkness to pass over them and let them be safe from all evil things. I ask, Holy Mother of All, place your seal of protection over their hearts to save them from any darkness that comes against them. Esvele raised her head to see the passing people and houses of the city going by. Please let them all be saved from this shadow.

The ride to the Citadel was bumpy from the uneven cobblestone streets. As they passed through the city, the high noon sun burned the tops of the homes and stores of Valistar and gave it a radiant gleam. As they passed by an alley, she saw a figure in a crimson dress, and it reappeared in the next alley. What they had seen from the bright sun striking the rooftops of the decorated homes had shimmered over the truth of the Xurinal. What should have been a glorious pyramid and holy palace of the Saints of the Sun to worship in and pray to the "Old Gods," as Miranda told them before they departed, was now a ruin of unkempt stone. Myrcle's eyes teared up at the sight as he looked upon it.

Organa was looking out of the window to her right as she watched the people pass by. The horses must have been at a trotting pace. As they passed by an alley, she saw a figure in a crimson dress that reappeared in the next alley. Again, she saw him—tall and thin, with a shadowed face and clawed fingers. She saw him again as they passed another alley, and he was closer, in the crowd and high above them, but no one looked up. Another time, and he was closer as they passed. Another, and then the figure appeared just a few feet away. Organa moved in her leathered seat as fear entered her heart. As she leaned away, she touched a slimy substance behind her. When she slowly turned to look, she saw a dead thing. Its face was like a rotting corpse, and a cold aura seemed to drain the light from the space around it. There was no movement, but she heard a foul and deep voice.

So red shall burn the flames of thy ruin.

The screams of the multitudes who perish in thy wrath shall haunt each footstep thou takest. Great casks of blood, spilt by thy own hand, shall drown the world. No salvation awaiteth thee... only death shall still the torment of thy mind.

Its voice was like a drowning person in the depths of the sea. It stretched forth a hand made of barnacles and foul growths of the sea. Water ran over its dead skin and filled the coach. Organa screamed in horror.

The coach halted instantly in the middle of the street. Miranda came down from her seat and threw open the door with a spell charged in her hand, ready to attack the assailant. Myrcle and Esvele were trying to comfort Organa, who was weeping as she lay across EV's knee.

"What happened?" Miranda asked, here eyes wide. "Was it one of the street scum?"

"No, no, no. Nothing of the sort. Just…" Myrcle trailed off as he thought.

"She has moments like these often at home," Esvele began in her fake voice. "She just needs a moment. We can continue on."

"Are you sure, m'lady?"

"Of course, go on," Esvele bid her.

"As you wish, m'lady," Miranda bowed and went back to her seat and drove the coach forward.

"I saw something," Organa said through her tears.

"Another vision?"

"No," Organa sat up in her chair and wiped her tears from her eyes. "It was real here." She looked at the emptiness beside her. "I don't know what it was. But it was real."

"What did it look like?"

"Like a dead person, still rotting and decaying. There were torn red robes, and from under them came tentacles like some beast of the sea."

"Organa," Esvele said, worried, "did it speak?"

"Yes," she said with curiosity. "The screams of the multitudes who perish in thy wrath shall haunt each footstep thou takest. Great casks of blood, spilt by thy own hand, shall drown the world. No salvation awaiteth thee… only death shall still the torment of thy mind."

"It was a Weave Oracle," Esvele answered rather quickly.

"What are they?"

"They are servants to the Crimson Moon—mortals who go through an agonizing transformation to heighten or even awaken their Far

Sight. They delve into the very Web of Fate."

"Esvele," Organa asked, "what did it mean?"

"I do not know, but I assure you, it was nothing good."

The Morning Glory Inn

Velkin, Florie, and Talos walked westward for seven miles and made their way through the city. Noon had now come, and the sun was beating down upon them. Gutter Street was a foul place that smelled of decay and shit—naturally. Most of the poor and homeless were confined to this area, as the trio discovered when a guard forbade one from leaving, only for another person to slip past while the guard wasn't looking. Although tempted to take down their hoods and escape some of the heat, they did not in fear of revealing themselves to any guard who may know their names or faces.

People had been passing by them all day, and no one looked up. Talos had noticed some of the homeless on Gutter Street as they passed. He saw a small child, maybe twelve years old, reach into the bag of a sleeping human who was lying on the wet and browned stone. He tapped Florie's shoulder and chuckled as he watched the child slowly creep a hand into the bag. Florie stopped, paying no attention to Velkin, who was struck with awe and continued walking forward.

Florie and Talos watched the kid closely; they had once been where this young child was. The young boy was wearing torn brown slacks and had no shoes. A simple dirty red vest was wrapped over his shoulders and covered most of his gray skin. His hair was long, dark, matted, and filthy, and his eyes were bluer than the Old Sea itself. The thief finally got hold of something and pulled it out, and, given the smile across his face—wide enough it might drop off—he had struck gold. He stood but lost his balance and landed on the sleeping woman, who jerked awake, and the boy screamed in fear. The woman pulled him up, making him drop a small sack that sounded like coins when it hit the floor, and shouted at him. Talos and Florie sprang into action, arrived at the struggle, and Talos pinned the woman against the wall while Florie held the boy.

"He stole from me! He stole from me!" the woman cried out.

Talos struggled to hold back from vomiting at the horrible smell of her breath and body odor, but he composed himself and said, "He needed some help; everyone is trying to survive."

He shoved her away, and the woman fell to the ground, scurrying away like a rat.

"He stole from me," she repeated and crawled away on the filthy street back toward the main street.

Florie set the young boy down, and he would have run if not for Talos holding out the sack of coins for him to grab. As the child's hand hesitantly approached, Talos could feel a wave of heat getting closer. The boy took the bag in hand and smiled at Talos.

"What's your name, little fella?" Talos said as he smiled.

"Max, short for Maxilian."

"What a kingly name," said Florie. "Are you nobility?"

"If I were, I wouldn't be here," he giggled.

"Well, maybe you're a long-lost prince of an ancient bloodline long forgotten. Wouldn't that be grand?"

"Yeah," the boy giggled again.

"Here," Talos reached into the bag on his belt and pulled out an empty sack. He stuck his hand back inside again and this time came out with a few gold pieces and some silvers as well. "Take this and use it to help the ones you love and yourself." Florie gave a shocked look as Talos placed the coins in the second sack.

"You give this freely?" The boy knew to be wary of strangers, especially living the life he had.

"I used to be in your shoes, little prince, and once there was a friend of mine who helped me steal a great hoard of money." He pointed to Florie and pulled a silly expression. "We used that money to form a band of friends, and we traveled all over Rethial to relieve people of their burdens."

"Should I do that?"

"With some coins and some passion, anyone can do anything," Florie said, smiling at him again. Max went and gave both Talos and Florie a tight hug and waved goodbye as he walked back down the street.

"You really told him about us forming our thieves' guild?" Florie laughed.

"Hey, there's always a child dreaming of being a criminal, just need a little shove." They both laughed for a moment and reminisced about their memories, and then the laughter died, and Florie realized that Velkin was gone. "T, where's Velkin?"

Talos turned around, seeing the pacing crowd. "I thought she was behind me."

"Shit."

The two bolted out of the alley and looked around at the sea of people. They called out her false name and then, as they looked around, they saw where she must have gone.

A blinding light made it hard to make out the fine details as they walked toward the Xurinal. A great pyramid made of sterling stone rose ahead, with four obelisks—one on each corner—of the same material, save for a pure golden apex of magnificence. The top of the Xurinal was made of a blue, purple, and red stone that caught the sunlight and looked as if it were aflame. At night, it caught the moonlight and shone a white light like a beacon of hope in the darkness. On each face of the pyramid were angled skylights that funneled sunlight or moonlight into the chambers. No shadow could ever have touched the holy place in the days before the Menitheal Dynasty.

The blinding light faded as they passed in front of the building, revealing the truth. A decaying pyramid of unclean and unkempt stone. A decrepit building from days gone by. Florie and Talos moved quickly through the crowd to find Velkin. Even though Talos no longer believed in the Pantheon, it made him sad to see such a holy place left to die. Eventually, they reached the stone stairs that tiered up to the base of the Xurinal. They came upon a great archway carved with Stellevarian runes of protection and holy rites. The symbols were barely glowing in the radiance of the afternoon sunlight, and they passed through them into the Xurinal.

They ran through the entrance and into the main chamber. The afternoon sun faintly shone on the stone and the dilapidated decorations of gold and rusted silver. Marble statues of the "Old Gods" were overgrown with ivy and moss. Some had cracks and were chipped; one was cut in half, and its ruin sat as a pile of white marble. Those who once served devotedly to the Pantheon would pray at the altars and light the sacred incense. The afternoon sunlight should have illuminated this holy place fully, but it could not. As they continued to look around, they saw a shaded figure receding into the shadows and heard a sniffle from the center of the room, down the staircase of the chapel.

Velkin stood on the pulpit, where a rotting wooden podium rested. The place where the high priest or priestess should be praying or teaching the laws of the Pantheon of Dawn. She was looking around what used to be Rethial's Cathedral of Dawn. Her eyes were full of tears, and trails of water lined her cheeks. Her blue hood had fallen, and she was in a state of shock as she looked at the reflection of her old home across the sea. "It fell. I fell," she whispered just loud enough for her companions to hear the first two words.

"Velkin," Florie calmly called out.

"It fell," she repeated. "I fell," she kept under her breath. "Father… Talmon…" His old face flashed into her mind. "I'm sorry."

"Velkin, are you okay?" Florie's voice was tender.

Velkin did not respond.

Florie approached her slowly and held out her hands, "Velkin."

"Ascroth," the paladin's voice echoed in the vacant chamber.

"Take my hand, let's go." Florie said.

"It fell, Florie."

"I know, and I'm sorry. Take my hand."

"I already took a hand when I was promised absolution and reunion." Velkin's tone sagged as her heart fell.

"Yes, when you pledged yourself to Calikan. Now take my hand and let's go find Bendrit," Florie kept her voice calm, knowing that Velkin was in a very fragile state and could shatter at any moment. Florie continued to hold out her hand, waiting for Velkin to take it.

Velkin whispered to herself, "I already took a hand."

"Take mine Velkin."

Talos watched with anticipation and held tight to the bottom of his bow on his back.

"Velkin, take my hand," Florie commanded a final time.

Velkin's eyes were so fixed on a single point that they could have melted the stone. Her mind was filled with doubt, fear, and disappointment, all in or about herself. In her mind, she confided a new truth to herself: *This is what it takes.*

Her defenses reacted immediately as she felt an unknown hand close to her, and a shimmer of light flashed as her holy sword came into existence. Her blade moved with such speed that, had Velkin not been paying very close attention to what she might be attacking, Florie's head would have been lopped off with a single stroke.

Florie's eyes were wide and her breathing short and quick as her heart pounded throughout her like a war drum.

Talos had an arrow nocked and let it loose as the blade came around. The arrow soared through the air across the chamber in the Xurinal, and a wall of protection formed in the space between them.

Talos' shot was deflected upon a rippling wall of nothingness that landed against the floor with a *clink*.

"You ought to know better, Paladin of Calikan," a female voice echoed in the chamber.

She descended the ruined staircase in sterling white robes stitched with golden holy symbols. Golden pauldrons with silver swirls sat on her shoulders, connected by gold chains across her torso. Her skin was a deep brown and her black hair flowed like waves. Her eyes were metallic gold that shone every time they caught the sunlight that managed to enter the sanctuary.

"Who are you, that you would know me?" Velkin asked.

"I am Grove Warden Ofelia of the Druids of Valkiel," her voice was like a running stream of calm water.

"Who?" Talos asked.

"She is a Guardian of Lorial," Velkin said with frustration as she recognized her face.

"And you are the ones who protect the Child of Starlight."

"How do you know us?" Florie asked.

"I have been keeping a close eye on Organa and her travels since she left the Living City."

"What do you mean? How could you? You're dead." Velkin straightened her posture, gripping the hilt of her blade tighter.

"No," she laughed, "I am not dead."

"You fell in the siege of the capital during the Cataclysm."

"Yes, I did, but I endured."

"Impossible. You're an imposture!" Velkin raised her blade to strike, meeting the throat of the Lady Moonlight, who disappeared in a wisp of mist and reformed behind her.

"I am not dead."

"Then where have you been?" Florie cut with her words. "If you're a Guardian, why haven't you done your job?"

"You all will be formidable adversaries of the Dark One," the woman smiled.

"Organa told me about why she left the Living City. She said that the Elders wanted to have her do a task. For her to Ascend." Florie said.

"Yes, that is correct, but I would never allow that. Now that I have taken control of the Living City and expunged the fantatics from it, I can assure you, she will have no part in some doomsday cult's plan to usher in their age. I even freed her old friend, Gerith, from their influence."

"Why are you only showing up now?" Talos glared.

"I did not know who she was in the company of exactly. But, through my observations, I have determined that you are worthy companions and loyal friends of hers."

"Then why haven't you helped us?" Florie was skeptical.

"My time for aid has not yet come, but I will assist you when you have returned her to the Living City. A Darkness is coming—one that you cannot hope to stop alone. There will be another Cataclysm, that no one can stop, but, together as Guardians, we may yet prevent the destruction of all things."

"What do you mean, 'a Darkness'?" Velkin finally spoke. Her voice had returned to normal, and her blade vanished.

"Things are in motion that cannot be undone. You"—she motioned to Florie and Talos—"will protect Organa with all your might." Ofelia looked to Velkin, "Your fate is still undecided. You made a choice, but you need not follow that path. You will decide this fate, and I only hope you choose wisely."

Velkin's heart nearly stopped as she listened to Ofelia's words.

"My time is up, I have said what I needed to." Ofelia continued. "When you have left this city, and the War for Eternity has begun, come to the Living City. There we will draw battle plans and together, we might defeat the evil that rises." Then, she disappeared in a swirling column of golden light.

"Velkin?" Florie asked, "What did she mean, 'you made a choice'?"

"Something that I have yet to decide," she replied as she walked out of the sanctuary and through the shadows toward the doors out to the city.

Night had almost fallen upon the City of Valistar. Dark clouds moved in from the east, and rolling thunder trailed through the skies as they came. A few flashes of lightning went off in the Old Sea, but they carried themselves to Valistar along the crests of great waves. The golden gleam that had shone about the city had fallen, and, where the Element Moons faintly shone through the black clouds above, a silver and blue spotlight was cast upon those who it graced with its radiance and kindness. All the while, the great Fire in Heaven loomed above. Many had wondered what had happened to that world. A Cataclysm like their own, or a great drought that befell that land, and brought it to the knees of desolation? The few stragglers left in the night were either shade of darkness that wished to pass unseen for their nightly machinations or the lost tourists of the city. Those who lived there learned long ago to never stay out after dark if they could help it. For the locals knew in those shadows were beasts of evil and temptation.

Velkin walked toward where the Morning Glory Inn had to be,

with Florie and Talos behind her. They trekked through the alleys and streets, avoiding whom they could when they could. A sprinkle of rain fell in the darkness, and the Element Moons were gone, along with the war-colored Fire in Heaven.

Half an hour later, they reached their destination. A sign with a sunrise over a green country was colored yellow with a few trees along the edges for some flavor to its design. The trio arrived with soaking wet clothes as they entered the place where Bendrit was meant to be. Velkin had a flame in her eyes—a mission that needed to be completed, a rage to be let loose. Florie wanted to ask her if she was okay, but Velkin moved to the bar where the innkeeper poured a few mugs of ale.

"Is there a man by the name of Verit staying here?" Velkin asked.

The man's voice was light and higher pitch as his voice shot up to her from a few feet below. "Let me check the ledgers," he said as he waddled over the wood flooring with his small feet.

The man was short of stature, around three feet tall, and barely reached the top of the bar where he placed his tray of drinks flawlessly without spilling a drop of the ale. His ears and nose were long and pointed. A tacky purple vest covered his rag of a shirt. His slacks were green, and he wore small brown leather shoes. Despite his formal clothing, his hair was quite matted, and he had a foul odor. He made his way around the bar and disappeared from sight and then reappeared as his shoes bonked against the wood of a stool that he stood on to get to his ledgers. He pulled out a small monocle held by a chain from his left vest pocket and placed it on his eye. His four-fingered hands turned the pages of a dusty tome that seemed as if it had not been opened in many months, if not years. He turned the old and creaking pages where many names had been marked through with a solid and thick black line. He turned every page from beginning to end, easily scanning every name, but when he reached the last page, he disappointed them.

"I'm sorry, sweetheart, no one by that name here. Not that I know of." The innkeeper shrugged.

"Are you sure?" Florie asked from down below the bar.

The pale-skinned Halfling looked over the edge of his counter. "Listen, if my records are wrong, it is because I've been running this joint for over seventy years. My mind isn't what it used to be. Either that or my shithead son forgot to write someone down. He's over there at the gambling table." The Halfling pointed over to a round table with seven people sitting around it. Among them was a small, fiery red-haired young man. He was clinging close to his cards and watching nervously around the table.

"Poor fool doesn't bear any resemblance to a game face," Talos sighed.

"That I can agree with my friend," the father laughed. "If you want to know, go ask him, but if you need a room, find me."

Velkin's eyes evinced her irritation with the older Halfling, but before Velkin could say a word, Florie spoke, "Thank you so much. We'll let you know."

"Take care now."

Florie looked up at Talos. "Go over to the table and wait for them to finish their round, then talk to him." Talos nodded and made his way over while Florie held Velkin back from following after him. "What has gotten into you?"

"What are you talking about?"

"You looked like you were about to kill that innkeeper," Florie's worried voice barely cut through the shouting jubilation from the gambling table.

"He wasn't giving us proper information," she said rashly.

"Velkin, you saw the ledger. He was looking through the pages, and Verit wasn't there. How isn't that proper?"

"He didn't look fast enough."

"Velkin," Florie's worry was apparent all across her face, "Are you okay? You were acting strange when we were making our way here and at the Xurinal -"

Velkin cut her off. "I'm fine."

"You tried to cut my head off!" she shouted in a whisper.

"You snuck up on me," she defended herself. "I didn't know who you were."

They were going to continue arguing, but Talos interjected, "His dad may not think that he has a game face, but man does he have a good hand."

"We're having a conversation, T," Florie sighed.

"Yeah, but we need to find Bendrit, so let's get moving," Talos shrugged his shoulders. He turned, walked away, and they followed him over to the table.

Florie pulled him back quickly though and whispered, "Does the fact that she almost killed me not bother you?"

"Of course it does, but I don't want to dwell on it just yet. She was probably just going through a phase. She hadn't been in that building in ages."

"I know, but I am worried."

"Don't be. All we need to do is find Bendrit and meet back with the others. Don't worry."

"We have a lot to worry about."

"Yeah, but," he paused, thinking of what he could say, "just don't," he shrugged again. Their attention was drawn to the table, where shouting and excitement were radiating from the young halfling. "Told you he had a good hand," Talos smiled.

Florie's worry ran through her mind. They needed to get inside the Western Obelisk to figure out if the Sepulcher was even in Valistar. Were Organa and the others okay? Had they been found out? Every question imaginable ran one-hundred miles around and around in her head.

Talos walked forward and took a seat at the table across from the son of the innkeeper. Florie bolted to his side and slammed against the back of the chair. "What in the name of sanity are you doing?"

"Getting information."

"You're in," a shrill voice called out across the table. Talos looked over at the young halfling, who was maybe in his early twenties. "Yeah, you. Are you in? I'm on a roll, so let's keep going."

"Yes," Talos smiled.

"I hate you." Florie hit the back of his head.

"Don't worry, this will work."

"You'd better hope so," she hit him again.

"Oi," the Halfling called to her, "if you're going to be hitting him, take a seat, so it makes sense to hit him once he bleeds you dry."

"No, I am not playing," she smiled back.

"Then move out of the way."

Florie was tempted to insult him back but decided not to since they needed information. The cards were dealt, two to each player, and three cards in the middle. Florie now wished she were playing instead. Talos' poker game was awful, but he had already put two hundred gold pieces into a pot that held at least twelve hundred already. The cards in the center were a jack of diamonds, a queen of diamonds, and two clubs. Florie looked at Talos' hand and saw the first two cards, a king of spades and four diamonds.

Her fear spiked; he was surely going to lose.

Each of the players around the table looked at the cards and placed a few coins in the pot, with two of them folding to reveal worse hands than Talos'.

The innkeeper's son raised the value by fifteen gold pieces when it came round to him, and a player after him called his bet. Each of them placed the same up until Talos, who placed twenty gold pieces in the pot. Florie's eyes got very wide, and she worried. On the other end of the table stood Velkin behind the young boy, who shook her head back at Talos' action.

The innkeeper's son smiled greedily. "You've got some stones on you, dragon boy?"

"Indeed, half-man." To Talos' delight, the anger on his opponent's face was clear as day; so he raised the bet by three more gold pieces. The other four players instantly laid their cards bare and revealed some good hands and some bad ones.

"Your move," the shrill voice said. Talos placed down three more pieces. "You must have a hell of a set over there. Deal the rest of the cards, Seraph," and a Hawkina with blue feathered hands placed out three more cards to the two opponents. Talos was given the nine of diamonds, the three of clubs, and the ten of hearts. Florie turned around so as not to give away his bluff and swore under her breath. She recovered and saw Velkin across the way, shaking her head again with disappointment.

"You ready?" he asked.

"I'm doing fine and dandy," Talos smiled back, and together, they revealed their cards. A cry of laughter came from across the table as the halfling collected his prize of gold.

"You really are a fool," he said through his excitement.

"I just tested my luck."

"What more do you have to offer?"

"A few more sacks of coin."

"And you think you'll win?"

"Yeah."

"Good luck then. I always win."

"And if you don't?"

"I will."

"Then you're a cheat."

"What?" he cried out in outrage and stood on his chair to make himself just a little taller. "You dare!"

"Yep, and when I win, I don't just want money."

"You won't, so there is no point in begging for more," he said as he sat back down.

"I will, and I want information."

"You think I'm some master of whispers in this city?"

"No, but you check a lot of people into this inn, and I'm looking for someone."

"Then check the ledgers."

"I did, and he wasn't on them, but your dad said that if they weren't written to come talk to you. The best way to get information is through friends or money. So, when I drain you dry, the only thing you'll have left to bet with will be that information," Talos said with all the confidence he could muster.

The Halfling was clearly ready to explode with rage at the insolent comments of his adversary but contained himself. "Deal us back in, Seraph," and the Hawkina did as he was bid.

On the first hand, Talos won with a large straight in his hand and then some on the table. The second, he won again in two pairs. The third, though, he lost and found himself scrambling for some coin after the massive pot of seven-hundred and eighty-two gold pieces within.

He whispered to Florie, "Give me some coin."

"No," she answered back, "you're losing your own money on this one."

"If we want to find Bendrit I need to win this last hand. He's shorter than me," and as Talos said that, Florie saw the boy only placing three pieces in the pot. "Please, Florie, I can win this."

"If you lose, I will place a knife so deep in your neck you will feel it from whatever eternity you end up in."

"You're a diamond, dear," he said as he patted her feathered cheek.

"Don't screw this up, please."

"No promises," he trailed off under his breath.

"All right," the shrill voice said, "last round. We've bled each other dry, so let's settle the wager. I'll bet the rest of my coin," and he landed a bag on the table that was much more than what he led on to be, "and the information you want."

"Against?"

"Your coin," Talos was pleased to hear, "and that nice recurve bow of yours."

"What?"

"You heard! That bow and your coin against my coin and the information you're after. Deal?"

"Talos," Florie eyed him, "don't; we might need that."

"Oy! Over here. Deal?"

"Deal!" and the final hand began.

The dealer placed the three cards in the center and revealed a six of clubs, seven of hearts, and a king of clubs. Talos' hand was pure and sublime luck, a four and seven of clubs. Florie was actually very hopeful. All he needed was a five. She looked at Velkin, who was nodding her head up and down. Talos had a chance based on these next two cards.

"All in," the Halfling said and placed his money into the pot.

"All in," Talos mirrored and placed his bow on the other side of the table.

The final card was placed on the table. A four of spades and five of clubs. Florie did all she could to contain her excitement, and Talos felt a wash of ease come over him. The final two cards were dealt to the opponents. Talos reached for his cards and pulled them back, one by one. The first, a queen of hearts, and the last, an eight of diamonds. Though it did not matter, the hand he already had ensured his success. His opponent was sweating so much that it was clear to him as the droplets of salty liquid caught the light of the torches and shimmered just a little.

"Ready?" Talos asked with confidence.

"Ready," the Halfling smiled back, "You first." Talos showed his cards. "You are quite the gambler, aren't you? But you'll never be as good as me, even though you won this time." He showed a bluff hand of rubbish odds. A roar of laughter and cheers erupted like an explosion around the inn. Talos jumped to his feet and placed his bow around him. Florie jumped all over him with relief and disbelief. A hand pulled his arm from below as the Halfling stretched out his for a shake. Talos obliged him, and his debtor made a slight move away from the crowd at a free table. Talos nodded and made his way with him over. Florie quickly followed with Velkin coming as well after noticing her companion's absence and spotting them. They took a seat together, and through the roar of the patrons, discussed business. "So," the Halfling began, "what is it you want?"

"We're looking for a friend of ours who said he would meet us here. His name is Verit," Talos explained.

"Ah, an alias, of course?"

"What do you mean?" Florie asked.

"Sweetheart. If anyone is not written down, they come through me. I have many connections through some mutual friends of mine in the Conclave of Daggers, poor souls." Florie and Talos tried not to show their hurt at the mention of what they used to be a part of—their old family. "After what happened in Itheca, though, what a mess," he laughed. "I lost quite a few of those connections. But a few I still maintain, one in each of the other taverns in the northern half of the city here and a single operative, who I sadly haven't heard from in a while, inside the chapter of the Children of the Crimson

Moon."

"Get to the point, half-man," Velkin said, hitting the table hard.

"V, shut up and control yourself," Florie said, hitting her shoulder, and swore she saw another hand ready to stab her with some unseen blade.

"Listen to your friend, 'V', she has the right idea," the Halfling threatened, "As I was saying, I have heard through the grapevines, that the ones who were responsible for the deaths and destruction at Itheca had an agent in the great library of Gavis Vel'Stratis. But a few moons ago, a conquering force of the Flames of the Sphinx, and that bitch of a commander, Merith, went to that old spire and put the place to the torch. Although that agent was seen still alive until two days ago, right when you and your lot arrived in the Red Baron."

"Excuse me?" Florie felt a flutter of fear.

"Yeah, I know exactly who you are, and how many you've killed, you and your friends. But I don't know the reason why you attacked Itheca, and frankly, I don't care, but you owe me."

"Then keep your money and tell us where our 'agent' is," Talos pushed his comment aside.

The Halfling laughed. "Oh no, no, no, you will do something for me to wipe off the red in your account. Go to the chapter of the Children of the Crimson Moon and make sure my contact is still there. The chapter is up near the Citadel, that way, so if they get hired to kill the king or queen, it's much easier." He laughed at his own joke: "Return to me with the seal from their ring, and I'll tell you where Bendrit, the Flame of the West, the Guardian of Lorial, is." A foul smile crept across his face as he held out his hand. "Do we have an accord?"

"We don't have time for this!" Velkin shouted and picked up the Halfling by his shirt and held him in the air. A shimmer, followed by a shadow from her hand, brought forth her blade, though it looked much more rusted and jagged than it had ever before. Florie pulled her blades from her sheaths as she saw the patrons remove their weapons from their own, and Talos held on to a blade's hilt on the side. "You stand between a mother and her children, and I will not allow some half-brained twit to remain there long before I kill them. So tell us! Where—is—he?"

The one she held aloft said in a calm voice, "You might want to put me down before you and your lot here die."

"Velkin, put him down," Florie shot at her.

Velkin looked around at the horrified faces of the bystanders and the war-torn faces of those ready to defend their friend. Her anger subsided, and she slowly lowered the barterer to his seat. He was smiling at her and waved a hand to dismiss his guards.

"The rage of a paladin," he began, "is just as many said it is—raw, untamed, and deadly."

"Speak again without telling us what we need to know, and you'll see," her rage returned.

"Do as I asked. Find my contact in the chapter."

Talos looked over at him. "We are on quite a schedule, so we don't have time to run your errands."

"Well, run mine fast and you'll still be on time."

"We will," Florie finally interjected. "Let's go, you two!"

"Come back soon!" the halfling shouted as they walked away. "And good luck."

A single finger came up from Talos' hand as they exited the Morning Glory Inn.

Letters of Welcome

The coach came to a stop an hour after their encounter with the Weaver. Miranda brought them before the gates of Castle Black Rose. The massive fortress stood in three separate tiers, each built behind the other, and each with a massive, chiseled staircase that led to the next terrace. The first was a massive barracks where the royal guard stayed. In the center of the rectangular courtyard, formed by the four buildings, was a single massive oak tree. Simple and sterling, the walls themselves, unlike anything in the city, were solid white marble. Windows lined its outside, decorated with pristine white wood. The wall directly beyond the gates mirrored their shape, with an arch serving as the entrance to the castle. Six towers lined the tall seventy-foot walls that surrounded the royal domain, each of them with cone apexes made of black shingles and topped with golden flagpoles that sported the crest of the Menitheal Dynasty.

The second tier was the Great Hall, where any of the guests would stay, and where the Crystal Thrones stood vigilant. Five tall towers extended from the walls of the Sol Hall and surveyed the city. Each of them was mighty and carved with ancient runes and symbols of the bygone age before the Cataclysm, written in Stellevarian. The roof of the hall was glass and supported by flying buttresses decorated with gold and silver ornaments. Painted figures on the glass, stained blue and red, told of Rethial's founding. The final tier was the most famous of them all, the Silver Spires. Great towers were connected by bridges of Orisian Iron, a black stone that gleamed like the night, pricked with a few stars. The King's Pillar was the grandest and highest of them all, and where the Lord and Lady Menitheal rested. The Sunset Tower was dilapidated and ruined. Most of it had fallen into the sea and bashed against the cliffs below. Where they could find purchase, massive tendrils of ivy crawled along its sides, and the marble had faded into a dim shadow of what it had been.

Their goal, the Western Obelisk, stood proud and majestic, its rotating pieces held aloft by magic, casting twisting shadows upon the sea in the light of the setting sun. Castle Black Rose was a marvel of engineering and a masterpiece in the craft of mortals. In the days of old, in the Age of Silver, when the East still stood, the Lux guided peoples in the craftsmanship of magic and built every town and city from the sheer will of creation. But when the Lux left, the teachings of their ways were lost, and only the masters of that age still retained any resemblance to that magic.

Miranda shouted for the gates to open, and the two massive metallic portals opened slowly into the courtyard of the Citadel. She drove them along the cobblestones around the grand oak tree. Guards clad in black and silver armor stood watch at the entrance leading into the maze of corridors inside the citadel. The dark oak wooden doors opened, and out came two figures, both bearing crowns. A tall Elven man with a sharp golden crown on his head seemed to be on fire when it caught the sunlight. His robes were black and red, with a golden cloak trailing behind him. Pale skin clung tightly to him, appearing almost corpse-like. His bride walked beside him, and her crown was a silver circlet around her brow decorated with radiant golden accents and chains that hung on the sides. Her dress was blue and yellow with beautifully stitched swirls.

The trio's driver descended from her station and opened the doors of the coach, revealing Esvele, Myrcle, and Organa as they stepped out.

"My Lady of Nefis," the Lady Magis curtsied, "welcome to Valistar." Her voice was rough but kind. "I hope your travels were not too troublesome."

"Not at all," Esvele replied in her posh voice, "merely lengthy, but not too troublesome."

"I am very glad to see you escaped that awful mess in Itheca. I assure you we will catch those responsible."

Worry crossed their faces quickly and faded as they recovered. Myrcle held his grief and shame close to him, thinking of his desolation, but Esvele responded and broke his thoughts.

"Yes. It was quite a tragedy indeed. However, we all know they were a bunch of thieves and miscreants."

"Of course, but our agent had not contacted us for a few days. Only a short while ago did we receive word from them that they had made it to the city and were taking refuge till the Council of the Nine had completed," the Soulflame King informed them. "Well, Miranda, thank you for your service." She bowed to him. "If I might inquire about another, please escort the Lady and her advisors to their chambers. We'll meet you for supper in a few hours in the Sol Hall and eat together. You are aware that you arrived early, my Lady?"

"Of course, but the early bird gets the worm, and the information," Esvele laughed, and the king and queen did as well.

"Take them on, Miranda," the Lady Magis commanded. "Welcome to Valistar, my Lady."

"Thank you, Your Graces," Esvele said with polite and proper courtesy, her "advisors" doing the same.

Miranda led them on into the lion's den.

As they passed through the gates of the massive castle, they saw a broad staircase that led directly to the immense doors of the Sol Hall. The walls were lined with torches that gave light to the darkness, but the darkness lingered still. Guards stationed along the railing of the staircase bore the same black plate armor as the ones outside.

Miranda led them to the right and up a spiraling stone staircase that wound broadly around a central pillar. When they got to the top, Miranda opened a door and led them across a stone bridge between two towers. The sides were lined with crafted metal rails that they held onto as they walked across the expanse. The wind blew fairly hard, but not hard enough for one to lose their balance. Down below, they could see the roof of the barracks and the great oak. High above stood the Western Obelisk, its shifting apex of floating celestial spheres and rune-carved bricks holding the answer to the secrets they had been seeking. Miranda opened a wooden door and held it there for them to ascend once again up a large and lofty tower, big enough to hold suites for the royal guests and their families.

Miranda led on, took them up more stone stairs, and passed a few large wooden doors, but stopped a floor before the main room.

"You two will stay here, in the advisor's chambers." Miranda looked at Myrcle and Organa. "Feel free to call on any servants to tend to your needs."

"Thank you, Captain Miranda. You have shown true hospitality to me and my advisors," Esvele said, her accent almost fading. "Go on, you two. I'll see you in my chambers in five minutes; we've much to discuss."

"As you wish, my Lady," Myrcle said and bowed. Organa stuttered, not paying attention, and quickly mirrored Myrcle. Miranda and Esvele continued up the stairwell and toward her room.

Myrcle placed his hand on the long, vertical door-latch and pushed forward, opening into their quarters.

Four chiseled pillars of fine white marble bent up into the ceiling. There were two large beds with red sheets and golden accents. Large canopies above them with colored silks draped down. The floor was mostly covered in fine animal skins and wool rugs to combat a night's frosty floor. Two separate doors on each side of the room led to individual privies. The open doors of a hearth against the far wall held a mass of stacked logs ready to be burnt. A balcony provided a pleasant breeze into the room, and the last few rays of the sun fell below the mountains and gleamed upon the decorated stone. Myrcle snapped his fingers, and the candles and hearth burst into flames, illuminating the rest. Organa saw a long table in the center where letters bearing each of their names caught their attention— not "Advisors of the Lady of Nefis," but Organa and Myrcle. Myrcle instantly closed the doors with a gust of wind, and Organa felt a cloak of fear surround her.

Myrcle stepped forward and inspected the letters on the silver platters sitting on the table. He looked over at Organa and held out his hand as he saw her reach out to one. He shook his head at her, and she took a step back. With a swift motion, the letter bearing his name flew into the air and came closer to him. He turned it around and saw instantly the seal of the Children of the Crimson Moon. A skull with red ruby eyes protruded from the ink itself and manifested before him as a full skeleton. The other letter shook as well and lifted itself on its own, landing on the floor, backside up, and another skeleton manifested from its wax seal. Their visages were like dripping, rippling blood. Crimson shadows fell from their bodies, and their eyes were solid ruby gems. Both sorcerers held their hands back, reading spells of fire and ice, and then the skeletons started cackling.

They spoke in unison, in a single raspy, dry and dead voice. "The Shadowlight cometh!" Then, their voices broke into a hundred screams as the Oracles leaped forward.

One of the creatures gathered a sickly web of shadow threads that erupted and struck Organa, singeing her skin like a raging fire as an infestation of decay began to spread. Its glowing eyes penetrated beyond her physical form and deep into her soul, crawling around it as if it were tearing her very being apart into pieces.

Myrcle called threads of fire from the torches in the room, but as they wove together, he felt the power cease as the other Weave Oracle cut them.

Just as Myrcle's flames died, the Oracle stitched a burning tapestry of its own and unleashed a stream of frenzied flames, coiling around him like a snake, scorching his skin.

He matched the Oracle's burning waves with a ward of chilled winds as he stitched water and air together. Still, a few firebolts broke through and scalded him.

"Thine fate has been written! You will not save her from the fire of his rage!" the Oracle prophesied.

Organa reached into the Flux, grasping for whatever magic she could conjure, pulling from within, a blade of blue ice that she plunged into the neck of the rotting corpse holding her.

A shrill cry rang out as the creature released her from its rotting grip. Where the blade had cut, the arm had frozen into solid, transparent ice.

The Weaver broke off its frozen arm, shattering it into a hundred shards of glass. There was no cry of pain from the severance, but a screech of hatred as the Weaver lurched forward again, missing the young woman and crashing into the stone wall beside her.

The second Weaver's threads of flame ceased and Myrcle fell to the ground, a few patches of fur singed off and his whole body smoking. It took its free hand and conjured a pool of black liquid that sank into Myrcle's clothes and flesh, setting in an instant decay that ate away at his innards. A deep laugh from beyond anything Myrcle could imagine echoed in his ears as the Weaver reveled in the ecstasy of his pain.

A winter storm blew with the fierce, cutting winds of Menagerie, as shards of ice penetrated the dead flesh of the demon. The power of the blizzard threw the Weaver off of Myrcle, forcing the abomination through the table in the center of the room, scattering candles around the chamber, igniting the curtains on fire, but pinning the Weaver to the wall with spikes of frost.

Organa's Weaver levitated back up and soared across the room, latching onto her back. The Weaver's teeth sank into her shoulder, infecting her muscle with the same corrosion as Myrcle. Her own blood felt like it was solidifying within her veins, clotting and ready to kill her in an instant. Yet, a ray of light released from Myrcle's hand burst through the head of the Weaver, shattering the skull and splattering black blood along the walls and in Organa's hair.

Myrcle panted as he hunched over, feeling the infection within him growing with each passing second. The body of the Weaver fell to the ground with a *thud* as it dismounted Organa, dragging her as well. Rushing to her side, Myrcle placed his hand on her gushing wound, filling her with golden light. Her poison was banished instantly— thankfully not a work of dark magic.

A scream from behind them shattered the frozen blades impaled in the body of the undead being. Within the blink of an eye, the Weaver appeared in front of Myrcle and extended the nails of its bony fingers into thrashing claws. Slicing away at his exposed flesh, the Weaver cut away at Myrcle's mortality. With a lightning-fast thrust into his chest, Myrcle felt his bones crack under the pressure of the blow and his organs tearing as the talons sliced within him.

With her arms against the stone floor, Organa bent the stone to her will, forming it into a stalagmite that pierced through the heart of the reanimated thing. Though the creature pulled itself free of Myrcle's body, it continued to thrash about like a demon. Organa stood to her feet and called another blade of ice to her side. With a swift stroke, she plunged the cold sword into the Weaver's skull, shattering it as Myrcle had, and covering her face in black blood. Organa fell to the floor beside Myrcle and called upon the healing words of the ancients. Though she could feel the dark magic taking hold around his soul, Myrcle's chest rose and fell as he took another breath of life.

"What was that?" Organa let her spell go.

"Nothing good," Myrcle breathed out heavily.

"You don't say," she glared.

"Not now, Organa. We have to get into the Western Obelisk tonight. We must have accelerated their plans enough for them to think of killing us as their only avenue. We're out of time."

"Let's not fuck it up." Organa stood to her feet and held out her hand. She pulled Myrcle to his feet, and then they heard Esvele scream.

* * *

"Here is your room, m'lady. If you need anything at all, we will see it done. Enjoy your supper with the king and queen tonight. They have been looking forward to seeing The Nine for some time."

"Thank you, Miranda," Esvele said, trailing off. Miranda walked away, but Esvele called out, "You have been very kind to us, Miranda. As one of the Nine, I dismiss you for the next few days. Go travel the country. Leave Valistar tonight."

"Why, thank you, m'lady," she bowed back to Esvele. "I would very much enjoy that."

"You're very welcome, Miranda," Esvele uttered painfully, hoping that she might escape before they discovered the truth, and the Sepulcher was destroyed, or worse, opened. Esvele entered her room and found it to be massive as she lit the candles and the hearth. Many pillars supported the ceiling, and a large bed rested against the right wall while a grand hearth was against the other. Extravagant cushioned chairs of red and gold sat on either side of a table that held a chessboard.

The pieces were carved stone, pristine and polished, in white and black. The black king was far in the corner, looming behind two knights. The matching bishops stood before five white pieces. Two rooks and a bishop, a queen, and a knight were standing valiantly before the dark forces.

A gust of wind blew open the tall shutters to her balcony, and she went to close it. As she stepped away from the doors, she turned back to see a letter with her name on it, set in the center of a table in the room.

She looked around every corner and under her bed quickly, and in all the places someone might have hidden. She opened her door out onto the stairwell and looked for anyone, but only saw the gloomily lit stone walls of the tower. Esvele closed her door back and locked it with the metal latch. She walked across the floor toward the table, her boots *clopping* forebodingly against the surface. She stretched out her hand and lifted the letter into the air, examining her name and the make of the letter. The letter turned, and she saw the crest of the Children of the Crimson Moon's eyes glowing brightly and dropped it to the ground. A skeleton of crimson shadows and blood manifested like many grains of sand forming into one.

"Thou hast come far, but no further, Child of Starlight," a thousand voices spoke together. "Master Esvele, Master of the Earth, what doest thou believe thou canst do against the rising tides of doom?"

Esvele remained silent.

"Wouldst thou like to be free of the Dark Song—that accursed melody which haunteth thine footsteps?"

Esvele still did not respond as the shadow of the Weaver passed in front of the curtain she hid behind.

"Oh, thou art trembling with fear. Mine senses understand so. Hear me Esvele, Master of the Earth, thine coming unto this city is as the footsteps of doom. Thou hast brought us thine key and the one who wouldst release our Lord."

"I think not," and she cast a spell that canceled the magic channeling through the letter and brought the skeleton into reality. It lost its balance and shuffled back a few feet, passing through the table as if it were air, then catching itself and correcting its posture.

"Your magic is weak, Master Esvele," it taunted.

"That is not my name. Not anymore." Esvele's guilt played in her head.

The many voices laughed, "Ah, but it is. It was you who failed the people of the East. You who allowed the Cataclysm to devour that land of dreams. But we thank you for your role, Master Esvele. Without your ignorance, our Lord would never have been brought into this world." Esvele could hear the Weaver smiling.

"Your words mean nothing," Esvele shot back, the Dark Song playing louder in her head.

"But images tell a thousand stories," it laughed in a deep and impossible tone. A cloud of red dust erupted from the creature and enveloped Esvele before she could summon gales to cast it away.

Pure air struggled to enter lungs as the spores tainted it and the surrounding room became like pitch-black ink, falling like smoke around her before forming into ruined buildings, flames, corpses,

Soulless, demons, undead—evil—the Cataclysm.

A Soulless caught Esvele's scent and turned to her. Its loose, pale flesh sagging and clinging in different areas. Shadows whirled around it, and its eyes were burning yellow hollows of nothingness. It ran across the bloodied streets at her and leaped into the air, sprouting wings of black night. A loud screeching, shrill and low roar came simultaneously from its circled and toothed maw as it descended upon her. Esvele held up her hands and cast a spell, twisting the stone street around her into spears of rock that shoved themselves through the chest of the Soulless. The fire in its eyes faded, and it fell still. From behind her, she heard a great explosion and saw the shadow of the North landing on the city, crushing all beneath it. Its dark visage stood tall over the ruined buildings. Its purple eyes gazed into Esvele's soul, and she saw it open its mouth to unleash a dark inferno of death and decay.

Esvele held up her hand and cast a ward of protection between them. Its breath met her shield and collapsed it instantly, shattering around her like glass. A whipping and whirling sound came from her left as she saw a swirling mass of clouds and purple, green, and white fire puncture reality.

From within stepped two figures: Golgorot and Kethir, who moved into the light of their dark magic. Both of them wore long black robes with crowns on their heads. Their veins pulsed with a green and white light, and their eyes poured out a mist of death and decay. The gauntlets of the Lady of Bones were carved metallic claws that formed an exoskeleton around her hands and a majority of her forearms. Golgorot's staff in his right hand was topped with three black skulls, each eye a different precious stone, all sitting on a charred piece of wood acting as a foundation.

"You are weak, Esvele," the Lord of Shadow's hundred voices declared to her.

"You are nothing," the Lady of Bones smiled and she held up her hand and cast a spell. A beam of rippling purple lightning met Esvele's ward she instinctively cast. Esvele was able to hold her dark advance back, but she could feel her heels digging into the cobblestone street.

"You failed before, and you'll fail again tonight," Golgorot's hand moved grossly, the skin barely clinging to it. He cast a spell of fire and frost that intertwined as one, catching the edge of Esvele's ward and pushing her back further.

Esvele felt herself failing, weakening, and falling into death's hands.

"You will never redeem your soul; you are damned," they said together with their thousands of voices. Esvele screamed as she felt her arms buckling in from the force of their spells and her ward fell. The two streams of magic struck her chest and flung her across the room.

Esvele stood to her feet with a grunt and gasped for breath. "You are nothing," the Lady of Bones said as she knelt down in front of her. She moved a single finger, and purple and black shadows quickly wrapped around her, forming dark and burning chains that seared her skin.

The others outside of Esvele's room heard her scream.

Esvele was lifted into the air and saw people being slaughtered. They were ripped apart, slashed, gashed, beheaded, and eaten, but ultimately all died around her. She could not fail again, so she let go.

The ground around them rumbled and shook.

Esvele's eyes ignited with chromatic fury. Her skin began to fragment and lifted from her in small patches, like soot from a burning log. Her hair floated around her as if she were submerged in water, and her veins pulsed as a purple and black glow ran through her. Kethir and Golgorot had foul smiles across their faces, and then they looked into her eyes. Esvele held up her hand and lifted it into the air. She pulled them close to her and, as she did, they dissolved.

There was no cry of agony, no sound at all from her attackers, just deadly grins of greed and glee. Esvele threw them away from her, and they diminished into floating ashes of nothing.

Esvele looked to the Shadow of the North and held out both her hands, sending forth bolts of dark magic, one at a time, that exploded upon impact with its scales. The great beast roared in annoyance and let lose its breath weapon upon her, but she deflected it with ease and redirected it back at the crumbling ruin around her. She focused her power into a single form and let it shoot from her hands—a beam of purple, green, and white fire that wrapped around the dragon like the tentacles of a kraken of the seas.

The Shadow reared back its head in agony as burns across its body consumed it.

A thousand voices cried out in terrible agony as the beast was turned into a great statue made of shadowglass.

The ground cracked. Many guards had now come to the door, trying to get it open. Myrcle pushed them out of the way and cast a powerful spell that disintegrated the door. They saw Myrcle and Organa quickly run into the chamber, finding the room in disarray. Gravity had been made an uncertainty, as if the rules of the physical realm were malleable rather than absolute, and even reality itself around Esvele seemed to diminish.

"EV!" he shouted as he reached for her.

She could not hear.

"EV!" he called again.

Still, she could not hear.

Organa then reached out and pulled Esvele to the ground, accidentally causing her to hit her head on a nearby marble pillar as she fell.

"What the hell was that?" Miranda asked.

"She was cursed!" Myrcle shouted dramatically as he lied to the commander.

"We must get her to the infirmary."

"Now then, guards, take her," Organa commanded like a queen, and they carried her out of the room.

Miranda and the guards left the room with Myrcle and Organa following close behind them to the healers. "This is a viable opportunity," Myrcle whispered.

"What?" Organa asked.

"It is imperative that you make your way to the Western Obelisk and retrieve the scroll. Once you've confirmed the Sepulcher's location, we need to safely extract it from and transport it to a location that is more secure. Go now!"

Organa shook her head and, while the others were not paying attention, broke off from them and wandered the halls toward the Silver Spires.

The Chapter of Valistar

Night fell fast as Talos, Florie, and Velkin left the Morning Glory Inn, thundering clouds rumbling overhead as a deluge soaked the streets and buildings. Cracks of lightning and rolls of thunder echoed as they traversed the muddy paths between the homes and shops of Valistar. Florie and Talos pulled up their hoods, Talos' horns puncturing through cut-out holes. Velkin embraced the rain, hoping it would wash her clean of her anger, her rage, her hate, her pain—everything she felt in abundance now that she was so close to what she had lost. The light of the moon rarely broke through the small patches in the clouds above. In the distance loomed the Citadel, and Florie prayed for her friends to be safe. The rotating and shifting tower of the Western Obelisk shone out there in the darkness with a changing light from blue to red, then to green, and finally purple. The runes' glow was like a lighthouse—fainter, but still unmistakable. Those walking in the rain and dark seemed unsavory—thieves and criminals—though Florie and Talos could not judge, being the same themselves.

"We need to find a faster way through the city," Talos said, stopping the others. "Who knows what Myrcle, Esvele, and Organa are doing right now. We need to get this done, get Bendrit, and then go to the Citadel and help them."

"We should have just beaten the words out of the little rat and then killed him out of sheer annoyance," Velkin scoffed.

"What is going on with you, Velkin?"

"You're worrying me," Florie said with a sad look in her eye. "I haven't known you for very long, but I know that this doesn't sound like you."

"You don't know me." Velkin eyed her with fury.

"I know that before Itheca, when Merith attacked, you were hellbent on helping Organa, finding her brother, and the Sepulcher. Now, you're bloodthirsty and vengeful. What happened?"

"Nothing." Florie's words reminded her of what she was once before, and she tried to play it off. "It's just a lot at one time."

Florie wanted to believe that but could not bring herself to let Velkin fall more into herself. "Tell us what is wrong."

"Let's just find the Chapter, and get Bendrit, and go."

"No Velkin! Tell us."

"You wouldn't understand; you weren't there," Velkin spun her lie.

"Try us," Florie begged. "We can help you. I don't want you going into a dangerous area and doing something dumb because you are so out of it."

"You didn't live through the Cataclysm; you don't know what it's like to be standing here." Velkin began to cry, thinking of her sons and the husband she had lost.

Velkin sat on the muddy street against a nearby wall, her armor darkening as it was covered. "This city is a replica of Husieàkritae. Preservation of the memory of what should still be standing. A shadow of what should be and what I should have protected. And I fell. It fell." She looked up at the Xurinal, its stone becoming visible with a few flashes of lightning from the sky.

"I lost my family!" she shouted into the night and sobbed, "I lost everything I loved."

Talos and Florie stood there over her, letting her let go. Florie then crouched down and stretched out her hand to place it on Velkin's shoulder, but Velkin recoiled from her touch.

"I told you, you wouldn't understand."

"I wish I had a story to tell you," Florie began as the rain fell against the hood, "but I don't. My whole life has been with the Conclave. I have had a good life; things have only gone south since I got involved with you all. I know I should hate you all. Myrcle's magic destroyed everything Talos and I loved. But I know that there is a bigger problem at hand; the fate of Lorial itself is at stake. And though I want to just leave and forget about you and the others—trust me, I do—I can't abandon Organa nor Lorial, and neither can you. You are a Paladin of Calikan, a righteous hand of divinity, and you can conquer all."

Florie's speech touched Talos, and he knelt down beside her. "What she said," he smiled at Velkin.

A moment of rain-filled silence passed between them, and Velkin smiled falsely. "Thank you." She stood with a sigh, and they continued their way toward the Citadel.

"What do you have in mind?" Talos asked.

"There might be a tavern nearby with horses," Florie thought out loud.

"Stealing horses?" Velkin raised an eyebrow. "Are you sure that's wise, Florie?"

"That will be the least of our sins to worry about. We are trying to save the city."

"Fair enough," Velkin laughed back, and they walked on down the wide streets of Valistar.

The trio walked for a few miles and eventually came upon a roaring sound from within a tavern with a few good horses tied up out in the side stables. They were already saddled and ready to go.

They each snuck under the windowsill of the tavern and into the stables, untying the steeds. They mounted them and took off down the street at a brisk gallop. The rain fell harder, and the lightning picked up in its ferocity. Within only a few minutes, they had passed the Xurinal, and as they did, a figure caught Florie's eye—a tall person in red, torn robes. They rode on nevertheless and reached the northern stretch of the city. Castle Black Rose stood absolutely grand before them.

Talos felt the urge to run inside and find the others. Something was wrong… and then he saw a flash of fire from a balcony, but he forced himself to think nothing of it. Yet, something was still wrong. They dismounted their horses and ran back down the street toward the tavern. Velkin looked around, her boots sloshing in pools of muddy water, for any semblance of the crest of the Children of the Crimson Moon. Florie shouted at Talos to help, and he was drawn away from the Citadel. Together they went from door to door, looking for any chance of finding the crest they sought. A creaking sound came from behind them, and a sharp prick of pain struck each of them as they fell to the ground, sleeping.

* * *

A faded light came into view through a burlap sack over Florie's head. There was extreme heat radiating not far from her. Her hands were bound to a piece of wood that she struggled to free herself from. A dripping sound echoed through the chamber. She heard a shuffling noise from close around her and looked as best she could, but she could make out two other shadows to her left. They were moving—slowly, but moving. A flickering light was on the far side of them, and the tips of flames shot up from a few braziers. From a carved stone portal came another silhouette. The gleam of a red robe shone as they passed by the flames, and Florie discerned white hair that fell past their shoulders. They walked surprisingly fast with the regal posture of a noble-born. They stopped in front of the middle shadow on Florie's left.

"After Itheca, I went to find you," a male voice spoke, "as our 'Righteous Mother' demanded I assist you fools in your errands." He removed the bags from each of them with a simple wave of his hand. Florie twisted her head, not paying any mind to the burn of the sack against her face being removed. Beside her, she found Velkin and Talos tied to massive wooden shafts. It was a cold stone chamber only a few yards in length, but the heat from the blazing braziers pushed the chill away. "You are responsible for the deaths of hundreds in a single night. I thank you," he smiled. "You've only sped up our plans."

"What plans?" Velkin asked.

"Surely you are not naïve enough to believe that this hasn't been by design. Although not much has gone exactly according to our will, nevertheless, we have kept the endgame in sight, and it's all fallen into place." They gave no response, only annoyed looks at his masterful conniving, which he was very proud of. "Well, better to keep you in the dark. You'll all die down here, anyway."

Velkin went to summon her sword and cut her bonds, but it did not come at her call.

"Oh," he laughed. "You did play your part well. With all the illusory magic, I am surprised that you still have your head on straight with the separate facades you had going throughout our production."

"What?" Florie asked.

"Velkin, you must be quite the actress. Did you never slip up once?"

"Fucking tell us or kill us. Quit being so maniacal and get to the fucking point," Talos grumbled.

Corvin paused for a moment and glared at the Drakemen. He took the blade from within the sheath on his hip and knelt down in front of him.

"So direct. So strong. I wonder what it would take to break you. Tell me, Florie," he said without breaking his gaze from Talos' eyes, "did Talos weep when Natalia died? When Merith shoved her accursed blade through her chest and devoured her soul, did he mourn for her?"

Florie gave him no answer.

"I cannot simply believe that his oldest friend being killed wouldn't have sparked some emotion." Corvin had not blinked once since locking eyes with Talos. His innate focus peered beyond his physical form and pierced Talos' soul. "Aban," he shouted, "bring her in."

A man in black and red clothing entered behind a woman in a white robe of sacrifice. Esvele stumbled like a walking corpse with the point of a dagger at her back.

"What do you think of the work we've done, Talos?" Corvin grinned.

Talos could only stare at the emaciated body of the one he had come to care for. Where Esvele's long fiery locks once hung to her shoulders, her hair had been shaved with shears to the root. Her once-long horns broke off forcefully, leaving dried trails of blood down her gray face where her sunken skin clung to her bones like a rotting cadaver. Esvele's eyes, cold eyes, had lost all color, now turned white from whatever the Children had done to her since their arrival. Scars along her face, neck, and arms from torturous instruments that had dug into her skin covered nearly every inch.

Corvin smiled, watching Talos' mind crumble, and then released the threads of night that formed his illusion. The form of the false Esvele dissipated in a burst of purple flames, sending a writhing feeling within Talos, making him vomit beside where he sat.

"Weak and pathetic. Nowhere near the valor that Natalia always described. A pity." Corvin chuckled.

Florie's wide eyes and racing heartbeat nearly caused her to do the same as Talos, but one thing kept her focused: Velkin's blank face. No tears, no frowns, nothing at all. Her eyes were sullen, as if she didn't care. Her oldest friend, tortured and burned right in front of her, and she didn't even blink when she caught fire.

"I would love to continue our game, but I believe it has run its course," Corvin straightened himself. "Velkin, come now, we've work to do."

Velkin gave a sorrowful look as the rope around her hands fell. Talos thrashed about like some wild thing. Florie could not move as she watched Velkin stand and walk to Corvin, bowing before her master.

"You have played your role sufficiently, Velkin. Your just reward will come soon by the promise of the Shadow Monarch."

"Thank you," she replied through her tears, breaking her façade.

"Why do you weep?"

"I do not know my Lord."

"Wipe them away, Child of Truth; you need not weep for salvation. Do you have the Glass Key?"

"Of course, my Lord," and she reached into her satchel and removed the amulet.

"You lying bitch," Talos shouted, "You said you got that from thieving."

"I did." She turned on her knee. "I stole it from that old man, who was Bendrit. But I modified his memory to never realize it had been in his possession at all."

"Well, he'll remember when we find him," Talos glared.

"No, he won't." Her eyes trailed off. "I killed him in Gavis Vel'Stratis as we laid siege to the Wizards of Corthal. We put it to the torches, and now it rests as rubble and ashes," Velkin said back rather simply.

"We?" Talos glared.

"She was lost when her sons died. So much grief, pain, and suffering, a soul cannot bear the weight of such toil. So, to preserve herself, knowing that the *Vitu'Lux* was leaving her, and that the Pantheon had not answered her prayers in centuries, she sought us out and made a deal. We performed a ritual that shattered her soul into two beings. One sustained by pure magic and what could be considered an illusion, and one the true form of the light bearer— or whichever infinite power is strongest in them. When the lesser image of the original form is destroyed, they will be conjoined once again. Now she is whole, and her pain will end with the rising of the Shadowlight."

"Why?" Florie asked Velkin, her eyes tightening.

"I had to," she said without hesitation, "for my sons. I-"

"All right, I'm bored now," Corvin interrupted her. "Velkin, go to the Citadel and bring the Lady Magis and the Soulflame King to the chamber. Together, we will achieve the Final Shape the Shadow Monarch has envisioned, and we will see the world remade. Go now, do as you're bid." Velkin turned from her friends and bowed to her master, leaving them behind as she exited the stone room. "Come and see," the Crimson Priest said with a foul smile.

The Crimson Priest caressed his amulet. A trail of sparks flowed from it and wrapped around Florie, Talos, and himself. In the blink of an eye, black-and-white flame erupted around them.

The flames died away, and a dark place took shape around them. In the middle of the large space was a white marble pyramid that clung solidly to the roof. Small trails of shadows flowed up onto it from a glossy structure that mirrored its shape. Those tendrils that reached out from their own abyss stacked upon one another, forming a fine and shimmering dark pool where stars seemed to blink ever faintly for a brief moment before being extinguished by that devouring shadow. Four staircases stood, one leading up to each face of the Sepulcher. At each corner were lightless flames that moved in the darkness like eldritch evil above oil pans that held nothing. They sat upon pillars of scarred skulls and shattered bone. Four massive Orisian stones held up the ceiling high above them. The chamber was cut perfectly in the form of a square, its tall walls carved into a vast mural.

Florie could make out a few images in the darkness. A crystal with many jagged edges and what looked like spirits trapped within it, a glaive whose blade twinkled with starlight, and a crown of gold with galaxies at the top of each pinnacle. They shone faintly, giving just enough light to reveal some of the room they were in. Each one glowed differently and was pulsating, the darkness overcoming and then being driven back.

Talos and Florie felt their rope bonds loosen and fall to the floor behind them. Then the four flames near the Sepulcher ignited. Each held a different color, red, blue, green, and white, that revealed the entire room. They looked around to see everything in its truth and final shape that had been meticulously carved to perfection. As they circled, their eyes caught a figure rising in front of a stairwell that ascended into deepening darkness. Corvin manifested from the black and white flames that clung to him and released him fluidly.

Florie and Talos both jumped to attack him, but before they could reach him, chains made of purple and black shadows shackled them to the ground and burnt their skin as they gripped them. "Now, now, no violence shall be had here, yet," he said through his grimace.

"You serve the Blood Mother. You were meant to help us," Florie said, glaring.

"The Blood Mother died with all the rest of the gods when the Fire in Heaven tore apart the Great Beacon. What you saw in the Chapter was a puppet of our Greater Will, a manifestation of the Shadow

Monarch. If she still lives, she's holding on to the last strands of power left from those who still venerate the lesser goddess."

"That's not possible. The Shadow Monarch cannot enter our plane without a vessel. Myrcle said as much."

"Our master never took a physical form," Corvin said, shaking his head with disappointment. "It sent an image, an influence, not a tangible being. Now Organa's brother is a vessel. A piece of the Shadow Monarch still lurks within him, filling his rage and his hate for those who betrayed him those many years ago. And now he will be set free. A chosen herald of shadow and perfection. The maker of a pure universe of order, where the chaos of life and choice is no more. A world where the disease of freedom has been cured and violence and evil are no more. A *pure* world."

Talos and Florie both tried to snap back at him, but he raised a finger to his lips and their mouths made no sound, nor could they struggle against their chains.

"You will soon understand. When we awaken the Shadowlight, you will see its power and glory shine. And when we have found the Instruments of Chaos, we will remake it all into its Final Shape. We shall have perfection at last. All we need now is for Organa to open it." He fixed his glare on them for a moment and then walked away toward the Sepulcher.

The Western Obelisk

Organa ran through the halls of the castle, remaining hidden from the guards and patrols. She moved through the shadows and past the light of the torches. The fierce storm thundered outside and hit the castle hard with sheets of rain. Lightning flashed throughout the skies and struck the sea with power. Organa found a door that led outside to a bridge that connected to the base of the Silver Spire. She could see out a barred and colored-glass slit, the rain falling hard upon the bridge. She pulled back on the silver bar and the wooden door opened, letting in a wild, spiraling wind of violent force. The gusts nearly threw her against the wall. Organa steadied herself and faced the storm head-on.

She walked out the door and was instantly drenched in water as if she had fallen into the sea. The drowning sheets flung large drops over the entire city, and Organa could see the Xurinal looming in the distance. She hoped that she would find the answers she needed. Was there truly a Sepulcher there? Was her brother this close? What would she do? She pushed those thoughts from her mind and clung to the railing, pulling herself toward the base of the Silver Spires. She saw a shadow pass across a lit window, then withdraw, and a figure gazed out at her from the far end of the bridge. Though she could not see them in detail, she heard a female voice calling out to her, but she could not make out the words through the raging storm.

Organa continued her trek across the bridge. A loud clap of thunder shook the air as clear white lightning flashed through the clouds overhead. She pushed against the cold and wet that fought against her advance. Her hands were turned white by how hard she was gripping the railing, and as a loud clap of thunder sounded, she lost her footing and slipped, crashing onto the Osirian stone floor and sliding before she pulled herself back up to her feet. Finally, she found a place for her feet on the bars of the railing and pushed herself up, sticking the landing before pressing on. She heard that voice again, calling out to her from across the way, but still could not understand it. Organa held tight and pulled herself across. As she reached for the door, it opened and a shadow pulled her inside.

"What the hell were you doing out there, you fool?" said an old man in blue formal clothes with a white beard that fell a few inches below his chin. He let her go and Organa fell back onto the stairs, but before she hit, she held out her hand and caught herself with magic, lowering herself easily the rest of the way. "What compelled you, pray tell, to walk through a storm?" His voice was coarse, his skin a copper tone, and even though he was furious, she saw the kindness in his eyes. Arcane symbols and red accents were stitched onto his fine dress clothes. Even though it was the same, his cloak's colors were inverted. "Speak, child."

"I need to get somewhere, and that was the way I saw it," Organa replied.

"Well, you are a fool! But at least a *brave* fool, nonetheless."

"Thank you," Organa said as she stood, the water from her clothes dripping like a small waterfall. Her silver hair had gone dull and gray with water, and she wrung it out over the stairs.

"What are you doing?" he slapped her hand. "Trying to kill someone on the stairs tonight? It's not a polite fall down these stairs, believe me, I know."

"I beg your pardon, sir," she stuck to the performance.

"Who are you?"

"My name is Mariana Picklea, and I am an advisor to the Lady of Nefis," she said, trailing off as she nearly forgot Esvele's false name.

"'The Lady of Nefis,' you say? She isn't meant to be here for some time, for the Council of the Nine."

"We arrived early to find a healer for her guard. He has a terrible memory, and certain potions, which we cannot brew on our island, could cure such a thing."

"Well then, if you are indeed who you say you are, I am very glad to make your acquaintance," he said with a smile. "I am Lord Mavius, Sorcerer Lord of Valistar, and advisor to the Soulflame King and Lady Magis." He bowed to her with great respect. "Well, I know I'm an old man, but I mean no shenanigans when I say, you are more than welcome to come with me and dry off. I swear to you on all I am as a decent man, I will do you no harm."

"That would be very kind of you," she smiled and was grateful that her mission just got much easier. They ascended the stairs and walked for about fifteen minutes, taking the long and dry way to the Silver Spires. They passed a few servants, who wore fine and tailored clothes, along the way and many guards stationed around the Citadel. The stained glass only revealed its colors when the lightning outside flashed or the light of the torches and chandeliers hit it enough to get a glimpse of its intricate design.

"So, Mariana, tell me, when were you brought on as the Lady of Nefis's advisor and Mistress of Spells?" he said as they ascended the last stairwell up to the Western Obelisk.

"Yes, I have served the Lady of Nefis for many years now. I grew up with her. She was practically my sister after my mother died, may her memory live in the Dawn Eternal. My mother was the advisor to the previous Lord of Nefis," she responded properly.

"Is that so?" Mavius said with an impressed raise of his eyebrow. "You come from a powerful family."

"I suppose so," she laughed.

"Well, it is my honor to play host to you for a short while," he said as they reached the door to the Western Obelisk. He pulled back his hand, and the door opened at his graceful command. Organa entered the space and saw before her a grand library filled with hundreds of books and scrolls extending over three separate floors connected by ladders of current and bygone ages of the Elder Days of Lorial. The roof was no roof at all, but an endless yet controlled expanse of stars, nebulae, and the heavens that gave light to the room. Celestial spheres drifted around the outside of the tower, suspended with effortless grace as they rotated.

It was then, as she looked out at those marvels, that she realized she heard no sound of rain or thunder. The storm had not passed, as she could see the rain and the flashes, but they were silent. In the center of the room were padded chairs, and against a wall was more fine furniture near a roaring fire inside a hearth. Organa shook off her awe, stuck to her role, and made her way quickly to the fire. Its heat surrounded her, and she felt its warm embrace as Mavius entered the room and began walking toward the young elf. Organa wished to speed things up, and she pulled the fire from the hearth and bent it to her will, wrapping around her in coils of red, orange, and yellow. Within a few seconds, she was dry and returned the flames to their origin.

"You are a student of the arcane, I see," Mavius said. "Or rather, you must be her Master of Spells then, or Mistress," he corrected himself.

"Mistress is correct," Organa confirmed.

"How wonderful to see another magic user in the courts again. I need to go get myself changed out of my wet clothes, which I owe to you," he smiled, "but no matter, feel free to look around anywhere you'd like, then we'll head to dinner with the king and queen. I am sure they invited you and the Lady of Nefis?"

"Oh yes, that would be very kind of you to escort me."

"Then I will be right back," and he walked toward another door across the room into his chambers.

Organa's awe returned to her as she gazed around the dazzling room. She walked toward the bookshelves on the floor she stood on and ran her hands across the bindings.

Land of Clay: The History of Balinor and the Great Wastes.

The Great Unbeheld: An Account of the War of Old and the Eldarin.

Gold plates with carved words were pinned to the shelves below the scrolls.

Scroll of the Planes.

Account of the Luxian Magics.

Historia of Shadows.

The names went on and on. Scrolls and tomes of spells, histories, legends, myths, everything anyone could ever want to know was written here. Organa passed through every aisle and read the names of so many books, even opening a few to see their words.

One passage from *The Compendium of Stars* read:

Upon those vast expanses of endless light and night are the greatest of mysteries in which possibility has no limit. The days of the early worlds of the universe are unwritten and the pathways through that astral sea are uncharted and will always be. Such things that wait in that night are beyond comprehension and any sight of mortal power. Only the Eldarin dared to look into that beyond, and only they knew what they found. A mystical phrasing of words continued on, and she was frightened by her own image of what could be there in the night and closed the book, placing it back on the shelf. She looked around for more interesting material and saw a book titled: The Land and Peoples of the North: A History of Menagerie. She opened it, remembering Florie's old comment about her people coming from that land, and read: According to legend, the race of the Hawkinas came from the mountains of the northernmost land of Menagerie. Their people, being shifters of both human and bird forms, survived the land by cultivating those few places they could and living as nomads as the seasons of winter went from mild to extreme throughout the year. Organa skipped toward the end of the book. When the Cataclysm ravaged the land of the east, the Hawkinas of Menagerie welcomed those who they could save and provided teachings in their way of life, and the magic of the Dremicans brought to those people many areas of viable land to cultivate as farms, shielded from the frigid northern winters.

Organa closed the book and continued to look around and then remembered she was on a mission to find particular information.

She looked for the tome or scroll she needed, but that would be impossible to find in a decent amount of time. Organa then had an idea. She went back to the shelf of spell scrolls and looked for a Scroll of Finding. She pulled scroll after scroll off the shelves and came upon one that caught her attention: a Scroll of the Traveler. Breaking the seal, she unraveled it to reveal the name Amsu, the Traveler. The words were of an ancient tongue that, for once, she recognized, Stellevarian. She looked around the room for Mavius and, noticing he wasn't there, began to teach herself the song—the ability to Flash. It took a few moments, but the melody was simple enough, and she believed the words were correct. As she put the scroll back on the shelf, she found the one she was looking for.

She unfurled the parchment horizontally and began to read, thankfully, common speech words on casting the spell. She took the scroll to a podium nearby that was carved out of Osirian stone that absorbed the light around it, almost making it invisible at certain angles of sight. Reading the words for the casting, she noted its required ingredients.

An item that pertains to that which you seek, with the concept penned upon it, and a knowledge of minor casting abilities.

She looked around and saw a scrap of paper on which she had written "Sepulcher." Organa muttered the words under her breath before casting, unaware of a shadow emerging from behind a door in the tower. She read the words of the spell aloud, the scrap of old paper held in her hand.

As the words left her mouth, she closed her hand into a fist, balling up the paper. The reality around the paper swirled and bent to her will as the magic flowed from the Flux, tingling her hands as it passed into the new form being made. A burning sensation, not terrible, but still painful, warmed her hand as the paper caught fire. An instant chill came over it, not of her own affinity with winter, but of the spell's design, instantly freezing solid, forming itself into a purple and yellow stone that was smooth to the touch as she opened her hand.

Organa opened her eyes and saw the stone in her palm, pulsating with a wild and unnatural light. She moved in closer, and the light lost its gleam. She moved it away, and it rejuvenated itself with life. As she moved from the podium, Mavius revealed himself from the doorway, unbeknownst to Organa, who was focused on the stone. The light bounced inside the conjured rock as she moved about the space, speeding up and full of life, then slowing down and dying—a compass pointing toward what she sought.

She followed its brightening arrow up a ladder onto the second floor and then across the wooden balcony toward a door in the wall, but still, the stone beckoned her upward toward the stars. She ascended another ladder and reached the top of the tower where she could clearly see the thundering storm outside and the massive rain that fell upon Valistar. Following her stone again for a few moments, Mavius's eyes tracked her the whole time until eventually, the gleaming stone was pulsating so rapidly that she feared it might explode in her hand. She turned back toward the spot on the shelf where the stone burned brightest and saw a black and red tome.

The Children of the Crimson Moon: A Single Hand of Darkness.

Organa placed the stone on the shelf and removed the book from its place, looking upon the ruby-eyed skull in a black wispy-painted hand. Her heart thumped loudly in her chest as she feared what she might find inside, and she flipped it open and skimmed the pages until she saw what she sought. A black pyramid was sketched onto the pages, and the four braziers lit with four colored and black flames. Two figures were chained to the ground with black shackles.

and two souls shall be required to awaken the eye of the Glass Key and contain the raw power within this sanctuary of torment, but they must be there of their own accord, ready to die to break the chains of eternity. Her heart quickened even further as she read on, Upon the Glass Key must befall great power of life and death and can take the place of the two willing souls of sacrifice. She dropped the book to the floor and found that as she did, a hand caught it before it hit the wood.

"Are you all right?" Mavius asked.

"I... I," she stuttered.

"Come, dear," he said, wrapping his arm around her, placing the book under his other, and bending the realm of the Western Obelisk with a simple outstretched hand that caused the wood to contort itself into stairs that they descended to the base. He sat her in one of his padded chairs in front of the hearth and fire. "Now, what has you so struck?"

Organa took a moment and then fell back into her character. "Oh, I am terribly sorry. I was just finding a book, and it was so interesting, I lost myself in its words."

"They can often do that to you," he laughed it off, "but such a strange book to read indeed."

"I had never heard of them and saw that sketch. It caught my eye particularly. I read its words beside it and was dumbfounded."

Mavius took the book from under his arm and opened it to the page he saw her reading. He repeated it out loud and gave a false shudder. "A dark passage indeed, Mariana. What drew you to such a text?" and he repeated its title after flipping to the cover.

"It sounded interesting."

"Ah, I understand," he said with a small smile. "So, Mariana, tell me, when were you brought on as the Lady of Nefis's advisor and Mistress of Spells?"

"About seven years ago," she lied.

He caught her lie. "Wonderful, it has been some time since anyone has had a Mistress or Master of Spells that wasn't in direct service to the Menitheal Dynasty."

"How strange, why?"

"Well, many believed that the ones from the earlier days of the Dynasty's rule were Magiqas in hiding. Which had them in constant flux with their Balance of Chaos, which has been a term for far too many things, I believe. Thus, they were wildly unpredictable. Too little magic was used, and they went catatonic, and too much ushered in the same fate, often resulting in the deaths of many and even themselves. So the position was disbanded from the royal courts, and the Sorcerer Lord was placed as the only magic user in any courts across the kingdom. So, if I might be so bold, 'Mariana', how did you come to be in her service as such?"

Organa controlled her panic and tried to recover from her misstep. "The Lady of Nefis has always had a soft spot for magic users in her heart, and I was practically her daughter, so I believe she made an exception."

"Except, 'Mariana', you are more than a simple magician and the Lady of Nefis lost her sister and mother to a blood mage's ritual. Lady Veilstom has a distinct hatred for magic," he said simply. "Oh, and she's been dead for nine years now, going on ten. There is no 'Lady of Nefis,' it's a Lord now, Lord Bernis." Organa's heart was beating beyond anything she had ever felt in her conscious life. "So," he began as he twisted the flames nearby in the hearth, "I ask again, who are you, and why are you interested in this?" he held up the book.

"I–" she started.

"No, you can't lie; I'll know." He waved his hand, and a golden pulse shone from his palm and engulfed her in an arena of candor. "I don't do well with liars on the first encounter, but you were brave enough to face a storm like that head-on, so I thought you had a reason to be here. So, don't lie, and tell me who you are and why you want this book."

"My name is not Mariana," she said.

"I gathered," he smiled.

"My real name is," she paused and did not know what to do for a moment and then came out with it, "My real name is Organa Evenstar. My parents were of the Starlight Dynasty."

The flames in the room died, not in a slow manner but instantly.

"Ah," he stuttered, "a…a Child of Starlight…in my chambers." He stood to his feet and paced around for a few minutes.

Organa sat in her chair, relaxed enough now to speak clearly, "Okay, so yes, I am here and frankly very tired of people either harassing me or not knowing what to do with themselves when in my presence, or hiding things from me they shouldn't—but that last one is a different topic. What I need is this book to know how to stop this from happening, and to know if there is a Sepulcher beneath the Xurinal."

The man stopped dead in his tracks. "The Xurinal?"

"Yes, before… well before a lot happened, I met a man named Malorian–"

He cut her off. "Malorian, he's alive?"

"Well, I don't know. The last thing I know that happened was a raid on Turnmot, where he was hiding out, and the death of his… the death of his wife and… kids. They took Malorian hostage. I don't know where he is."

"Malorian's family. They were murdered. By whom?"

"Merith, I think. I didn't have the vision."

"Forgive my threats, m'lady," he bowed politely.

"I don't have time for that," she shouted. Mavius shot up with a surprised look. "I'm sorry, but I believe that someone is going to try to open a Sepulcher, and I need to know if this thing is actually here. If not, that is great because we can go find it properly, but if it is, thousands of lives are in immediate danger and millions more if we don't stop whoever is doing this."

"That would be the Children of the Crimson Moon and their false 'goddess.'"

"What?"

"None of the gods, lesser, greater, or the Pantheon of Dawn survived the Fire in Heaven. There has been no proof that any of them did. The one they follow now is not the real Blood Mother, but some conjured thing."

"My friend, she is a Paladin of Calikan. She has the power to summon her holy sword and everything. How could she do that?"

"You know a paladin? One that can still use the holy magics?"

"Yes."

"What's her name?"

"Velkin."

"You have to find her, and you have to keep her away from Merith!"

"Why?"

"It was part of the plan to get you, the Guardians, to Valistar."

"I'm not a Guardian."

"Not yet, but you will be. Which is why they must have tried so hard to get you here. The Web of Fate has shown it according to a source of the Lord and Lady. It was planned by Organa from the beginning. I was there when this was set in motion, but the details were scarce. If I had known this involved a Child of Starlight and a Sepulcher nonetheless, I would have voted against it, spoken out, done everything in my power to stop it from coming to fruition as it has."

"Why did you support the killing of random people—the 'Guardians'? What if they had not been in the presence of a Child of Starlight? Would you have supported their murder?"

"I don't know," he said quietly.

"Well, figure it out because you have a choice now." Silence fell over the room for a moment, and then Organa realized something. "You said the Children of the Crimson Moon were being led by a false goddess. Who?"

"I do not know."

"What do we do?"

"'We'? I can't do anything. The Vow of Lords is sacred and unbreakable. You die if you do."

"You said you would do anything to stop this from happening. There are millions of lives at stake. So, do me this favor and help me."

"How?"

"Get me to the infirmary–now."

"Why?"

"I need to get Myrcle and Esvele. They are the ones who came with me, and we need to find Florie, Velkin, and Talos before Merith, whoever she is, gets ahold of them."

"Then to the infirmary we go." He walked over to her and held out his hand. "I assume you're familiar with Flashing?"

"Yes, now get me to my friends."

"All right," and he cast the spell, but as he uttered the last words of the arcane tongue, it fizzled.

"I knew one of you would be around here sooner or later, Organa," said the Lady Magis from the doorway into the Western Obelisk, her hand raised and a dim light fading away as she cut Organa's threads. "No matter, I'll cast it for you, but mine is much darker." She smiled. Black and white flames wrapped around them both and the Lady Magis as they felt themselves turn to ash.

A Song of Sorrow

The room around them disappeared, and the Sol Hall came into view. The grand chamber was empty; only the towering pillars that supported the roof remained, and the stained glass above, flashing to life with each strike of lightning. Across the polished floor, and descending from the great ceiling, great extensions of crystal flowed separately like rivers of white light. They branched from two apexes that fell from the rafters of white marble. The Crystal Thrones, great, gleaming white seats of power that held meaning from the time they were sculpted, now held nothing but what should have been a prosperous and fair kingdom that had fallen into the hands of darkness and deceit. A land that would soon die, and an Inquisition waiting if the Guardians failed.

Across the hall near the thrones, Myrcle and Esvele were chained to the floor with dark and burning shackles. Organa and Mavius ran to them. A sound from behind stopped them in their tracks. A sudden sound of flame brought with it the Lady Magis and the Soulflame King.

"Welcome, Child of Starlight," the Lady Magis called out, holding out her hands as though basking in the light of the storm outside. "We have long awaited your arrival, and to see you walk into our midst so willingly was truly something," she laughed. Her voice had changed from what Organa had heard before. The voice was lovely and rejuvenated, whole and pure. They walked close to them, and Mavius stepped between Organa and the royals. "Careful, Mavius, I know you value your life."

"You never told your advisors who we agreed to hunt and trap like some rabid dog."

"No, I didn't, because you would have done something incredibly stupid—which you are doing now."

"Please, Mavius," the king asked, "step aside."

"No, I will not. She is an Evenstar, and she will be protected."

"Like some rightful queen," the Lady Magis laughed, "waiting for her throne and the grand revolution that follows her to cast me down. That will not happen, and this city will be ash by the dawn. The Inquisition of the Damned will begin."

"You've no right to deny the return of the Starlight Dynasty!" Mavius boomed. He reached for the Flux, but the Oath bound his fingers from weaving anything against his sovereigns.

"Oh, Mavius, you are a soldier of the days of yore, but you forget yourself, and your guard is down." And she cast a dark spell in her palm and summoned a blade made of moving, bursting shadows that Mavius barely perceived. He cast a ward between them that pushed the Lady Magis back into the room. She gracefully skidded across the floor and steadied herself before a wide and arrogant smile gleamed across her face. The Soulflame King simply stood there and let the assault on his lover happen. "That was lucky," she snickered.

"Tell me who you are," Organa intervened and stood in front of Mavius.

"You haven't figured it out yet? You are dull," she laughed as she walked forward.

"I've been in this city for only a day and met you once. What more do you want from me?"

"I didn't mean myself personally. I meant, who we are?" Organa saw, in the shadows, a choir of black-robed entities and three of the Weave Oracles, caught in a flash of lightning. As the flashes of lightning died, the Lady Magis and the Soulflame King were gone. Organa turned around and saw them on their thrones. The robed figures pushed forward, and Organa and Mavius moved back toward their enemy.

Myrcle woke and saw the king and queen upon their thrones. A sharp pain shot through his body as the flesh on his arms singed and died. Esvele was to his right, and he felt a hand on his shoulder that caused some pain, but it was eased when he looked up and saw Organa above him. Esvele felt her wounds and bolted back into consciousness. She glanced around the room wildly, and her eyes focused on Organa near Myrcle. A strange man beside her caught her eye, and she tried to break free of her bonds, to no avail.

The Lady Magis took all of their attention with her laugh of a thousand voices. It sounded like men, women, children, all people laughing out of time with one another, the voices rising and falling separately. The haunting voices lingered in the room a short while and faded as she stood from the throne. In that room, the choir enclosed about them even tighter.

"All right, enough of the fanfare," the Lady Magis said. "We'll get to the rub. I brought you here to watch as the new order is ushered in, but I need a vital piece of the puzzle. You," she smiled at Organa, "I need your power to help open the Sepulcher that holds your brother."

"You won't get it," Organa spat back.

"Who said anything about your being willing? When the Dark Song takes hold, all the senses are so overloaded that one can barely function, much less control their power. But the Shadow Monarch's gift to their servants is control. Control over chaos and form. Control over that exulting song. With your brother's help, it will all be possible, and the Final Shape will be achieved, an everlasting peace to the universe."

"I won't help you kill millions."

"It isn't murder. It is freedom from a universe of cruel chaos that holds no true form of perfection. But we can achieve this! Through the Shadowlight, through your brother."

"What makes you believe that he would help you?"

"He's vengeful. Despises those who betrayed him and locked him away in that prison. He hates those who have wronged him. Why wouldn't he join those who can give him vengeance and peace?"

"You can't open it without the Glass Key, and we don't have it."

"You are right, my dear, you do not, but she does." The Lady Magis looked back toward the entrance to the throne room as the carved metal and wooden gates of the Sol Hall began to open.

A faint light from the torches illuminated the foyer further, and a figure cast its shadow through the light as they walked forward. A woman with hair as white as snow stepped out from that place. Armor of disgustingly beautiful design, edged in silver, came into view. Pauldrons with rising ornaments of spiraling, broken shadowglass twirled around her shoulders, covering a layer of thick, leather gambeson, stitched to look like black scales underneath the plated armor around her body. The byrnie met the gauntlets and was consumed by silver, the metal etched with dark symbols carved into its deepest foundations. Claws covered her fingertips as their own weapons, sharp enough to cut through the flesh of a fully grown demon.

Covering her chest was a black breastplate, lined with more silver accents that shaped an ancient Vodrian symbol across her torso. A leather tunic made of the darkest leather fell beside her legs and behind her, just kissing the floor of her false masters. Her legs were guarded by silver greaves that rose up to her knees, with a pinnacle on each that sharpened to a point.

Looming behind her was a great blade of Blood Iron poking out of a rune-carved sheath that wasn't quite long enough for the massive sword. Its pommel was made of the whitest wood imaginable, contrasting her dark appearance. Held within its four metal fingers, the pommel contained a gem that swirled with black and white smoke, ready to be deployed either as a toxic fume or a swift means of diversion for her and her dark commanders as they made their escape. Her eyes had changed from that beautiful sea blue to a burning green that illuminated her face slightly. "Welcome, Velkin," the Lady Magis said with pride and went down the stairs that flowed from the Crystal Thrones.

"Organa," she nodded, her shoes *clopping* along the floor. Organa felt rage flow through her body and a faint melody in her mind, but she held herself steady.

"You traitorous bitch," Organa said, scowling.

"Please, Organa, don't make this all any harder than it has to be," Velkin pleaded. Her new green eyes passed from Organa and over to Myrcle, whose face sagged, only allowing himself to blink as his chest rose and fell with each gasp. Esvele's shackles clanked against the floor as her eyes burned with nearly the same heat as the dark knight before them. Melodies of rage, pain, and fear sang in her mind as her eyes scanned the woman of darkness and light.

"You're a coward," Esvele gritted her teeth.

"Coward?" Velkin stopped in her tracks, turning to her friends on their knees. "Is it cowardice to fight with all you have? To do everything you can, give up all that you hold dear, forsake the gods you once believed in, so you can have what you lost back in your arms? To be able to hold those who were taken from this world far before they reached their prime? To see their eyes look up at you with joy, knowing that they are safe in their mother's arms because now she can never fail them again? To know that I did everything - regardless of consequence to myself - to save the ones who were stolen from their potential to grow, cast into the reaches of some eternity that I do not even know is there anymore?" Velkin's gasps for air in between every question left her staggered for a moment.

The Black Knight's breaths echoed as her chest rose and fell. She closed her eyes and let the air fill her lungs properly again.

"No Esvele. Cowardice is believing in that which you know is no longer there to comfort you. Cowardice is believing your own lies, well-wishes, and unheard prayers because the truth hurts too much to admit and accept. That is you, and Myrcle, and all the rest of them that still believe that the Pantheon of Dawn ever gave a single *fuck* about any of us in their creation. We're just pawns for them in their great game. And no matter what we do, when we pray and sacrifice and trust in them, we always lose more than we could have ever imagined possible."

"Velkin," Myrcle whimpered. "You…" he had to stop his voice from cracking, but it did anyway. "You …you…" he couldn't hold it in, and drops of water spattered the cold floor in front of him.

"Run out of words, have you, oh wise and illustrious Myrcle Coast-Born Son?" the Lady Magis laughed from her throne.

"Give it a rest, you pompous bitch," Esvele sneered. Like the crack of a whip, the Lady Magis unleashed a stream of black and white fire that kissed Esvele's face, instantly cauterizing a scar up her right cheek and across her eyes and upper forehead.

"I would watch that spiteful tongue of yours," the dark witch spoke. "You may find it gone if you're not careful." The witch rose from her seat beside her husband and descended the stairs, caressing Velkin's armored shoulder as she spoke, "Well done, my champion."

"Give me what I am owed," Velkin shot at her.

"Oh, my dear, the war has but just begun. There is much more the

Shadow Monarch will use you for. You have a role to play in the grand scheme of this drama. I've seen it. The hand that rises high to strike down the god of the new world comes from you. Your hand will bring death to the false god."

"You gave me your word that my sons would be alive. Where are they?"

"They will live again; this I have seen. You will embrace them once more. Simply fulfill all that the Shadowlight asks of you; then you shall have your paradise. Trust me, my champion, and step aside." The clank of Velkin's armor sounded through the quiet hall as the metals scraped against one another with each step she took down the stairs.

"Now then, my love," she turned to the king, "summon the Valiant. The day they have waited for is at hand." Her husband gave a hesitant nod as he spoke in an ancient tongue of old. Swirling columns of flame shot up all around the walls of the great Sol Hall as the Cult of Blighted Souls assembled themselves for their savior's arrival. Donned in red and green cloaks, the cultists chanted as they entered: *"Re'ame Ratul Amsur Gal'bein Loaktax!"* and their dark mother repeated the old adage of their people. "My friends, Children of the Crimson Moon and Children of Shadow, I bring glad tidings: the day of reckoning has come."

"Children of the Crimson Moon?" Esvele asked.

"Hush. I'm speaking." The Lady Magis turned to the acolytes again. "Now we shall bring forth the one who will lead us into Finality. The universe will be set right once again with perfect darkness and endless nights. And the Daughter of Starlight will lead us into the new age: the First Age of Darkness. The Shadowlight cometh!"

"The Shadowlight cometh!" the dark cult raised their hands with their priestess in their dark proclamation.

"Corvin, High Priest of the Blood Mother, Black Hand of the

Darkness, bring forth our prayers," the Lady Magis smiled with pride.

The Crimson Priest appeared from the blackness of a door, met the dark queen with a graceful bow, and delivered his sermon. "Sons and Daughters! The night we've dreamed of has come at last. Tonight, our Lord returns to us. The Herald of Hatred; the Vengeful Son of Sorrow; the Forgotten Brother; the Burning One; the Unending Flame of Chaos shall return to this world and bring about the Dark One's Finality. Now we have the Daughter of Starlight, we've the souls of those we need as the sacrifice, the time is nigh!"

"You were meant to help us!" Myrcle spat at him. "You are sworn to the Blood Mother."

"Her powers wane and fail. Through the Dark One, I will have everlasting might and command of my own fate. The Mother of Vengeance has no power over me, and I will drive my Dusk Blade through her heart before all is done."

"You will pay for this," Myrcle glared back. "You will die, and she will take your soul into the deepest hell to torment you for eternity."

"I rather doubt it," Corvin smiled back. The priest looked upon the congregation again. "My children, sons and daughters of shadow. The Daughter of Starlight will free our lord, and we will behold his might-"

Organa's laughter filled the room. "I will not help you. What makes you think I would?"

"He's your brother, Organa. You wouldn't free him from the agony they put him in?" he pointed to Myrcle and Esvele. "He suffers more than you can imagine in the time that it takes you to blink. Free him. Save him."

"I can't," she said, shaking her head. "If he gets out, he will burn the world to ash."

"And that is how it should be," the Lady Magis's eyes gleamed as she knelt beside the young Elf. "This world was a mistake. It was not meant to be and should never have existed. The Shadow Monarch's creation is the perfect world. Mass orders on a vast scale. Unity. No war, no suffering, no pain. A paradise for the forlorn who have been forsaken by the false god Arratir who invaded the perfection of the Void."

"The lies you believe," Esvele chuckled.

"The lies you believe," Velkin said. "Truth is sadly relative once the lie has been told and then persisted throughout history as the truth."

"Your eyes have been opened, sister," the queen smiled, rising to her feet and cupping Velkin's cheek in her hand. "You are getting closer to becoming a Pure Soul. Maybe the first of our new age to come."

"Thank you, Lady of Bones," Velkin took a deep breath and bowed.

"My love," the Soulflame King said as he descended the stairs, "shouldn't we quit toying with these insolent fools and take them to the Sepulcher?"

"A most excellent idea, darling. My children," she turned to the cultists. "Tonight, we bring about the first glimpse of perfection."

"We live together in the heart of the Dark One. His power and might protect us, and his servants shall smite the Dawn," the Blighted Souls called out.

"My king," the queen turned to him, "take them to the Xurinal. The Shadowlight cometh."

"The Shadowlight cometh," he smiled falsely, taking her hand in his and kissing the top. The king spoke in the foulest of tongues to the corrupted ones, giving them a dark command. Shuffling feet under the colored robes echoed through the great hall. Squeezing pairs of multiple hands pulled Myrcle, Organa, and Esvele to their feet.

The Soulflame King held Myrcle and Esvele both around their upper arms. "Be ready," he whispered in Myrcle's ear. *"Dya'chatlav."*

Myrcle directly recognized the Word of Power for "shatter"—an ancient rite and form of magic lost and forbidden long ago. But as to why the man knew this, it did not matter. The chains that bound Myrcle and Esvele snapped loudly, echoing through the chamber as the Soulflame king stood and released them. "Run, Guardians."

The Soulflame King hurled a series of rays of fire at the cultists and the Lady Magis, who raised a shield of darkness to swallow the spell. Some of the followers were incinerated instantly. The king pulled a Dusk Knife from under his robes, and its blade gleamed like a thousand stars at once, banishing the shadows from the room. Beside him appeared the Weave Oracles, one was instantly killed with a stab to the chest, and its scream was unlike anything of the material realms. For another, he cast a spell to distract and then cut the entity's throat, banishing the beast to its eternity. He raised his blade again to kill the last Weaver, but the Lady Magis appeared in front of the blade, twisting his arm, and reaching to catch the knife. Small trails of steam as the blade's hilt burned her hand and gave a loud *clang* as she disarmed him, throwing the Dusk Knife to the floor.

As the blade tumbled down the stairs, Esvele snatched it from the stone. Myrcle grabbed her, and the Guardians made their way toward the exit.

A cultist ran at them, readying a spell of binding, but found a shard of ice lodged in his chest quickly from Organa.

Another shard struck Mavius and sent him flying back into a pillar with a sharp *snap*. Esvele clung tightly to the blade in her hand and followed the others toward the gate. As they reached the bottom of the stairs, another cultist hit Myrcle's knee hard with her club.

The cultist then felt a sharp pain in her chest as the Dusk Blade pierced into her from Esvele. The cultist's face lit up as streams of darkness filled her veins and poured from her eyes, nose, and mouth. Her flesh was broken and veiny as the shadow was driven out from within the dead host. Her body then lost its ashy and broken complexion and returned to a clear and beautiful tone of life.

"Thank you," she muttered, and fell to the ground dead.

They ascended the stairs and, to their left, a voice called out, "Stop." It was Velkin. Her voice had changed and didn't sound like one, but instead at least three others inside her. They complied for a brief moment out of love for their friend but ran again before she stood in her way. "You will not leave."

"Please, Velkin, move." Myrcle pleaded.

"No." Esvele stepped before the traitor and held out the Dusk Blade in opposition. The Cult of the Valiant surrounded them quickly at the exit. Velkin stood above them on the stairs, and the robed figures formed a dark circle around them.

"That was a good attempt, my love, but you are a fool if you thought that you would win by yourself," the Lady Magis said to her dead lover as she dragged the corpse of the Soulflame King behind her, parting the sea of black robes. She thrust his body forward, and it slid across the floor and up onto the first few stairs, leaving a trail of crimson in its wake. "Now that we've all met one another, it's time to get the night's main event underway. Valiant," she called to her disciples, "take them to the Xurinal, prepare the Sepulcher, and make ready for the arrival of the Shadowlight and the beginning of the Inquisition of the Damned."

The Lady Magis raised her hand, and the gate out of the Sol Hall creaked and rumbled, shaking the ground around them; collapsing under the weight of her magic. The stone, metal, marble, and wood splintered itself and then reformed into an archway of mangled elements. With a simple snap of her fingers, the center of the archway ignited with fury and punctured reality, tearing the schisms of the planes apart with a swirling whirlpool of lightning and purple and black flames. The cultists walked in front of the Guardians, and they entered the inferno before them. Corvin took the Dusk Blade from Esvele and sheathed it in an open strap. Organa watched as the Lady Magis lifted the king's body and followed behind them as they entered the portal. They appeared in a large stone chamber with a black glossy pyramid in its center that sent upward shadowy tendrils that had now covered most of the mirrored white marble pyramid above it, only a few feet away from total consumption.

The Guardians looked around the room and saw Florie and Talos chained to the floor with those draining shackles. Organa bolted for Florie and slid across the stone, landing at her side, and wrapping her arms around her friend.

"Ouch, careful, love," Florie chuckled. Organa looked closer and saw Florie's face had nearly lost all vitality. Chains, slowly pulsating like a heartbeat, bound them to their knees before the relic. The crimson color of shadows flowed down her bonds toward the red flame on a column at the corner of the Sepulcher. Florie's life was being siphoned into the flame, and Organa looked over to Talos, standing to her feet, and saw the same. The flame he was closest to pulsed a deep crimson color with the rhythm of a heartbeat.

Myrcle ran to Talos and examined him, sending Organa a telepathic message. *He won't last much longer.*

Organa felt her heart nearly explode at that moment. She had already lost Brok; she would lose no one else.

Corvin appeared from the shadows beside the gateway that the Lady Magis had opened. Upon his head was a simple crown of Blood Iron and a few amethysts. The queen exited the portal, and it collapsed behind her as she pulled forward the corpse of the king. The duo stood there above them all and descended toward the Sepulcher, taking no notice of their adversaries tending to their friends. Corvin reached out his hand and pulled at the earth, forming a stone table near the base of the great black pyramid. The Lady Magis moved her fingers in a fluid, ethereal manner, controlling the body like a puppet, and the king's bones snapped and popped with each forced movement from her curse. With a thump, the Soulflame King's husk fell on cold stone, molded by the Crimson Priest. The Lady Magis thrust the body onto the platter, letting it lay limp, and the Crimson Priest and Lady Magis raised their hands, closed their eyes, and drew forth from the Flux.

From the Sepulcher came four shadows that held no true form but were humanoid in nature. In their darkness, Esvele saw a slight resemblance of eyes that burned with a white ferocity of rage. The Lady and the Priest stood at the head and foot of the table, and the shadows waited at the corners for them to finish the words of their incantation. Green light emitted from their palms, stretching into the sludgy darkness that flowed onto the body of the dead king. It did not seep into his garments, but into his flesh. His body fluttered lightly for a moment and then stopped. It moved again, and again, and again, until it was fully seizing and contorting itself, the bones snapping and breaking with loud *pops*. The sounds from his voice came on the ear like wild screeches as he tried to reject the darkness entering his body.

The shadows stretched forth their limbs, and one grasped his eyes, another his mouth, another his heart, and the last, his mind, each entering in unison. His body seized even faster, and the bones in his body broke and shattered. As the wisps of darkness settled, his back arched, and he let out another cry of agony and fell limp on the stone table. Within a few moments, his eyes opened with a burning green flame surrounding his iris and green smoke that flowed from them.

"Behold, the first Pure Soul," the Lady Magis rejoiced, and her acolytes spoke in their foul tongue: *Praise be the Shadow, the Final Form of one achieved.* The body of the king sat itself up, walked back toward the Guardians, and took Organa by the throat, choking her, dragging her to the Lady and Corvin. Myrcle bolted from Talos' side, and the queen held him in place with her gaze against his will. Esvele reached for her and from the ground raised vines and roots of the earth that tried to entangle the assailant, but Corvin held out his hand and burned the vines with a green flame that combusted them. He flowed the energy from the vines into one of the black flames, which gained a green glow.

The once-king arrived at the table, but the Lady Magis crumbled it, its service already complete. "Let her go," she thought up a name for her new ward, "Glirik, that sounds nice." She smiled, and he dropped Organa to the ground gasping and coughing, straining for air. The queen knelt down to Organa's side. "You will play your part," she said calmly but strictly, and she picked up the Child of Starlight with a wave of a few fingers. "Free your brother." The Lady Magis pulled Organa forward with an invisible grasp.

A gesture from Corvin summoned Velkin from the shadows. He placed the Glass Key into the hands of the Shattered One, and the darkness enveloped her as she got closer to the Sepulcher. A carved slot fit perfectly as she placed the key into it, and the dragon's eye in the center lit up wildly with purple flames and moved around as if it were alive.

"No," Organa shot back through her shallow breath.

"I told you I didn't need your complacency, but it would make it much, much easier and less painful for you," she said back.

"No."

"All right," she smiles, "More fun for me." The Lady held her palm up and curled her fingers inward, igniting the stone below Organa, and letting the heat surround her, burning her skin and clothes. She tried to contain her pain and refuse its attack, but the fire enveloped her, and she let out a cry. Esvele and Myrcle fought valiantly, but the

Valiant overcame them by sheer number. The Lady let her flames die and recede enough not to cause harm. Velkin stood in the shadows of the room, half-illuminated, and ready to strike upon command.

"Free your brother," the queen said again.

"No," and Organa felt the flames searing across her skin again.

"Open the Sepulcher!" the Lady shouted, her fury beginning to show.

"No." More burns.

"Do as I say or-"

"What?" Organa cut her off through her painful breath. "What will you do? Kill me? You won't because you need me."

"It just works more smoothly if you cooperate," she said and burned Organa again.

"I won't do it," Organa screamed.

"Leverage it is, I guess," the Lady Magis grimaced. With a flash of her fires, she appeared beside Myrcle with a blade of fire at his throat. "You will, or you will watch your friends die. One by one. Until we get what we want."

"You'll kill us all anyway when Kyriel is free."

"You dare speak his name!" Corvin shouted in anger.

"He is my brother. I've every right."

"He is a *god* among us mortals and will outlive all things in all creations. With his power, the Shadow Monarch will remake the universe. The Final Form shall come."

The choir erupted in their song again, "Blessed be the Shadow Monarch and the Final Form of Unity. Peace shall come."

"'Peace'?" Myrcle's voice called out, straining against the hot blade of the knife at his throat. "You say 'peace' and you strive for war as an 'inquisition'. You are no peacemakers but dark fiends of the Void! What you will bring is the destruction of all things. You bring terror and death to everything. Your faith blinds you from seeing your 'salvation' for what its true purpose is."

"And your own devotion to the Dawn does not blind you? You cling to a creation that was never meant to be," the Lady Magis shook her head in disappointment.

The husk of the king spat out in a thousand voices. "We are liberators! We will remake the universe as a new world with a single identity. That all will come to one mind and one heart. Unity everlasting. War, death, sorrow, all things of the Primeval's false design."

Myrcle trembled at the sound that burned his ears but remained resolute. "The Pantheon is not 'primeval'."

"There are far older and worse things than the Pantheon of Dawn, Myrcle. You've believed for so long in the Sky that you barely know of its equal," Velkin shuddered at the very idea.

"And you have?" Esvele scolded.

"I have stood on this line for some time," Velkin emerged from the shadows, walking to Esvele. "I have been torn and shattered because of the Pantheon." Velkin appeared half inside the darkness as she stood at the entrance to the dark room. "Light and dark are the same sides of a coin that has been tossed in the hands of a greater being than we could ever understand."

"That's enough, Velkin," the queen glared.

"We are nothing alike," Organa quivered with pain from her burns.

The Lady Magis nodded, and Velkin silenced herself, moving forward into the dark room. "Light and the Void are twins," the false queen began, "Born of the Sky and the Deep. To all of us who can shape their forms with our magic, they are just tools. We can free all things through the Greater Will's power. The Balance of Chaos will be thrown aside, and a new order empowered," the Lady Magis' speech aroused the acolytes, who shouted words of praise. "Now, Organa," she said, "you will open the Sepulcher. Unleash your power into the Glass Key. Corvin, prepare the two souls." He complied with her command, making his way between Talos and Florie, and slowly out of his hand came three clusters of red sludge tendrils that made their way toward them, across the space. "Begin to siphon your power, Organa, or they will die for nothing."

"I can't."

"Let go. Let the Dark Song fill your mind and use it to reach out and shatter the bonds of your brother's torment. Free him."

"I can't let him loose upon the world."

"Do you want them to die in vain? Let go."

Myrcle and Esvele waited, and the room fell into a heavy silence, like death.

The tendrils from Corvin reached a few feet away from the two souls, and Organa shouted, "Stop. Use two of your own, and I'll open it."

"We can't; they have no souls; they are part of the one binding soul of the Shadow Monarch, the unity and freedom from chaotic choice."

"Then I won't."

"So be it," she said plainly. "Kill them. The Dark Lord doesn't want them anyway."

The Crimson Priest thrust his power into Florie and Talos, and their bodies fell limp as the shadows that bound them pulsed faster, pulling their life force from them. But the black and crimson flames fled in fear of what had been unleashed.

Organa summoned a dome of protection around herself and those near her, pulling Florie and Talos' bodies inside. With her other hand, she unleashed a concussive blast of force, fire, and ice that shattered the pillars holding the ceiling, disintegrated the cultists, hurled the stone of the Xurinal high into the sky, and demolished the area around the sacred temple. The buildings around were blown like leaves in the wind, and those who were around made shadows against the stone as it left the Xurinal. A raging inferno erupted from the already deep crater and drove them further down, the immolation eradicating what it could. A cold winter followed last and covered the mountains and forest nearby with spears of ice and a cold wind that froze everything around it. Her power was so great that the storm that had drenched the city was vaporized and banished.

When the dust finally settled, Organa, Florie, Talos, Esvele, Myrcle, and their enemies survived. Organa fell violently to the ground, hard and violently, as the sheer volume of power she used left her drained. Esvele rushed to her and helped her onto her legs. In the silence of the desolate city, there was a *crack*.

The Sepulcher withstood every amount of force she could conjure, and The Glass Key glowed with a vibrant radiance full of her power. The glass around the dragon's eye broke shard by shard and formed in different places above the Sepulcher. A shining beam of light from the eyestone floated at their apex, reflecting through the lenses and creating four rays of light that placed themselves on the columns of black and red flame. They watched as the top of the black pyramid broke apart like the shards above it and a blue beam shot into the sky that curled inward to the clouds above it. It unmade itself slowly, and more and more pieces of its precipice floated high into the light.

"Thank you, Organa," the Lady Magis's voice was full of awe. "Behold! The Shadowlight cometh!"

Esvele gave a vengeful scream and made a cut against the Lady Magis with her summoned green blade of fire, striking against her and cutting her shoulder. Corvin turned back, pulled a Blood Iron dagger from its sheath, and, as he did, he ran the edge across his chest, cutting through the fabric and flesh with ease, setting the edge ablaze with a deep red fire. He shoved the blade forward and barely missed as Esvele countered him with her own. Esvele heard a melody in her head as her emotions overtook her, and she calmed herself quickly as their swords clashed.

Myrcle had given in, however, and when she saw Velkin rising from the ground, he formed a wild and unstable ball of blue and white fire in his hands that grew as he expanded them. Velkin, seeing him charge his spell, unsheathed a new dark sword, conjured from the Void itself, and held her hand behind the blade, waiting for the attack. With a cry of anger, Myrcle unleashed a terrible and violent immolation that struck Velkin's blade and pushed her back through the rubble. He let out another shout and launched a barrage of lightning called down from the skies above. She deflected two of the bolts, but the other three struck her armor and coursed through her body.

Velkin fell to the ground on her knees and breathed heavily as her armor smoked. She raised her sword with great fury, and from its blade came a bolt of black and white necrotic energy that wrapped itself around Myrcle's body like snakes. Myrcle sustained himself through his Song of Power, took the damage in whole, and replied with another spell of viciousness. A guiding bolt of radiance struck Velkin's blade and deflected into a pile of rubble.

Corvin saw Myrcle's power flowing through him and raised his hand, calling forth weapons from the Void. A bow of purple shadows and an arrow of Osirian Iron that came from the ruins of the city like glass shards on the ground formed clearly in his fingers. Corvin pulled back on a string of shadows and let the arrow fly across the sky, striking Myrcle in the shoulder and throwing him to the ground with a loud *bang*.

The Pure Soul's eyes, once the Soulflame King's, burned with rage. He pulled from under his shredded and burned robes two curved blades and he charged over to Esvele and cut against her left shoulder, igniting the blade with a black fire, and then struck again across the chest, pushing her to the ground with his force. Esvele raised her hand against another incoming attack from the Pure Soul and reached deep into the earth for roots to entangle him with, but only found bedrock. She then held her hand up to brace herself, but a stab from Mavius's dagger in the Pure Soul's side caused him to fall to the ground with a shout. He reached out a hand to Esvele, and she cautiously took it, and he helped her to her feet saying, "Get the Dusk Blade from that Crimson Priest."

"What is the point? We need to get the others out of here."

"No, use the sword to kill him and the queen. Avenge my people and your own."

"No," Esvele said. "It's not about vengeance; it's about saving my friends." And she ran to her old student. "Wake up, Organa!" But the young girl gave no answer. Esvele placed her hands on Organa's chest, and a radiant light shone from her palms, pulsating life into her body. The streams of light moved into her flesh and filled her veins with radiance, but her heart remained still.

The Sepulcher was cracking from the top down and shattering slowly, but at least one-third of it had revealed itself. The Lady Magis basked in the glory of her coming savior and said, "Come, Shadowlight, we beckon you to usher in a new age." As she finished her sentence, she saw her breath, and the air turned frigid. The Lady Magis turned around and saw the open and glowing crystal blue eyes of Organa Evenstar as she rose from the ground.

* * *

Organa did not see the world of reality around her; instead, she was standing on a green mountainside where a tall oak tree had grown nearby. Behind her loomed a great silver monastery. High above the rolling hills and forest below her, she stood, and she could see a gleaming city and a swift sunrise illuminating it like a beacon of hope upon that land. Life flourished where she stood. She could feel the heartbeat of Lorial around her and the murmur of waving trees from the wind. She could feel the *thump* of the hooves of horses, deer, and the scratch against the trees from clawed animals as they climbed. The buzz of bees and the rush of streams. The crashing waves of the coast and the great rumble of the earth. Peace overcame her like a great tidal wave, and she wept, a tear falling from her face in reality.

"Brok," Organa called out desperately, her voice echoing over the hillside of Mount Doloroth. But the only reply was the wind rushing alongside her, swooping around and taking a few of the leaves with it. "Brok!" Organa called for him over and over again, but he wasn't there. "Brok! Please come back. I didn't mean it!" The wind picked up again, but this time like a cyclone around her. High above, the blue sky turned black. Like a curtain being drawn over the heavens themselves, blinking each star out of existence. The leaves of the great oak shriveled and died, falling to the ground and crumbling into ash. Blades of grass fell to the blight that rose all around them, turning brown and dead, then finally black, dissolving into a layer of dust along the rolling hills before the lonely Mount Doloroth. Not even the blue and silver light of the Element Moons could break through the growing darkness above, drowning all light from reaching her world.

Organa took a few steps forward, kicking up ashes from the ground. Total darkness surrounded her. Pitch-black nothingness. Though she could not see them, Organa could feel her hands and placed them a few inches apart. With a few ancient words, she reached out into the Flux for whatever power she could to call the light beside her, but there was nothing. Not even the Dark Song would sing to her here. When Organa looked back up from the darkness around her, two crimson eyes stared back through the shadows.

Suddenly, the hidden earth around her rumbled and roared, cracking to the foundations of Lorial itself. Streams of fire deep within shot up geysers of immolation, illuminating the world around her. Those crimson eyes vanished, and in their place, Organa saw trees fall into the lake of fire below. The flames that rose around the breaking and tearing earth revealed hordes and hordes of foul, malicious, snarling, and terrible demons of the Void. The growling of a creature raised her heart rate instantly as a *click, click, click, click, click,* chirped in her ear. Organa turned to see the same creature that she now remembered attacking her and her mother when they were trying to escape the City of Light during the Cataclysm. In its large, mangled jaws, the creature held her still-bleeding body. Organa felt her heart racing in her chest as the creature inched nearer. Then, Mount Doloroth exploded.

A great plume of ash flung up into the sky by the throat of the western land, reaching the highest cloud it could. Red and blue streaks of lightning rained down upon the mountainside, providing flashes of an ancient burning temple of stone with hundreds of people running from a legion of demons. There in those flashes, Florie flew away from the temple, but a bolt of energy struck her down from the heavens and she fell into the darkness.

The hungry earth continued to eat away at the world until the entire visage of reality bent around her, transforming into a great city with hundreds of buildings with green rooftops. The night had come to swallow this place as well, with no stars or moons in the sky to provide any comfort above. Within moments the scene changed as the houses were lit aflame with green, blue, and red fire. A horde of demons demolished the southern walls, throwing great heaves of stone into the sky, and an unseen hand lit them aflame as well. To their delight, the crashing meteor exploded with such power that areas of the city were leveled entirely. A woman's scream dominated the screams of hundreds as the foundations of the city cracked and opened up to devour the city into the lake of fire below. Then the image changed again.

Organa stood in the darkness once more, lit only by the torches along the battlements of the Living City. Druids in many-colored cloaks stood ready with swords, shields, axes, bows, and arrows, and their magic ready to fight against whatever emerged from the blackness that threatened to end all life across Lorial. The cries of the Order of Valkiel shot into the night with courage and heart to face the evil, but they quickly distorted in Organa's ears into screams.

A tremor crawled through the earth as an aftershock to some quake far off in the darkness at the edge of the Forest of Bravica. The druids looked at one another, unknowing of what was getting ready to happen. Organa could see the fear in their eyes. A voiceless man shouted and pointed high into the sky above them where the stars had broken through the shadow over Rethial. But with each passing second, the stars got bigger and bigger until reality hit them too late. From the black heavens above came a rain of fire. Falling stars shot through the darkness and crashed into the Living City.

Massive explosions and sundered earth riddled the landscape as this cascade of desolation fell upon them. The walls splintered under such force, and a wave of demons revealed themselves from behind the black curtain of night, laying siege to the Living City. Screams of the slaughtered rang out as Organa saw different images of the butchering of the people she once called her family. Her mind focused on one image quickly, the image of Esvele, Florie, and Talos standing beside others she did not know in the Hall of Elders guarding Myrcle as he kneeled under the Heart of the City. Standing together, they defended him gallantly with daggers, swords, spells, and courage, slaying demon after demon until they all stopped instantly. Not frozen, but ceasing to attack them.

From behind her, Organa heard the clopping of heels along the stone stairs. She could see the look of horror in her friend's eyes. Organa turned to see the one who had made themselves known, and she saw three figures: the Lady of Bones, Kethir, possessing the body of the Lady Magis and holding dark blades in her hand of shadow. Organa surrounded herself with the winds of winter with eyes glowing bright blue, washing away her natural emerald, and in between them, a few steps ahead, was her brother, Kyriel, wearing black and red robes sewn with ancient symbols of Vodrian and runes of power with bright crimson and fiery eyes. Two black wings of night wreathed in shadows dragged on the stairs behind him. In his hands, he held his rage in red and yellow flames. Kyriel descended the stairs without saying a word, his eyes focused on the ones in front of him. Organa tried to scream at him from beyond the vision she saw, but her voice could not break through the walls of reality and fate. With a swift motion of his hands and a smile across his face, he released his flames upon them, but was met with a great barrier of light.

In front of her friends stood a woman with dark skin and white robes decorated with silver and gold embroidered and stitched with holy symbols of the same make. She pulled back the string of an ethereal bow of pure light she summoned to her hand. Kyriel's rage surrounded the golden dome of light, washing over it like water over the stones of a river. Kyriel intensified the flames and pushed harder to break her barrier, but he could not. Finally, his screams of pain and anger broke through the schisms of time and space and penetrated Organa's own ears, as did the sound of the rushing tides of immolation upon her friends. Organa watched herself stand there beside her brother with a smile on her face as Kyriel broke the golden globe of protection.

Shadows clouded her once more, but an isolated and lonely jagged ray of gleaming, radiant light shone. Within the blink of an eye, Organa was behind it, something holding the light, but not alone as she had thought. A gloved hand guarded by gauntlets held tightly to the golden hilt of a glistening dagger. The pommel's diamond orb caught the light of the shining stars above that now called from the black heavens. This holy relic's guard, carved with Stellevarian runes of protection and assault, met at the center where a shadowglass sphere rested. Within its darkness, swirling white lights flashed their luminous rays like lightning in a bottle. The stars above were restricted to a single circular space surrounded by a purple and green corona, providing enough light to see the top of the white hair tied in a tight braid of three sections pulled together and falling behind her head.

Organa reached out to touch the silver pauldrons, but the hand holding the glistening blade rose above the woman's head and came down in a single swift stroke upon the back of someone in black robes who manifested from the darkness in front of her. The moment the blade tore through the fabric an explosion of light rained down through the circle of stars above, reaching the diamond orb at the base of the dagger and filling the runes with pure glorious light that broke the shadowglass orb at its center, and unleashed the darkness within. The light and dark became one within the body of the dark figure.

The explosion of light lasted just long enough to see that betrayal, and the light blinded her for a moment more, bringing her back to a familiar hell. She found herself back on the hillside where Brok had died, remade and rejuvenated from the darkness that had devoured him. She was not alone.

A hand touched her shoulder, making Organa jump as she turned to see her brother. Kyriel stood there in silver and gold robes, wearing a crown with amethysts to match. His eyes were as blue as the Old Sea, and his smile as happy as she had seen in the memories she dreamed. "Hello Organa," he said with a tear in his eye. Kyriel wrapped his arms around his sister and hugged her tightly. Organa blinked, trying to wake herself from what she knew wasn't real, but Kyriel held on to her still. After a few moments, Organa wrapped her arms around him too, and she wept with her brother on the mountainside. Kyriel pulled away from her. "It's so good to see you, sister."

"Kyriel," Organa smiled at him, "It's you."

"It's me," he laughed at her snidely. But his face went serious quickly. "But I am not here. I'm stuck. I'm trapped within."

"I know."

"Then free me so we can be together again. So we can both go home."

"Kyriel," she sighed and cupped his face, "there is no home. Our home is gone."

"Then we'll make a new one. We'll rule a new land as the Twin Gods if we want. We can do anything together."

"Kyriel," Organa sighed again, shaking her head. "No, we can't."

Kyriel's anger began to show through him, his eyes kindling into crimson fire. "You side with them. The ones who betrayed me. The ones who betrayed you."

"Yes."

"They stole your memories, Organa! They hid your true self from you!"

"Yes, to protect me."

"You actually think they care about you? How could they? They threw me in a prison for four hundred years because of something that was done to me." With every word, Kyriel's clothes tore apart and were replaced by the same black and red robes she saw in the Living City. Kyriel backed away from her, and the sky above darkened with each step. "You take their side in a war you will never win!"

"Then I'll lose. But I'll lose knowing that I stood for what was right."

Kyriel could hold his anger within no longer, and he let loose a torrent of flame that shot into the sky like a tornado, surrounding them both in red, yellow, orange, blue, and green flames. Kyriel smiled with delight as his destruction dug into the earth around them. "Come on. Strike me down. Do it."

"No. I won't."

"You're that afraid of me? Come on! Do it!"

"No. I won't," she repeated.

"Why? Afraid that you'll kill me? I've been dead to the world for centuries, but soon they'll know I'm back."

"I won't."

"Unleash your fury on me!"

"I won't."

"Gods above! Fine," he rolled his eyes and hurled two huge fireballs at Organa. The young woman held up her hands, creating a vast wall of ice that absorbed the heat and shattered like glass upon impact, leaving her unscathed but with a few scratches from the shards. "Fight back!" Kyriel pulled from the twister around them two blades of green flames and charged at her.

Organa pulled the shards of ice around her to her hands, creating two cold blades, and met the fires of her brother with them. Slash after slash, Organa defended herself from his strikes without making any offensive movements. Her blades quickly melted away with each strike from her brother, and she molded the earth beneath herself, allowing it to carry her away from him. Kyriel dispelled his blades and reached high above himself into the burning cyclone, calling forth waterfalls of fire upon her. "Fight back, you coward! Fight me!"

Organa called forth her power, focused on the light from the fire around her, and she separated the flame from its luminous beams and pulled them around herself, imitating the spell that the woman in the Living City defended herself with and creating an invulnerable sphere around herself of pure silver and golden light. The fires engulfed her barrier like they did the woman in the white robes and Organa endured the assault, dispelling her ward when the fires subsided. "Come on, Organa! Fight me! Stop me before I can't stop myself." Kyriel lashed out again, screaming at her as he unleashed his might. "Come on! Do it! Wreak havoc! Kill me like you killed Brok!"

Organa shuddered at his name being uttered by someone else. The image of Brok's charred and mutilated body lying on the rocks of the destroyed camp flashed in front of her eyes. She turned on the spot, breaking the very earth beneath her into shards, and she froze them into solid blue fractals of ice with a wave of her hand, sharpening them into spears. The swirling fire slowed as Organa summoned a blizzard hitherto undreamed of in all the minds of Lorial, her Dark Song's melody singing louder than she had ever heard it before.

And she let go.

* * *

The ground around Organa's body froze solid, the stone changing form into ice. The surrounding air swirled with a mighty wind of cold and ice. Mavius pulled Florie and Talos'bodies from across the way.

The Lady Magis shot a spell of flames at Organa to subdue her, but it was extinguished by the surrounding winter. Corvin mirrored her spell, but again, to no avail. He shouted an order to Velkin. The dark knight made her way onto the ice.

Corvin gave another order to the Pure Soul, and he stepped willingly into the blizzard surrounding Organa. Within moments of touching the vortex, he almost turned into a statue of ice, taking only a few more seconds to complete his transformation.

Organa cut the air with her right hand, shattering him into a million pieces that joined the surrounding storm. Organa raised one hand, and her spell expanded to the east. Far across the city, another blizzard sparked. She raised her other hand and did the same, freezing the land around it. Organa's eyes met the gaze of blood-red ones from within the half-opened Sepulcher. Her brother's rage poured out onto the land in enveloping and devastating immolation. But against Organa's storm, there was no victory, and it was frozen into black columns of solid stone like solidified magma. Her power surrounded the Sepulcher, and the four pillars at its corners changed to ice. Organa shattered the bond between the two Soul Flames, releasing them from their bondage. The sparks traveled back into the bodies of Florie and Talos, who shuddered as they returned to themselves, still asleep and weak.

She saw the Sepulcher in front of her and her brother's eyes as his power tried to overcome hers, and it very well would have, had he not still been mostly contained? Black wings of night and shadow rose over the light, overcoming it in his prison. She then looked for her friends and saw Esvele and Mavius over Myrcle, Florie, and Talos' bodies. Organa smiled at them. Her eyes met Esvele's. Esvele looked back at her old student with confusion, but then she heard Organa's voice begin to sing the Song of the Traveler. Esvele shouted at her and stood to her feet, getting ready to sprint to her old student. Before she could take the first step, her body disintegrated, and Organa hoped she had cast them all away from that place in safety. Peace, a sensation of acceptance, filled her, for if she had failed in saving them and instead killed them, she would see them soon if she failed in stopping her brother.

She closed her eyes again, and the Dark Song's enticing promise of forgiveness was there. She could feel a hand outstretched in her way from the Void before her.

A new voice spoke, echoing over itself in a chorus of whispers. *You are free. Save them all.*

Organa could now see with clarity in the darkness, strikes of blue, green, and red lightning slowly stretching themselves from within an endless pit of blackness and swirling clouds. A cold wind pulled itself around her, and she could feel a hand outstretched to her. She could not see from where until one of the flashes reached its climax and created a burst of light in the night.

A beautiful form of radiant light exploded in the night and shone with the power of a thousand suns. At least fourteen feet tall, a figure emerged from the illusion before her, and the darkness recoiled itself for a moment before it began to try to make its way back to the figure, stretching out long shadows like the grasping arms of some sea beast. Beautiful copper skin stood out against a white gown of silk with golden trim. Their eyes were metallic gold that glowed with a trailing light. Long white and black hair fell from her head behind her ears and down a few inches past her shoulders. A diadem of woven silver and gold wrapped around her brow bore three gems: a ruby on the left, a diamond in the center, and a sapphire to the right. *Let go. Be free. Save them.*

Organa let go.

With a second pulse of unimaginable energy, Organa stood on the precipice of divinity in the eyes of mortals as her form rose up into the sky. Her hair flowed like water, and her skin crackled with energy, her veins pulsing blue and bright light. Her eyes glowed with the power of a star, their ice blue shining radiantly, and she felt everything at once. Happiness, sorrow, regret, pain, peace, rage, serenity, hate, and forgiveness. Her body emitted a glorious light and became like crystal blue ice.

A living and swirling vortex of ice and snow spun around her like a hurricane. The stone, marble, foliage, and everything within the immediate area of Valistar turned into a tundra, like the frozen wastes of Menagerie. The clouds overhead shot with lightning and struck the ground with devastation in its wake. Her blizzard grew and grew, expanding its reach from the center to the edge of the city. Her enemies stood there with terror in their eyes as their bodies began to solidify from the ice creeping in.

The buildings around the city crumbled as they froze, and long streams of ice pushed against the wind and formed sharp spears. With a crash, the great foundations of Castle Black Rose gave way, falling into the sea and taking part of the city. The ground caved in beneath the massive weight of the keep and buckled down with the natural wall of stone that held the sea back, and the ocean devoured its new domain. The winter met the sea and its cold was so great that the waves that rushed into the crater froze as they were and the weight of the water before it crashed against the ice, shattering it a few times before the winter won its battle with the deep and froze it solid, continuously expanding.

But in a single moment, the storm dispelled.

The Sepulcher was open, and Kyriel was completely visible. He wore black clothes, and his skin was pale as snow. His silver shaggy hair embraced the dying light of the Sepulcher's walls around him, the chains weakened, and they broke apart like glass. Instantly, the light from Organa faded in his darkness, and it flooded off of him like a wave of the Old Sea. The surrounding reality warped itself from his presence, and then he solidified it. Organa's winter thawed, and her Song of Forgiveness, though playing loudly in her mind, was being overcome by vengeance. Kyriel's blood-red eyes gazed upon his domain, and the Shadowlight had come.

Organa's power faded in his presence, and she fell to the ground with a *thud*. Kyriel's wings of shadow and night retreated into his back, and he floated gracefully to the lowest stair of the Sepulcher. His servants waited for him to speak, but he said no words, only looked upon the desolation that his sister had wrought.

The Lady Magis stood to her feet, and she approached her lord, bowing before his majesty. "My Lord Kyriel, Shadowlight, and Usher of the Final Form, your servants venerate you. I am Lady Kethir, the Lady of Bones. I have been granted form through this mortal's flesh and have set you free to begin the Inquisition of the Damned and help you honor our Monarch's wishes."

"It could not have been you who freed me," his blood eyes gazed at her. "No, it wasn't you. Where is she? Where is my sister?" and Organa rose from the crater of her ruin, meeting his dark gaze. "Hello," he smiled.

"Hello, Kyriel," she glared back.

"Why do you look at me like that? Isn't it good to see your brother alive and well after four hundred years of imprisonment?"

"Kyriel ... I," Organa tried to contain her hurt at his words.

"You can't have fallen for their lies about me, did you?"

"I didn't." and she broke down in tears. Her brother walked across the ruins of Valistar to her. Only a few feet away.

"Speak to me, sister."

"What then? Why do you look at me with such pain in your eyes?"

"Because I know what you're here to do. I know what it will cost."

"And the universe will be better for it. Besides, if you plan on blaming anyone, blame yourself; you opened the gates of hell. There's no closing them now."

"You don't have to do anything," she begged him. "You can choose who you are going to be remembered."

"I choose the tyrant," he said without a second thought. "The Dark Throne was mine by birthright, and now I will have it. All will bow."

"And those who refuse?"

"They don't get to choose," he said, shaking his head.

"I can't let you do this, Kyriel. I'm sorry." Organa pulled back her hands and touched the schisms of the Flux, her fury burning inside her.

"*Val'Qor!*" her brother's voice boomed across the sky like thousands of cracks of thunder, and her eyes quivered with fear. She heard nothing in her mind. Silence surrounded her. The Flux left her.

"Now, you cannot harm me." He smiled.

His Word of Power echoed through her, restricting her flow of magic with the shimmer of his crimson eyes. Organa collapsed onto the cold stone as Kyriel smiled and walked forward toward his sister. "The Words of Power are unbreakable unless you can match my might," he scoffed. "Even Myrcle couldn't unravel them." Kyriel's eyes flashed around the ruin of his sister's power. "Where are they? Where are my traitors? I've a debt to repay."

"They are far away from here; I sent them away." She saw his eyes light up with fury.

"You dare prevent my revenge?" His eyes shone as brightly as the morning sun.

"I won't let you kill them."

"And how will you stop me? You cannot harm me. You have no allies among you. You are alone in the dark." Kyriel raised his head to the twinkling heavens above and spread his arms wide, holding his palm up to the night. The sound of rolling thunder echoed overhead, drawing Organa's gaze as she saw the stars go out one by one. A curtain of nothingness devoured each light above, eating away every star in the sky and expanding further with an insatiable hunger.

With the passing of each glint, Kyriel's smile grew wider and wider as he relished the glory of his power.

"I am the God of a new age. All will bow before me."

He lowered his arms and, just as they relaxed; he thrust them into the fabric of reality, tearing apart the schisms of time and space. A sudden ignition of bright red and orange flames sparked in his palms as he removed his hands from the foundations, leaving two holes in the universe. Kyriel fell back with a heavy breath, chuckling through the last few wisps left within him, and with a cry of anger, he drew more power from his Dark Song that rang out with pleasure in his mind. With one final spell, he tore open two swirling infernos that bridged across the planes of existence into the Void itself. Organa's heart skipped a beat as a mangled hand reached out, and then another, and another, exponentially multiplying and exiting their reality into Lorial. The bodies of charred, frozen, broken, slaughtered, dissected creatures of an elder nature long-awaiting their chance to devour this world once again stumbled into the mortal realm. Legions of undead, demons, and other foul things of the Void manifested beside the Herald of the Night.

"Now I will have vengeance!"

Epilogue

The Guardians felt themselves reforming on the hillside as they gasped for air. Myrcle looked around and saw Florie and Talos' bodies, both breathing faintly. He ran to them and knelt on the mountainside, holding his hands over Florie's chest and shining a radiance through his palms into her laboring lungs. Esvele and Mavius made their way to them, and the druid cast a similar spell, filling Talos' body with stable life once more.

"It worked," Esvele gasped through her smile, "she heard me."

Myrcle rose to his feet and took a few moments to catch his breath. The old wizard, who had arrived with Organa, helped Esvele to her feet as she finished her incantation.

"Who are you?" Myrcle asked. "Why did you help us?"

"My name is Mavius. I was the Sorcerer Lord of Valistar until a few moments ago when the city was destroyed."

"But why did you help us?"

"Because, unlike most magic users in Rethial, I still believe in the Pantheon's power, and when Organa revealed her identity to me, I was sure there would be a return of light to our world."

"You served the Menitheals," Esvele said, holding her hands over Talos.

"I did, but I swear to you, when the plan was made to bring the Guardians back to the city, it was presented to the Flame Council as a mission to reignite faith in the Pantheon. So, naturally, there was a unanimous decision, save for the Crimson Priest—"

Myrcle cut him off. "The Crimson Priest was on the Flame Council?"

"Yes. The Children were the hired assassins of the crown, so they were granted power on the Council—a motion I voted against, but I was overruled."

"Okay, we'll get more information about you later. Let's heal them," Myrcle said, trembling. Life pulsed from his fingertips, and he saw Florie's chest rising more rapidly.

Florie took a wild gasp of air as she sat up. She saw Myrcle at her side along with Esvele and some mage she didn't recognize. Her mind instantly went back to the mission, and she turned to Myrcle.

"The Sepulcher is under the Xurinal, keep Organa away from it." she shouted.

"We know," Esvele answered.

"What?" Florie looked past Esvele and saw rising pillars of smoke.

Talos woke from his coma gasping for air, his body shaking from the trauma. Esvele helped him to his feet slowly. He looked upon the ruin of Valistar and saw what everyone else did. He looked around and shouted, "Where's Organa?"

"She's down there," Myrcle sighed.

"You left her?!"

"Not willingly," Esvele shot back, tears in her eyes. "I would never leave her."

"You did once," he muttered under his breath, but she was just close enough to hear him. She jumped at him and punched him hard on the side of his face, thrashing him to the ground. Florie went to pull Esvele off, and then a roar of dark voices, screams, shrieks, and howls filled the night. They ran across the rise and to the edge of the cliff, where the ruin of Valistar shone with a few bright fires that escaped Organa's winter. The shouts pierced their souls as the cries of the damned rang along the mountainside under a roaring thunder that soared above with every inch gained as the ancient darkness was unleashed upon the world.

Myrcle's lip quivered as his hands trembled and he looked upon a familiar sight.

"We failed. The second Cataclysm has begun."

About the Author

Matthew E. Johnson grew up in Church Hill, Tennessee. Since his early days of elementary school, he has always loved to write short stories that he wanted to share with those around him. On the playgrounds he would weave tales like any other child, but wanted to make something out of it. Throughout his schooling, he learned to write properly and took masterclasses with famous writers like Margret Atwood, Dan Brown, and others on the craft. In 2017, Matthew was a Sophomore in high school, and this was the year that he would be pulled into D&D through the show, *Critical Role*. Getting some friends together, Matthew began making a world and the outline of a story he wanted to tell with them. Over the first few sessions, the number of players grew and the story truly began. From 2017-2020, the *Guardians of Lorial* lived in the minds of Matthew and his friends, coming to life around a long table in the bonus room of his house. But before the campaign ended, Matthew decided that this was a story that others needed to hear; and so he decided to write about it. Originally, the *Guardians of Lorial* was going to be a trilogy, but as Matthew mapped out the major plot points that happened throughout the game, he realized that it would be much, much longer than what he hand planned. The *Guardians of Lorial* became a saga of six planned books. In 2021, Matthew finished *The Dark Song*, and now in 2022, it's in your hands dear reader. There are more installments to come and dangers to be conquered. Be on the lookout for *Inquisition of the Damned: Book 2 of the Guardians of Lorial Saga.*

"Writing *The Guardians of Lorial* has been one of the most amazing experiences I have had. It was amazing to feel the world and the stories my friends and I made transferred from my mind to the page. But it could not have been done without the help of you, my fantastic reader. You, who took a chance and picked up my book. You, who turned the pages and read to the point where you are now. But this story is far from over. Kyriel's wrath is unleashed and he is coming for his traitors. Book two in *The Guardians of Lorial Saga*: *The Inquisition of the Damned* is on its way. Know that the Guardians have even further to go after that to see the end of their journey."

-Matthew E. Johnson

You can connect with me on:
 https://www.facebook.com/profile.php?id=100009285911760